Carried Away

BY KAMERY SOLOMON

Praise for *The Swept Away Saga*

"Amazing! The best way I can think to describe it is **Pirates of the Caribbean meets Outlander!** There is action, adventure, romance and so much more! You will not be disappointed!"

~Heather Garrison, *Amazon Customer*

"This book has so many twists and turns that **will keep you reading all night long**. I love the characters and the mystery. The author does a fantastic job weaving every part in this story that will leave you wanting more. I highly recommend!"

~Laura Collins, *Amazon Customer*

"I was pulled in right away and **I did not want to put the book down**, nor did I want the story to end . . . a must read!"

~Holly Copper, *Amazon Customer*

"This is the book you **MUST** be reading **NOW!**"

~Julie Engle, *Amazon Customer*

"This is a story I will read time and time again."

~Angie Angelich, *Book Banshee*

"What else could you want?!"

~Vonnie Hudson, *Amazon Customer*

Other Books by Kamery Solomon

Forever

Hell Hall (A Halloween Novella)

The God Chronicles

Zeus

Poseidon

Hades

Adrastia

Dreams Novels

Taking Chances

Watching Over Me

The Swept Away Saga

Swept Away

Carried Away

Carried Away

By Kamery Solomon

*For those who have suffered in silence.
Don't ever be afraid to talk about what
happened.*

Mark Bell, Present Day

The old Mission building at *Los Olvidados* had been one of the lucky ones, escaping destruction from the Native Americans. While most of the others had been abandoned, burned down, or torn apart by attackers, the priests here had somehow managed to keep the peace. We weren't exactly sure how, or why, for that matter. The Spanish conquest of the New World had been a brutal one for all involved, resulting in the almost complete annihilation of several peoples. For whatever reason, though, the warring nations had managed to coexist here at the southernmost tip of modern day Texas, helping to begin the Spanish colonization of North America.

Missionaries didn't excite me, to be honest. Indian wars kind of did, but I was here for another reason entirely.

It had been a little less than a year since Samantha Greene had followed in her father's footsteps and was claimed by the Treasure Pit in Maine. Understandably, I knew why she had snuck onto the land owned by Duke McCrery, awarded to him after their legal battle. I'd felt the thirst to discover the treasure at the bottom of the Pit as much, if not more, than she did—we both owed it to her father. But something always went wrong on Oak Isle, and, with Sam's accidental drowning, the state declared the area protected land. Not a soul was allowed to dig for anything, whether they possessed the island or not.

I'd spent years studying and searching for answers on Oak Isle, earning the title of Pirate Historian Extraordinaire. In my mind, I was still plain old Mark Bell, the man who knew (or at least thought he knew) all the answers to the island. Now, all I had to show for it were two dead friends and an empty bank account.

When October break arrived six weeks after Sammy's death, I caught the first plane out of town and headed south, meeting up with some of my buddies in Florida. The university I taught at hadn't been very happy to hear I was leaving mid-semester, but there was nothing they could do.

Everyone knew what had happened on the island; it was no secret what I'd lost and never found.

With its fresh, humid air, Florida turned out to be just what the doctor ordered, the Caribbean only a short distance away. It made a man knowledgeable about pirates a good thing to have around, especially when your friends owned a dive and salvage company and wanted to look for lost ships.

So, we set to work, combing the ocean for anything and everything. Business wasn't bad—we took tourists out on dives every now and then—and I finally started to feel like maybe I could find a new passion besides Oak Isle. Life was simple there. It was a welcome respite from the endless imaginings and failed attempts at trying to solve the Treasure Pit.

Maybe it was my lot in life to always have some mystery that couldn't be solved hanging over my head, though.

It was hot. Of all the things I could have remembered about the night that set all of this in motion, that seems the clearest. Tangled in sweaty sheets, I tossed and turned, shrouded in the blackness that filled the little shack we called home, the wood walls barely held together enough to keep mosquitoes out. The house wasn't bad, not really, but it felt much more like a fishing hut at times. Every penny the business earned was spent on equipment or food and, as a result, the living quarters suffered. Sometimes, I wondered why we didn't ditch the hovel all together and live on the boat. It would have been slightly more cramped, but at least then I would have had the breeze off the ocean to brush against me, while the rocking motion of the waves lulled me to sleep.

Nine months. Two hundred and seventy days, give or take. That was how long it had been since Michael's funeral. Only a month less than that since Sam had been caught on tape, climbing into the hole that would flood a short time later.

They never found her body.

Somewhere in my thoughts, I finally drifted off to sleep, dreaming of the young woman. Her body floated eerily in the ocean, arms spread out, eyes wide and locked on me, brown hair fanning out around her head like a halo of darkness.

"Mark," she whispered, her face somehow still unmoving. "Mark!"

Jerking awake, I tumbled off the small mattress, taking the sheets with me as I rolled across the wooden floor. "Good gods, Joe!" I yelled. "Are you trying to give me a heart attack?" Glaring up at the man who'd actually been saying my name, I began trying to untangle myself from the cotton mess I'd gotten into.

"Sorry." The beefy, bald man didn't seem all that regretful of his actions. In fact, he appeared to be the most excited I'd ever seen him. His hands shook some as he licked his lips, his feet doing a slight dance of anticipation.

"What is going on?" Frowning, I paused in my Houdini-like actions, letting the covers stay as they were for the time being.

"Stephens, the guy I told you about, who you replaced—he just called." He was worked up about something, that much was certain. It didn't seem to be anger, like the last time he'd talked to me about the man who had up and left with only a day's notice.

"About what?" I asked grumpily, rubbing the spot on my elbow that had connected with the floor in a very unfortunate fashion.

"He's at the Mission they asked him to come help with." Joe's thick, brown mustache twitched as he smiled and licked his lips again.

By this point, I was almost dying with anticipation—or annoyance—at what he would say. Eyes narrowing, I watched the way he bounced up and down, his tan skin even darker in the night. "Would you get to the point?" It was as polite as I could muster at three in the morning.

"They found a ship sunk in the bay! They

thought there had been mostly fishermen in the area, but he said this is a big one—a galleon. Their equipment suggests that it was either sunk on purpose or taken down in a battle. Some of the hull shows signs of fire damage."

"Really?" My interest spiked, but the thought of returning to bed was sounding more and more promising. *Only if Sam stays in her grave,* I thought suddenly, my skin prickling uncomfortably at the memory of her in my dreams. Trying to shake the feeling of the ghost, I focused on the man in front of me. "What's the ship's name?"

"That's the best part," he answered almost giddily, staring at me with renewed fervor. "It doesn't have one."

"What?" I stood up straight as a board, tripping until the sheets lay forgotten on the ground. It didn't even matter that I was only in my boxers, my body super exposed in the cramped space. All I cared about was the seemingly nameless vessel. "You mean they don't know the name because their equipment isn't good enough, or it actually doesn't have one?"

"Their equipment isn't good enough, but they were able to get preliminary sights with a diver. She checked the stern. There's no name painted there." Joe grinned, the hair above his lip twitching as his eyes nearly bugged out of his head. "Of course, there is a chance that the name could have been burned or rotted away, but still."

Could it be? An unknown pirate ship, sunk right where we could get to it? If that were the case, it would be extremely lucky for us. Those vessels were the hardest to find, with only two or three ever being

13

loosely confirmed. Unless the ship had been stolen from someone and already had a name, pirates didn't give their boats one. The anonymity of attacking with an unnamed craft aided them greatly in their escape, since no one could say who had confronted them specifically. Of course, no name was a dead giveaway to the Navy, but the buccaneers didn't seem to care.

"Mark," Joe said happily. "They want all of us to come. They want the equipment—and they want you. Stephens told them that you're the best Golden Era expert he's ever heard of."

"That was nice of him." I chuckled, not caring that I'd never even seen Stephens, let alone met him. Joe had made him sound like a level one prick, but I was sure we'd be singing his praises from now on.

A small voice in the back of my mind whispered to slow down, to forget the excitement. *Remember what happened to Michael and Sam?* it whispered. *Their treasure hunt killed them. You left to get away from that. What if you're next?*

Steadying myself with a deep breath, I looked Joe in the eye and smiled as wide as I could. This was no mystery pit waiting to be solved, but something sitting in the plain light of day. Swallowing hard, I grabbed his hand and shook it firmly. "When do we leave?"

Bursting into enthusiastic laughter that could've woken anyone within three miles, Joe clapped me on the shoulder, pulling me into a hug that made me feel like I finally had a team again, after months of running away from the ghosts of the ones I'd left behind.

Brown eyes stared back at me now from the front

window of the boat. We were sailing Joe's *Explorer*, the one and only ship in our "fleet." In the two days we'd spent making our way to our final destination, I'd had a lot of time to plan what our newest job would entail. Yet, all I could think of was Michael and Sam. It was as if signing up to help find this treasure had triggered everything from the last one. Half the time I looked at my reflection, I saw theirs staring back.

Blinking hard, I checked myself in the window again. It was my own eyes I saw, though, and my short, black hair, spiked up like usual. The face was my own, tan from working at sea for so many months. It wouldn't have been so bad to see Sam's smile in the place of my own goofy one—she'd always had the type of grin that could make anyone feel happy—but I was relieved to look like myself all around.

Glancing down at my hands, the tattoo of the skull and crossbones on my wrist appearing in the corner of my gaze left me needing to banish the thoughts of Sam once again. It wasn't the memory of her that made me uncomfortable; she was a good friend, always willing to listen and help out. In the short months I'd known her, she'd become like a little sister to me. The brotherly love I'd acquired for her was what made me wish she was gone from my mind. How many times could I think about her in the bottom of that pit, dead, before I went crazy?

"You doing all right, Bell?"

Sighing, I looked over at Joe. He was steering, his large hands wrapped around the tiny helm of the boat, large, black aviators covering his eyes as a slightly smoking cigar hung from his lips.

"Yeah. Just thinking about some stuff. Trying to decide what all we're going to need for our first surveillance of this boat." Taking my own sunglasses off the collar of my shirt, I slid them on and shoved my hands in my pockets. "I imagine it's going to be pretty fragile. It's a miracle that it even survived at all."

"I was thinking the same thing," he replied, nodding. "The salt count in the water is just barely low enough. Anywhere else and the wood would have dissolved within a hundred years."

"And it's just cold and deep enough. If it hadn't buried itself in the ground, there probably still wouldn't be anything left."

"What are you thinking? Will you want to raise it if we can?" He glanced away from the ocean stretching out in front of us, taking the cigar from his mouth and blowing out a puff of smoke.

"There might be wood worms in anything that's left," I answered, shaking my head. "I don't know if we can bring it back up at all. It could be that everything under the sand is charred and fallen apart anyway. I've never dealt with a ship that was burning when it went down."

"Either way, we're in for the find of our lives." Grinning, he placed the cigar back in his mouth and turned his attention to driving, leaving me with my thoughts once more.

The shore was visible in front of us at this point. We'd decided to leave the coast and travel in open water to save time. The sight of land made me feel comfortable, even though I didn't mind being on the ship.

"Stephens is going to meet us at the dock a few miles from the site," Joe continued, smoke curling out around his cheeks. "They don't want us sailing right in just yet. Don't want to tip off other treasure hunters, you know." He laughed slightly at that, shaking his head. However, it was a real threat, and one we constantly had to be on the lookout for. If someone else came in and tried to claim the find, they could seriously damage the ship and even steal any artifacts that might be on board.

We sailed up to the harbor as the sun was setting, the lights of civilization twinkling around us. As Joe had said, we had a welcome committee, with a tall, gangly looking man at its head.

"Joe!" The man raised his hand in greeting, his suit looking extremely too formal for the dingy dock he was standing on. A gold ring graced one of his fingers, shining almost as brightly as his slicked down, white blond hair. Joe had said Stephens was only a few years older than me and in his early forties, but he looked ancient, like he'd spent every day in a tanning booth, purposely making his skin appear the same consistency as a crocodile's.

"Hey, Stephens." Joe smiled and waved back, leaving the captain's cabin and hopping onto the wooden planks beside him. The other member of our team—Hal—was already on deck, waiting to toss a rope out so we could tie the *Explorer* down.

Hal, by contrast, really was in his early sixties, with light blond hair that was blowing all over the top of his head, but looked to be about my age next to Stephens. I half expected the latter to open his mouth and suddenly reveal that he had fangs and drank

17

blood to survive, he looked so out of place.

Following Joe out, I hesitated on deck, waiting to see if Hal would need help tying off. My presence was immediately noticed, though.

"And this must be the famous Mark Bell," Stephens said, beckoning me toward him. "We're very happy you could join us, sir."

"Thank you for the opportunity," I replied warmly. "When will we get to see this ship of yours?"

"He doesn't beat around the bush, does he?" The group laughed at my expense, friendly smiles greeting me from the men and women behind him.

"Mark is serious about his work. It's what makes him so good." Joe winked at me as he passed, heading down the dock. Stephens, who apparently hadn't been ready to leave the spot just yet, hurried to catch up with him, the rest of the group doing so as well.

"He's a mystery, Stephens is," Hal said as we watched them all go on without us. "There was always something about him. I can't quite describe it. He's a nice man, though, despite his appearance."

"You're talking like you're my dad again, Hal." Laughing, I looked back at the man, comforted by his remarks nonetheless.

"And you better listen up, sonny!" he teased, finally hopping over the rail and onto the dock himself. "We'll see the wreck tomorrow. Stephens may have some theatricality to him, but he's as anxious as any for a good find."

It was decided we would send the cameras down first, after scanning the entire bay with a special machine that would create a map of the wreck for us. Ashley, one of the archeologists helping sort through the items at the Mission, had been the diver who found the ship to begin with. She looked more like a super model than a scientist, but it was instantly clear she knew what she was talking about.

"It was my day off," she explained, tucking her long black hair behind her ears. "I hadn't been for a dive in a while and the water looked calm enough. The site is about one hundred feet under water, just inside the opening to the bay. The only reason I found it was because of the metal detector I'd brought with me; I'd been hoping to find some artifacts linked to the missionaries that lived here, maybe uncover how they interacted with the water."

"What pinged the monitor?" I asked, watching as the printer slowly pushed out a sheet detailing the area. "A cannon?"

"I'm not exactly sure." Her tone was apologetic and she shrugged. "It might have been. Once I saw all the stones laying in a row, though, I knew it must have been a boat. There's not much left on the surface. Not of the actual craft, anyway."

Nodding, I continued to watch the map forming before us. "Just things that were on board." We'd driven over the location five times with our equipment, hopeful that we'd get a good enough scan to really see what was there. So far, it looked like we were stumbling into the find of a lifetime. "Good catch with the stones, by the way. Most people would have thought they were just rocks sitting funny."

"I *am* an archeologist," she said, laughing. "I know ships had big stones like that in the hold to help keep balance. Nature doesn't really make perfect lines, either."

"I guess you wouldn't be most people, then." Looking over at her, I smiled warmly. She was very pretty, intellectual, and didn't seem to shy away from the fact that she knew those things about herself. Confidence was very appealing to me; maybe I'd ask her to dinner one night.

The printer made a final ding and the large map slid the rest of the way out, onto the table, a mess of lines and numbers. In the middle of it, though, plain as day, was a vessel lying on its side.

"It looks like there's quite a bit left under the sand, if these readings are correct." Gingerly, I picked up the map, holding it so we could both examine it better. "This is where you tried to look for a name, right?"

"Yeah." Moving closer, she pointed to a spot on the ship at one end. "I didn't dig very far, though. It's pretty stuck in there. There was no sign of extreme decay, but I didn't want to risk it. Based off what I was seeing, it looked to be a good size site, as well. There wasn't exactly enough oxygen for me to stay down there all day and search through everything."

"Do you want to? I mean, when we send divers down. You can help me catalog everything, if you'd like." Blushing slightly, I cleared my throat, aware that I'd phrased it like I would have if I were asking her on a date. I hadn't meant it that way, but I could tell from the expression on her face that she had heard the proposal.

"We'll have to see how the work on shore goes. There's a lot of books here. Maybe I'll just keep an eye out for something about your mystery ship." Grinning, her hand brushed across mine as she leaned in to study the sketch I held again.

"Bell!"

Turning, I waved at Joe, who was waiting to deploy the camera that would give me my first glimpse at the site below. "I have to go." Focusing back to Ashley, I smiled, feeling a few butterflies at her presence.

"I can see that." Gracefully, she left the cabin, moving to get on the jet ski she'd rode out on. "Let me know if you have any more questions."

"Thanks, Ashley," Joe said, beaming like an idiot as he watched her climb over the side and zoom away. After she was gone, he glanced at me knowingly. "Who knew they made the smart ones so pretty now, eh?"

"Everyone, Joe." Chuckling, I carried the map over to him, discussing a few key points of interest. "I can't wait to get down there myself," I added eagerly as I rolled the sheet up.

"Me either. But we need to see what is down there first before we go running off like school kids. There's no telling how old this thing is. I've seen them pull things up that were down there for almost five hundred years. Granted, there wasn't as much salt, but who knows, right?" Falling silent, he helped position the expensive lens over the side of the boat, waving when he was ready for it to go under.

Nodding, I watched as the high tech camera was carefully lowered, Hal working a small crane mechanism above us. Once everything was set, he'd join us in the cabin to steer the craft and see what showed up on our screen.

As I went back inside and took my seat, I silently marveled at Ashley. Normally, it wasn't recommended for divers to go below one hundred and thirty feet. It was surprising that she'd even gone as deep as she had, especially for a simple, unplanned dive. We were partly using the camera now because we wanted to make sure it was worth risking going down there. If there were a large amount of the ship buried, we'd be taking an even bigger chance on our lives to uncover it.

"Is there a picture in there yet?" Hal called from above, still working the controls of the crane to drop the equipment while Joe watched.

Shaking the anticipation and wonderment off, I leaned over and turned the television on, a vision of water filling the screen. "Yeah!" I yelled, scooting the metal seat I was on over so there would be room for all of us.

The two men joined me, settling back as Hal took the remote control in his hands. "And they said video games weren't worth the time," he muttered, laughing. This elicited snickers from me, which I quickly masked as a cough. Hal had probably played three video games his entire life, and yet he still cracked the joke every time he used the deep sea camera.

Silence fell over the room as the descent to the ocean floor began, nothing on the screen but some white flecks and lots of water. The deeper we got, the darker it became, until the overhead lights on the machine were triggered and lit up the space around the tiny craft. Along with the sunlight that still managed to penetrate the distance, the illumination gave us almost perfect vision.

"Look, there," Joe murmured pointing to a small object as the lens drifted over it. "That look like a bottle to you?"

"Kinda," I agreed softly, leaning forward. It was dirty and half buried, with organisms growing on it, but there was a faint outline that looked like a regular, glass bottle.

"We're coming up on the bow now, according to our last scan," Hal stated, slowing down some.

"Look, boots!" In awe, I watched the leather items as they lay on the ground, undisturbed for who knew how long. The sand around them swirled gently as the motion from the camera's propellers moved over it. Suddenly, it occurred to me that there could be more than just artifacts here. What if there were human remains buried in the sand as well?

"There's the first stone from the hull," Joe replied, already moving on to the next thing he saw. "And look at that bit poking up right there. Looks like a box to me. See the metal corner, coming up out of the mud? The rest of the chest could be buried in the sand."

Everything was covered in growth from the ocean, as was expected, and only a small portion of the actual ship was visible above the silt. After three hours of careful exploration with the camera, it was clear that we would need to dive to the wreck ourselves.

"Pistols, cannons, dishes—I can't believe how much stuff is down there!" Popping some candy into my mouth, I smiled happily, leaning back in my chair. The ship was definitely from the same era as the Golden Age of Piracy, based on the outlines of the weapons we'd seen. Once we'd raised a few things and studied them, I was positive we could give the vessel a date.

"It does look like she was taken down in battle," Joe said, continuing the conversation. "If they'd burned her to the deck and sank her on purpose, don't you think they would have taken those things with them? Why destroy all of the stuff as well?"

"I think the greater question is what were they doing here to begin with?" Hal interjected from the doorway, having just hoisted the camera out of the water and set it back on deck. "This isn't a good place to careen. If it came in the time frame we think it did, all that was here were the missionaries. What would pirates want with them?"

"I suppose the battle that sunk the ship could have been with the Mission." Joe looked doubtful even as he said it.

"Because missionaries are the burning and

sinking type." Hal barked out a laugh, shaking his head. "No. I'd bet good money that there was another ship here, one that would have been a fair fight for No Name. Not some dinky fishing raft ran by religious types."

"But that leaves an even bigger problem, doesn't it?" I interjected, standing. "One ship could be a coincidence. But two? There's no way. A fight suggests they were enemies, or a reluctant partnership that went bad. What were they looking for that brought them both here?"

No one had an answer for that. As we all stood there, contemplating what could have happened in this place so many years ago, I suddenly felt as if the ghosts of my friends were nearby. The notion sent a chill through me and I could practically feel the color draining from my face.

"You all right, Bell?" Joe asked suddenly, lurching forward to grab me as if I were tumbling over.

"Yeah." The reply was stronger than I meant it to be, but it stopped him from saving me like some fainting woman. "My, uh, stomach suddenly doesn't feel so well."

"There's a storm blowing in." Hal covered for me, changing the conversation as he looked out at the clear horizon. "I can smell it. The waves are picking up some, too. We'd best get back in to shore. The visibility below will be gone before we could get down there."

"A touch of seasickness?" Joe was joking, knowing that I had fine sea legs as he looked at me with slight concern, but I nodded all the same.

It's happening again, the tiny voice in the back of my mind whispered. *You're getting yourself into another mystery that could kill you.*

Pursing my lips, I tried to steady myself, banishing the voice and ghosts from my head. It was ridiculous that I kept feeling like I was on the brink of death. How many dives had I been on since I'd come to Florida? I'd never felt danger through any of them, besides the occasional things that all divers experienced. Sure, Michael and Sam weighed on my thoughts a lot, but this was . . . different.

Why did I feel so terrified?

The radio on the dash beeped in, saving me from the complexities of my own brain.

"This is *Explorer*," Joe answered, talking into the mouthpiece and steering the boat at the same time.

"Are you guys planning on coming in soon?" It was Stephens, his high voice as smooth as silk. For some reason, whenever I heard it, I had to fight the urge to frown.

"We're on our way back now. Why?"

"We've been going through some of the manuscripts here," Stephens answered offhandedly. "Records, journals, that kind of stuff. It looks like we've found a couple entries about your ship."

"What year?" I immediately asked, holding my breath as Joe repeated the question.

"These entries are dated sixteen ninety-seven. Once in a log book, another in a personal journal."

Shocked silence fell between us. There it was—the boat, if it was the same one, was indeed from the period we wanted.

"Well, I'll be damned," Joe said softly. He

looked at Hal and I, thinking over something before he turned back to the window and pressed the button to reply. "We're going to need to call someone about this, right, Stephens?"

"I've already contacted the local authorities and informed them of the historic value of the site. Hopefully, they'll get back to me soon and send some help to keep it secure."

"Can we see the documents?" I pressed again, impatient as the message was relayed.

"We've got them in a holding room for you. Ashley is looking at them right now to see if there's anything we could possibly match to the wreck."

"We'll be in as soon as we can," Joe announced. "Thanks, Stephens."

"These books are from right before the Mission was abandoned," Ashley said, leading us through one of the many work tents that were set up outside the old building. "Around seventeen hundred, the missionaries packed up and moved down the coast. We think they were headed for Veracruz, but we aren't exactly sure what prompted them to leave in the first place." She paused, a frustrated look passing over her before she shook her head and sighed. "There are stories that relations with the indigenous people were becoming more difficult, but I personally feel that there had to have been some type of catalyst to make them run so suddenly. I was hoping to find some answers in this journal that was left behind, but it stops before anything occurs. For some reason, all of the records stop at sixteen ninety-eight. It's like they decided what they were doing wasn't worth saving anymore."

"That's why you're so interested in what happened here," I continued, trying to fill in the blanks she was leaving. "There's two whole years missing."

"Yes. There's some things here and there, but it's

not enough to really understand why it was abandoned. I mean, look at it! It's beautiful—a real oasis, surrounded by green forest that leads off into desert and mountains. This was a good place to put down roots. Why did they run?"

We left the work area and moved into the actual building, following an already excavated path to the holding room we'd been told about. It felt like the building was going to fall down around us; it looked so worn and old. The government had put it under protection decades earlier, constructing a large fence that surrounded the entire area, but they'd never brought anyone out to go through everything. Preliminary findings had made them conclude that the building was empty—that is until someone broke in one night and discovered a door beneath the rubble of one wall. The secret basement behind it had immediately drawn curious eyes and the team that was working in the space now.

"Here's some gloves," Ashley said, pulling them out of her pocket and passing them out. "Don't touch anything without them. The room you'll be in is just a holding area, but we've filled it with a lot of artifacts."

Unlocking the padlock of the entrance in front of us, she stood to the side, allowing us to scoot by her. The room itself was small and boring, the walls carrying a somewhat crumbled appearance. The workers had lined them with tables, though, all of which were covered with various odds and ends that had been brought up from the basement. In the center of the room, one long bench sat with only a few items laid out, among them some very old looking books.

"It's all written in Spanish," Ashley said from behind us, watching as we slowly gathered around the table. "Do any of you speak it?"

"We each know a little," Joe replied.

"I read it better than I speak it." I felt confident that I could decipher anything, as long as it gave me the answers I was searching for.

"I'll leave you to it, then." Smiling, she closed the door, the sound of the lock never clicking shut on the other side.

Carefully, I pulled my latex gloves on and picked up one of the books, slowly thumbing through the pages. "This is the log," I murmured. "This line is saying they bought fish from someone. This one about herbs picked from the garden."

"The brothers were good housekeepers," Hal said, smiling. "They would have needed to keep track of everything, especially their stores." He frowned then, glancing down at the objects on the table. "But that makes it even more strange that they just stopped writing it down."

"Maybe they had a change in leadership?" Joe guessed, shrugging.

I continued my perusal, ignoring their banter, hunting for any signs of a galleon, but all that was mentioned were fishing boats. Then, finally, on almost the last page, I found it. "Here!" Excitedly, I set the book down for the other two to see, pointing to the entry. "One galleon, nameless. Paid to drop anchor; ten pieces of silver."

"Sounds like a lot to just let your ship sit out in the water." Hal frowned, obviously put off by the price. "Doesn't it?"

"There's no mention of it leaving, either," I said, ignoring him. "The log ends with it still there."

"Let's look at the journal," Joe suggested, picking up the other book and flipping it to the back. He perused the pages for a few moments before nodding and sitting down in the chair beside him. "Here, I think I found it." He struggled over a few words for a second and then began reading the passage out loud, translating as he went.

I do apologize for not writing for so long—this past week has been filled with so many strange occurrences! It has made life here something I have not experienced in quite a while; exciting.

It began on the Sabbath. We had just finished evening prayer, when there was a knock at the chapel door. A married couple—an Irishman and his wife by the name O'Rourke—had arrived seeking shelter. Apparently, they had been looking for a friend of theirs, a Father, whom they had been separated from in Mexico City. Their informants had told them he might have headed this way, but none of us had ever seen or heard of him.

All in all, they were nice people. The man helped care for the animals while the wife assisted in making dinner. They were quite put off by the ship in the bay, though.

Oh, the ship! I forgot to tell you about the ship. I didn't think it important until I saw how nervous it made them. I also suspect that the men who anchored here are pirates, and I did not wish to write too much about them, should they indeed turn out to be of a vicious nature.

It was some weeks ago when the galleon arrived out of nowhere. I confess, up until I saw it in the water, I did not know the bay was deep enough for a craft so large to come in so far.

Now that I think of it, I wonder if the couple were also of a pirate's mind? Why else would they have been so put off and so secretive about any information they had on it? All they would say was that it would have been better if we'd never set eyes on the thing.

To continue with my narrative—the ship came into harbor and dropped anchor. A long boat appeared almost immediately, full to the brim of men who looked as if they'd just experienced the worst time of their lives. We fed them, even though we had very little, and inquired as to what brought them so far north.

(Some of them were French, I am certain. They didn't ask after any settlements by their people, though.)

It became clear that they wanted to leave their ship anchored for some time, however, they wouldn't say how long. It was all very secretive. They paid a handsome sum and we entered it into the logbook.

I do wish to mention here that the ship had no name and the men refused to tell us what they called her. They also refused to give any of their own names, which was alarming to say the least. We didn't dare refuse them at that point, not when we were so obviously working with evil men. However, I would listen when they weren't paying attention, and believe I managed to hear their captain's name.

Thomas Randall. He was a very fierce man, though not as menacing in appearance. His hair was long, black, greasy, and the only thing that really made him look like a man who should be left alone when it hung in his face. Still, I remember the ring he wore on his finger; gold, with a cross etched into it. In the middle of the cross was a black dot. It seemed out of place on his person, but strangely his at the same time.

I digress. The O'Rourke's only stayed the one night, thanking us warmly for the accommodation. We tried to warn them of the natives and traveling on alone as they wanted, but they wouldn't listen. One can only hope that they will find their friend and make it home alive.

"The rest is just stuff about the natives. I guess it was exciting for him." Joe shrugged, closing the book and frowning. "There's nothing that ties the ship we've found to this one, other than the fact that we don't have a name for it."

"Have you ever heard of this Thomas Randall, Mark?" Hal stared at me expectantly, like I would suddenly spout out the man's birthday, home, and every other fact about him.

"I have no idea who he is," I confessed, rubbing

a hand over my face. "But I might be able to find some information on him. If we can tie him to something we salvage from the ship, then we'll have it identified for sure. Otherwise it will all be guesswork."

"Where do you plan on going to look? Surely not anywhere around here." Joe was still frowning. I knew how he felt; here was the evidence we needed, but it was maddeningly out of reach.

"Probably the New York City Public Library. They have a really extensive naval history section there." Except that New York City was much closer to Maine and the Treasure Pit than I wanted to be. Scott had been trying to reach me for months. If he found out I was nearby . . .

"I say take as much time as you need," Hal said, agreeing with me. "Turn over every rock until you find him."

"We'll get started on the diving here, so we have something to match him to when you get back." Joe stood then, shaking his head. "We'll solve it. I know we will."

Disappointed about missing the dive, I nodded, knowing I needed to go find *something* out. This was just like Oak Isle; every answered question spouted fifty more unanswered ones. Thinking over the entry, I hedged, coming across something I didn't understand.

"Why would he mention the ring?" I was talking mostly to myself, but the other two men stopped to listen, watching me expectantly. "I mean, it's not important. Why would a missionary feel he needed to describe the ring the man was wearing?"

"Because it's important?" Hal guessed. "Maybe you can find him with that information."

"Ask Stephens," Joe said suddenly, laughing slightly.

"Why?"

"Because he's got the same symbol on his ring. I should have recognized the description earlier, but I was too involved in trying to find something about the boat. I bet he can tell you what it is. He treats that thing like it's his baby. Remember that time he took it off and almost lost it in the sea, Hal?"

"Oh, yeah! He acted like he was going to die without it. Big baby." He chuckled with Joe at the memory. "I suppose it's the same symbol, isn't it?"

"I'll ask him before I leave." Smiling tightly, I exited the room. Something about Stephens made me uncomfortable, but I still hadn't been able to put my finger on it. What were the odds he would magically have the same kind of ring as our pirate captain? It all sounded very fishy to me. "I'm going to turn in for the night, guys," I said, glancing back from the doorway.

Leaving the two of them behind, I made my way through the Mission and into the tents outside, lost in my own thoughts about the journal entry as I trudged through the sand. It was all very strange.

An Irishman? The Spanish were the only ones in this area at that time. What was he doing here, and with his wife nonetheless? Why hadn't more questions been asked about the mysterious ship and her crew? What did the symbol on the ring mean? Why was it so important that it was recorded in a journal? Did the priest just really like the trinket, or did it hold a higher meaning?

"Find anything interesting?"

Jumping, I turned and forced a smile for Stephens. He was sitting at a desk, examining an old vase with what appeared to be gold inlay. The cautious feeling I'd always had around him grew with force.

"No Name still has no name, if that's what you mean."

"I didn't have a chance to look at the books before Ashley let you at them. I was simply curious as to what they said." He smiled nicely, folding his hands on the tabletop, the vase put aside for the moment. I could clearly see the symbol on his ring, matching exactly the description of the one Thomas Randall had been wearing. All of my intuition was saying that something was wrong.

"Cool ring," I said nonchalantly, nodding in his general direction. "What's the symbol mean?"

"Oh, this? It's nothing. I picked it up at a pawnshop in Florida. Thought it was cool."

He's lying, the voice in the back of my mind said. *You can see it in his eyes.*

"You should have it checked out." My mouth was going dry for some reason, my heart hammering in my chest. I knew I shouldn't say anything else, but he would most certainly look at the books and find out later. "It matches a ring the journal described. It could be worth a lot of money."

"I see." His eyes seemed to darken some at my comment, a slight shield appearing to fall over them.

In an instant, I suddenly felt like I was being pulled into a trap. I needed to escape, and *now.*

"Anyway," I continued, trying to act as normal as possible as I faked a yawn, stretching dramatically. "I'm going to hit the hay. I'll see you tomorrow, yeah?"

"Sleep well," he replied cordially, going back to his examination of the vase.

Turning on my heel, I left the encampment as quickly as possible, all the while cursing myself for being so jumpy. What was it about this project that had me so keyed up?

Once I was in the rental car I'd driven over that morning, I pulled my phone out of my pocket and dialed the number to the airport.

"Yeah, I need a flight to New York City, as soon as possible. Return date?" Glancing out the window, I saw Stephens again, his form moving slowly toward the parking lot, the glow of his own phone lighting up his face as he raised it to his ear.

"No return date," I told the woman on the other line. "I don't know if I'll be coming back."

You are crazy. Running off like a kid in trouble! And over what? Some ring? Stephens literally did nothing to warrant you flying across the country right this second.

"Yeah. I'll call if I find anything. Talk to you later, Joe." Sighing, I hung up the phone and ran a hand through my hair. I'd told him I couldn't sleep, so I'd flown to the city instead. He'd said to take all the time I needed.

I didn't think he believed me.

All around me, the metropolis was bursting with life and action, people hurrying in the various directions they wanted to go. As I stood outside the library, taking it all in, I felt another wave of sadness. Had Sam ever seen a place like this?

She was haunting me. Why, I didn't know, but the alternative was that I was insane. What was she trying to tell me from the other side? Why did I feel so awful about my latest job?

These questions, and many more, had prompted me to call Scott myself and tell him I was coming to New York. He'd wanted to meet up, as I'd suspected, and would be here the day after tomorrow.

Guilt flooded through me as I thought of how I'd dodged him for the better part of a year. The older, balding man had been one of my best friends as well, working as hard as everyone else to solve the Treasure Pit, and feeling as traumatized by the deaths that occurred there.

"Don't think about it now," I muttered to myself, startling a young woman as she passed by. "Sorry!" I waved apologetically and turned to go inside the building, face burning.

I was losing it.

There was a lot to go through in the library. Starting online, I spent the better part of the day reading through old logs, both computerized and not, until my eyes felt like they were going to roll out of my head from exhaustion. After an early dinner break, I hit the books, turning through volumes that hadn't been touched in decades, it seemed.

And there was nothing. No mention of a pirate named Thomas Randall, no gallant exhibitions by a ship with no name and a mystery crew, and no galleon that sailed into the Gulf of Mexico and never returned.

"Sir, we're closing now." One of the workers kindly tapped me on the shoulder and smiled as she spoke, an armful of novels balanced in her grasp. "Did you find what you were looking for today?"

"Unfortunately, I didn't." My breath was short and frustrated from a day of work with nothing to show for it. Now I would have to remember every volume I'd been through, so I didn't repeat the process tomorrow.

"Can you tell me what you were researching? I

can see if we have anything that can help."

"I'm searching for a man named Thomas Randall who was alive in sixteen ninety-seven, or right around there. He was supposedly a pirate, which is what I'm trying to verify." Smiling tightly, I glanced at the woman again, taking in her curly black hair and dark skin. Her grin was as genuine as any I'd seen of late and I instantly felt calmed for some reason.

"Will you be coming back tomorrow?" She set the stack in her arms on the table and pulled a pad of sticky notes out of her pocket, grabbing the red pen that was tucked behind her ear at the same time.

"Yes."

She wrote down everything I said, nodding her head as she did so, a contemplative expression covering her features. "I'll see what I can find. It might be nothing, but we have a few books that we rotate in and out of the collection. I'll do a search and leave anything I find right here for you in the morning. Sound good?"

"That sounds wonderful! Thank you so much for your help, really." For the first time in weeks, I felt genuine relief flood through me at the thought of someone helping out. All of my crazy imaginings and thinking about the past had really wound me up.

"Not a problem. What was your name?"

"Mark," I replied, watching as she wrote it down.

"Okay, Mark. I will hopefully have something here for you in the morning." Picking her stack up again, she smiled once more and left, leaving me slightly less keyed up than I'd been moments before.

That night, I dreamed of Sam again, floating in the ocean, but she didn't speak to me. Instead, she remained lifeless, the bottom of a large ship passing through the water above her. It was a galleon, huge and menacing. As its shadow overtook us, the cannons started firing into the water, barely missing me. Fear encapsulated me, my muscles screaming for relief as I continually tried to flee the attack. Covered in sweat, I finally woke, feeling as if my life had truly been on the line.

With tired eyes and aching bones, I made my way back to the library, halfheartedly hoping that something would have turned up in one of the books the librarian had mentioned.

Thomas Randall was starting to feel like a figment of my imagination. It didn't help that the missionary could have recorded the wrong name, either. What if it was something completely different, and the reason I'd found nothing was because no pirate by that title had existed in that time?

As I walked through the front doors, I sighed, adjusting the strap of the backpack on my shoulder. The bag was filled with the few notes I'd taken yesterday, as well as some information Joe had emailed me about the ship. The table I'd sat at before still had some of the books I'd gone through earlier still sitting in their stack. Next to them, though, was a single volume with a sticky note on top.

"There were a few men by that name in here, some not in the right period, though," I read out loud, my heart instantly speeding to the same pace as a galloping horse. Pulling the memo off, I examined the volume. It looked like a copy of a logbook. Flipping through the pages, I could see that it was full of ship manifests, listing the names of all the crews and passengers that had sailed from one particular port in Spain. Glancing back at the message, I went to the first page number listed.

Thomas Randall, aged forty-five, surgeon. However, the entry for this ship was too old, more than fifty years before the man described in the journal back at Texas.

There were six entries total, two of which I thought could be the man I wanted. One had been employed on a fishing boat, the other on a merchant ship called *Adelina*. Both were young—in their late twenties— and both had been riggers. The year of enlistment was sixteen ninety-two and ninety-four, which meant that it could be either of them.

Stumped, I sat down and tried to think of how I would pick the right one. I could research them both, but that would waste more time than I had. There was no telling what Scott wanted or how long I would be tied up with him tomorrow. No, I needed to pick one and hope it was our man.

Pursing my lips, I looked over the two manifests again, hoping that something would stand out to me and—

As my eyes landed on another name among the *Adelina's* crew, I felt an electric shock shoot through me.

Tristan O'Rourke, aged twenty-three, quartermaster.

It was as if I could hear Joe's voice again, detailing the Irishman who had come to the Mission, the one who had been put off by the ship in the harbor. His name was O'Rourke.

"Got him!" Laughing, I slammed the book

closed, leaning back in the chair and clapping a hand to the top of my head.

"Shhh!"

The woman who hushed me glared furiously, but I couldn't even care at that moment. I'd found our pirate! Even better, I'd found another person who was tied into history with him. If I couldn't find anything about Randall, I'd hopefully be able to learn more about O'Rourke. For all I knew, the ship lying on the bottom of the ocean could be the *Adelina* herself.

At that thought, I left the table and claimed another computer, doing a quick search for the ship. It took some digging, but I finally found her mentioned offhandedly in another log book. She had sailed from a port—yes, one known to have been used by many pirates—and been burned in battle before sinking.

"Where did she sink? *Where did she sink?*" It felt like I was flying through the documents catalogued, but there was no more information to find. It seemed that the only reason she had been listed was because the harbormaster had expected her back soon.

Another wave of intuition hit me and I returned to the Caribbean log, checking to see who the captain of the vessel had been.

Tristan O'Rourke.

The grin that was plastered across my face only grew. It wasn't hard to imagine what had happened. O'Rourke had staged a mutiny and taken over the merchant ship, turning her bad and becoming the captain himself. But when did Randall take charge?

I was missing something. The log still had the Irishman as the leader when she burned and sank, yet the missionaries had been certain that Randall was at

43

the head of the men. Was there another ship I had lost in the writing?

For several hours, I went back and forth between everything available to me, hoping to catch the moment where Randall had stepped into the position of authority, but, like I'd struggled with before, there was almost no mention of him. As far as the records were concerned, he was nobody. O'Rourke was the star of the show.

Stretching my mind to max capacity, I tried to think of other ways the two men could be connected. "Childhood friends?" I muttered, bringing up an ancestry page and typing in O'Rourke's information.

Very little came up; it appeared that no one else was really looking for more details on the man, other than what was already known about his pirating. There was one extra thing recorded that I hadn't seen yet, though—a type of marriage certificate. It looked to be signed by a priest and was very official for so early, which suggested that the man had something even more important than just a boat to his name.

Could Randall have been related to the wife? Who was she? She had been included in the journal; she didn't like the ship. Would a relative have been upset to see her kin's belongings?

Quickly, I read over the lines of the document. The man had been a prince! His family fled the country after the English invasion . . . no wonder the marriage was so official. The woman had married into Irish clan royalty. Even with their kingdom lost, they would have treated the union with the utmost care.

"Where's her name?" I mumbled, scanning the

rows.

Samantha Green of America.

Everything in the world stopped. I was frozen, unable to move if I wanted to, staring at her name.

Samantha Greene. Just like my Sam. Both dead. The coincidence was so large that I couldn't even wrap my head around it. Were they relatives? Was I reading about Sam's long lost ancestors?

Slowly, the sound came back, fading in as if I'd turned a television all the way down and then slowly set it as loud as it could go. My heart restarted, sputtering as I shoved away from the desk, my mission forgotten. I could hear her voice in my head, calling to me.

"Go away," I whispered to the ghost, fighting the urge to cover my ears.

The Treasure Pit was everywhere.

Sam was everywhere.

Death was everywhere.

How did I get away from something that covered every inch of my existence?

"You don't look very well, Mark."

Scott's voice was full of concern, his brow furrowed as he examined me across the table of the Italian restaurant we'd agreed to meet at. The man was just as I remembered, with a kind air about him, his bald head shining under the light. He seemed to have aged further than a year, though, his skin more wrinkled and pale than I recalled.

"I don't feel very well, to be honest," I replied, smiling weakly. "I've had an interesting trip."

"Do you want to talk about it?"

"Not here."

An uncomfortable silence stretched between us as we watched the other patrons enjoying their food. Sipping my water slowly, I studied the man over again, wondering just what it was he'd come all this way to say.

"So you've been working in Florida?" Scott smiled at the waiter as he brought us some salad, waiting for him to leave before regarding me expectantly.

"Yeah. It's been nice."

If we'd been sitting together like this before

everything happened with the Treasure Pit, we would have had no problems talking with each other freely. Now it felt like we had a past we couldn't mention in public, for fear of someone else suddenly dropping dead beside us at the mere mention of the death trap.

How many times had I shared a slice of pizza with him in the back room of the twins' restaurant? We'd sat next to each other at business meetings in Michael's house for years, becoming great friends, despite our varying ages and interests. We had one thing in common and that was enough for us. What were we now without it?

Eventually, our food came and we ate it over small talk. It was obvious that meeting in public had been the wrong thing to do. He didn't want to tell me his news, and I didn't know how to tell him what I was working on, or that I thought I was being haunted.

"If you have time," Scott said, signing the check at the end of our meal. "I brought something I thought you'd like to see. It's back at my hotel, a few blocks from here."

"Does it have anything to do with the Pit?" I sounded so bitter—and scared. That was somewhat surprising. I'd thought I'd be able to hide my feelings for the place better than that.

"It does. You'll want to see it, though. Trust me." He smiled, standing and nodding toward the door. "What do you say?"

Mulling his request over, I suddenly felt like I needed a distraction from O'Rourke and his bride more than anything else. "Yeah, I'll come."

We left the restaurant, heading to our destination

in silence, allowing the noises and sights of the skyscrapers and busy streets to fill the void. When we reached the hotel, Scott showed his key card and we were let on the elevator. Only when we were finally in his room, the door locked and curtains closed, did he sigh and turn to stare at me.

"We've missed you in Maine. That's not to say that we don't know why you left, but the twins and I have had a rough go of it without you."

"And Michael and Sam," I added for him, smiling weakly. "What have you even been working on? I thought the state shut everything down."

"Oh, they did." He took his light jacket off, laying it over one of the seats at the dining table in the corner, before sitting in the chair next to the couch I sat on. "And Duke raised hell about it. He was never able to get them to reverse the decision. No one has been on Oak Isle since you left."

"So you haven't been working on the Pit?" It gave me a cold feeling to even think about the place, like a ghostly hand running up my arm. Suddenly, an image of Sam flooded my mind again and I slammed the doors against her.

"No," Scott continued, not noticing the distress I was in. "The search and rescue team went out a few more times after you left, to see if they could find anything related to Sam, but they haven't been back out in months."

"So, what? You've been trying to find the treasure by standing on the beach and looking out at the island?"

"No." He laughed, reaching back behind the chair for something. Carefully, he pulled a black duffle bag up, setting it on his lap. "One of my longtime friends was part of the search crew. As you know, they never found Samantha's body, but they did find this."

Carefully, he opened the sack, reaching in and retrieving something swaddled in thick, dark fabric.

"This was in her carrier, which they discovered just after you left, stuck on a root growing through the wall of the tunnel. It was deeper than the divers had really gone before, and hard to see down there, but they did find it."

"What is it?" Normally, I would have been ecstatic over anything unearthed in the Pit. This time, it had a bitter taste to it.

Slowly, he unwrapped the object, revealing the oldest vase I'd ever seen. Ancient markings covered it, the lid apparently stuck tight together. "My friend gave this to me. Do you realize what this could mean for us and the Pit?" He grinned, cradling the object carefully. "If we can prove that this is as old as I think it is and that it came from Oak Isle, the state will have no choice. They'll have to let us excavate. McCrery will agree to work as a team when he sees that we're the ones with the proof."

I stared at him for a moment, feeling a slight surge of adrenaline at finally solving that blasted hole in the ground. At the same time, overwhelming dread washed over me.

"I'm not going back to that place, Scott." My voice was quiet, but held enough authority that my message couldn't be mistaken. "I can't get it out of my mind as it is. It's like Sam's haunting me. I see her in my sleep, in the mirror, even as random people standing on the side of the street. I can't go back to where she died. Michael was buried in that thing. Sometimes I see him, too. It's not in me to return. I just can't."

"I know what you mean." He smiled sadly, pulling the cloth over the vase. "Sometimes, I think I hear one of them saying my name. They are not far from us."

"No, you don't understand," I replied forcefully. "I literally can't go anywhere or do anything without Sam. I've felt her touch me, heard her, seen her in places that she shouldn't be. And every time, all I can think is that I'm risking my life. I need to get away. Even the ship I'm working on right now seems to have her fingerprints all over it. I can't explain it."

"You don't have to," he rushed to say, concern in his eyes. "I had no idea that her death had hit you so hard. Were there . . . feelings you had for her?"

"No! Maybe. Just at first, though. She was pretty. But we weren't each other's type. That was immediately clear to me. She was more like my sister than anything else at the end." Groaning in frustration, I rubbed my face with one hand, shoving to my feet. "I don't understand! Michael was my friend and mentor for years. Why am I not seeing him as much as her?"

"Have you spoken with anyone else about this?" There was classic Scott, always trying to analyze and offer his opinion. When he saw the expression on my face, he sighed, nodding in acceptance to the answer I hadn't spoken. "No, you wouldn't. What can I do to help?"

"Why did you come here and show me this?" I

asked, gesturing to the vase. "What did you want me to do? Come and help?" Embarrassment burned my face. Why had I told him I was being haunted? I looked even crazier than I felt now.

"Actually, I was hoping that you would take the vase to your professor friend in Arizona." He stood, coming over and placing a hand on my shoulder. "It hit us all hard, Mark. There's no shame in what you're feeling or experiencing. We're all grieving together. I didn't think you would want to come help again. I can even try to contact the professor on my own. I just thought he might listen to a friend more than me."

"Oh." Suddenly, all the weight that had been piling on me as soon as I knew we were meeting began to lift. No one was asking me to come back. I could still be done with the island, if I wanted.

"Will you do it? I thought someone with a degree in ancient civilizations would know just how to study this. We don't exactly have the funds to pay for it to be tested and examined, either." He laughed, shaking his head. "You know about that, though."

Sighing, I looked at the vase, resting on the chair, the top of the lid just barely showing. "I can take it. I'll fly that direction on my return to Texas. It'll only be a few hours difference. I haven't seen Steve in a long time anyway. He might have access to some files I need for my current project."

Scott clapped me on the shoulder, a watery smile covering his face. "Thank you, Mark. You have no idea how much this means to me."

"It's your life's work. I understand that."

Going to the chair, Scott carefully packed away

the ancient relic again, sighing in what sounded like relief.

"What's inside it?" I asked, sitting down once more.

"No one's opened it," he answered. "We were worried it might break if we tried to take the top off, not knowing how old or fragile it is. It's light, though. I don't think there's anything at all."

"I'm sure Steve and his students will figure it out."

It was already too hot in Arizona for my liking, and they hadn't even reached their warmest season yet.

"How do people live here?" I muttered, wiping my forehead with the back of my hand as I left the terminal and got into one of the waiting cabs.

Steve had been more than happy to look at the vase, though he informed me that it would have to wait a few days after my arrival. Normally, he would have been at home in Tucson, teaching at the University of Arizona. This particular weekend found him in the state's capitol, Phoenix, instead.

"There's a big conference this weekend," he said over the phone when I'd called a few days before. "If you come on Sunday, we should be just wrapping up. I'll look at it for you then, if you'd like."

"That sounds fine with me." To be honest, I wanted nothing more than to be done with the project and never think of it again. The only reason I'd agreed to help Scott out was because he was my friend and I knew how much the vase meant to him. Ever since I first picked it up, it was as if a dark cloud were hanging over me. There were no more dreams or impressions of Sam, for which I was grateful, but after having decided her spirit was floating around, it was strange for her to suddenly just be gone.

"Crazy," I muttered, staring out the window at the desert scenery passing by. When had I decided to believe in ghosts? I'd entertained the stories a few times, but never gave them much thought. Something was different now.

I couldn't help but feel that Sam had gone because of the vase.

Sighing, I peered down at the bag in my lap, imagining the object carefully stowed inside. So much trouble and pain for one item.

The cab took me downtown, into the more business-like part of the city. There were a few skyscrapers and a public transportation system, but other than that it didn't really appear like any other huge metropolises I'd been to.

Steve was staying another night at his fancy hotel before driving back home in the morning. They had a nice restaurant in the top of the building, and it was here I met him, comforted by the nearly empty space.

"Mark!" Steve was my own age and plump, to say the least. He carried the weight well, looking somewhat like an overstuffed teddy bear as he rose from his seat and motioned me over. "How are you?"

"I'm good." Grinning, I remembered a few of my graduate school days that he'd been a part of. We hadn't seen each other in some time, but it was as if we'd not spent a day apart. "How was your conference?"

"Boring, but informative." Chuckling, he slid a menu across the table to me. "I was actually presenting some of the findings from my department. We worked on an exhibition in Egypt this semester and found quite the cache."

"Oh, really?" The food here looked good, if the pictures in the menu were any indication. What I could smell from the kitchen was giving me that impression as well. "New stuff, or just reinforcing what we already knew?"

"A little of both, actually."

After the food was brought out, Steve finally cleared his throat and asked to see what was in the bag.

"The markings seem Greek to me. What do you think?" Pulling the jar out, I carefully uncovered it partially and held it over for him to study.

"Wow." It was whispered, his eyes growing large as he gawked. "Where did you say you found this? That pit you've been laboring on?"

"I actually don't work there anymore, but yes. One of my former associates asked if I could get you to take a glance at it." I pushed the thoughts of my friends in Maine to the back of my mind.

Keep it business, I coached myself as I watched him.

"I can definitely see where the markings look Greek in origin. I haven't seen anything like this in . . . I don't even know when! It's an extraordinary piece, Mark. Really. Do you think you could send it to the

University for testing and analysis? I don't want to tell you something right here and now without thoroughly going over it." His fingers reached out, but he held back, obviously worried about harming it.

"I think that's what they were hoping you'd do, test it at the school. They want proof that it's an ancient artifact."

"Of course! I can even take it with me in the morning, if you'd like. Or would you rather bring it yourself? I wouldn't trust any post service with something like this." He leaned back in his chair, eyes still trained on the vase, and smiled. "It wouldn't be any trouble for me. I can stop by wherever you're staying."

"I'm actually just down the street. If you don't think it will be a bother, that's fine with me." Carefully, I put the object away, feeling relieved that I would soon be done with it.

"I can't believe that was there waiting for you to find all those years." Steve was still stuck in wonderment, staring at the wall as he spoke his thoughts out loud. "What else could be down there?"

"Careful," I joked. "That's how you get sucked in. It's better to not ask questions and just go with it."

He seemed to come out of it then, looking at me with a dazed expression. "You said you don't work there anymore?"

"I've been helping on shipwrecks and dives for almost a year now."

"Still a treasure hunter at heart." He chuckled, waiting for the waiter to leave our food before continuing. "You know," he said, cutting his steak. "Arizona has its own lost treasure. Maybe you could take a try at that, too, eh?"

"What do you mean?" As much as I didn't want or plan to do any hunting here, I did love a good story.

"The Lost Dutchman's Gold Mine. You've heard of that one, of course." Spearing the meat with his fork, he dragged it through some sauce and popped it into his mouth.

"I have, vaguely. It's just a gold vein that's supposed to be in the mountains around here somewhere, isn't it?"

"It's a lot more than that. The Dutchman claimed the deposit was eighteen inches wide and that there was so much of it, he could pick it up off the ground. He'd go up alone, in secret, making sure no one followed him. He confessed to eight murders, one of whom was his own nephew, which he committed to keep the location confidential. He died before he could tell anyone exactly where it is, but he did leave some clues. They aren't very good, mind you, but they're hints.

"People still go missing in those mountains to this day. Bodies have been found without their heads. Some people think the Apache are responsible, that they don't want anyone to find what's up there."

He made an expression that I assumed was meant to be suspenseful and playful at the same time.

"That sounds racist and absurd," I laughed. "Maybe in the Wild West, but not today."

"Who knows?" he countered. "The only way to really find out would be to go up there and see if anything happens, now wouldn't it?"

"What were the signs?" I asked, chuckling as I

tried to steer him in another direction.

"You're supposed to follow an old government road and find the rock that looks like a man. Near that is the remains of the hut the Dutchman built for himself. Just beyond that is the entrance, which he covered with planks and buried." He was really getting into it now, his eyes wild and excited. Steve had always been a good storyteller. It was part of what made him such a great archeologist.

"Specific." I knew he liked it when I said just enough to keep the story going—as long as he was the one who got to tell it.

"More people have claimed to have found the place than any other lost treasure in the world. Yet, it still remains a mystery. There's a nice little museum about the mountains, with more details, out in Apache Junction. You should check it out while you're here."

"I only hunt one treasure at a time now," I replied seriously, feeling tired and full. All of my traveling was really wearing on me, and I wasn't even done yet. "And it's the one I get paid to do."

Saying our goodbyes at the end of our meal, we set up a time for Steve to come pick up the vase in the morning. Sore from all the time I'd spent sitting and researching, I walked the few blocks to my hotel. As soon as the door had opened, I found myself falling into the bed, sighing. Despite being exhausted, however, I couldn't sleep.

There had been a moment, when I could have told Steve everything that happened on Oak Isle. I hadn't wanted to. The words seemed to stick in my throat. Sam and her father were dead. Why was it so hard to talk about them still?

Sighing, I rolled out of bed, flipping the television on to some random show I didn't really watch. Instead, I stared at the bag holding the vase from the Pit. The jar could very well have been the last thing Sam ever touched.

Curiosity getting the better of me, I wandered over, settling into the armchair and pulling the container out of its cloak. Why would she have picked this up, out of all the other things she could have possibly seen? Had the lid been on it then?

"What happened to you, Sammy?" I asked quietly, wrapping my fingers gently around the top of the vessel and opening it.

There was nothing inside, which was both relieving and disappointing. Closing the jar, I placed it back in its carrying case and went to the window. It seemed that the walls were closing in around me, the air escaping from the room. Without another thought, I threw open the door and went outside, sucking in a deep breath.

The wind had picked up, blowing forcefully through the open walkway I stood on. It felt refreshing. Closing my eyes, I allowed it to just whisk past me, carrying my stress and anxieties with it.

After a few moments, my skin started to burn. Eyes flying open, I coughed as I inhaled a mouth full of dust; a massive wall of dirt, or a "haboob" as the locals called it, had blown in full force in the time I'd been outside. Surprised, I looked around, amazed that I hadn't seen or heard any warning about the event.

Sand clouded my vision, blocking out the entire hotel in an instant. Blinking furiously, I tried to wipe away the offending material, succeeding in only blinding myself further. Chocking, I covered my face, trying to block the tiny rocks and grains scratching ferociously at me. Fingers reaching out in desperation, I coughed, the dirt filling my lungs no matter where I turned. Panicked, I continued to feel for something that would anchor me back to the world and give me some sense of stability.

I never found it.

Samantha Greene O'Rourke, 1697

"Sit up straight, my dear. Ye're part of the family now and I expect ye to act like it."

Frowning, I did as the woman, my own *seanmháthair*—grandmother—by marriage, ordered. It wasn't that I didn't think she knew what she was talking about; she had been a queen, after all. I just didn't think sitting up straight was as important as other things in the long run.

"I swear, lettin' ye run around as part of that pirate crew," she continued, clicking her tongue at me. "What was the lad thinking?"

"That I'm his equal? You didn't have any problem with it when I was here last time." I replied under my breath, smiling apologetically when she shot me a look that could've cut glass.

"Equal or not, I'll not have any granddaughter of mine dressed in breeches and gallivanting around the world. If we'd still been in Éire, ye'd have been a princess, and I intend for ye to act that way."

"*Seanmháthair*," Tristan chuckled from the doorway, announcing his presence. I'd been married to him for a year now and he still took my breath away whenever I saw him. "Leave the lass be, aye?" he continued. "Ye'll teach the roughness I love about her away; I didn't marry a proper princess, and *I* intend for it to stay that way."

"What's that supposed to mean?" Smiling in a teasing manner, I rose, the skirt of my heavy dress brushing across the floor, and moved to kiss him in greeting.

He was dressed for our official wedding—the one his grandmother insisted we have, just as he'd said she would. We'd been hand fasted a year earlier, which was more than good enough for me, but now we were to be married by a priest and have an official record of our union made. The gold pattern on his white coat suited him very well, seeming to bring out the dark color of his short hair even more than usual. Butterflies formed in my stomach as I looked over his handsome face, strong and tan from being outside so often. He looked like the prince he should have been.

I had indeed married into royalty.

Memories flashing back to the night he'd told me about his history, I could almost feel the tossing of the waves we'd endured, sea sickness claiming both of us as we sat in the tiny cabin. His face had been so pale and drawn, but his happy laugh still managed to permeate the gloom of an upset stomach while we spoke. The fact that he was a prince hadn't really settled in until I met Gran for the first time, however.

Her dinner party dress was still lodged firmly in my mind, the skirt swishing over the doorway, the look on her face that of pure glee as she saw her grandson standing before her. Throwing her arms around him, she'd clutched him to her as she shouted to the rest of the house that he'd finally arrived for another visit.

Then her eyes found me, filled with confusion, some distaste, and definitely disapproving of my attire. Dressed as a man and stinking like a pirate, I couldn't really blame her.

That was the last time I'd been here, at her home in Southern Africa. After that, events had led to me becoming a member of the pirate crew Tristan commanded. Technically, I'd already been a part of the crew, but they'd all thought I was a man named Samuel. Only a select few really knew that I was Samantha.

"I didn't mean anything," Tristan replied, smiling kindly. "Only that I adore ye just the way ye are."

Blushing, I ignored Gran's snort of humor behind us. "You're sweet," I told him, grinning like a school girl.

"Yer both lovesick," Gran spoke up. "But we have a wedding to get to!"

As Tristan and Gran talked about a few details beside me, I felt my mind going back over the past two years and everything I'd been through. The icy cold water of the Treasure Pit gushed over my skin, everything instantly becoming a blur as I found myself, once again, struggling for breath in the torrent of flood waters. The next day, my entire form had felt as though I'd been squeezed out of a toothpaste tube, squished and cut up, my head pounding. Everything was the same—except it wasn't.

Hauled onto a ship in the bay, I was quickly kidnapped by pirates, Tristan taking orders from his captain to bring me along. My heart still sputtered when I thought of how scared I'd been, how unbelieving that I wasn't being pranked by a group of talented actors.

Fear of being lost in another time quickly became fear of rape, the face of Captain Rodrigues still etched in my mind. His drunken laugh would sometimes echo through my dreams, his slackened face drooling toward me as Tristan continued to pour alcohol for him, not stopping until the man passed out. Whenever I was visited by those memories, the comfort of Tristan's touch would push them away. He'd been my only ally then, and he was the best one I had now.

Fate had separated us for a time, when I was put ashore in Spain, but it led me to another man, one who would help me facilitate my disguise as a male.

Grinning, I thought of Father Torres and his excited spirit. He'd protected me when marauders took the ship we were on—the very crew that had kidnapped me across the ocean. Tristan had recognized me instantly and helped me join the crew as Samuel. Those months that we spent on the water, while terrifying, were some of my fondest memories. We'd fallen in love then, and he had confessed his feelings to me right here in his grandmother's garden.

Thinking of his words, of the way he'd so desperately and truthfully told me he loved me, I smiled to myself. Glancing up, I watched as he talked animatedly with Gran, his happiness filling the room. We were already married in my eyes; today was a formality for religion's sake. We were already bound together, by both affection and blood.

Captain Rodrigues's face slammed back into my mind, his putrid breath washing over me, his fingers

63

clawing at my clothes as I screamed for help. My disguise was busted; he knew who I was, that I'd been hiding under his nose for months. Fear wrapped around me, my breath catching, the memory so strong that I felt like passing out all over again.

"Are ye alright, lass?" Tristan asked in alarm, immediately coming to my side. "What's wrong?"

"Nothing," I replied quickly, brushing the horrifying incident away. "I was just thinking about how we got here." Smiling tightly, I motioned for him to go back to his conversation.

Hesitating, he watched me for a second longer, as if to make sure I was telling the truth, and then turned to his grandmother, picking up where they had left off.

Sighing slightly, I mentally pushed the attempted rape further into the depths of my mind. Tristan had arrived in time, eyes blazing, a challenge on his lips.

Captain Rodrigues had been dead within a half hour, beaten in a duel. It felt like there wasn't a man alive who wasn't grateful to see him gone, except for Thomas Randall.

Thomas.

Frowning, I easily brought the man's image up in my mind, his dark, greasy hair, and the evil look in his eyes. He'd burned a whole village to the ground, etching his name into the bodies as a calling card, ransacked another settlement, burned our ship and sank her to the bottom of the ocean, kidnapped a member of the crew and tortured him, among many other things. Every time I thought of him, my skin grew cold and clammy. We would only be safe and worry free when he was dead.

All of this had happened because my dad wanted to know what was at the bottom of the Treasure Pit. I didn't blame him for looking. It was a mystery that deserved to be solved. However, it had taken both of our lives in return. While he'd been laid to rest, everything I knew was suddenly gone. I'd opened the vase in the bottom of the vault—which I would later learn was technically not a vase at all, but was the ancient artifact often referred to as Pandora's Box— and, after almost drowning, I woke up on the beach surrounded by pirates.

If only I'd known then the adventure I was about to set out on. I'd probably still have been as terrified. It would have been nice to know that I was embarking with more than pirates, though.

Glancing back at the man I loved, I felt wonder at who he truly was, yet again. Never in my life did I think I would meet a member of The Order of the Knights Templar. Yet, here I was, married to one. His form practically exuded all of the regal and important titles he carried. Randall, on the other hand, had belonged to the same order and showed no such honor or peace.

Power. That was what came to mind whenever I thought of our common enemy. Not because he possessed it, but because he wanted it so desperately. His eyes always seemed to be searching out the treasure the Order was hiding on Oak Isle, never able to discover how to get to it.

His face glared at me now, the image backed by the men who had joined him, the group that called themselves Black Knights. They looked like villainous traitors to me, covered in the blood of their victims. They were the reason we'd returned to Oak Isle, to fight for our lives and the protection of the artifacts hidden there.

The island was finally in the condition it would be when the Treasure Pit would be discovered, a little less than one hundred years from now. Thomas had gotten away with a few members of his crew, but the pit he'd dug was filled in and booby-trapped by Knights who stood on the side of good. I'd supplied them with all my knowledge of what it was like in my own time and they followed my instructions to the letter. It felt strange, to finally know exactly how everything worked.

Sometimes, I wondered if Dad had been able to solve the riddle that had beaten every man for two hundred years because I was the one that set it up. Time had come in a full circle in that aspect.

If only he'd been able to see what he'd been searching for before he died.

"The lass is going to meet the King of France, Tristan," Gran's voice said, interrupting my thoughts. "She should be presented and act as who she is now."

"She'll be fine," he assured her. "We spoke about it much on the journey here. Ye forget, Gran, we've known we were going to France for over a month."

"Tristan has been educating me on how things work with the Order and what's considered polite," I added, wanting to help him as well as defend myself. "I may live and dress like a pirate, but I do know how to act like a lady."

Gran contemplated the two of us, Tristan's arm around my waist, and then threw her hands up in the air. "Ye're as stubborn as my grandson," she said, shaking her head. "Lord help ye face the courts. Have ye even been to France?"

"I haven't," I replied smoothly. "But I know what an important visit this is."

"The head of the Order!" She looked like she wasn't ready to give up any time soon. "The Grandmaster is an advisor to the King! Everything you do will reflect back on our family, in the public eye and the society that we are all secretly tied to. Do you not understand how important it is for you to shine as brightly as possible?"

"With all due respect, Gran, Sam has helped the Order in more ways than one. With her history, I'm sure meeting a King will be just another day for her." Tristan chuckled, leaning over and kissing my forehead. "We leave tomorrow. Unless ye have more ye'd like to harp on her about?"

Gran's face softened, and she gave him a small smile. "I know ye picked well, lad. I can't help the mothering nature I have. Go now, to the church. I'll see the two of ye wed properly before ye take off to save the world again." She turned to me, crossing the space and taking my hands. "Ye'll do well, lass. I'm not used to having more than one grandchild to take care of. I apologize if I offended ye."

"You didn't," I replied warmly, laughing at her suddenly polite nature. "You want what's best for Tristan. I'll do whatever I can to help him, including wearing a horrid corset every day so I look proper."

She laughed, pulling me into a tight hug. "I know ye'll take good care of him. Ye've been doing it for a year already." Stepping away, she looked me over again, smiling at the gold fabric of my dress. "Ye look beautiful, lass. Now, off with ye! I want to have a word with my grandson."

Nodding, I stepped out of the room, pausing in the hall as she started speaking to him.

"She's a spitfire spirit, that much is certain," she said to him, sighing. "But she loves ye. Any fool can see that."

"She's a good soul, Gran," Tristan agreed. "The Lord has put her through a lot."

"And ye'll still not tell me what it is the Order knows about her? Brian would only say that it was surprising, but not to be shared. I'm the lass's grandmother now. Surely, I can be trusted?" She sounded almost pleading, which I immediately recognized as a tactic to get information. Tristan also seemed to grasp it.

"Gran." He laughed, sighing happily. "I'll say nothing. If Sam wants to tell ye in the future, that will be her choice. I'll not take that from her."

"Don't be keeping secrets from your *seanmháthair* now, lad," she scolded. "Is she breeding? Ye've been married for a year and no babe to warm yer family with. She can conceive, can't she?"

"Aye, I'm sure she can. We don't want a baby yet. Not while we're on the hunt for Randall. Ye can understand that, can't ye?"

"Hmph." She didn't sound too happy about that, but there was no more argument from her. After a few moments silence, she cleared her throat and dismissed him, an excited sadness to her voice. "Go and be with yer wife. Heaven knows ye've met yer match in her."

The ship rocked gently on the small waves, lulling me into a kind of restfulness that I never wanted to end. Tristan lay beside me, one arm thrown over my waist, chin resting on the top of my head. The tiny area we'd been allotted was cozy and warm, the wood beams that sat around the makeshift pallet bed seeming to stretch up into forever. Various parcels sat around us, waiting to be delivered to the harbormaster when we arrived at our destination. I was grateful for the space, though, and the privacy it allowed us, cramped as it might be.

"Sam?"

"Hmm?" Snuggling deeper into his embrace, I kissed the fabric of his shirt, breathing in his scent. Though our trip had been short, I enjoyed the time spent with his family. Ever since leaving Oak Isle, Tristan had been absorbed in finding Thomas, talking with other members of the Order and questioning those who might have seen or heard from him. During the month we'd spent on our current trip, he'd done the same. It would be worse in Paris; he didn't have to tell me that. With the unlimited number of Knights there, and the intelligence they possessed, he was sure to be preoccupied with what he felt was his duty.

I, on the other hand, would be expected to spend occasions with the other ladies, talking about dresses and raising children, or whatever it was the women talked about now. Tristan had sounded somewhat sorry when he told me. When it was just he and I, we lived by a system of trust and equality. The one instance he'd broken that vow had almost cost us our marriage. So, while he would tell me everything that was discussed in the secret, male-only society, I wasn't allowed to be part of the group, even though a good number of the leaders now knew that I was from the future.

Apparently, I was another special treasure to be kept away from the world. My history was addressed when they needed something from me, like the plans to booby trap the Treasure Pit. I didn't mind helping, but I was miffed that I was still being treated as a "delicate woman," as it had been put to me on our voyage to South Africa.

"What are ye thinking?" Tristan mumbled into my hair, kissing it softly. "Ye've not spoken for a while."

"I was sleeping." I yawned. "And then I was thinking about how things will be for the next little while."

"Aye. Don't worry about it, savvy? We won't be there very long, I'm sure. Of course, we'll have to make the proper appearances, but I don't intend to do much more. Randall needs found, everyone agrees on that." Rolling away slightly, he glanced at me, smiling his handsome grin. "It will be nice to take ye away and let ye be yerself again. Every time I see ye in a dress, I want to laugh!"

Playfully, I slapped him on the shoulder, chuckling. "What, I don't look good in a dress?"

"Not that," he stated, grabbing my hand and holding it against his chest. "Ye're downright gorgeous, lass. It's the thought of ye wielding a sword in such a contraption that humors me. How would such a fierce, protective thing move about like ye do? Ye're the first woman I ever met who I thought was more suited to pants." Raising my captured fingers to his lips, he kissed them softly, his eyes burning.

"I could fight in a dress if I needed to," I retorted, squeezing his hand slightly. "Anything for you."

"Aye. Anything for you."

Scooting closer, he brushed the side of my face, touching his mouth against mine. It was like breathing, being with him like this. Every time we touched, each look we shared spoke to my heart. I'd found my soul mate, born more than three hundred years before me.

Hooking a finger in the front of my bodice, his lips crossed over my cheek and down my neck, his tongue licking my collarbone. I hummed in encouragement, pushing my hands into his hair as he rolled on top of me and reached down for the bottom of my skirt. Upon finding it, he slowly pulled it up, his hand sliding to my thigh as he settled back on his knees.

"Sir?"

Groaning at the knock on the door, I scooted away from him, sad that our time together was being interrupted.

"What is it?" Tristan called, grabbing my hand

and keeping me from rising.

"The captain wanted me to inform you we will be arriving in port within the hour. He requests you and your lady join him for a drink to toast our good voyage."

"Tell the captain we'll join him shortly," Tristan replied. "Thank you."

"Aye, sir."

The cabin boy's footsteps faded slowly away and Tristan yanked me back into his embrace, kissing me thoroughly once more.

"I love ye, Samantha," he whispered fiercely against my lips. "Don't forget it. Things will be different here, but that will never change. No matter where ye are, or when, my heart belongs to ye."

Smiling, I suddenly felt a little teary at his words, touched by the sentiment. It was odd, after fighting pirates and traveling through time, that I felt so worried about having to spend a small period away from him. We hadn't really been apart since I arrived here, though. The few weeks I spent on board a different ship had all occurred before I knew I couldn't live without him. Now, I felt like I was being thrust into a situation I wouldn't be able to handle on my own.

"And I love you," I whispered back, holding him tightly. "Just don't be gone long, okay?"

"Ye'll do fine," he assured me again.

"Even meeting the King?"

"I think ye'd be surprised." He chuckled. "I've met him once before. He's a very energetic and opinionated man, but smart. Ye know that he's been at war with Spain and England for some years?"

"I had heard that, yes."

"Aye. Well, he's calling for peace now. Ye'll be meeting him when he's on his best behavior—and ye're married to a man from the country he tried to liberate. True, he wanted his own relative on a throne that sat over all of the Éire, but he fought for the people. Gran was quite interested in knowing how that turned out. Had he won, we might have returned to be members of his court. But, alas, it was not meant to be. Ireland belongs to the English now, and it will always be that way."

"It won't," I replied, smiling slightly. "I don't know a whole lot about world history, but I do know Ireland is its own country in my time."

He chuckled, resting his chin on my head once more. "Then it will have to be enough for me to know that they will have their freedom someday."

"Does King Louis know that the Knights are in his court?" I asked. "It was a French monarch that tarnished his own name and saved them all those years ago, after all."

"I don't think so. If he does, no one is sharing that information with me. As far as I know, the man is simply a king, but what king doesn't own his share of secrets?"

Mulling over his words, I fisted my hand in his shirt. I'd never been one for politics. It gave me anxiety just thinking about how people ran countries, and here I was, about to be thrown into a hierarchal society I couldn't even begin to understand. What was worse, I knew almost nothing about what was going on in the world. Thank heavens Tristan had thought to mention to me that peace was now being sought after. All anyone had been concerned with was telling me when I needed to bow and what fashion was like. It wasn't very likely I would be discussing war at length, but the women would know what was going on, wouldn't they? What if it was brought up?

"Ye're working yerself up again," Tristan commented, rolling away from me. "Honestly, ye'll be fine."

"I don't know anything. If someone were to ask me what I thought about some situation or place, I wouldn't even know what to say." Frowning, I stood, straightening my skirt and running a hand over my long, pulled back hair. There wasn't much in the way of grooming on a ship, so I'd taken to tying the brown locks into a bun every day, a few wisps hanging around my face. I would have killed for a bath at this point, but had made do with what I had. Cleaning myself could wait until we were on shore, as gross as that made me feel. I wanted to look presentable when we arrived.

Gran had supplied me with a number of dresses, her personal team of seamstresses having worked night and day to finish them in the short amount of time we'd been there. Among them was a maternity dress, much to my embarrassment. Hopefully, we wouldn't have any children until this was all done with and we could feel safe. I faithfully took herbs to protect against a baby every day. The loose dress was the least of my worries, though.

The gown I wore now was simple enough, a white fabric with little blue, silk ribbons accenting my waist and chest, but some of the gowns were fit for royalty. They had huge skirts and fancy tops, embroidered and covered with lace. The underthings looked like an ungodly contraption meant to torture me; there were massive hoops, padding for my hips, and corsets that had designs all their own. There was no way to get dressed by myself, let alone undressed. Gran had insisted she send a maid with me, as was proper, but I refused. As a result, we were now carrying enough money to hire one in the city.

I'd never felt so pushed into anything in my life—politics, dresses, and now a live-in servant? How would I ever survive without Tristan with me every step of the way?

Suddenly, I realized he'd been talking to me and I'd missed it. "I'm sorry. Could you say that again?"

"If ye don't know, ye tell them the truth, lass." His voice was soft and caring as he got to his feet and came over to me, cradling my face between his hands. "Ye were born in America. It's all ye know. No one would expect any more explanation than that."

"So I just play dumb." That didn't make me feel any better. I'd be the "stupid girl" who was lucky enough to snag Tristan. No one would care to ask about me personally; everything depended on whom I was married to in this time.

If that weren't enough, I would now have a paid slave following me everywhere. That part made me the most uncomfortable. At least we would be paying the woman. The only comfort I got was in knowing whomever we hired would get money in exchange for helping me.

"Don't think about it, aye?"

"That's all you keep saying!" Frustrated, I moved away, breathing heavily.

"It's the best advice I can give ye. Be yerself, Sam. Let the other things do what they will."

Nodding, I looked at him over my shoulder. His smile somehow made my anxieties lessen, aided in part from his hair, which was poking up from our nap. Resisting the urge to giggle, I marveled at how someone so strong and daring could look so innocent and young in that moment. At the same time, the line of his jaw held the roughness of the sea in it, his hands, resting on his hips, those of a pirate who did whatever he needed to get what he wanted. He was everything to me, each breath I took and every sight my eyes saw had him in them. Continuing my appraisal of his appearance, I bit my lip at the sight of his white shirt hanging out of the waist of his black pants, the front untied and hanging open in a very enticing manner. Barely visible, the saber scar Captain Rodrigues had given him across his shoulder, during their fight to the death reminded me of what he would do for me—lay down his life without another thought. The memory both thrilled and terrified me as I looked down to his bare feet, seeming to grip the floor.

"Here," I said, turning back and taking the strings of his shirt in my hand. "Let me tie these for you."

"Pity," he mumbled, watching me work. "I'd have liked to undo yer laces for ye."

"There's time enough for that later," I replied, snickering. "The captain is ready for us now and we have a whole city waiting to greet us."

"This isn't Paris?" I whispered the question to Tristan who grinned like an idiot and pulled me aside.

"No. We'll board another, smaller ship here and sail the Seine into Paris. The water is too shallow for a big ship, savvy? It's not much further, though; we should be in the city by tonight, tomorrow morning at the latest. The wind is good." He nodded at a crewmember that was carrying one of our trunks down the gangplank and motioned for me to follow. "We're in Rouen now."

Looking out over the large city, I felt some trepidation at having to travel even further; I had really been looking forward to a bath.

Shaking myself, I stepped off the vessel and onto the plank that reached to the shore. Tristan had said we might be in Paris tonight, which meant I could still rediscover some relaxation, if at all possible.

Rouen was a bustling mass of trade and transport, being the last stop on the river that large ships could get to. Our own captain had informed us that he would be returning to the Channel in the morning, headed for London. With talks of peace being entertained, it was now considered safe to travel between the two countries without the fear of being bullied into the Navy.

We didn't stay to see any more of the city than the dock, immediately booking passage on a boat leaving for Paris within the hour. It felt like I'd hardly had any time to blink before we were on our way again, sailing smoothly down the river.

The closer we got to our final destination, the more excited I became. I'd taken Tristan's advice and put the political aspects of our journey out of my mind and instead focused on the city itself. Paris had been a place I'd always wanted to visit. What would it be like now? Would I be allowed to explore Notre Dame? Would there be trees lining the avenues and statues dotting the landscape? This was when the beautiful Paris I longed to see was being constructed. How much of it was available already? The Eiffel Tower wouldn't be built until the eighteen hundreds, but I wasn't too upset over missing it.

When the sun had set and we still sailed on, Tristan beckoned me over to him and we strolled around the deck, watching as the small crew steered our ship. There wasn't even a hold, since the vessel was so tiny.

"When we arrive, we'll go find an inn to stay in for the night." He took my arm. "The Order has arranged a place for us to live while we're here, but I don't want to be searching them out in the dead o' night."

"And in the morning?"

"We'll get settled in. I'll have to meet with the Grandmaster right away, for a new assignment."

"Do you think there's a chance he'll tell you not

to go after Thomas?" My stomach clenched at the thought, and I instantly felt ashamed for wishing we could let everything go in this instant. Thomas had all but marked Tristan and I as his nemesis, though.

"Aye, I do. I don't plan on letting him. I need a ship and crew, which I could persuade him of easy enough. However, he'll need convinced of the situation. I imagine he'll be wanting to meet ye as well." Smiling at me, he patted my hand. "Ye'll have to wait to be called."

"I expected as much," I mumbled, sighing.

"I'm sorry, Sam," he said softly. "I know ye don't like being treated as a secondary person."

"It's a man's world," I replied evenly. "As much as I don't like being allowed to not make decisions on my own, I understand things are different here. I'm sure there are plenty of strong willed women helping their husbands behind closed doors. I'll just have to learn to do so discretely, as they do."

"Ye're something else." Laughing, he leaned over and kissed me, stopping our walk. "Sometimes I think ye might still be a witch of some kind."

"If I were a witch I would have conjured myself some hot water and candle light days ago."

Gasping, one of the crew members, who had heard our easy talk of witchcraft, crossed himself in earnest and scurried away, glancing over his shoulder every few seconds.

"Well, he didn't like that, did he?" Tristan mused as I snickered.

Eventually, Paris began to emerge out of the darkness around us, candlelight flickering in windows and gas lamps illuminating the streets. Even in the shadows, I could tell how beautiful it was. There was such exquisite architecture everywhere I looked. The only dim part of town seemed to be the poorest, and even the tall, skinny houses there had lights in the windows facing the streets.

"Welcome to Paris, love," Tristan said, wrapping his arms around my waist from behind. "Our home for the next little while."

"We've never had a home that wasn't a ship," I replied conversationally, my grin growing wider by the moment. "I'd never thought of that before."

"I have. Someday, I will bring ye home to a house more beautiful than ye can even imagine. It will have a garden and more than enough land to raise animals. Our children will run through the halls, filling the space with laughter and love. And I will tell ye how much I love ye every day, until ye're old and can't hear, and then I'll shout it at ye."

Laughing, I leaned against him, letting my head rest on his shoulder. "Where will this house be?"

"Anywhere ye want. As long as I'm with ye, I couldn't care less where we are." Kissing my neck softly, he continued to hold me as we sailed to the shore.

"Do I have to?" I moaned, sitting down in the small chair by the window.

"If ye want to be able to get dressed and leave the house." Tristan's mouth twitched as he obviously tried to hold back a smile. "It's only a maid, lass. Not the end of the world."

"I don't like the idea of having a servant," I replied sourly. "It feels . . . wrong."

The window of our room at the inn was dirty, but everything else felt very comfortable and clean. I'd had my bath—finally—and dressed with Tristan's help. A delicious breakfast had been served to us, the remaining dishes of which I could smell in the kitchen below us still. However, it was time to sort out our business now, which mean Tristan was leaving to speak to the Order. In the meantime, I was to hire my maid.

"It's not wrong," he continued, straightening his long tailed coat and buttoning it. "Ye're paying her for a service rendered. Ye'll not tell me that people don't do that in yer time?"

"That's not fair." Pouting, I peered out the window again. The street was alive with activity, despite the early hour.

He was right. There were still nannies, housecleaners, cooks, drivers, and all sorts of people who made money by working for someone in their home. It hadn't ever been a luxury I'd experienced. I'd always felt bad for those who had to put up with those kinds of duties.

"We'll not be here long." Tristan's voice had softened and I turned to stare at him, taking in his entire formal apparel. Black buckle shoes, white stockings, blue pants that covered down to his calves, and a matching coat that covered his white shirt with the frilly neck piece. Lace peeked out of his sleeves, finalizing the look of the period.

"I know we won't." Glancing down, I twisted the green fabric of my dress between my fingers. "I just—I don't like knowing that a stranger will be helping me get dressed. I feel like it's something I should be able to do by myself. I would in my own time, why not here?"

Smiling gently, he crossed over to me, squatting beside the chair and taking my hand. "It's a different time, Sam. Things are not the same. Ye know that better than anyone. Find a lass and give her the money and care she needs. Let her help ye in return. Savvy?"

Nodding, I held back the tears I desperately wished to shed. I'd felt ridiculously emotional of late and I didn't like it. At first, I'd wondered if I was pregnant, but that time of the month had arrived almost immediately after I thought it.

"What's bothering ye? I know it's not the maid. Ye've always handled the differences here with ease." Tristan stared at me expectantly, as if all his plans had suddenly been canceled for the day and he had every moment to listen.

"Nothing," I muttered, looking up and blinking hard.

"Ye're still upset over what happened on Oak Isle? With James?" He waited for me to answer, watching my face with love and worry in his eyes.

Lip trembling, I sucked in a ragged breath, instantly able to recall the horrible images from the bottom of the Treasure Pit. In one second, Thomas was shooting James. In the next, it was Tristan at the end of the barrel. Then there was the end—James opening Pandora's Box and being killed by it, his mouth hanging open in a silent scream.

"Sometimes I have nightmares about it." The whispered confession left my lips with great relief. It was hard, going to bed knowing James might be waiting for me in my sleep. Of all the things that had happened to me here, it was his death that bothered me the most. It had been so far out of my realm of control. If I'd been any closer to him, the jar might have taken me through time again, or killed me as well.

"Me too." His tone was soft, fearful even, but it held all the comfort I'd needed from him.

I cried then, the weight of what we'd been through crashing down around me. It hadn't been so bad when we were in Africa, but now we were getting ready to throw ourselves back in the whole mess. What if it was Tristan who was captured and killed this time? What if our ship was burned and sank again? Just the thought of ever seeing Thomas made my skin crawl. I would have given anything to forget him and the horrible events he orchestrated.

We had a duty, though. Tristan knew him better than any of the other Knights, having served on the same crew with him. He knew how Thomas worked and thought. Our friends had been killed. A portion of the treasure of the Knights Templar that Tristan had been trusted with had been stolen. Things like that couldn't go on and be forgotten. We had to do something to make it all right. Not anyone else.

"I dream that the wind grows and takes ye away from me," Tristan whispered, gripping my hands in his.

"Never. Never!" Pandora's Box was still in the

bottom of the Pit, where it would remain until I found it again in the future—a future that was now my past. Only heaven knew if someone had pulled it out of there after I vanished.

I hoped not.

"I'll never go, not willingly." Leaning forward, I kissed him, squeezing his fingers.

"I know ye wouldn't." Standing up, he pulled me into a hug, brushing a hand over my unbound hair. "But I can't help the fear that one day ye'll be gone, and there will be nothing I can do about it. Ye'll be okay while I'm away?"

"I'll be fine," I said against his shoulder. "And I'll go find a maid." He laughed at my sour tone, releasing me and moving toward the door.

"Ask the lady of the house here. She might have some good suggestions. If ye want, I'll make some enquiries on my end, too."

"That would be nice. How long will you be gone?"

"I haven't the slightest idea. Ye'll be wanting to explore some?" When I nodded, he continued. "Don't stay out after dark, aye?"

"I won't. I love you."

"And I love ye." Kissing me briefly, he straightened his coat once more and turned for the door, off to do the work I'd always known he would have.

The city was as amazing and beautiful as I'd imagined. Cobblestone streets led the way past tall buildings with designs that seemed to have been forgotten by my own generation, trees lined the avenues, and all of it left me gaping. Paris even had a sewer system, which I hadn't been expecting. It was a relief, not having to watch where I stepped, for the most part. Walking through the space was like going back in time all over again.

Upon leaving the inn, I still wasn't quite ready to hire a maid. I wanted to see the city on my own and didn't know if she would immediately start following me around. While Tristan had been right about my major anxiety being over something else, I was still uncomfortable with the thought of ringing a bell and having a woman appear to serve me.

Slowly, I made my way through town, stopping at merchant carts and watching the people. It felt like a maze of sorts, with some of the structures set into the old walls that had been erected around the city. I arrived at places with no idea of how I'd gotten there, despite having just passed through the area. At one point, I suddenly realized I was on a bridge; one side of the path was all houses, built up tall and skinny, but when I turned around there was a perfect view of the river. Eventually, I found myself standing before one of the sights I'd most wished to see—Notre Dame.

It was more than I expected, probably due to the pictures I'd seen of the place. In my mind, it was just the iconic front facade and towers, but the whole edifice stretched out behind that, apparently bustling with people doing their religious work. The cathedral was huge, reaching into the sky, her painted glass windows shining in the sunlight. Bells rang in the tower and I closed my eyes, taking in the moment.

"*Señorita?*"

Gasping at the familiar voice, my eyes flew open and I turned, bursting into the widest grin I'd worn in ages. The man was wearing the plain, brown robes I'd met him in, his dark hair still fashioned in a bowl cut. He looked every bit the pious priest, and yet I knew him to be one of the most fun loving, romantic men on Earth.

"Father Torres!" We stepped together, laughing, and threw our arms around each other. "How are you? I didn't know you were in Paris!"

"*Sí, sí,*" he said, squeezing me tightly. "I came on the ship from the island."

"Of course. We went on one and you were on the other. I thought they would have dropped you off in Spain, though."

"No. I had to speak with the men—you know which ones—about keeping the secret." His voice lowered as he stepped away, peering around cautiously. "What happened on Oak Isle—"

"Was horrible," I interrupted him. "Thank you for your help. I know you were worried about working with an organization you didn't feel you could support."

"The Lord commands evil men be stopped, *señorita*. I did what I felt was right." Pausing, he studied me over, smiling at my dress. "You look very lovely. I suppose I should call you *señora*, no? How is your husband?"

"Wonderful," I replied warmly. "He'll be sad that he missed you. He's working now, unfortunately."

"At the Temple?" He watched me expectantly, clearly thinking I had some idea of what was going on.

"I'm sorry, Temple?" I asked, confused. "What Temple?"

"The one built by the Knights Templar," he stated. "It is across the river some way. Of course, I don't think they openly admit the Knights are still there, since they were cast out from the church. I believe many artisans live and work in the area. It has been standing for centuries."

"Really? I had no idea anything like that was even here." Staring in the direction he pointed, I bit my lip. Would the Templars hide in plain sight like that, using a building they had erected and been removed from hundreds of years before? Had the Temple been the very place that was ransacked when King Philip demanded the Knights arrested?

"It is very large," he continued. "It served as the Knight's prison when they were captured as well. I thought *Señor* O'Rourke would have told you about it."

"We've been a bit more preoccupied as of late." Laughing slightly, I turned back to him, pushing the Temple to the back of my thoughts for later. "I am to meet the King. As you can imagine, I've had to learn how to be a proper lady for the occasion."

"His Majesty, the King!" He appeared both flabbergasted and pleased at the same time. "What an honor! I've always wanted to visit the gardens at the palace, but I have never been called to visit. Maybe someday I will get to serve in the chapel there. I hear it is very beautiful."

"Do you plan to stay here in Paris? I thought you wanted to be a missionary."

"I did," he replied, chuckling uncomfortably. "I am somewhat ashamed to admit that my time as a pirate was not what I'd expected it to be. It was a romanticized version I wished to play out. Now that I have experienced the real thing, I do believe I am done with traveling the high seas for a time."

My expression fell a little at that, guilt overtaking me. "I'm sorry for what I put you through, Alfonso," I said quietly, looking at the ground. "If we'd never run into each other on that dock, you might have had the life you wanted."

"If I hadn't found you on that dock, you never would have made it on the ship and back to your husband. The pirates would have killed me when the boat was overrun. You have nothing to apologize for, my friend. I would not change the past for anything."

Glancing up, I caught the end of the bow he had honored me with. All the memories I had of him began flooding my mind and I suddenly wondered if there was as good a library here as the one he'd left behind at the abbey in Spain.

"Would you like to come in for mass, *Señora*? Or do you have somewhere you need to be?"

The question interrupted my musings and I smiled. "I would love to. All I have left to do besides sightseeing is hiring a maid. To be honest, I don't even know how to go about that."

"A maid?" He didn't seem stunned by the notion, but he did look contemplative. "Do you have specific requirements for her?"

"That she knows how to tie a knot? I don't know. I really just need help getting dressed. Tristan's grandmother thinks I need someone to accompany me everywhere, though."

"It would be wise to have someone with you," he agreed, nodding. "Paris can be a dangerous place, Samantha. I think I might be able to help you."

"Really? That's surprising."

He made a face, halfway between amusement and offense.

Frowning, I laughed at myself. "I didn't mean that the way it sounded. I just didn't expect a priest to suddenly have a girl who can help me."

"Come inside." He chuckled, motioning for me to follow.

Leading me through the wooden doors, Father Torres smiled as I gasped at the interior of the building. High, vaulted ceilings took my breath away as I stared up at them in awe. Magnificent pillars stretched from the floor to the top of the room, carved with such elegance that I couldn't even think of any words to describe them out loud. Looking to the congregation space, I watched the small crowd gathering in the pews, getting ready for the mass Alfonso had mentioned. Priests scurried around the front of the room, behaving as if they were trying to be reverent, making sure all was in order. Religion had always made me somewhat uncomfortable, but I would have come to sit in this room every day, whether there was a mass being performed or not.

"This way," he whispered, going through a door off to the side. A spiral staircase greeted me on the other end, the Father's footsteps already echoing down from above. Hurrying up the steps with ease, I met him at the top, momentarily stunned by the balcony view stretching out in front of me.

"A few weeks ago, a young woman came here seeking sanctuary from her abusive father." Shaking his head, he motioned to someone standing at the edge of the balcony. "She's too afraid to return home, but she can't stay here much longer; there isn't room to take in every person off the street. I've spoken with her many times and find her to be very pleasant. She's been helping with the cleaning, but we will have to put her out soon. Perhaps you would like to meet her?"

Surprised, I nodded, wondering what condition I would find the woman in.

"Her name is Abella," Father Torres said, gesturing for me to go ahead.

Taking a deep breath, I took a step forward, ignoring the slight breeze that ruffled my hair. The air didn't seem to bother the girl either, her long, black, curly hair blowing away from her face. Studying her, I tried to guess how old she must have been. Sixteen? The plain dress she wore did nothing to hide how beautiful she was, either. With a sickening twist in my stomach, I suddenly wondered how her father had been abusing her.

"Abella?" I spoke softly, not wanting to scare her. It didn't look like she'd heard us come up at all.

"*Oui*, Madame?" She didn't turn, simply staring out across the city, what I could see of her eyes locked on something far away.

"My name is Samantha O'Rourke. Father Torres tells me you might be needing work?" Hesitating, I remained a few steps away, not exactly sure how to act in this situation. I'd met abused people before, right after the offense had happened. Some of them didn't want to be touched or stand too close to other people.

"*Oui*, Madame. What kind of work did you have in mind?" Her voice was high and sounded like tinkling bells. Did she like the bells here? Was that why she fled to the church, instead of leaving town?

"I need a maid, mostly to help me dress."

She nodded, the expression on her face never changing.

"You'd live in my house while you were employed," I added, wondering if her living situation was the issue. "And accompany me on outings. Really, I guess I'm looking for . . . a friend. You won't be treated like a slave, and it's only for while I'm in town. My husband is refusing to help me get a corset on every day. I'm to meet the King and something tells me I should probably be wearing one when I do."

She did peer at me then, smiling lightly. "Did Father Torres tell you why I am here?"

"You ran away from your abusive father. I'm sorry for your hardship."

"I stole bread," she said quietly. "They wanted to cut off my hand. When Papa found out, he tried to do it himself, to restore the family honor." She looked down at her wrist, touching the dirty bandage tied around it. Carefully, she pulled the cloth away, revealing a mostly healed hack job of cuts that made me want to pass out. "Would you want a disgraced thief working in your home?"

Swallowing hard, I looked away from her wounds. The thief part did throw me off some, but Tristan and I didn't really have much to lose. Her crime suggested she'd been starving. I could accept her actions in that case. "Madame," I said in as strong a voice as I could. "As long as you did not kill someone or sleep with my husband, I do not care what crimes you are accused of. Stealing bread because you are hungry does not warrant having your hand cut off, and I will stick to that statement till the day I die. Now, do you know how to tie laces, or not?"

Father Torres snorted behind me, hastily trying to cover it up with a cough. In spite of myself, I grinned at her, raising an eyebrow as I waited for the answer.

"*Oui*," she responded, her teeth shining as she truly smiled for the first time. "I worked as a maid for a lady, once. I can help you. The King will be very pleased with your corset."

Laughing loudly, I clapped my hands together. "Good. Come with me and we'll get you fed. We're moving from an inn to our permanent residence today. You can help with all of that, too. There isn't much."

"You aren't worried I'll steal from you?"

"All I have are corsets. If you want them, then by all means take the blasted contraptions."

Father Torres emitted another hacking cough as she chuckled, turning away from the ledge and looking at me fully.

"I have plenty of corsets, Madame."

"Wonderful. Do you want to stay for mass? It doesn't matter to me either way."

"I am hungry, since you brought it up before. I missed breakfast." She seemed very calm and in control, but there was a fire in her eyes that I recognized. I'd seen it in myself many times.

"Let's go, then. I could eat."

"*Merci*, Madame." She moved to follow me out, tying the dirty rag back around her wrist.

"Please stop calling me that. It makes me feel like an old maid."

"What should I call you, then?"

"Samantha." Smiling at her once more, I turned, knowing she would stay right behind me now that she'd been hired.

"Thank you, Alfonso." Curtseying, I flashed him a grateful smile, too. "I'll take good care of her."

"I know you will, *Señora*. I would not have let her leave here with anyone cruel."

"You didn't tell me there'd be more servants!" I hissed under my breath in the doorway of our new bedroom. My face was positively burning as I fell silent, waiting for the woman who had suddenly appeared in the hallway to leave. After a moment, she disappeared inside another room, humming softly to herself and barely even giving us her notice.

"I thought ye knew." Tristan glanced at me. There was an enormous amount of humor in his eyes, and a grin playing on his lips. "Every well off house in Paris has servants, lass. They're getting paid to be here. It's their job. Do ye even know how to run a household like this?"

"I took care of mine for years, thank you very much!" I snapped, turning and walking across the hall. Leaning against the banister, I peeked down to the floor below, watching Abella stand near the front door, acting like she didn't quite know what to do. She'd been quiet since we left Notre Dame, only glancing over my clothes when we got back to the inn. We'd left shortly after that, and I'd had barely a moment to speak with her since walking into the house.

"Ye know that's not what I meant." Sighing, Tristan joined me, covering one of my hands with his. "Do ye know how to run a house with hired help? I know ye can cook and clean, ye lived on a ship with me for over a year."

"Pardon me," a small, female voice interrupted. It was the housemaid, her arms carrying an empty basket. "I put new sheets on all the beds, Madame," she said, curtseying. "And closed all the windows. The house should be aired out well enough now. Do you need anything else before I go help with dinner?"

Gaping, I stared at her, trying to think of what to say. "No?"

"Perhaps your Lady's Maid would like to be shown to her room and change for supper?" Tristan suggested, but I couldn't seem to form a coherent thought, so he answered her for me. "That would be very nice, thank you. Would you please tell Mr. Claudel that I'll join him shortly, as well?"

"*Oui*, Monsieur." She curtseyed again and slid past us, hurrying on to her other tasks. Just as I heard her greeting Abella below, Tristan took my hand and led me into the bedroom, closing the door behind us.

Despite my horror at having even more servants, I couldn't deny that I had no idea how to run the house we'd been put in. It wasn't like I could order everything we needed online. The home was beautiful—hardwood floors, colorful rugs, delightful wallpaper, and the most ornate furniture greeted me at every turn. The outside was a magnificent façade of architecture that I probably couldn't have ever dreamed up, even if I tried. It was like I was living in an old dollhouse, transported through time.

I suppose I was, after all.

Our room was rather large, with a sitting area and desk to work at. Resting in the armchair in front of a large mirror, I inhaled deeply, trying to take comfort in the smell of the bouquet of flowers arranged on the table just beside me. "How many are there?"

"The maid ye just met, the cook, and Monsieur Claudel, who is in charge of running the finances of the house," Tristan replied, knowing I was still uncomfortable over our hired help. "He will bring everything to you for approval, of course. There's also a coachman who can be called, should you wish to go anywhere."

"That's it?"

He smiled at the relief in my voice. "Ye are very peculiar about having people work for ye, Sam. Aye, that's it. They take care of this place whenever someone comes to stay and are well acquainted with all her corners and needs. Ye won't have to do much."

"Just approve everything."

"Aye. Ye are the Lady of the house." Sitting on the edge of the bed, he began to undo the ruffle around his neck, pulling at it slowly as he watched me.

Muffled voices filtered through the closed door. It sounded like Abella was being instructed on how things went in the house, should she need help with anything.

"Abella," Tristan said thoughtfully, tugging the lacy cloth completely off and tossing it on the mattress. "Father Torres introduced ye?"

"He did." Nodding, I stood and went to look out

the window, staring over the rooftops of the city stretching out in front of me.

"She will be good for ye," he said decidedly, removing his jacket with care.

"Oh, really? And how can you tell that? You only just met her when the carriage you sent to the inn dropped us off." Smiling, I turned to him, trying not to laugh as he set to undoing the many buttons on his long vest; Tristan wasn't really the type who liked dressing up.

"Ye've both got that same defiant air about ye," he replied, chuckling. "Though, come to think of it, defiance seems to get ye in the most trouble." Pausing for a second, he fumbled over a button, cursing softly at it.

"Here, let me help you." Crossing to him, I put my own calloused fingers to the task, moving through it with a little more ease than he had. "I guess our hands aren't very practiced for the finer things of life." Watching them together, his touch brushing over mine, I took in the wear and tear from years at sea, doing hard labor.

No, we had never been meant for the fancy court life we now found ourselves thrown into.

"Tell me about your day," I asked, wanting to distract myself as I moved on to the buttons of his shirt. "I haven't spent so long away from you in . . . I don't even know how long."

"What do ye want to know?" Grinning, he ran a finger down the side of my neck, watching me as I continued to undress him. Blushing slightly under his gaze, I knew what he was thinking. I'd seen that expression more than a few times since we'd been married. I'd seen it often enough before that as well, but he'd never gotten what he wanted then.

"Everything. Is the Temple still the Knight's headquarters?" My voice caught some and I grinned. He knew I was onto him . . . that I was trying to sidetrack him and find out what was going on. What neither of us knew was if it would work, and for how long.

"Yes. In part, that is. It's been overrun through the years and the city has built up around it. We are very easily able to conduct our business there without being noticed. I'll take ye, tomorrow, if ye'd like. The Grandmaster has asked for ye, just as I'd said he would." He stroked my collarbone, stopping on the spot he knew was most sensitive, teasing me.

"Well, I guess I'd want to meet a time traveler, if I ever got the chance," I joked, clearing my throat heavily. "I don't know much, though. I hope he's not wanting to ask me lots of questions."

"I'm not sure, lass. He only asked that I bring ye when it was convenient for ye."

"How polite of him." I snorted, pulling the last of the laces on his pants free. "Did you want me to get a bath set up for you?"

"No, I mean to just change for supper. I'm going back out once it's dark."

"What? Why?" I tried to hide the disappointment and frustration that had immediately blossomed at his words, the playful manner I'd been acting in dying away instantly, but he saw it anyway.

"It's a secret society, lass." He gently sat down, pulling me onto his lap. "And secrets are best kept after dark, aye?"

Sighing deeply, I leaned my head against his shoulder, remaining quiet. We'd only been in Paris for a day and already he was gone more than he was around. No wonder he'd wanted to be with me now— it was probably the only time we had for the foreseeable future.

"Will you be able to tell me what happens at your secret meeting?" I finally asked, tracing the veins on his arm.

"New members are being inducted. I'll be back before morning. I promise."

"Fine—"

A knock at the door interrupted the kiss I'd intended to give him and I moaned, standing up. "Who is it?"

"Would you like me to help you dress, Samantha?" Abella asked on the other side. "Monsieur Claudel says dinner will be served in half an hour."

"I'll help her tonight, Abella. Thank you," Tristan called. Turning, I saw that he had risen as well and was going through the wardrobe beside the head of the four-poster bed, pulling out a new outfit for each of us. Apparently, our teasing time had ended.

"*Oui*, Monsieur." Her footsteps faded down the hall and stairs, leaving us in peace once more.

"Come here," Tristan said gently, motioning me over to him. When I was by his side he smiled, taking my hands in his. "It won't be for long. The Order is in an uproar over the reemergence of the Black Knights. As soon as I can get the information and ship we need, we'll be gone. Then it will be just the open ocean, ye and me. Savvy?"

"And an entire faction of Knights bent on murdering us," I replied, smirking sadly. "Be careful, Tristan. I don't know what I'd do without you."

"Ye don't need to worry," he stated, releasing my hands in favor of rubbing his fingers along both sides of my jaw. "I'm not going anywhere without ye. Ye're as much my heart as the one that beats within me."

Leaning in, his lips pressed against mine firmly, fingers holding my head steady. His touch was warm and comforting, a reminder of the partner he was to me. Slowly, one hand slid down my neck, over my shoulder, past my arm, and onto my hip, pulling me closer.

Sighing, I let my body melt against his, wrapping my arms around his waist and opening my mouth, delighting in the sweet taste of honey on his tongue. His breath was hot, a small moan escaping him as he clutched me even tighter, seeming to match the yearning I had for more than just a few minutes together. We were both done with the teasing, the reality of how much time we'd have together settling in.

Almost desperately, he released his hold on me, lips still devouring mine, and began undoing the buttons on the front of my bodice, sliding the fabric off my shoulders and letting me take it off the rest of the way. Fingers found the tie for my skirt and ripped it loose, as well as the hip pads underneath.

Helping him pull off the bulky underskirts and silly, fashionable contraptions, I laughed, wondering how on earth I'd managed to wear so much for the whole day. It'd taken forever to get into, and here we were, taking it off with just as much effort.

Once I was free from the waist down, Tristan spun me around, pulling my back up beside him and kissing my neck, growling softly as he found a ticklish spot that made me twitch. Making quick work of the corset ties, he pulled the trap off me and swung me around again, tossing me onto the bed.

Trying my best to remain as quiet as possible, I squealed, scooting across the fluffy blankets in just my slip. He was having none of that, though, shaking his head as he climbed over me, pinning me beneath him.

"What about dinner?" I whispered, giggling. "It's going to take almost half an hour to get all of my clothes back on!"

"Ye're sick," he said in an official tone. "The heat o' the day made ye light headed. We'll take supper in our room."

"And we waited until now to tell everyone?"

"Aye, that we did." Silencing any further protests, he entwined our fingers above my head, sucking on my collarbone.

"We should probably tell someone, then" I whispered breathlessly, wiggling underneath him. "Or they'll come back to get us."

"Let them," he replied playfully, looking into my eyes. "Ye're my wife and I mean to treat ye as such."

"What about Mr. Claudel?"

"Hush yer mouth, Samantha Greene O'Rourke. Ye're mine for the next little while."

"Not so tight!" I gasped, grabbing onto the bedpost to keep from falling over. "I want to be able to breathe!"

"Are you sure?" Abella asked, the frown she wore obvious in the tone she used. "There's a lot of room for tightening. Your waist could look very thin." She pulled slightly on the cords of the corset to emphasize her point and I struggled for breath again.

"I'll take air over a slim figure any day," I assured her, a groan of relief quickly following as she loosened the strings a little. "Thank you."

"It will need to be tight when you meet the Sun King," she advised, moving around to grab the next layer of clothing off the bed. "Fashion is very important at Court. There are many rules for lots of things. If you're not careful, you could give yourself a bad name without even realizing it."

"Thank you, that made me feel much better about everything."

If she was offended by my sarcasm, she didn't say anything, merely smiling, beginning to sling hip pads around me.

"I don't understand this trend. Women are

supposed to have a skinny waist, but huge padded hips? What kind of sense is that?" Pouting, I waited for her to finish tying, watching in the large, almost floor to ceiling length mirror across the room.

"Some of your dresses don't need the padding," she offered. "The under skirts are padded enough without them. I'd take them to the Palace, if I were you; they are more French. Whoever made these dresses for you did it in the Spanish style. I hear they wear hoops under their skirts there!"

Raising an eyebrow I watched as she gathered the first skirt I would put on, getting ready to pull it over my head. "You know a lot about fashion."

It wasn't a question and she knew it. Carefully, she laid the fabric over me, arranging it around my waist and tying it securely. "*Oui*, Madame. I do. The lady I was a maid for before was a seamstress. She made gowns for Her Majesty, The Queen, before she passed."

"I was told the Queen died some years ago." Sincerely hoping I hadn't caught her in a lie, I waited for her to answer. I'd taken her into my home in good faith, knowing her past. If she were to lie to me now, though . . .

"*Oui*. She died when I was only a babe, God rest her soul. My Lady—the seamstress—continued to make dresses for members of Court until her own death, three years ago." She picked up the main skirt of the gown and helped me put it on as well, adjusting our position so she could look at me in the mirror.

Abella had already dressed herself for the day, a feat I had no idea how she'd accomplished, and stared evenly at my waist as she moved the skirt around. Her own brown skirt stood out in stark contrast to my blue, every bit of her outfit seeming to say that she was only a servant. She'd pinned her long hair back, with tight curls framing her face in a heart shape.

"Abella," I started cautiously when she turned to pick up the jacket off the bed. "How old were you when the seamstress died?"

"Thirteen." Holding the jacket out, she waited for me to slide my arms into the sleeves. All I could do was stare at her in the mirror, dumbfounded.

"Thirteen! How old were you when you started working for her?"

"Eight." Her tone was all business, but I was becoming more flustered by the second.

"Eight? Why so young?"

She met my gaze in the mirror, her mouth twitching some as she motioned for me to keep getting dressed. "My mother was her maid before me. When she died, I stepped in and took her place. My father needed the money and I was the only one who could obtain employment."

"That's a lot of responsibility for just a child to hold." Slowly, I did as she asked, putting the three quarter sleeve jacket on and holding still as she laced the back for me.

"Maybe, but I had a place to live, food to eat, and my father had money to pay his debtors." Coming around to the front, she handed me the fancy stomach piece, watching as I slid it into the opening of the jacket. When she was satisfied that my clothes looked presentable, she signaled for me to sit. "I'll do your hair now, if you'd like."

"No, thank you, that's okay. I don't mean to pry,

but how did you end up on the streets stealing food? Were you not able to find work after the seamstress died?"

"I worked at a shop for a year before my father made a drunken display of himself. It was obvious then that he needed more help than I'd realized. I had some money saved up, so I quit and stayed with him for a while. I thought—" She paused for a moment, frowning as she looked at the floor. As she struggled with the next part, I felt my feelings toward her growing; she'd had an absent father. Just like me. "He promised he would stop. Every week, he'd cry and promise to go out and find work. It'd been so long, though, that no one wanted him. He was too old, they'd say, too fragile. It hurt his pride. After a while, he stopped trying. When the money I'd saved ran out, I was able to do odd jobs here and there, but there's been nothing for several months now. The war changed some things. I guess my ability to find work was one of them."

"And so you resorted to stealing to feed yourself, until you got caught. Because your dad needed you to take care of him."

"A lot of good it did me, too." Snapping back to attention, she sniffed, blinking twice, and then looked at me evenly. "As soon as he found out, he declared me the ungrateful ingrate who had ruined his life and tried to cut off my hand for the law. He can take care of himself now. I won't ever go back there."

"You won't ever have to. I promise. Even if it means you come with me when I leave Paris. You will have a job and people who care about you." Turning, I picked up the brush on the table and ran it through my waist length hair a few times. A few uncomplicated twists and pins later, I was admiring the bun I'd created, a few wisps framing my face.

"You look beautiful, Samantha." Abella smiled gratefully at me in the mirror and I returned the favor.

"All thanks to you." I laughed. "Too bad you can't come with me to meet—er—Tristan's boss. I would have liked to have some familiar company."

"You'll do fine, I'm sure. He's not the King, after all. Otherwise, I would insist you wear a cap." She gathered my dress from the day before as she spoke, seeming to be in some type of rush.

"I highly doubt you could get me to wear one even for the King. Do you have somewhere to be?" I asked, chuckling.

"I thought I might take my first week's pay and buy myself a decent dress," she admitted, chuckling herself. "That is, if you don't mind?"

"Buy whatever you want," I assured her. "It won't make any difference to me."

A sharp knock at the door sounded through the room, startling me slightly. "Madame O'Rourke? Your carriage is waiting."

"Thank you, Monsieur Claudel," I called back to the kind, but stern man. "I will be right out." Turning to Abella, I curtsied some and smiled. "Thank you for all of your help. I'll see you tonight?"

"Before dinner, *oui*," she confirmed. "Go now! Don't keep that man of yours waiting."

Letting her usher me out of the room, I made my way down the carpeted stairs, smiling at Tristan, who waited by the door in his light green, fancy clothes.

"*Mi amore*," he said, clapping a hand over his

heart. "Ye look like an angel, lass, truly. Is that a dress Gran had made for ye?"

"It is," I confirmed. "Though, I don't think she meant for this angel to breathe in it. However, Abella was kind to me, so I live to see another day."

Chortling, he opened the door for me and motioned I should go out. On the street, just down the three front steps, waited a black carriage, complete with horse and driver. The man looked to be in his late forties, a cap pulled down around his large ears despite the warm weather.

Stepping around me, Tristan held a hand out to help me in, bowing slightly. "Lady O'Rourke."

"Thank you, Monsieur," I replied in faux haughtiness, taking his hand and stepping into the cart with ease. "Where are we off to today?"

"To the old Temple," he said to the driver as he climbed in. "We have business to conduct." Sitting beside me, he took my hand in his, squeezed it gently, and then took to examining the city as we passed through her streets.

We headed in a direction I hadn't explored the day before and I found myself just as caught up in the surroundings as I had been earlier, feeling like I could spend years in Paris and still never see all it had to offer.

"There's one of the old walls, from when the city was first built." Tristan pointed at a line of buildings as we moved through an opening between the houses. "The King had the only remaining modern one torn down some years ago."

"Oh? Why?"

"Paris is safe enough without them." Shrugging,

he looked away again, nodding in the direction of a building rising up in front of us. "That's it. The Temple."

I'd been expecting some type of fancy building, shining in the light with all the magnificent splendor imaginable. The Temple was actually more of a fortress, though, with huge walls built around it. Two towers peaked over the top, one higher than the other. Suddenly, I felt disappointed to be seeing something plainer than I'd pictured, like the Templars should have coated the walls in gold, or something. However, the Order had always been logical in my dealings with them, so it only made sense that they would build a sensible center to work from.

The gates were wide open, various numbers of people moving through them, the courtyard a bustling hub of activity. Carts lined the walls, some of the tiny shops extending into the rooms built into the brick behind them. Delicious smells wafted to us from some, while other tables held beautiful paintings and other types of artwork. There also appeared to be a large church built into the Temple, where several people sat praying or begging; I couldn't tell which.

The towers themselves appeared occupied more or less by the same things, people leisurely strolling through the large, heavy looking doors. The shoppers themselves amazed me as well; they were from all classes of income, come to buy and look at what was offered here. It was astounding to me that anything secret existed in these walls with the number of individuals who entered the space with such ease.

The cart stopped in the middle of the yard, much to the displeasure of some of the patrons, and we exited, Tristan taking my hand and leading me to the nearest table. It was covered in silks and pearls, the seller's eyes almost bugging out of his head when he saw us coming.

"Pretty necklace for your Mademoiselle, Monsieur?" He held out a string of the stones, eagerly nodding as Tristan slowed to examine it.

"I don't need anything," I told him, smiling uncomfortably. "Thank you."

"Hold on, lass," Tristan said, halting completely and taking the strand from him. "Ye may not need it, but I'd like for ye to have it."

"It's a good man who buys gifts for his lady," the merchant encouraged him, observing as Tristan clasped the strand around my neck.

"It suits ye. Will ye take it, for me?" Taking my hand, he raised my fingers to his lips and kissed them, smiling as he waited for a reply.

"If you really want to get it for me, I guess." Blushing, I watched as he turned back to the table and worked out a price for the jewelry. I hadn't worn a necklace today to begin with because I'd been trying to draw attention away from the low neckline of my dress. The lace edging of the jacket had done little to hide the enormous amount of cleavage I was showing off. Still, I was pleased that Tristan had wanted to buy me something. Our relationship wasn't one built on material things, which made such gifts even more of a surprise.

"Come this way," Tristan said once he'd paid the man, taking my arm.

We strolled through the courtyard, eyeing items the vendors were displaying, before we finally stopped at a table that apparently had some significance to it. Tristan examined the contents laid out before us intently, tapping his finger on the stand, but saying nothing. When the seller finished with the woman he'd been assisting, he smiled widely at the two of us.

"Monsieur O'Rourke, I was not expecting you back for at least another day." His voice was high and most definitely English, though he used a French greeting.

"Aye, my wife wanted to come see the place when I told her about it," Tristan replied, laughing. "I thought it would be best to humor her sooner, rather than later."

"A woman is not to be trifled with," he agreed. "But where are my manners? Jacob Williams at your service, Madame O'Rourke." Bowing to me, he swept his hat off his head and held the pose for a moment before standing straight again. "I have just acquired a marvelous painting that I think you would be interested in. Would you care to come inside?"

"Thank you, Mister Williams." Tristan towed me along behind him and into the room in the wall directly behind the table.

"Feel free to handle anything you'd like," Mister Williams called, his skinny form disappearing back through the door and outside.

There was no one else inside, the piles of merchandise left lonely. It looked like many things hadn't been touched in some time.

"This way," Tristan murmured, nodding to the back of the room.

I followed him, watching as he tapped on one

brick, the same rhythm he'd been tapping on the table outside. Slowly, a portion of the wall before us began to move, revealing the hidden door that had been there all along. Stifling my surprised gasp, I glanced back at Tristan, who was grinning his boyish smile at me.

"Welcome to the headquarters of The Order of the Knights Templar, Sam," he said smoothly.

The long, brick hall stretched on for what felt like forever, torches lighting the way every few feet. I felt more like I was lost in a dungeon, rather than moving through a hidden passageway to long forgotten chambers.

The man who had opened the secret door for us—Jacob Smith, he'd said—led the way in silence, a flaming stick held in his own hand. Silently, I wondered why we'd need a guide in the first place; there weren't any options but straight.

"A little further," Tristan murmured to me, still holding onto my arm.

Nodding, I kept my budding questions to myself. There would be time enough later to ask them, I was sure.

After a few more minutes, we finally were getting somewhere. Hallways started branching off in various directions, a maze of sorts that made me envision being stuck in here for eternity. The building hadn't looked this large from the outside, making me wonder if we had moved underground sometime during the trip.

We turned down the third passageway on the

right, moving past a gloomy set of stairs leading even further down, before we finally stopped in front of a plain door. It was only wood and metal, no ornate designs, no secret symbols, no anything.

Knocking on the door, Jacob waited for a reply before speaking.

"Who is calling?" a gruff voice on the other side inquired.

"Jacob Smith. Tristan O'Rourke and his wife are here." He smiled at me in what I assumed was an encouraging manner.

"Enter," the voice on the other side said.

Our guide opened the door and bowed slightly, ushering us in before securing it with a muffled click. Tristan, leading me into the space, took his time, watching as I glanced around.

The area was at least three times larger than I'd been expecting, with high ceilings and four beautiful pillars twisting up into the brick. Carved into them was what appeared to be a history of the Templars. Battles, treasures, and scenes that must have had to do with their undisclosed rituals covered every inch of the surface. Feeling like I couldn't tear my eyes away from them, I gaped at the artwork, until something in the corner of my gaze caught my attention.

The walls were painted with various acts as well, but accent pieces covered the work in places. There was a beautiful, gold shield in one spot, and in another an extraordinary carving that had to be made of diamonds. Other treasures sat here and there, their splendor almost causing me to miss the designs in the floor, laid into the brick.

"It's something, isn't it?" Jumping back to the

moment at hand, I turned and took in the old man seated behind the wooden desk before us, his white hair shining in the firelight. He was wearing the customary French fashion, a large, golden cross hanging around his neck over the purple cloth. Pale skin, extra wrinkled, made me think he must be very old. His eyes instantly drew me in, though, their deep gray gaze seeming to speak to me as much as the room around him.

"It was part of the treasure vault. The old Knights made no secret of their riches, as you well know. While the Temple was built to be a fortress on the outside, the inside was created to be as beautiful as the treasures she held."

Standing, he wiped a napkin over his mouth and I suddenly realized we'd interrupted his meal, the silver tray of meat and bread resting just within his reach.

"I'm sorry we disturbed you while you were eating," I said, suddenly remembering my manners and curtseying.

"It's no trouble." He waved his hand in dismissal. "How often does one get to meet a time traveler? I can eat any day. Besides, we have places to go." Smiling, he stood and bowed, coughing slightly before he straightened. "I am the Grand Master, Augustine Bevard."

"Samantha O'Rourke." Feeling awkward, I curtseyed again, elbowing Tristan in the side when he chuckled softly.

"Captain Abel told me you were beautiful, Madame, and your husband assured me of the same, but I find myself somewhat surprised by your looks still." He made his way around the desk slowly, making my guess at his age rise considerably. The man looked as if he could topple over at any minute and be gone from this life.

"You are very kind," I replied, blushing.

"Ye should see her in a pair of trousers," Tristan said easily, eliciting an embarrassed gasp from me and a laugh from the Grand Master.

"I have been told in detail of your exploits as a pirate as well, *oui*. You are very brave, Madame. Tell me, are all women in your time that way?"

"Um, I guess they could be, if they wanted. We tend to do what we want in my time, no man required."

"I've always thought women were just as capable as men," Grand Master Bevard continued, finally arriving beside the two of us. "But less . . ." He paused for a moment, searching for the word he wanted. "Extreme. They seem to trifle over daily things, with no real concern for what goes on outside their lives. I have often pondered what they could do, given the right power and circumstances."

"Ye've spent too much time with yer own wife." Tristan chortled.

"Perhaps," he agreed humorously. "Today we had a crisis because her dress for the ball is half an inch too short. I suppose it will be fixed by the time I return home."

"Isn't stuff like that really important in this era, though?" I asked, trying to remember all the things I'd been taught about high society.

"It can be." Bevard shrugged. "But I sincerely doubt a half an inch would have been noticed by many. Aren't you attending the ball as well?"

"We are," Tristan replied, smiling when I looked at him in surprise. "We plan to ride to the palace in two days."

"Wonderful. Perhaps you would like to share my wife's carriage? I do admit, I would enjoy the company."

"That is very kind of you." Trying not to laugh, I flinched as Tristan elbowed, his own eyes sparkling.

"It would be an honor to accompany ye," he said, bowing.

"Very well then. I will let the driver know as soon as I return home tonight." He motioned for the door, adding some speed to his step. "Would you like to see the rest of the Temple?"

"I would love to! Is there much more besides what I've been through already?"

"The Temple may have been over run and our legacy destroyed, lass, but there's much to this place ye've yet to see," Tristan answered, nodding for me to go ahead of him and follow the old man.

"I've been wondering about that," I said to the both of them. "Why did you reestablish your headquarters here, after everything that happened? Wouldn't you go somewhere else, somewhere that was safer and more secret?"

"The Temple of Paris is the best stronghold the Knights Templar ever built," Bevard replied. "It was the only one really made to withstand a siege. Even when the Black Knights fell, they were imprisoned here, because of how strong the fortress was. When the whole ordeal was over, we silently crept back in; it's still the strongest holding point we have."

"Much of the Temple is hidden, lass," Tristan

116

continued, closing the door behind us as we entered the hall again. "Initiation was always private and hidden away. The bank vaults were kept out of sight and guarded, to protect the money. While the world may think they know what this place is, they've barely scratched the surface of it."

The Grand Master led us back the way we'd come before, but instead of turning down the main hall we'd traveled down, he kept going straight, pointing out bricks that had things carved on them and doors that led to other treasure rooms.

"Of course, they're all empty now," he said conversationally, stopping at the bottom of some stairs. "The treasure is long gone—we are all aware of that fact."

"Do you know where El Dorado is?" I asked, the question popping out as soon as I'd thought of it.

Surprised, the man turned and looked at me, his gaze studying my face. "You were right," he said to Tristan. "She wastes no time, does she?"

"No, Monsieur." Smiling, he took my hand, squeezing it gently.

"Sorry," I said quickly, blushing. "I didn't mean to be so blunt."

"Of course you did. Thomas Randall tried to kill you and murdered your friend in front of you. He got away with the blood of the gods—you want to know if you can stop him. It's a natural reaction, dear." He waved his hand at me and began to ascend the steps, coughing one more after the first one. "As for your question, no. I do not know where the City of Gold is. I'm more prone to believe it doesn't exist, but there is truth in all things. The men who took their eighth of the treasure to that part of the world never returned. The riches of the Knights could be sitting on top of a golden pyramid, for all we know."

"Eighth of the treasure?" I questioned as we followed, suddenly remembering the voice of the priestess on Madagascar.

Eight is a magic number.

"*Oui.* When we fled with the treasure in the thirteen hundreds, it was split into eight parts. One was on Oak Isle. Another was taken to the new world by a few of the Spaniards among our numbers. However, they didn't return and their ship was never found. We can only guess what happened to them and the riches they carried. That's where we're going now, actually. We've been searching for the treasure there for centuries. Now that Randall is a threat to it, I've called in our man in charge of the hunt there to speak with the two of you."

"Do you think Randall is privy to information we don't have?" Tristan asked, surprised. "Surely he wouldn't know more about it than the Order. He would be operating on guess work only."

"These are trying times, Monsieur O'Rourke," he said, stopping just above us and turning to look. "Half of our number betrayed their oath and became Black Knights when Randall arrived and burned their city. I am not so sure that we don't have enemies among us even now." He watched us expectantly and then moved, heading on his way again.

"Did he mean us?" I whispered to Tristan, falling back somewhat to talk to him.

"I don't think so," he answered, frowning. "Perhaps he is worried the man we are going to meet is the traitor?"

"I guess we'll find out."

"Be careful, Sam," he cautioned me. "I've never met this man, and I'm sure he won't be happy that I've been asking into his business. This is supposed to be something secret. Not even the other Knights are to know where the treasure is hidden. They only know the one they are assigned to. He may be upset to see you."

"Why?"

"Everyone knows about Oak Isle now, lass. A good number of them know what ye are, too. They fear the unknown, but hunger for the knowledge ye possess. Watch what ye say and be wary of anyone trying to use ye, savvy? Even the Grand Master. Remember, when the Order fell the first time, the Grand Master himself had joined the Black Knights. Do not consider anyone safe."

"I understand," I replied, surprised at his sudden caution. "I'll do my best to make sure I'm paying attention."

"This is no different than the ship, lass," he murmured even softer. "They may look nice and wear fancy clothes, but these men are pirates at heart, in every way. Never forget."

Nodding, I tried to keep my eyes from widening even more as we finished our trek up the stairs and joined the Grand Master in front of another doorway.

"This way," he said, opening it for us and nodding. "Lomas is waiting."

Lomas turned out to be a Spanish man not much older than Tristan, with dark, tanned skin and black hair that was so short it almost resembled what was known as a buzz cut in my time. His face, while handsome, seemed severe, aided in part by a scar stretched across one cheek, reaching from under his ear to the corner of his mouth. It made him look like some sort of horror film creation when he spoke, as if the rest of his face was going to split open at any moment. Of course, it didn't, but as he bowed to us, the blue of his sailor's coat standing out against the red of the room, I felt a sudden uneasiness.

"Adrian Lomas, Captain O'Rourke," he said, introducing himself as we came to stand by the table with him.

"Captain of what?" Tristan laughed, tightening his grip on my hand slightly. "I have no ship, as I'm sure ye're aware."

"Regardless, you are still a captain in this organization and I will address you as such, as I would expect if my ship had also been lost." Despite the fearsome look he had while speaking, Lomas' voice was very proper sounding, the accent of his country strong in every word.

"I thank ye," Tristan replied, his own tone mimicking the politeness being displayed. "I hope we can work together in this endeavor without much conflict."

"I highly doubt that." For the first time, Lomas seemed to sneer at us, catching me by surprise.

Trying to avoid the awkward stare the two men were now giving each other, I turned to examining the room. It wasn't large by any means, but the high ceiling made it feel enormous. There were no windows, leaving me clueless as to whether or not we were finally above ground again. There were, however, large tapestries that hung down, displaying magnificent portrayals of more of the Knight's accomplishments. Some of the images seemed outlandish, men speaking with mythological creatures and battling dragons, but the fabrics gave the room a lightness that was missing without the sunlight. A large chandelier, filled with candles, was displayed over the centerpiece of the room—the table at which we all now stood.

It was almost too much for the space, leaving only a narrow walkway around its circular edge. For an instant, I thought of King Arthur and the Knights of the Round Table, seated together as they ruled a nation. Were the Knights Templar that same kind of organization—a group that worked together and held respect for all, regardless of their title?

Of course, the main focus of the table, itself, was the beautiful world map carved into it. Whoever had completed the task was a master at their craft, though I did notice a few things that were off, such as the shape of the Americas, which were somewhat squashed together. For the most part, though, it looked like any other map I'd seen in this time. Sea monsters were placed off in the ocean every so often, carvings of ships appeared as if they were traversing across the waters with ease, and the landmasses had their own markings, showing civilizations and other points of interest.

"You mustn't mind Lomas," Grand Master Bevard said conversationally, bringing my attention back to the present. "He only means that he isn't happy about someone else being brought in to search for his charge."

"I don't need any help," Lomas said through stiff lips. "Especially from a man who was so careless with his own duties that the Black Knights stole a portion of the treasure."

"He wasn't careless," I said defensively, catching him by surprise. "Thomas Randall kidnapped and tortured one of his men. He killed countless innocent people. He burned our ship and sank her after killing most of the crew. When he finally made it to the treasure, which he had to dig to, by the way, because Tristan refused to tell him where the entrance was, he had to use Medusa's head just to get away from everyone. If it weren't for Tristan, the entire treasure on Oak Isle would be in the hands of the Black Knights."

"You have forgotten your place, Madame," Lomas said, regarding me sourly. "Why are you even here? This is a man's conversation."

I felt like I'd been slapped, my mouth hanging open as I glared at him.

"I'll take it you haven't heard." Bevard chuckled. "I wondered if you would have, having just arrived from South America. Samantha here has been greatly discussed among those who know the story of Oak Isle."

"This is my wife," Tristan said coolly, pushing me forward. "Samantha Green O'Rourke."

"I'm from the future." I silently dared him to argue with me about it as his eyes narrowed, studying me truly for the first time.

He didn't really seem to believe me.

"Why is she here?" he asked Tristan, apparently deciding to ignore me.

"Because I opened Pandora's Box in the bottom of the pit that Randall dug almost three hundred years from now," I growled, feeling my defenses picking up more. Being ignored bothered me, especially when it was because I didn't have the same anatomy as everyone else in the room. "It brought me here, and so help me, if you keep trying to act like I'm not here, I'll give you a reason to remember me."

Tristan laughed, putting a hand on my shoulder and pulling me back. "I'd be careful, Captain. Sam's been a pirate for a better part of a year, as a man and a woman. I wouldn't put it past her to beat ye in a fight." His tone held a small amount of his own warning toward Lomas; he wouldn't stop me if I decided to fight him.

The Spaniard regarded us with cold eyes, his nose twitching once before he turned toward the Grand Master. "What is my part in all of this?"

"As you're aware, it is well known among our ranks that the portion of the treasure sent to the

Southern Americas was lost."

"I am." Lomas didn't seem to like that fact. Actually, he appeared to loathe it. Suddenly, I wondered if the men sent to find the missing portion were being punished somehow. In my mind, I would have thought the Order's best men were on the case, but Tristan was one of their best, wasn't he?

"Randall will know, too. It's the only lead he has on finding what he's looking for." Tristan was slipping back into his business mode, looking at the map on the table.

"You think he will go south?" Lomas was uncertain, but turned to the masterpiece as well, frowning.

"That's what the Black Knights have done in the past."

"Really?" I asked, surprised.

"Aye, lass," Tristan said, nodding. "They've sent at least two companies in the past two hundred years, that we know of. Ye've heard of Christopher Columbus?"

I almost snorted. Of course I'd heard of the man who "discovered" the new world. There must have been something in my expression that confirmed my knowledge, because he smiled, continuing on.

"He was a Black Knight. He and his followers never found the treasure, though, probably because of the extreme force they showed the natives."

"Cortés is the next Knight we know of," Lomas said, appearing to think it over. "He thought the treasure was with the Aztecs, which we now also believe to be true, but it was gone when he tried to take it."

"Why the Aztecs?" I asked, fascinated. These were stories I'd heard growing up. In fact, Cortés, himself, reportedly named the mountains just outside my hometown. He called them the Superstitions, after many of his men mysteriously died while traveling through the range. They were looking for a city of gold, but all they found was grief.

"We've uncovered some documentation that suggests the Knights who first arrived with the treasure became sick, or were already sick, when they made landfall. They were friendly with the natives, but none of them survived whatever it was they'd caught." Bevard sighed, shaking his head. "We can only assume that the treasure was then overtaken by the native people. They would have recognized its importance."

"Didn't Spain tear South America apart looking for gold, though?" I could feel it, the same kind of excitement that had overtaken me when I was studying the Treasure Pit with Dad. I wanted to know what had happened. I *needed* the pieces to the puzzle. It was as if he were standing there with me, drinking in all the information we could as the Knights told me what they knew.

"The tribes began hiding their gold together," Lomas explained. "They knew what the conquistadors were looking for. They used their riches for religious purposes and didn't want it tainted. It is my personal belief that Montezuma's treasure was that of several tribes, hidden together to keep them safe."

"And they would have hidden the Templar's treasure there as well, knowing it held sacred value to the men who had brought it," I added for him, the lines connecting together in my head. "What happened then?"

"Cortés tortured the people," Lomas answered simply. "All of his research had led him to the same place ours has. The treasure of the Knights Templar should have been in Mexico City—or Tenochtitlan, as it was called then."

"But it wasn't." I was no stranger to things not working out when it came to treasure. Nothing ever seemed to go right on Oak Isle, no matter how many signs you had saying something should be true.

"After Montezuma died, the Black Knights raided his palace and vaults. But whatever had been there was already gone." It was Bevard who spoke this time, watching my face carefully. "No one has seen it since."

"We believe that a large number of servants and guards carried away the riches, but we don't know where. There are so many different tales of fortune in the New World, it's like looking for a needle in a haystack," Lomas added, frustrated. "I don't understand how something so massive could disappear so suddenly!"

"Well, the Templars did it," I pointed out. "In my time, your treasure is considered a myth as much as anything else. No one has ever found it. Well, except me, but it's not like I got to do anything with it before I was sent here. And even if I had, no one would have thought that there was more hidden somewhere else."

"It seems that Cortés followed a few leads he found on his own, traveling up further into North America, but there was nothing. We don't even know what leads he was following. Due to the extreme nature of the natives now, we haven't traveled as far north as he did." Bevard finally looked at Tristan, who, when I turned to him as well, appeared to be absorbing all of the information quickly.

"Is there any way to go further north? Randall will do it for sure, if he believes that is where the cache is." He paused for a moment, apparently considering his words, and then went on. "I believe he's looking for the Holy Grail. When we first found him in the Pit, he was upset to find that not everything we'd carried to the island was there. He must not have realized that some of it was transported to other places once it reached Oak Isle."

"Why would he want the Grail?" Lomas questioned, surprised.

"He stole the ichor. If he drinks it from the Grail, he will carry the gods' immortality." Bevard's voice was crisp and to the point, but it still stung me somewhat. Thomas was bad enough now. If he were as invincible as a god? There would be no stopping him and whatever plans he had.

"What's in the missing treasure?" I asked out of curiosity.

"Not the Grail," Lomas said, sounding supremely thankful. "But there are plenty of things we don't want the Black Knights to get their hands on."

"Oak Isle had many Greek treasures," Tristan offered.

"Norse," Bevard said. "The missing treasure was full of Norse artifacts. Among them, Thor's gloves and hammer. Imagine, if the Black Knights could control lightning? We would never be able to get close to them again."

Slowly, I felt another line in my brain connecting. It was an old story I'd heard, from when I was so young it seemed like another hundred lifetimes ago. Frustrated, I tried to grasp onto whatever my subconscious was tying together, ignoring the chatter about what else was missing.

And then, suddenly, I remembered. Gasping, I turned to look at Tristan, eyes wide.

"What?" he asked, confused.

"It might be nothing, but I heard . . ." I stopped. Glancing between the men, I was suddenly nervous to share my revelation with them. Swallowing, I hurried to continue on. "I think I know where the treasure is."

The three men looked at me in surprise and disbelief. Well, all except Tristan, anyway.

"What do ye mean, lass?" he asked patiently.

"It's a lot of things tied together," I replied, starting to feel stupid. "I don't know a whole lot about any of it."

"Tell us," Bevard encouraged, entwining his fingers and resting his chin on them as his elbows sat on the table, his form leaning forward in his chair.

"Cortés visited where I was born," I said, watching their eyes widen some more. "He named the mountains around the valley I grew up in. So, we know that whatever leads he was following brought him there. There's a lot of reservations in Arizona—I mean, a lot of Native Americans live there. The Apache live in those mountains. They always have. Everyone thought that they were the ones who killed Cortés's men because they felt threatened by the newcomers."

Pausing, I tried to choose what part to tell them next. One was going to excite them for sure; it made me grin like an idiot just thinking about it. The other . . . the other was a far reach, at best. Pursing my lips, I decided to share the least helpful thought first.

"I was working in the library one day and came across another story about a man—a miner—who was hit in the head and claimed to have a vision. Supposedly, he saw thousands of Aztec slaves and warriors marching out of their city with their treasure. In his vision, they carried it into Utah. Cortés never went there, according to my knowledge, though. However, when the man went to dig and find the treasure, there wasn't anything. Well, that's not true. They found the armor of a Spanish conquistador in one of the caves he uncovered. That's all. The book didn't say much more about it."

"Are you suggesting that someone found the treasure in this . . . Utah you speak of?" Lomas stared at me, his gaze burning intensely.

"No," I replied, shaking my head. "I think a vision had by a man with a concussion is shaky, at best. However . . . I do think the treasure could be somewhere else. Somewhere that Cortés visited, but never got to explore."

"Ye mean the mountains outside yer home?" Tristan's eyes narrowed as well as he took in what I was saying. "Why?"

"A couple of reasons, actually." My hands were shaking by now, half out of excitement and half out of worry that I was about to lead them on a wild goose chase. "The Indians were protecting the mountains, right? Wouldn't they do the same if there was a massive treasure hidden there?"

"I suppose so," Bevard replied.

"Well, there is a massive treasure there, according to local myth. It's rumored to be a gold

130

mine, with so much of the stuff that you can pick it right up off the ground without any effort. No one has been able to find it since the original man who claimed to know where it was died."

"The treasure isn't a gold mine," Lomas said, some exasperation seeping into his tone. "It would be actual objects. Things that had been crafted by man."

"You said the natives used gold for their religious practices, didn't you?" I asked him. "So, why wouldn't they have hidden their sacred treasure in a place where more of it was?"

"They could have thought that it was a place designated by the gods," Bevard offered, his own thoughts hidden behind a mask of contemplativeness. "But that's all circumstantial at best. We believe there is truth in all things, but the only point you have working for your theory is that the natives killed the Knights to protect something."

"That's not all." Excitement rushed through me and I smiled, ready to reveal the thing that had made me tie it all together. "You said there were lightning controlling objects in the treasure? The reason the Apache hold those mountains sacred is because they believe their lightning god lives in them."

They all visibly straightened at my comment, just as I'd expected. Lomas looked as if he'd been clubbed over the head, no doubt because a woman had just told him several truths he'd never known. Bevard was smiling, as if it all made sense. Tristan was gaping at me in awe, as if he'd never considered that I might know more than just Treasure Pit information.

"That does lend some credibility to the thought

that the treasure might be hidden there," Bevard agreed.

"How far is it from these mountains to Mexico City?" Lomas asked, still skeptical.

Frowning, I knew that this would be a hard part for them to believe. I'd had a hard time believing it when I searched how far it was from Utah. "Almost fifteen hundred miles," I said quietly.

How could thousands of slaves and guards transport a massive treasure that far without being seen by anyone? How would they have done it without leaving some kind of trail? The thought seemed impossible, laughable even.

Then again, so had the idea of the lost treasure of the Knights Templar being at the bottom of the Treasure Pit.

The men seemed to be thinking along the same lines, each of them lost in their own thoughts, and I frowned, feeling stupid again.

"It could be nothing," I stated once more. "But what you were saying made me remember all of it. It's a reach, tying it all together like that, but it's the best I can do to help at the moment."

"It's good, Sam," Tristan said encouragingly. "At the very least, it gave us more information. What do ye think, Captain Lomas?"

The Spaniard stared evenly at me, lips pressed together tightly, whatever thoughts and feelings he had hidden behind his mask of a face. "I think . . . it's not a bad idea. For all we know, Cortés tied things together and followed the path they made. If we could find any more information on these particular mountains and the people who live around them, we might be able to decide more definitively."

"If you want to go and look, you mean?" It felt like my heart was in my throat. He'd said they didn't go north because it was dangerous, and here I was, telling them they should go there.

"What kind of place is it, Madame O'Rourke?" Bevard questioned. "Jungle?"

"It's a desert," I replied, grimacing. "Not like the Sahara, but hot. Really hot, actually. There won't be much water. The plants and animals aren't very friendly either."

"How far from the ocean?"

"Several hours by car." Closing my eyes in frustration, I shook my head. Thinking about my hometown was getting me mixed up with modern day things. In my time, it would have taken around six hours to drive to the closest beach. They wouldn't be coming from the west, though; I had no idea how far the closest eastern ocean was. "A while. I'm not exactly sure how long. A few weeks at the least, assuming we don't just march straight through without stopping for anything."

"We?" Lomas scoffed, looking between everyone in disbelief. "You expect to be part of a secret Order mission? Your place is here, with the other wives. It will be dangerous!"

My earlier annoyance at being treated as though I was less than him returned in an instant and I frowned, trying to hold back my anger. "I am as much your equal as either of these men, whether you believe it or not. The fact that it is dangerous makes no difference. If you can go, so can I. Besides, I'm the only one here who has actually seen the mountains and knows what they look like."

He stared at me, mouth gaping like a fish, and then finally turned to the Grand Master.

"She's right," he said, sighing. "She would have to go. I suspect that Captain O'Rourke wouldn't leave without her."

"No, sir. I would not," Tristan confirmed. "And Lomas can't be sure of anything without his witness to it all."

"I would do just fine with a map, thank you," the captain replied stiffly. "All Señora O'Rourke would have to do is draw one up for me."

"I don't know anything about making maps," I shot back just as haughtily. "Either I go, or you don't get to be part of the mission."

Lomas looked aghast at that, moving toward the Grand Master again, who merely shrugged.

"We'll go without ye." Tristan filled him in. "I mean to handle Randall myself, with or without the Order's assistance in the manner. He was my man. My mistake. I should have noticed the path he was on. I should have stopped him. Ye said yerself, I'm the one responsible for this mess."

"We will take care of the arrangements," Bevard said, nodding. "There are others we must consult and ships we must prepare. Captain O'Rourke, I do believe you should lead one of them. Be thinking of whom you would like on your crew. As for you, Lomas," he spoke, standing and moving toward the man. "Would you come with me? I should like to go through the records we have of past searches. Perhaps Madame O'Rourke's theory will play out more in them."

He began making his way to the door, his features contemplative, before stopping to look at me again. "You are a marvel to have around, Samantha."

"Thank you?"

He left then, Lomas following quickly behind, and Tristan and I breathed a breath of relief at the same time.

"I didn't know ye knew so much about lost treasures, lass," he remarked, teasing. "Are there any others ye're going to want to search out after this?"

Laughing, I wrapped my arms around him, hugging him tightly. I hadn't realized it until just then, but I'd been so incredibly nervous for this meeting and discussion. It seemed like luck that I had managed to be helpful at all.

"Let's find this one first." Falling silent, the memory of my hometown filled my mind. How different would it be now? There would be no budding metropolis, no manmade lakes, and definitely no air conditioning. Would the mountains look the same? Could I lead an entire group of men into a desert when I knew very well how dangerous it would be?

"What are ye thinking?" Tristan's voice was soft and calming, and I suddenly realized I'd been digging my fingers into his back as I held him.

"Arizona will be dangerous," I replied quietly, relaxing my grip. "The Apache Indians earned a very fierce and bloodthirsty reputation defending their lives and homes." It made my stomach drop just thinking about the warriors we could possibly encounter on the journey. "Besides that, the desert will be hard to handle."

"It is a desert, Sam." He chuckled. "I don't think anyone expects it to be easy.

"It's not just that," I said, exasperated suddenly. "The heat is one thing—one thing we should prepare for very, very carefully—but there are several other things we need to watch for. Dehydration—for example—how are we going to carry enough water for everyone with us? We'll need more than usual. And what if we run into rattlesnakes? I'm sure we will. They're all over the place there. If someone gets bitten, there won't be anything we can do to help. They'll be dead before we even have the chance to think of what to do. Wild boars could gouge someone to death. Even a spider bite could kill a man in a few days."

"I think the better question is why would anyone want to settle down there in the first place?" He laughed some, but I could hear the truth of the question in his tone.

Pulling away, I smiled at him tightly. "Gold. They wanted the gold. The mine I told you about isn't the only source by a long shot. There's lots of minerals there. Someday, they call it The Copper State, among other things."

Nodding, he sighed, contemplating something. "Gold drives men to do crazy things. It must be God's grace that we have ye with us to give us some foresight."

"Some foresight." I snorted. "All of the things I just told you about can easily be taken care of with modern medicine. My intel is practically useless when you realize that I have no way to circumvent things without items from my own time."

136

"The warning is enough, trust me. Many lives are saved when they have knowledge beforehand."

Frowning, I bit my lip and then looked down. "Sometimes, I wish I'd studied something other than English, like medicine or history. You know, things that would have been useful to me now. I feel so helpless, every day."

"Ye can't change yer past, Samantha." Taking my hand in his, he nodded toward the door. "It's best to look forward and do what ye can."

"Do you dance much, dear?"

Ripped from my anxious perusal of the French countryside, I turned and stared at Madame Bevard with wide eyes. She was a heavyset woman, adorned with the largest and frilliest dress I'd yet to see during my time in the past. The red fabric practically screamed elegance, though, and it matched her pale skin color beautifully. Her dark hair, streaked with gray around her temples, had been curled and piled into the latest fashion. She must have been at least thirty years older than me, but her personality was proving to be more around my own age. She sat across from me, flanked by her daughter and husband, all of them waiting patiently for my answer.

"Dance?"

"Yes! I thought you might, since we are on our way to His Majesty's ball, but upon meeting you, I felt I needed to adjust my initial thoughts towards you."

"Oh." What was that supposed to mean?

Next to me, Abella hastily converted her laugh into a cough, her gaze turned out the window of the carriage. Her light yellow gown seemed to mock me with its brightness as she left me to fend for myself.

"I'm afraid that I know very little about dancing," I stated carefully, smoothing the fabric of my own blue dress over my knees. The skirt was much larger than I was used to, which was apparently how things were done at Court. Everything was bigger and brighter, no matter the cost.

She nodded, seeming to accept my answer without question, and then turned to Tristan, who sat on my other side. "And you, Monsieur?"

"I know enough to get by." He offered his most dashing smile and I practically heard her sigh at the sight, along with her daughter.

"We should have dance lessons when we arrive!" The daughter—Gloria, I think was her name—clapped her hands in excitement, leaning over her mother to address her father. "Oh, please! It would be so much fun! The ball doesn't start until tomorrow. We could do it after dinner. You can get us a room, can't you, Father?"

"We'll see," Grand Master Bevard responded cryptically. Something about his tone made me think he would rather do anything but conduct dance lessons after dinner.

"His Majesty is very fond of dancing," Madame Bevard told me, casually. "He's been in a few ballets himself! I was at Court for one of them and it was simply magnificent. The theater at the palace is splendid; I hope we get to attend another show while we are there."

"Yes, the Sun King is quite fond of the arts," her husband stated. "He's started a school for dance and an opera company, as well as the projects he's had carried out to help beautify his palace and Paris. Though, he isn't too fond of the city itself, which is a shame. That's why he had the entire Court moved to Versailles, you know. So he wouldn't have to come into the city."

"And he loves dancing," Madame Bevard added again, coming back around to her original point. "So much that he's even had the entire Court take lessons. You need to have a lesson or two yourself before tomorrow, or you'll stick out of the crowd."

"Samantha can follow well enough." Tristan grinned, coming to my rescue. "As fate would have it, neither of us are much of a dancer, but together we manage." Taking my hand in his, he squeezed it gently and smiled the smile he saved just for me. The sighs on the other side of the coach were clearly audible this time, but I ignored them.

"I'll see if I can get us into one of the smaller ballrooms tonight," Bevard offered, much to the delight of the women he had in his life. "But I make no promises. I may be a Royal Advisor on certain subjects, but I wouldn't say I hold much sway at Court."

"How exciting!" Gloria was positively beaming.

"We should arrive just before dinner. There will be hardly any time to unpack before we'll have to set off." The mother and daughter started their own lively conversation, leaving me room to finally breathe a sigh of relief.

The palace was only a few hours outside of Paris, but it seemed like the trip was going by faster than that. I'd spent all day at home with Abella, making sure we had everything we would need while we were away. Tristan had been off doing who knows what with the Order, showing up right as the Bevard's carriage was arriving to take us away. After quickly changing, we departed, my nerves growing by the second. For some reason, the thought of meeting royalty had me on edge. I sincerely hoped I wasn't about to screw up and taint the O'Rourke name for the rest of all time.

It's only three days, I thought to myself, trying not to wring my hands in nervous dread. The king would be a busy man. I would only actually have to meet and talk with him for a few minutes. I could handle that. The rest of the trip would be spent with the members of Court and participating in the festivities. Most of all, I looked forward to having Tristan to myself for several days; the Order was in Paris and would have to leave him alone for a while.

I hoped.

"Samantha."

Turning, I smiled at Abella, my eyes drifting from the curled hair at the top of her head, and then downward to where the soft locks brushed ever so slightly against her face.

"I'll make sure everything gets unpacked while you're at dinner. Will you want to change for your dance lessons?"

"Don't be silly," I chastised her. "You'll come eat with us. You'll go to the dance lessons, too."

"I'm not sure that would be socially acceptable." She had an expression on her face like she was trying to advise me and I rolled my eyes.

"I told you when I hired you, I was looking for a friend. You are not my servant, Abella. You will

141

come with us because you are a guest, just like me. Besides, I thought a Lady's maid was supposed to go everywhere with her."

"It's not my place to be among the royals and dining with members of Court." She stared back out the window, as if the conversation was finished, her hands clasped firmly in her lap.

"The lass is nervous," Tristan murmured in my ear, apparently having been listening in. "Maybe try another tactic?"

"Oh."

Abella was always advising me on fashion and what was proper. It never occurred to me that she might feel out of her element here, as well, despite having helped dress the very people she was going to attend the ball with for years.

"You know," I said to her quietly, watching the back of her head. "I'm a little terrified of all this. I was hoping that you would come with me, so I would have some familiar faces to help keep me steady."

Slowly, she turned to watch me again, studying my face, before nodding once. "*Oui*. I will come, if you need me."

"Thank you," I breathed, suddenly realizing how true my statement had been. I wanted friends to be with in an unfamiliar place.

The Bevard women were still happily chatting together, so I turned my attention back to the window. We were part of several groups who were attending the ball, caravanning to the palace as one mass. The assembly stopped at the halfway point to stretch our legs, but the respite from the stuffy, red interior of the coach was short. Soon we were on our way again, bumping across the dusty road, and before I knew it, we were arriving at the Palace of Versailles.

I'd heard about the palace before, in my own time, and had even seen it portrayed in a few movies, but nothing could have prepared me for seeing it in person. The long, cobblestone covered stretch of space in front of us reached all the way to the gates of the palace, which were a flurry of activity. Everywhere I scanned, there were people. Courtiers and servants alike made their way across the area, the line of carriages I was in slowly being admitted across the barrier. As we inched forward, I did my best to not shove Tristan out of the way so I could see what was going on better.

As our coach passed through the gates, I gawked at the building around us, hardly even noticing as we left our seats and bags behind. Someone said something about our affects being delivered to our rooms, but all I could do was stare.

"It's quite the vision, isn't it?" Madame Bevard asked me, smiling knowingly.

Nodding, I turned to examine the official courtyard, the black and white tiles on the ground shining magnificently in the sunlight. "It's something, that's for sure."

"Wait until you see the gardens," Gloria gushed. "There's an outdoor ballroom there, too!" She continued to talk, reinforcing my impression that she was only here to dance, and nothing else. She didn't appear much older than Abella, but she lacked the maturity that the former had. She seemed very much like a naïve, innocent, little girl who thought only of dresses and parties.

"Perhaps we'll take a turn after dinner and dance lessons, aye?" Tristan asked, securing my arm in the crook of his. "For now, we need to get to the room they told us. They'll be dropping off our things and we both need to change for dinner."

"Again?" Flustered right out of my amazement for my surroundings, I looked down at my dress. "What's wrong with what I'm wearing now?"

"We're dining with His Majesty tonight," Tristan said, laughing. "I thought ye might like to wear something a little less traveled in."

"I do agree," Madame Bevard spoke emphatically. "I'll be changing as well, Madame O'Rourke. The King demands nothing but the best."

And, just like that, all of my fear and nervousness from earlier came crashing back. "Of course," I stated weakly. "Only the best." The sights around me seemed to tilt to one side, my head starting to pound as I imagined, yet again, how easily I could make a fool of myself here.

"Come, my love," Bevard said, hailing his wife. "We will see them again at dinner."

"Thank ye for yer hospitality," Tristan called as they hurried off in another direction. Then, turning back to me, his eyes widened and his grip tightened on my arm. "Are ye ready, lass? Do ye need a moment to breathe?"

"You look like you might faint," Abella said helpfully behind me, her hand instantly finding my back. "Shall I call for assistance?"

"No, I'm fine," I said, putting the painful swirling of my head aside. "Just overwhelmed, that's all." Suddenly, I felt as though I might throw up instead of pass out, but before I could decide, the feeling vanished. Heart pounding, I swallowed, hard. I hadn't been this nervous since we had gone to face Randall on Oak Isle.

No, I told myself firmly. *You are not going to focus on that right now. Not when you need to be completely aware and ready to meet the king.*

"I'd never thought Court would make ye nervous, Sam, especially after all I've seen ye do at sea." Tristan's eyes sparkled as he watched me, his expression showing he believed I was fine now. The two of us slowly started for the doors the Bevard's had disappeared through.

"Well, I could fight anyone I had a problem with," I said in a matter of fact tone. "And I could wear pants. And no corset."

Abella had the decency to look scandalized, but Tristan's laugh echoed in the large space, causing many people to turn and look at us.

"This is true," he agreed, chuckling. "I can only imagine the faces of everyone here if they saw ye wield a sword the way I have."

Grinning, I felt some of the pep return to my step. He was right; if I could handle myself among pirates, high society should be a breeze. Both situations were their own type of game, with different rules, but I knew how to adapt and survive.

It was how I'd made it this far, already.

Somewhere, bells chimed, marking the time, and the people around us increased their speed.

"Dinner is in an hour," Tristan informed me comfortably. "Everyone will want a good seat at the table. I, however, am content to wait and meet His

Majesty tomorrow, during the ball. What say ye?"

Breathing a heavy sigh of relief, I nodded. "Yes, please. I thought I was going to be sitting across from him making small talk when you said we'd be eating together tonight."

"No." He grinned, keeping any comments about my obliviousness to himself. "Everyone eats dinner in the Hall of Mirrors during the ball. It's a very large affair. We'll just be part of the crowd."

"Wonderful."

I really, very sincerely meant it, too.

The Hall of Mirrors only had looking glasses on one side of the long, rectangular room. However, they reflected the massive gardens through the large windows on the other side of the space, which made it feel much bigger than it actually was. Huge chandeliers hung from the ceiling, which was painted in magnificent scenes that must have been from the King's life. Golden statues and filigree lined the walls, the entire area truly fit for royalty.

It was my understanding that this place was normally only used for fancy gatherings and important meetings or parties, as well as for the King's daily use. Tonight, though not officially part of the ball, was apparently special enough that they had decided to feed everyone in elegance.

"So exciting," Madame Bevard was saying two seats to my left. "Doesn't His Majesty look splendid this evening?"

We were quite a ways away from the Sun King, but what I could see of him did fit the hype. He wore a long, dark, curly wig, the hair framing his pale face. Clothed in royal blue, his clothes seemed to be masterly crafted and adorned, as one would expect.

He was eating calmly, listening to someone seated closer, who appeared to be dishing out compliment after compliment in his favor.

"I do love it when there's a party," she continued confessing, loudly, for everyone to hear. "It breaks up the monotony of everyday life."

"I'm sure His Majesty enjoys the break from his schedule as well," another person I'd yet to be introduced to, agreed. "And he throws such lovely parties."

"Do you remember the last ball?" Gloria asked eagerly. "I felt I would never sleep again from all the excitement!"

And so began the conversation of the last time they'd all been gathered together. Tristan and I were ignored for the most part, for which I was grateful. I'd never been to any kind of ball before, unless you counted prom. Something told me it wasn't the same.

Abella remained quiet through the meal as well, eyes wide as she peered around, her food almost untouched. I thought she might have felt as overwhelmed by everything as I did, but she hid her anxiousness a little better. Every now and then, someone would ask her something, especially Madame Bevard, since they were seated right next to each other.

Frowning, I stared at my own plate, the bread and meat hardly even eaten. My stomach was feeling queasy again. Halfheartedly, I hoped I was coming down with something. Maybe then I could skip all of the lessons and important meetings without looking bad.

"Are ye okay, lass?" Tristan found my hand

under the table and squeezed it reassuringly. "Do ye not like the food?"

"It's delicious." Smiling, I made a show of eating a bite of bread for him, feeling like a dork when I realized the couple across the table was watching. Suddenly, a smell reached me and I felt my eyes go wide. "Is that . . .?"

They were bringing out dessert and drinks on trays, the first of which having been presented to the king. The unmistakable scent of chocolate made my mouth water and I gasped in astonishment.

"Chocolate?" I asked Tristan, grinning like a fool. "Really?"

"Ye've had it before?" he questioned, surprised.

"*So* many times. It's one of my favorite treats." I felt like bouncing in my seat as the waiter laid my own plate in front of me, immediately taking a bite as soon as they'd left. "It's even better than I remember."

Tristan chuckled, watching me, and took a bite himself. "Aye, it's good. One of the better things about coming to Court, actually."

A flurry of motion at the head of the table drew my attention then, as well as everyone else's, as the King raised his glass, waiting for silence.

"Welcome," he said warmly.

A tiny thrill shot through me at the sound of his voice. Being in the presence of someone who had made an important mark on history felt exciting, as nervous as it made me.

"It has come to my attention that some wish to practice dancing tonight, before the ball begins tomorrow. I find your enthusiasm heartening for the festivities."

Everyone laughed, clapping, and I followed suit, not knowing exactly why we were doing it. On the other side of the room, King Louis smiled, pausing for silence once again.

"Instructors will attend you in the Rocaille Grove, where the ball will begin in all its glory." He stood then, causing more of a conundrum as everyone moved to stand with him. I expected him to say more, but he simply turned and left, a line of people going with him.

"He won't be going to lessons?" I asked Tristan as the party moved through the doors into another part of the palace.

"No. King Louis usually follows a very strict schedule. I imagine he has meetings and papers to attend to."

Conversation resumed once His Majesty had departed, the courtiers and guests sitting back down to finish their meals.

"Lessons in the garden!" Gloria giggled, her face a bright pink and I suddenly wondered if she ever did anything but get excited about things.

Abella nodded politely, her hands folded in her lap, eyes fixed on the mirrors facing us. Looking into them myself, I could see some of the gardens in the dark, lights shining along the pathways. Again, I felt a tingle as I thought of where I was. Whenever I'd imagined running into famous people or places of the past before, I'd worried that I would somehow alter the future. This wasn't like some science fiction movie, though. Right now, it felt like I could do or say whatever I wanted and it would still be the same.

On the other hand, that wasn't really a risk I was willing to take.

Dinner came to an end shortly after that. It quickly became apparent that a good majority of people in attendance had decided to take the offered dance lessons, making it seem like the ball might actually start tonight anyway. Their excitement was catching, and I soon found myself smiling and chatting with Madame Bevard happily as we made our way out of the palace and into the gardens.

I'd heard of the gardens at Versailles many times, but felt just as blown away as I had when I first saw the palace. Even in the dark, I could tell that the area was massive. Sectioned off into different areas of design, the foliage was in the full bloom of spring, torches lighting the way to the open air ballroom. Under the sounds of talking and laughter, I could hear the rustling of skirts, footsteps, and the air moving gently past us. Statues of some god-like person appeared in a few places, many of which I paused slightly to look at.

"It's Apollo," Tristan murmured, his lips brushing my hair just above my ear as he stopped with me.

"To match the Sun King," I replied, catching on. "How very fitting."

"I'm sure he'll be happy to know ye approve." Chuckling, he turned me to face him and kissed me softly before leading me down the path again. "I've missed ye, lass."

"Me, too. It's strange. Everything here is so not like it was before." We were falling back from the group now, slowing our pace so we could talk in peace. It looked like others might have had the same kind of idea, slipping off down other paths. Lovers giggled as they made their escape. Did Tristan and I look like that, I wondered?

"We might not be here much longer," he stated easily. "Since our meeting at the Temple, the Order has sent out scouts to find Randall. I shared yer concerns about the trip with the Grand Master, aye? He agreed that we should do all we can before taking a step such as that. Going to Arizona will be our last resort."

"We'll be leaving as soon as they find him, then?" Resting my head on his shoulder, I took a selfish moment to drink in his presence, his touch warm all around me, his clothes smelling of the chocolate we'd eaten at dinner.

"Not a moment later. I want this taken care of as soon as possible." We stopped again, looking out over a fountain. Nearby, I could hear some music being played, mixed in with the sounds of the dance lessons.

"What will we do once Randall is . . . taken care of?" I couldn't bring myself to say "dead." Somewhere in my mind, I knew that was what Tristan's end game was for the villain, but it was hard for me to think of him being the one who would carry that action out. I'd seen him kill before, but this felt different. Only one time had I seen him kill out of anger—the captain whom he'd found trying to rape me—and even then, his actions had served a higher purpose. The fight had happened legally, according to pirate laws, and it furthered his position in the Order. But killing Randall? It seemed like pure revenge to me. Tristan had been betrayed; he intended to take care of it in the most final way possible.

"Sam?"

Looking up at him, I realized he had said something to me and I'd missed it. "Sorry," I replied, blushing. "I was thinking about something. What did you say?"

"I asked if ye thought ye could be happy on land, away from all the excitement of the sea and her ships? I cannot rightly tell if you like where we are now. I'd hoped . . . that is, after Randall is gone . . . I want to settle down and be with my wife. I want to have children to hold on my knee and tell them stories—to have a home that I live in every day and a garden to tend. But, if ye were to want none of that, I would go to the end of the earth with ye. Wherever ye are, that is where I have to be."

Tears stung my eyes as he shared his feelings with me and I laughed, stopping to throw my arms around him properly. "Of course I can be happy. I'd be happy anywhere as long as we are together. You are my home, remember?"

Clutching me tightly in his embrace, he rested his chin on top of my head, not saying anything. He didn't have to, though; we didn't need words to express how we made each other feel all the time. It was enough to just hold one another and be who we were. After a few moments, we broke apart, taking each other's hands, and continued our slow walk down the path.

"Do ye want to go to the lesson?" he asked, watching as I stifled a yawn. "Or would ye rather go back to our room?"

"I should probably go to the lessons." Grinning, I thought back to our handfasting and the celebration we'd taken part in afterword. To this day, I still hadn't experienced anything quite like a pirate party in a whorehouse on Madagascar. There had been lots of dancing—and drinking—and Tristan had pulled me around the room with ease. But, a formal ball was a different occasion. Secretly, I hoped it would be as rowdy and fun as our wedding. If it was, I could relax and forget about how nervous I was to be among royals.

"Ye're not so bad a dancer as ye think," he said, the look on his face telling me he was thinking of the same occasion. "I'd say ye're a right vision, in fact."

"And I'd say you were blinded by love," I retorted, laughing all the same.

"Aye," he agreed, his tone teasing. "I lost my eyes from the moment I first saw ye."

"So you've said."

"Come back to the room with me," he stated huskily, his thoughts obviously moving on to what had happened after our wedding celebration. "I can lead ye in the dances well enough tomorrow."

"What if someone else asks me to dance?" I asked innocently, toying with him. "Will they know how to lead me as well?"

"Ye know damn well that no one can lead ye as well as I," he replied fiercely, joining in on the game with me.

I'd missed him so much. Apparently, judging by his playfulness, he really had missed me, too. We'd never had time that was just for us before. It was always busy, always dangerous. Now that we had time to relax, well . . .

"I'm afraid that I'm not feeling well and have to go back to our room," I told him evenly. "I'm very sorry."

"And I'm afraid I'll have to escort ye back and make sure ye're not disturbed," he replied just as seriously, his eyes twinkling.

Turning me around, he set off at a much faster pace than we'd been going, chuckling under his breath.

"You know," I began, trying to keep up with him without jogging. "They say that Marie Antoinette used to meet her lovers out here for her secret affairs. She's a future queen of France," I added as an afterthought, realizing he would have no idea who I was talking about. "These gardens are notorious for things like that."

Pausing, he looked at me, surprise written in his features. "Ye mean, ye want to do it here?" he asked, looking around. "With all these people?"

"I'm sure we're not the only ones who snuck off to be together." Smiling, I nodded for him to keep going. "But you're right. I would much rather go back to the room than have someone like Madame Bevard come across us."

Laughing loudly, he began tugging me along with him again. "Ye'd never hear the end of it, lass. Ye'd probably make her whole year."

For the first time in what felt like forever, I woke up at a decent hour and with Tristan still beside me, his eyes closed in peaceful slumber. The room we'd been given at the palace was elegant, as expected, but larger than I'd thought it would be. This was more like an upgraded suite, with a separate sitting and receiving area, a dining space, and the bedroom all being part of our "small" accommodations, as well as an extra, added on place for Abella to stay. It was all decorated in yellow and purple, the latter of which I'd been told was a color reserved specifically for royalty and was a special treat to see. Fresh flowers sat on almost every surface and a fire burned in the hearths of each room, even though it wasn't even the slightest bit cold.

Servants wandered in and out after we got up, most of the time almost completely unnoticed. They tended to the warming flames, brought in food, made the beds, got rid of aging plants in favor of new ones, and all other sorts of chores. As I'd expected, being waited on made me even more uncomfortable, but there was nothing to be done about it here. The best I could do was make sure I didn't mess anything up that they would have to take care of.

"What do you have planned for the day?" Abella asked as she tightened the back of the jacket I wore with today's gown. "Or are we staying inside until the ball starts?"

"I thought we might do some exploring," I told her, smiling into the mirror across from the foot of my bed. "There's a lot here that I would like to see. Do you know when mass is?"

Surprised, she paused in her workings to stare at me with wide eyes. "You want to go to church?"

"Father Torres told me that the chapel here was beautiful." Laughing, I watched as she recovered herself and went back to the lacings. "I thought I would go see it, so I can tell him about it the next time I visit him."

"That would be very nice." She sounded like she would have believed I worshiped Satan before I ever said I wanted to go to church. "Do you mind my asking how you and the Father met? You seemed very close when he brought us together."

"He helped me out of a . . . sticky situation, before I was married to Tristan." He actually helped me get onto a ship disguised as a man and told a crew of pirates that I had my tongue cut out by aborigines and couldn't talk, but that was beside the point.

"He is a kind man." Her voice was soft and contemplative, and I suddenly wondered what it was she was thinking about. The air of sadness was a feeling that I suddenly didn't want to have anything to do with right now.

"What do you want to do today?" I asked, moving away to inspect my reflection after she was finished. I was in pink, with white lace accents. The sleeves gathered at my elbow, the frilly cuffs spilling down to my wrists in elegant loops. A low neckline accented my breasts as always, and the skirt made my hips look at least twenty times larger than they actually were. I liked this dress quite a bit, though, and smiled at my image. I didn't often feel pretty, instead thinking that I looked like a cream puff, but today felt different. I'd curled my hair—an exercise in patience without electricity to heat up the rod evenly—and pinned it up as I'd seen many women do last night, deciding against powdering it. It seemed I was a little tanner, possibly from my time in the sun on the way here, and I didn't want to cover it up with the latest fashion.

"You are positively glowing," Abella said from behind me, having been inspecting her work as well. "There won't be a person in Court who won't think so."

Smiling, I opened my mouth to respond and then blanched, my face obviously going white in the glass in front of me.

"What is it?" Abella asked in alarm, grabbing my arm as if I were falling over.

"What is today?" I inquired weakly, feeling like my head was spinning.

She told me, still holding onto my arm tightly. "Should I call for Monsieur O'Rourke?"

"No!" I'd kind of snapped at her, catching her by surprise, and she let go, stepping away. "I'm sorry," I said quickly, giving her a small smile. "You didn't do anything. Could I have a moment alone? Maybe go see if breakfast is ready?"

She nodded, obvious distress on her face, and left, no doubt to get Tristan from the other room anyway.

Catching a glimpse of her simple blue dress passing through the doorway, I sighed as the latch closed instantly behind her.

Forcing myself into some type of calm, I slowly counted the days back, feeling an uneasiness growing in the pit of my stomach.

Except, if I was counting and remembering right, that wasn't the only thing growing in my abdomen.

Slowly, all of my episodes of suddenly feeling sick or faint were making sense. I'd been more tired than usual the past couple days, but pushed through it because we had so much to do. Even today, as Abella had been tightening my corset, I'd felt like my breasts were extra tender, but attributed it to Tristan being somewhat rough with them the night before.

Fearfully, I placed my hands over my stomach. My period was more than a week late and I'd never even noticed. With all that had been going on, I'd focused on just trying to get used to my new routine.

Maybe I was off because of all the changes? That happened, right? Things could change in your life and it could mess with your cycle.

But it hadn't. Ever since I'd first started menstruating, I'd always started on the same day every month, almost down to the hour even. Why would it change now, after over ten years of regularity?

Tears gathering in my eyes, I blinked hard, not knowing what to do. There was no test for pregnancy in this time other than to wait and see if I ever started

159

bleeding. It would be at least another week or two before I would feel confident enough that there was a baby. How far would that make me then? Seven or eight weeks along? Did I see a midwife regularly, or was I on my own until delivery?

"No," I whispered, closing my eyes as a tear rolled down my face. Fisting my hands over my stomach, I tried to keep from shaking. I couldn't be pregnant now, not when Tristan needed me to go with him and find Randall. This wasn't part of the plan! We were waiting until the danger had passed, till we could settle down somewhere and stay forever. I'd taken the herbs I'd been given every day, without fail.

Yet, there was still obviously something going on, and my intuition told me what I desperately wanted to not be true.

Tristan and I were going to be parents much sooner than we wanted.

Taking a deep breath, I forced myself to open my eyes and stare at my reflection again. "There is no way to know, yet," I said firmly, my face somewhat fierce. "No way. You will keep it together. It could be a false alarm. No one needs to know anything."

After another minute, I felt I'd calmed down enough and reached up, wiping the tear from my cheek.

"Samantha?"

Abella's voice was small and barely discernable, but I turned anyway, motioning her in. Her expression was guarded and made me feel even guiltier for snapping at her.

"I'm sorry," I replied evenly, smiling. "I hadn't realized the date and it caught me by surprise. Today is the anniversary of my father's death. I didn't mean to alarm you."

Visibly relaxing, she seemed to accept my excuse without question. "I am so sorry. How did he die?"

"In a work accident." The real anniversary wasn't for another month or two, but that didn't matter. As long as she didn't say anything to Tristan about it, my white lie would go unnoticed.

An awkward silence stretched between us, myself wondering just how long I would have to go before I really knew if I was pregnant or not.

"Breakfast is ready," she finally stated, her eyes betraying how uncomfortable she felt. In that moment, I was her employer and she was nothing other than a servant. The sight made my heart hurt.

"I'm sorry, Abella. Really."

Sighing, she seemed to stand up taller. "You don't need to apologize for feeling, Sam. I understand. I would have done the same thing if I'd remembered something unpleasant like that suddenly. I am, however, starving. Are you ready to eat? Monsieur O'Rourke is waiting for us. He looked like he was ready to faint from hunger."

Laughing, I nodded, letting her lead the way out of the suite, glancing back at my form in the mirror once.

Breakfast went over without incident, with only the occasional odd look from Abella, before Tristan announced he would be leaving us for a few hours.

"Bevard asked me to escort him away from his wife and daughter before he went mad from their talking of dresses and fashion." He chuckled, shaking his head. "Do ye need anything while I'm away,

Sam?"

"No, I'll be fine." Smiling warmly, I watched as he left, a servant coming in and clearing his place.

"Abella," I said, once the woman left the room. "Thank you for not saying anything to Tristan. I don't want him to worry."

"Does he not know what day it is?" She was curious, suspicious even, her eyes narrowing some.

"I don't think he does." Swallowing hard, I stared down at the fruit on my plate, feeling a little less than enthusiastic about eating right at that moment. "I'd like it to stay that way."

"If that's what you want." She sounded all business again, like I was ordering her to do something.

"Will you keep it a secret, as my friend?" I asked her suddenly, very much wanting someone to confide in. "Not because you do work for me and think I'm your boss, but because you want to?"

She was surprised, her features softening into something that could only be described as kindly. "Of course, Samantha. I am your friend, after all."

"How awful must I be that I have to pay people to spend time with me?"

The joke broke the tension between us and she laughed, her eyes lighting up in her mirth. "You pay me to help you get dressed, not to be your companion. That I'll do for free."

"Good." Happiness flooded me at her comment and I started to feel like maybe—just maybe—I could handle being pregnant if I had a good friend at my side to help me through when Tristan wasn't around.

"This damn corset is too tight," I growled, trying to keep pace with everyone as they walked through the garden to The Ballroom that had housed dance lessons the night before. There would be no skipping out this time; tonight I would be formally introduced to the king.

Unfortunately, my hormones made me feel more like wrestling a grizzly bear at the moment.

"It's not so bad," Abella tried to reassure me. "I left room to breathe and move easily. It's a little tighter than normal, though, since your meeting is tonight."

"Thank you for that." Grumbling, I shot Tristan a look that could kill as he smirked at me. My grimace only made him laugh harder, aided in part by the ridiculous dress I was being forced to wear.

I would've been more than happy to attend the ball in the beautiful dress I'd started the day in. However, custom dictated I dress up for the party even more. What I wore now gave me the feeling of trying to land a plane blind. The massive, emerald skirt leaving no opportunity to see where I was stepping and shined like a beacon for all to see. Lace lined the edge and around the waist, matching the same design on my white jacket. A matching green stomach piece was sewn in, the laces on the back of this three quarter sleeve jail cell as tight as the horrid contraption holding my insides in underneath. To make matters worse, I kept wondering if I might accidentally be squishing the baby to death with all of this fashionable nonsense.

"Truly, Samantha. Ye are a vision to behold," Tristan said, trying to calm me some with his tone. "Corset and all. Just think, tonight ye get to take it off. Won't that be a treat?"

"I don't appreciate your teasing," I snapped back, smiling in spite of myself.

"Ye look beautiful," he responded sincerely, stopping our march to kiss me on the forehead. "It's glowing all around ye."

Smiling tightly, I felt my breath catch. What would he say when he found out? It was happening so fast. We'd been married for a little over a year. I wasn't old enough to be a mom! Well, not by my standards, anyway. Would he be mad? Probably not. Disappointed? Possibly. Would it matter? I was going to have to stay behind now, always waiting to see if he'd made it out of his missions alive.

I didn't know if I could handle that.

Thankfully, my thoughts were sidetracked as we came into the grove, a gasp escaping me as I took the area in. Hedges lined the space like stadium seats, a large, marble disk making up the floor. On the other end of the circular garden, a large fountain ran, the water pouring over rocks and seashells, some of it spurting into the air in places.

"Isn't it beautiful?"

Turning, I saw that the Bevard's had descended on us like hawks, circling our group with ease.

"They don't usually run the fountain. It wasn't on last night. Oh, how wonderful!" Wanting to stop Gloria before she really got going, I nodded and smiled.

"It's very pretty. Do you know what songs the orchestra will be playing tonight?"

Her eyes grew round and she promptly hurried off in the direction of the band, holding her skirts out of the way with one hand.

"Quick thinking," Tristan laughed, pulling me away from her mother and father as they watched her go. "I thought we were about to be regaled with the tales of how the shells came from far off countries by the hand of the navy."

"Were they?"

"Of course. Gloria could have made it into an hour long spectacle involving pirates and true love, though." He grinned, his eyes sparkling as he looked at me.

"You have to be careful about those pirates. I heard they can sweep a woman off her feet with just one look." His touch made my insides feel warm and fuzzy, calming the rest of the earlier anger I'd been battling with.

"Aye, ye would know that story best, lass."

More people filtered in, the musicians tuning their instruments, until finally, a still seemed to settle over the crowd. And then, suddenly, the king was there, a beautiful woman at his side, his golden outfit shining like the statues of Apollo that dotted his lovely gardens as he was announced with a fanfare and applause from everyone. It was like looking at the sun as he made his way through the crowd, taking hands here and there, pausing to speak with a man whenever he wished. Curtseying as he passed, I took the time to notice that even his shoes were gold, with what appeared to be real gold buckles.

King Louis was lucky his people wouldn't be angry about how much money the monarchy spent until he had been in his grave for quite some time.

Once His Majesty had made his way to the other side of the dance floor, the music started up, he took his escort in his arms, and the dancing began. It was a waltz, which quickly became stunning as people joined in around the king on all sides. Letting myself be lost in watching, the music hummed lightly in my ear while the laughter and conversations of others drifted to the background.

A tug at my hand brought me back to the present, Tristan inspecting me happily.

"Do ye want to dance? Ye look like ye're in another world."

"I think I was," I answered, laughing slightly. "And, yes, I would love to dance."

Taking my waist in his other hand, we fell into the formation easily. He was more than faking his way through the steps—he knew just what to do and led me through the movements gladly. I almost didn't even notice when the song ended, I'd been having so much fun.

Clapping for those around us, another number started up and we drifted back to the sidelines, watching as the king, yet again, proved his skill and love for dancing.

The night felt like it would stretch on forever, my feet beginning to ache after a few hours, but I couldn't seem to care. The party had given me an excuse to let my stresses go for a while, and I was embracing the opportunity with open arms.

As Tristan and I danced happily together, I suddenly caught sight of the king, heading our way. Eyes wide, I whispered as much to Tristan, who immediately turned and bowed. Following suit, I curtseyed low, staring at the ground and waiting for something to happen.

"Tristan O'Rourke," the royal voice said above me. "How long has it been? Five years? I was beginning to think you were a stranger to us here in France."

"No, Your Majesty," Tristan replied warmly. "Just a man busy with work and love."

Feeling him rise beside me, I came out of my show of submission and carefully glanced up. Surprisingly, King Louis was staring right at me, a wide smile on his face.

"So I see!" Laughing, he motioned to the woman beside him, who melted into the crowd behind him with a blink of eye. "And you are, my dear?"

"Samantha Green O'Rourke, Your Majesty," I replied, trying to keep my voice from shaking.

"Such a strange accent," he mused.

"I was born and raised in America, Your Majesty."

"How extraordinary." He regarded me for another moment before holding his hand out. "I wonder, Mrs. O'Rourke, if you wouldn't mind abandoning your husband for one dance?"

My heart practically leapt out of my chest at his words, fear freezing me on the spot. "Um. I mean, of course I wouldn't! However . . ." Biting my lip, I tried to think of how to phrase the next part. "I'm afraid I'm a much better follower than I am a dancer, Your Majesty."

He chuckled at that, as did his party of people behind him, and waved his hand in dismissal. "I assure you, Madame, I will lead you just as finely as your husband has been all night."

Glancing at Tristan, who gave me a nod, I swallowed hard and took the king's hand, hoping I didn't look like a frightened schoolgirl as he touched my waist and began moving me across the floor.

"Are you enjoying your stay at the palace?" he asked me, as if this were any old dance and he was someone of no importance.

"I am." I knew I should say more, but the words seemed stuck in my throat. How did I talk to a king? Right then, it dawned on me that this was a regular old dance for him. I was the new one at his house. I'd been "trained" for this moment for months. What had I learned?

"The Sun King loves to be praised," Tristan's grandmother had told me while we were in Africa. "Give him enough of it, and ye can get anything ye want while ye're in his care."

Smiling, I latched onto that one tidbit of information and held on for dear life.

"Your home is very beautiful. I can see why you moved it out of the city. It was very wise and becoming of you to do so."

King Louis grinned at that, moving effortlessly to the music, carrying me with him. "Do you not like the city?"

"I love what you've done to it," I replied instantly. "People will be talking of the Sun King and his glorious creations for centuries to come."

Well, that part was true.

"Wonderful!"

The advice I'd been given was spot on; the more compliments I gave him, the friendlier he became. One moment we were talking of the gardens and the next he was sharing stories of his other homes, to which I emitted approving noises whenever necessary.

When the dance came to an end, he bowed, as was custom, and I curtsied, feeling a little like I'd just won a game of Russian Roulette.

"My dear," he stated, holding his hand out to accompany me back to Tristan. "You simply must stay after the ball is finished. The Royal Ballet Company will be performing in one of my theaters and I have a feeling you would wish to see the show."

"Will you be performing? I heard you are extraordinary as a performer, as well."

"Oh, no!" He tittered, obviously pleased with the amount of sucking up I'd done. "Not this one. You will stay, though? The performance is in two weeks' time."

"I am honored that you would even invite me."

Tristan, having caught the end of our conversation, bowed as I was deposited safely back in his care. "Thank you, Your Majesty," he spoke kindly.

"You will stay, too, of course," King Louis said, in an air that made it sound more like a command than anything else. "You've picked well for a bride, Monsieur. Do not remain strangers for so long again, *oui*?"

Tristan bowed again and I hurried to curtsey, watching as the Sun King casually strolled away from us.

"Ye did wonderfully, Samantha," Tristan breathed as we both straightened. "He took to ye like a ship to sea."

"Is that a good thing?" I asked nervously, feeling somewhat faint from all the spinning around.

"Ye couldn't have done any better." Grasping my hand in his, he smiled.

Rather badly named morning sickness grabbed onto the edge of me then, warning that I was about to hurl in front of the entire party. "I need some air," I croaked out, desperately searching for any way out of the mass.

"Tristan!" Grand Master Bevard was waving him over, a grin plastered on his somewhat drunken face.

My poor husband was aghast at what to do, mostly because he didn't seem to know how to tell his boss to leave him alone for a moment.

"Go," I rasped. "I'll have Abella come with me."

She appeared at my side, as if saying her name had magically summoned her, the red of her dress making her skin look somewhat flushed and aroused. Carefully, she led me from the grove, instructing me to breathe slowly as we walked down the paths, leaving Tristan behind without another word.

Once we were far enough away that the sounds

of the party were only a haze in the background, I let my knees buckle, threw my head in a bush, and emptied the contents of my stomach.

"How far along are you?" she asked pleasantly, helping to hold my skirt out of the way.

"I don't know," I moaned, laying right down on the path and resting my face against its cool surface. "I just realized today. I think I'm about five or six weeks along. Too early to know for sure."

"I wondered if that was what had happened. You've seemed sickly and tired, but I didn't know if that was just how you were."

"Gee, thanks," I replied humorlessly. "I don't think I've ever been described like that before."

"You are with child. You will be sickly and tired for a little while longer." There was laughter in her voice, but compassion as well.

"Abella" I looked up at her with pleading eyes. "Tristan doesn't know yet. Please don't say anything."

"It's your news to tell," she replied simply. "I would be surprised if he doesn't already suspect."

"I want to be sure before I say anything. I—"

Voices on the other side of the hedge were coming closer to us, arguing. As they neared, I was able to make out some of the conversation.

"—doesn't just go right for the treasure is a mystery! What is he waiting for? The Natives to hand it to him?"

"You know Randall," the other voice said coolly. "He wants all of the crew to be the best he can get. This isn't going to be another crackpot mission like Columbus and Cortés put together. We're going to

171

get it this time, and Thomas Randall is the man who's going to get it done."

It felt like all the blood had drained from my body. Treasure? Thomas Randall? The conversation we were overhearing could only mean one thing.

The men on the other side of the hedge were Black Knights.

Abella, having become frozen at the look on my face, listened intently with me to the continuing conversation. She didn't show any recognition of the voices, which meant she was probably clueless to the entire plot unfolding in front of her.

I, on the other hand, felt my insides growing colder and colder as the unfamiliar men spoke, their voices rushed, but not discreet. They must have thought they were alone in the maze.

"Why England?" the first voice asked bitterly. "What is he looking for there?"

"Not what, you dolt! Who! There are members joining up there. By the time we make it to the Americas, we'll be more than one hundred strong and ready to fight!"

"You mean to tell me that old Joseph, who spends the vast majority of his time three sheets to the wind, is considered strong and ready to fight? The man has a bloomin' peg for a leg! If O'Rourke so much as looks at him, he'll faint dead!"

"Quiet!" the other man growled. Silence filled the air, and I wondered if the pair had left, when suddenly, the talk started up again. "Shark bait,

O'Rourke is. I heard Randall say it himself; he knows the man is coming for him. When he does—"

There was a sound like I heard people make in the movies, whenever they mimicked slicing someone's throat. It felt like I might faint from hearing it, just the thought of Tristan killed by Thomas Randall making me wish I hadn't heard the entire conversation. Abella clapped a hand to her mouth, understanding that someone she knew was in trouble.

"He'll be sleeping in Davy Jones' Locker before that wife of his even has time to scream."

I was ready to scream and yell right then, but it wouldn't have done any good. The men would get away before anyone would come, if they even heard me over the festivities.

"How long till Randall makes landfall in England?" the second man asked.

"They sent word he'd be there by next weekend. After that, it's another month or two to the Americas, where we'll be living like kings."

The men laughed, their footsteps starting to fade down the path, until there was nothing but silence in our immediate area.

"Sam," Abella said, fear in her eyes. "Was that Tristan they were talking about?"

Feeling sick, and this time not from pregnancy, I nodded. "It was. We need to go find him right now."

Helping me to my feet, the two of us stumbled back down the path, practically running, slowing at each corner as if we thought the Black Knights would suddenly appear and take us away. When we finally reached the grove again, it felt like I'd danced there in another lifetime, not less than an hour before.

Tristan was still with Bevard, laughing with a drink in his hand. He appeared so happy and peaceful.

And then he saw me.

It was like watching a storm overtake his features. I didn't know what I looked like, but whatever it was, he instantly switched from his calm, personable member of court appearance to that of the man who had killed the *Adelina's* captain in a duel on the beach of Madagascar. This was the man who worked in a secret trade, slept among pirates, and knew what dangers the world truly possessed.

Striding through the crowd that easily parted for him, some of the courtiers gawping at him in surprise, he reached me within seconds, taking me by the arm and leading me away.

"What happened?" he asked tightly, surveying Abella once as well.

"They're here," I spoke breathlessly. "The Black Knights. We heard them talking, going over plans that they had."

"Oh, Monsieur O'Rourke," Abella gulped fearfully, her eyes showing signs of overflowing with tears. "You are in terrible danger."

"I'm not the one in danger, believe me," he reassured her. "Tell me everything ye heard."

We relayed the conversation to him the best we could, glossing over the part where they'd been talking about his murder, as he led us back to our rooms in the palace.

"And ye didn't see either of the scoundrels?" he inquired again, locking the door behind us.

"Not even once." I was as apologetic as possible,

but it didn't feel like enough. Why hadn't I jumped through the hedge and confronted them? Why hadn't I at least tried to look somehow? I'd had no weapon and no way to do anything to help and it made me so angry I could have slapped myself.

He paced the room for a moment and then turned abruptly, going to the door. "Stay here," he ordered us. "Do not open the door for anyone but me. I'm going for Bevard. Who knows how many of the villains are here at Court tonight. We can't wait to make a plan."

The door closed hard behind him and we both flinched, my own heart still racing. "Black Knights at Court," I whispered. "This is bad—really, really bad. How high up could it have gone?"

Balking, I remembered Tristan's earlier warning. The Grand Master had joined the Black Knights. Kings had been part of the secret before. Was the Sun King a Black Knight in disguise? Did he know of the secret pacts that existed right under his nose? Did he facilitate them himself?

"Black Knights," Abella replied, breathing slow and deep. "I don't understand. Who are they?"

"Bad people," I answered shortly. "That's all I can tell you, right now."

She regarded me with a cautious expression she'd never aimed at me before and then nodded, seeming to accept it for now. Something told me she may have understood a little more than she was letting on, but I pushed that thought aside.

England was close. If the Order could get there and intercept Randall, this fight would be over before it really got the chance to start. I wouldn't be able to go, not when I could be pregnant, but Tristan would be back in no time at all.

Randall may have been making talk about killing my husband, but we all knew at the end of the day Tristan was the better fighter. Thomas would need God on his side to beat Tristan, and I didn't think the Lord was one to help the scum of the earth.

We didn't talk much after that, huddled together as we waited for Tristan to return. The longer it took, the more I began to relax. If we were in real danger, he would be here in an instant to take us away. I highly doubted he'd opened fire on anyone and accused them of being evil, so the only other alternative was that he was helping to sort things out.

Several hours passed before there was a light knocking at the door. Tristan stood on the other side, tired and angry, but whole. Silently, I let a breath I didn't know I'd been holding loose.

"Ye should have gone to bed," he said upon seeing me. "It's nearly dawn."

"You knew I'd wait for you."

Nodding, he smiled at Abella, who had regained some of her formality and composure after being scared by the both of us.

"Aye. Methinks it will be best to sleep through the day, anyway. Come to bed with me, lass?" He took my hand, helping me stand from the seat I'd been resting in, and then turned back to Abella. "All is well," he assured her. "It's taken care of. Ye need to rest as well. Thank ye for staying with her."

She curtsied, slipping away to her own room in a flash.

With a sigh, I went into our room with him,

watching as he locked the door and leaned against it.

"The scouts are on their way to England," he said roughly, with a note of impatience. "They will wait to see if Randall makes landfall. When he does, we will leave to get him."

"You don't like this plan." It wasn't a question; the feelings were all right there on his face.

"No, damn it, I don't! We shouldn't be waiting and wringing our hands like old maids! Who knows how long he'll be there? He could be gone before word even reaches us that he's arrived. Where will we be then? He'll have more men to his name and we'll have lost the trail." He slammed his fist against the door, making me jump some, and then ran his fingers through his hair, shoving away from the entrance and going toward the bed.

"I understand what you're saying, what you're feeling," I assured him. "But I understand why the Grand Master wants to be careful. Thomas is a dangerous man. It's best to think things through before acting."

"I know," he mumbled, undoing the buttons on his vest. "But I don't have to like it, savvy?"

Motioning me over, he began releasing all of my numerous laces, helping me out of my dress without saying anything else. Only when he saw me standing before him in nothing but my shift did he truly seem to relax, his eyes suddenly drooping in exhaustion.

"I'm sorry I wasn't with ye, Sam," he said quietly. "That ye had to hear men talking about me like that. I know if I'd heard anyone say those things about ye—"

"It's okay," I interrupted, pulling him to me in a

strong embrace. "I'm okay. You're okay. Everything is fine. I've heard much worse than two men babbling together."

My bravado and smile didn't do anything to cheer him. He simply continued to hold me, his fingers pressing into my back, his face buried in the crook of my neck as he breathed heavily. After a few moments, he let me go and continued to undress, climbing up onto the bed and collapsing against the pillows.

"Tristan?" My heart had started pounding again as I laid down beside him and I closed my eyes tight, trying to work up the courage to tell him what he needed to know.

"Hmmm?"

"I don't think I can go with you to get him."

His lazy breathing stopped, his form becoming more alert, and he rolled over, reaching out to touch my face with care.

"Why not? Is something wrong? Do ye not want me to go?" The questions poured out of him so quickly that I suddenly realized he'd been worried about going after the Black Knights as well. While I'd been afraid to be without him, he'd feared me not being at his side.

"It's not that," I said quickly. "I mean, I don't really want you to go, but I understand you need to. I want to go with you. I just . . . can't." The ending was lame, my mouth feeling like it was getting drier by the second, my words getting tongue-tied.

"What is it?"

His eyes were so startling green and full of love, and his hand warm on my cheek, which suddenly made me feel like crying again. He wouldn't be mad. Oh no, he would be happier than I'd ever seen him.

"I'm pregnant."

The words hung in the air between us, having caught him completely off guard, and his face went blank, his body freezing. After a few seconds, he seemed to come around, staring down at my stomach, the hand on my face traveling down to rest on the flat surface.

"Truly?" he whispered, wonder in his voice. His fingers traced my skin through the fabric of my shift, his eyes never leaving my midriff.

"I think so," I answered unevenly. "I was going to wait a few more weeks to be sure before I told you, but with everything going on I thought now was the time."

He gazed at me then, and one of the largest smiles I'd ever seen him wear covered his face. With a loud whoop and a laugh, he smashed his lips against mine, holding me to him tightly. "I'm going to be a father." He broke away, suddenly. "I'm going to be a father!" Sitting up, he put both hands on my stomach and leaned over, kissing it. "Hello in there," he said softly. "Child of mine."

His happiness was overflowing, the laughter, exclamations of surprise, and joy, made me feel like I could float away on a cloud of happiness.

"You aren't upset?" I asked, laughing as he kissed my stomach again.

"Why would I be?" He seemed appalled at the very thought. "My wife, the woman I love more than anything else in the world, has just told me I'm to be a father!" Lying down, he pulled me into his embrace, kissing the top of my head. "A child—a real child. That ye and I made! Our child. Our baby."

"Our baby," I repeated, tearing up a little. "I thought you would be mad that it happened before we were ready."

"I was ready from the day I married ye," he answered energetically. "I've been ready to be a father since the day I left home and joined the Order. It's all I've ever wanted, to settle down with ye and have our own little Tristan or Samantha. I would never be mad at ye, lass." Kissing me on the mouth again, he brushed his hand over my stomach once more, laughing against me. "Is that why ye've been so sick? I was worried ye'd caught something on the ship!"

"I guess," I replied, smiling. "I didn't think it was that obvious."

"Lass, ye would hardly eat sometimes. It doesn't take long to know that's not normal for ye."

Playfully slapping him on the shoulder, I finally allowed myself to feel the warm, fuzzy thoughts about having a child that I'd been shoving aside since I first discovered what was going on.

A baby. Our baby. Tears of happiness rolled down my face and I cuddled closer to Tristan, wanting to feel his heat all around me once more.

"Monsieur O'Rourke!"

The yell came from the front door, followed by incessant pounding as whoever was outside continued to shout. Startled, the two of us practically fell out of the bed.

"Wait here," Tristan ordered quietly, grabbing a lit candle and going into the sitting room.

Frowning, I nodded, upset that our time together to bask in this moment was being cut short. He didn't seem too excited about it either, but there was only one reason someone would come banging on our door just before sunrise.

"What is it?" I heard him grouchily ask once the door was open.

"A scout returned from England—one who was already assigned there. Thomas Randall has been spotted in London."

"What about you, Madame O'Rourke?"

Drawn out of my nervous musings, I looked across the room, to the woman who had grabbed my attention. She sat on the edge of her chair, every bit the proper lady, a teacup and saucer held delicately in her fingers. The dress she wore made her look like some kind of angel, the golden brown fabric layered exactly perfect for her skinny form. Lace brushed her elbows and neckline, the high collar a change from what I'd seen most women wearing lately. A matching hat graced her blonde curls, pinned expertly against her head in a way that simply made her entire appearance scream royalty.

Lady Chastity, the duchess of some place or another situated some distance from the palace, stared at me expectantly, her glass held just below her lips, as if she were waiting for me to answer before sipping.

"I'm afraid I don't quite understand what it is you're asking." Smiling tightly, I lowered my head, carefully tasting the hot liquid I grasped in my own hands.

Everything was too fancy here. All of the chairs

were hand carved and painted, the seats covered in beautiful works of art sewn into the fabric. Pink walls with gold inlay surrounded us, mirrors reflecting the scene, tall statues stood guard at every corner. Enormous bouquets of flowers cascaded over their vases on end tables, and a harpsichord, set right in front of the window overlooking the gardens, gleamed in the sunlight. This was a place for the visiting members of court to relax and spend their time, but it felt more like an overly decorated prison cell while occupied by our present company.

"Oh, come now," the older woman replied, laughing as she glanced at the other ladies in the room. "Surely, someone born and raised in the colonies would know whether or not their loyalty remains with England. You've traveled extensively with your husband, as well. Do you really claim to know nothing of the state of your homeland?"

"I think what Samantha means is that she's not been privy to the political leanings and desires of her representatives." Abella responded coldly, coming to my aid yet again. "Why would she be? She grew up on farmland. Her travels with Monsieur O'Rourke have been that of a merchant captain's wife."

"Why are you here?" Chastity asked, her voice snapping like a whip. "You should be with the other maids."

Feeling like she might as well have slapped us both across the face, my mouth popped open in surprise. "Abella is my friend, not a servant." Sitting up straight, I stared at the duchess, finding my voice at last. We'd been listening to her belittle and condone every other person in attendance for the past

184

two hours, and I'd had enough. "She's here because I asked her to stay with me. His Majesty has invited us to stay after the ball has ended, as his guests. You stay because your husband wants more time with his mistress."

The royal stared at me in astonishment, apparently having never been spoken to like that before. Those in the room whispered behind fans and hands, watching me with wide eyes.

"Samantha!" Abella scolded me, giving me the same horrified appraisal.

"Everyone knows it's true," I replied defensively. "We all saw him with her."

"*Oui*, just as everyone saw you spirited away by your husband on the first night." Lady Chastity's cup clattered as she set it on the table, picking up her fan furiously and practically throwing it open. "Tell us, what startled you so?"

"It must have been my lack of political knowledge and power," I replied smoothly, setting my tea down and standing up. "Now, if you will excuse me, I do believe I have somewhere I need to be."

Turning, I ignored the further gasps that followed behind me; if I'd been proper, I should have at least asked for her permission to leave, since she was a higher class than I. However, I also shouldn't have spoken out of turn, but there really wasn't any coming back from what I'd done now. It didn't matter in the long run. If the women hadn't been happily putting others down, they had been dragging England through the mud, directing many of their insults to me—the only English person in the room, or so they thought.

"Well, I never!"

Lady Chastity's voice carried after me as I brushed past the servant at the door, Abella right behind me. As soon as I was in the hall, I felt as if I could breathe again, sighing as my shoulders slumped. Facing her, I smiled sheepishly.

"I'm sorry. I know I shouldn't have said it, but I couldn't stand listening to her any longer. Who is she to make everyone else feel like garbage, intruding into their lives without so much as an excuse me?"

Abella closed her eyes as if she were trying to calm herself, lips pressing into a thin line. "She is a duchess, Sam," she muttered. "It doesn't matter what you think, what you did back there was very inappropriate. What's worse, it will spread like wildfire to everyone in attendance."

"Only because I said what everyone else was thinking!" Giving her a pleading look, I shrugged my shoulders. "How bad could it be?"

"That depends on what she wants done about it." Breathing heavily again, she took my arm in hers, the two of us walking slowly down the empty hall. "Lady Chastity is one of the King's cousins. If she were to ask him for something, she would most likely receive it. It could be nothing, or we could find ourselves thrown out of the palace before the ball is even over this evening."

"This stupid ball," I grumbled, feeling my earlier anxiousness fill my mind once more. "How are we supposed to go around, acting like nothing is wrong? Thomas Randall is so close we can almost touch him, and everyone is just sitting here, twiddling their thumbs while they wait until it's socially acceptable to leave."

"You know that's not what's happening," she replied, her voice taking a type of mothering tone. Despite being the older of the two of us, I found great comfort in her presence and suggestions. She had a way of making the situation sound better than it was, which I desperately needed right now, because she was right.

At this very moment, Tristan was with the other members of the Order that were here, meeting somewhere in secret. They were making a plan of action, sending messages back to the Temple, working to get a crew together that would depart in the morning. In truth, it was the earliest they could get the men and resources together. It was the last night of the ball, as well; there was no reason for them to have to stay any longer than tonight. Their presence here gave the illusion that we didn't know what was going on, which I assumed was imperative to the plan.

"They will catch them. Monsieur O'Rourke will return in no time, a few weeks at the most. Surely, you don't doubt his ability to catch these Black Knights?" Abella was trying to convince me again, noticing the signs of distress I'd been exhibiting since we overheard the conversation in the garden.

"Of course I know he can do it." Quietly, I continued on, not wanting any prying ears to overhear, should they be listening just out of sight. "It's only . . . I've never sent him off to fight alone. We've always gone together. Now, because of the baby, I have to stay and wait. How do I sit around and not know what's happening? If he's alive or dead? It doesn't even seem possible to me, knowing that while he's out at battle, I'll be here, pretending nothing is wrong."

"No. You'll be here fighting your own mental war—trusting everything will be fine while he is away." Smiling encouragingly, she kept us moving forward, through the doors and out into the gardens.

Silently, we started down no particular path, letting the beauty of the plants around us fill the space that our silence left. It was a warm day and there were many people outside, but it was like they were in another world. They didn't know what dangers could be lurking right around the corner. Every man I saw made me question whether or not he was a Black Knight, or some random person, out enjoying the light and air. Eventually, we reached one of the magnificent fountains and sat down on a bench beside it, content to remain away from Court and its inhabitants for a while.

It was there that Tristan found us, some time later, his face tired and drawn, but happy.

"There ye are! I've been looking all over for the two of ye. How was yer day?" Striding over, he beamed at me, kissing my hand and wrapping it in his grasp as he sat beside me.

"Oh, you know. I insulted some royalty and got a lecture from Abella about it." Laughing slightly, I felt a blush creep over my face. I'd promised to do my best while we were here and something told me I'd crossed that line by a large distance.

"I did not lecture you," she said sternly, glaring at me. "I simply told you that you shouldn't have said what you did."

"Ye mean to Lady Chastity?" Chuckling, he shook his head. "I thought that sounded like something ye'd say. Did her eyes look like they were going to fall out of her head when ye said it?"

"You mean you already heard about it?" I asked, surprised. "I thought it wouldn't get around until tonight, during the ball gossip."

"I'd be surprised if there was a soul who hadn't heard about it yet, lass." Eyes shining, he watched me, his nose twitching with suppressed merriment. "Ye made the servants' day, and many of the ladies, too, from the sounds of it. They've been singing yer praises since I came to look for ye."

"What?" Abella's voice mirrored my own shock.

"Mind ye, I imagine they only told *me* how much they liked ye. They'll be properly upset when required. However, Lady Chastity has had a reputation of saying more than she should, savvy? She's none too many friends here, despite the show she puts on. There's a reason she only comes to the palace when there's a party."

"You don't think the King will ask us to leave, then?" I asked, hesitantly.

"The King? No. He'll probably be upset he wasn't there to witness the spectacle for himself." Sighing, his happiness diminished some, a cloud covering his features. "It'll be best he doesn't ask ye to go. Ye'll be safer here, while I'm away."

"How did the meeting go?" I questioned anxiously, scooting closer.

Shaking his head, he stood, pulling me up after him. "Walk with me?"

"I'll go get things ready for tonight." Abella,

189

taking her cue to leave, curtsied slightly and left, not looking back even once as she went on her way.

"When are we going to tell her everything?" I asked Tristan, frowning as he guided me in the opposite direction, toward a hedge grouping.

"When the time is right, I suppose. She's a strong lass, to go along with things she knows nothing about. Very trusting."

"And the plan for you to leave?" I inquired again, pushing the girl from my thoughts. "What's going on?"

"It's not so much a plan as it is a raid," he replied carefully, staring forward. His fingers tightened around mine, tugging me closer, and his voice softened. "Randall has men joining up, aye? We'll wait for them to all be together before we attack. If all goes as it should, we'll be back just as ye're heading for home, in the city."

"And if it doesn't?"

He shook his head again, glancing over at me. "It will, lass. It has to. I'll not have ye left alone for longer than is necessary." He paused, whatever he was about to say seemingly stuck in his throat.

"What is it?" Encouragingly, I squeezed his hand, smiling.

"I've asked the Grand Master to relieve me of duty," he finally said, the confession whooshing out of him on a long breath of air. "Randall won't be our problem after this. Ye're going to have a baby—I'm ready to put my days of pirating behind me. We'll move wherever ye want and start our family."

"Tristan!" Shocked, I stopped dead in my tracks, gaping at him. "You didn't have to do that. I know how important the Order is to you, to your family."

"Being a father is more important," he replied evenly. "It's true, my relatives have aligned themselves with the Order for hundreds of years. That's not a life I'd want for my son, though, should it be a boy. I couldn't bear it, thinking of him doing all the things I've had to. It's time we became simpler folk, relying only on ourselves to make it by. I know we can do it, Sam. Will ye stand by me?"

"Of course I will," I responded immediately. "There's not anything that could stop me from supporting you. Are you sure this is what you want?"

"I've never been more sure of anything in my whole life, save the fact that I love ye." Smiling softly, he pulled me against him, resting his forehead against mine. "I'm ready to be a father, Sam," he said quietly. "Nothing will make me happier than ye and the babe, in a house of our own, not bothered by anything."

Kissing me lightly, his lips brushed over mine with a tenderness I'd rarely seen in him. It was as if his heart were displayed for all to see, clearly bonded to me.

"We'll leave before dawn," he murmured against my lips, one hand caressing my jaw while the other pressed against the small of my back. "Be safe, savvy? I have a bad feeling about this fight and I can't quite figure out why."

"You're the one who needs to stay safe." Taking a deep breath, I closed my eyes, trying to memorize what it felt like to be held by him. The thought of having to spend weeks apart made my heart race with anticipation, mirroring the ill thoughts he had about the time away from each other. "I'll be here waiting for you."

It was all I could do to hope that he would return quickly and unhurt.

"Stop fidgeting!" Abella chastised me for probably the twentieth time that day, watching me stand at the window as she sat in her chair with some needlework. "Staring out the window won't tell you anything and you know it."

Frowning, I glanced at her, hating she was right. However, I wasn't feeling sick today and I was ready to find out some news.

It had been two and a half weeks since Tristan left with a ship full of Templar Knights, bound for England and Thomas Randall. Abella and I had stayed at Court as the king requested, making excuses for my husband's absence and being as charming as possible, until it was time to come home. I'd expected to hear immediately what was going on, but not a word had been spoken to me about the mission from anyone. Abella still remained in the dark as to what was really going on, but she knew it was something important and dangerous. Each night, she lit a candle for him and put it in the window, a soft prayer leaving her lips. I was more grateful for that than I could ever have expressed.

After spending all of that time together, never

parting except to sleep, we'd become the fast friends I'd hoped for. She was younger, but matched my age mentally, and I soon found myself regarding her as a kind of sister. We would help each other dress now and decide what to do for the day together.

Yesterday had been a very nasty case of morning sickness. There was no denying it now—I was pregnant. All of the symptoms were there, which I was grateful for. It gave me comfort to know that my body was still going through a wonderful change.

But Tristan had not come home.

Had something gone wrong in London? It wasn't that far away, so I didn't think the time was being spent traveling. Was he hurt? Had Thomas gotten away and they were chasing him? All these questions and more swirled through my mind day in and day out. But, today would be different.

"Do you want to go to the market with me?" I asked Abella, moving from the window. "Tristan took me to a nice one at the old Temple before. I'd like to look at some of their stuff again."

"Are you feeling well enough to go?" She spoke skeptically, giving me the once over. "You could hardly stand yesterday."

"Fit as a fiddle," I replied, smiling. Truthfully, I did feel somewhat worn out from being so sick, but I desperately wanted news of what was going on. If the Order wouldn't come to tell me, I would go drag it out of them.

She thought it over for a moment, looking at me like a mother would a small child, and then nodded, putting her work aside. "Fine, but we're taking the carriage. I'll go let them know we want to go out."

"Wonderful!" Clapping my hands together, I tried to reign in my excitement. Hopefully, the news I wanted was good.

The city passed in a blur as we rode to the Temple, my mind on the secret entrance to the Order's headquarters. Tristan had tapped a special sequence on the wall, but could I remember it?

Finally, we arrived at our destination and I set out, slowly passing each cart and examining their wares. When we came to the table I recognized from before, there was a different man, who smiled and asked if I'd like to see any of the silks he had for sale.

"Actually, I believe there is a painting inside that my husband is interested in," I replied, unable to remember the rhythm I needed. "Could I possibly see that?"

"Of course, Madame," he said cordially. "Please, look all you want."

Frustrated with myself, I went into the back room, making a beeline for the hidden door. Tapping on it, I waited for it to open, but nothing happened. As I'd suspected, I needed the code to get it.

Abella, who was watching with mild curiosity, raised an eyebrow and folded her arms. "Shopping?" She may have sounded miffed, but she was smiling, catching on that there was something more here. "Anything else you need to inspect?"

"No." Pushing past her, I went back outside to the booth tender, smiling as nicely as possible. "I need to get inside," I said under my breath.

Confusion flashed in his eyes, his brow furrowing. "You were just inside."

"Not inside the shop, inside the Temple," I

whispered furiously.

"I'm not sure I know what you're talking about, Madame."

"Oh, good grief!" Throwing my hands up, I turned around, shaking my head. He obviously wasn't my way in.

And that's when I saw him.

He was standing at the gate, watching me evenly, a smile on his face, his long black hair concealing some of his features. He looked dirty and ragged, like a beggar, the hat on his head full of holes, but Thomas Randall's face was one I would have known anywhere.

The world stopped spinning in that instant, everything zooming in to focus on just him, the thud of my heart ringing in my ears. It was as if the breath I desperately needed to live was stuck inside me, my throat closing tightly under the scrutiny of his gaze. Then, with a pop, it all went back to normal, my mind imagining the sound of his boots crunching through the gravel as he started toward me.

"Abella," I said sharply, grabbing her by the wrist as she stood beside me. "We're leaving. *Now.*"

There was no way out of the courtyard except for the gate he hovered in front of. If we were going to escape, we would have to go right past him and into the city.

"Is something wrong?" Abella asked in alarm as I practically dragged her across the ground.

I couldn't even answer her. The wrong man had returned to me, the villain instead of the hero. Where was Tristan? What did I do? Fear tore at my entire being; both for the man I loved and myself. There wasn't any time to stop and think things through, though. It was time to pick fight or flight, and I was ready to run for my life.

There was another man I recognized already in the Temple courtyard, his hat pulled low over his face. Panic threatened to overtake me, but I shoved it down, instead relying on the adrenaline I felt underneath it.

"We can't take the carriage back to the house," I told her quietly, slowing as we approached the gate. "Someone is watching us. Randall."

Her eyes grew wide and I felt her step falter before she pressed forward with renewed vigor. "Monsieur O'Rourke?"

"I don't know," I replied evenly, trying not to cry. "We don't have time to find out now."

Looking back toward the table I knew was ran by the Order, I wondered why the Templars weren't pouring out to take control of their enemy. Had they not realized who he was? I couldn't exactly scream for help, not when no one was attacking me. Everyone would think I was crazy, Randall would run, and I wasn't willing to get close enough to him to let him touch even a millimeter of me.

Going back to the exit in front of us, I spied a cart getting ready to pass through from the other side. Timing it just right, we slipped through as it blocked us from the pirate's view, hurrying down the street in the opposite direction of home. The streets were packed and hard to maneuver—a blessing in our time of need.

"We have to lose them in the crowd," I explained quickly. "Stay right with me. We're going to run now."

To her credit, Abella didn't even look faint at the prospect. Her jaw set tightly as she nodded, her hands grabbing her skirts out of the way as we both increased our speed, darting down the street.

People yelled at us as we passed, bumping into them without apologizing. Rude gestures were flung our way, but I couldn't even care. My chest felt like it was ready to explode from being overworked, but my fear led me on, my feet slapping against the cobblestone roads mercilessly.

Ducking under an archway and onto the path on the other side, I looked over my shoulder, a scream lodged in my throat. Randall was still there, his face stony as he shoved a man pulling a wagon to the ground, knocking the items that were being transported into the street. Despite the raucous he made, his eyes never seemed to leave me, their darkness reaching out and touching me with icy fingers.

Trembling, I turned my attention back to my own route, taking Abella's hand and moving in the opposite direction we'd been heading. Slipping some, we shoved through a crowd of people watching a street performer, ignoring the exclamations of indignation and anger still. My feet were begging for me to stop, my fancy shoes flapping helplessly against my heels with every step.

Desperately, I tried to think of where we could go that would be safe. Home would have been preferable—a safe house, under the protection and care of the Order—but I didn't want to lead Randall and his men there. The door wouldn't hold them long and we needed to get word to someone we needed help.

Tall houses and shops all melded into one as we continued on, gasping for air, sprinting away from those who would harm us. The streets seemed never ending, our flight taking us down whatever path emerged in front of us. It felt like we'd been fleeing for hours, my body crying out for rest. Frustrated by my own lack of strength, I pushed on, trying to ignore the red color of Abella's face as she too struggled. The fine food and sedimentary lifestyle of living among royals had made us groggy and slow. In that moment, I would have given anything to be in the shape I'd earned during my time as a pirate. The months sailing from Oak Isle and spent trying to be a proper lady had softened me too much; I didn't even know if I could win a fight against Randall again.

Daring to look back once more, I barely caught sight of the horrid hat Randall was wearing. It turned every which way, frozen in a sea of people. Relief coursed through me at the sight—he'd lost our trail.

Slipping down a side alley, I persisted in driving the two of us at full speed, wanting to capitalize on our newfound disappearance. Practically carrying her down the street, we passed through another part of the old city wall, the river visible ahead of us.

"Stop!" she gasped. "I can't run any longer."

Collapsing against the side of the building, I nodded, chest heaving as I tried to catch my breath. It felt a little like I was going to throw up from all the exertion, my face covered in sweat. The bones of my corset were poking into me painfully, my skirt torn near the bottom. Abella looked much the same, dirt covering her hem, her cherry-colored skin covered in a sheen of moisture.

"There," I said, the sound barely a whisper in my dry mouth. Pointing to another alley between buildings, I stood up straight, basically dragging my feet across the ground until we were safely concealed in the space.

Staring out over the crowd, I felt another wave of relief. Randall was nowhere to be seen. Wanting to make sure we'd truly lost him, I scanned the area for another half hour, feeling secure in our hiding spot. All I saw were the normal city folk, though, going about their business. We'd lost the pirate at last.

"Come on," I croaked, stepping out from our hiding spot and into the mass. "Let's go home."

"I know a shortcut," she said wearily, fanning herself with her hand. "I'll show you."

Finally, bodies aching, we made it back to our house, halfway wondering if we'd imagined the whole thing. The façade was as welcoming as ever, smoke curling from the chimney and bright flowers in the windows. It was as if we hadn't even spent the last little while scared for our lives.

Swallowing hard, I looked both ways down the street, noting how much emptier it was than the paths we'd just traveled.

"Get inside, quickly," I urged her. "Lock all the doors and windows."

Nodding, she dashed through the doorway, almost knocking over the cook in the process.

"Come inside, we're in danger," I said quickly, helping the woman up. "All of the doors and windows must be locked."

Within seconds, the whole house was locked down and I found myself sitting at the window I'd been so eager to peer through that morning. Now I feared what I would see on the other side.

Minutes slipped into hours, the sun setting and darkness covering the street outside. Closing the curtains, I dared to hope that we had truly lost the Black Knights and were safe.

Thomas Randall didn't give up easily, though.

Abella sat at attention beside me, her hands clasped in her lap as she anticipated some kind of sign that everything was okay. "Should we send for someone?" Her voice was tired and soft, but the fear I still felt was there in her tone.

"The carriage driver will have noticed that we disappeared," I replied, hopeful. "Someone will come. I don't want to send anyone out, not when they could be hurt."

Silence stretched between us once more. Exhausted from our run, I felt my eyes drooping, my head nodding slightly as I drifted off to sleep, unaware that I was even slipping away.

It was the crash that woke the both of us. We'd fallen asleep in our chairs, waiting for something to happen, and now that moment was finally here. Several bumps and muffled shouts reached our ears as I shut and locked the bedroom door.

"What do they want with us?" she asked, trembling, her face white.

Grabbing her by the shoulders, I shook her hard, getting her full attention and looking her straight in the eye. "They're coming for me," I said evenly, having put the pieces together as I'd sat expecting them. "Tristan is a member of the Knights Templar. He's either been sent on a false mission, or he's been captured or—" The word stuck in my throat, but I forced it out anyway. "Killed. It was all a trap to get him away from me."

Her eyes were wide and filled with misunderstanding, but I didn't have time to tell her delicately.

"I'm from the future. I know things no one else does and they want me to tell them those things."

Her eyes grew even larger, if that was at all possible, and her mouth popped open, but no words came out.

"Hide in the dresser," I told her, shoving her toward the giant piece of furniture. "They don't want you. Hide and after we're gone, run to the Temple and tell them what happened. Shout it into the night if you have to. Do you understand?"

Stunned, she stumbled toward her designated hiding place, ripping the doors open and climbing inside. I'd just shut her in when the banging on the door started.

"I know you're in there," Thomas Randall's voice sneered, my hair standing on end. "Open up, Sam. This doesn't have to be difficult."

"Like hell," I muttered, grabbing the gun that Tristan had hidden under the mattress. I shoved it in the pocket of my dress, pressing myself against the curtains.

Suddenly, the wood splintered and the entrance flew open, revealing a gang of cutthroats and murders. Randall stood in front, smiling, a pistol aimed right at me. His expression was triumphant, excited even as our eyes met. In the time since I'd last seen him, he had changed clothes, his form now covered in threads fit for a sea captain. A long, red coat hung around him, a gun belt slung across his shoulder. His hair had been tied and braided, leaving his face clear and open for all to see. "We meet again," he said smoothly, stepping into the space.

"It's not my pleasure, I promise," I snarled in return.

"Come now," he scolded me. "There's no need to be rude."

The man behind him caught my attention for a split second, and I recognized his face as the driver who had taken us to the Temple that morning. My stomach clenched at the sight. Tristan had been right; I shouldn't have trusted anyone just because they were part of the Order. Anger washed over me at the betrayal and I looked back at Randall, giving him a half smile.

"Of course there is." In a flash, I had the blunderbuss out, aimed, and fired, missing Randall and dropping the driver to the floor. Chaos erupted in front of me, the group lunging forward and grabbing at me, but I was determined to not go down without a fight.

Clawing at the eyes of the closest man, I kicked out at another, shouting as I was knocked off my feet. With the weapon in my hand, I clubbed Randall over the head, desperate to put at least some distance between the group and myself.

There were too many hands, too many feet kicking me. In fear, I tried to roll away and protect my stomach, but had the wind knocked out of me first. They were dragging me away, my screams and curses echoing off the walls as I fought tooth and nail, tears streaming down my face from pain.

Across the room, the wardrobe doors flew open and Abella launched herself on the closest man, pulling his hair and biting his hands, shrieking as she foolishly tried to help me.

"Abella, no!" I shouted, but it was too late.

The smoke was curling from Randall's gun, the barrel pointed in her direction. She went limp, sliding to the floor as a red stain stretched over her chest. The sound of the fired shot rang in my ears, blocking out everything else.

"No!" I cried, over and over again as they picked me up, carrying me away. "Abella! She needs help! Abella!"

They hauled me down the stairs, quickly tying my hands together and shoving a cloth in my mouth. Outside, a large chest waited. When they threw me inside, I felt like I was going to pass out from lack of air. All I could see was Abella, collapsed on the floor, her blood seeping into everything.

My baby. Was it okay?

Crying, I tried to assess the damage to my midriff. I'd been kicked a few times, maybe even had a broken rib. But I didn't know if my baby was alive or dead.

Head knocking against the wooden cell, I tried to calm my nerves and assess what was happening. Every time I felt like I might be able to relax some and think, though, I was jostled violently, knocked around like a sack of potatoes. After the third time, I began to think they were doing it on purpose. The fourth fall left me seeing stars and I would have bitten my tongue badly if it weren't for the gag in my mouth. Finally, though, I recognized the gentle sway of water and realized we were on a boat. The thought gave me some calm, knowing we were on our way out of the city and toward the seaport, where I assumed they'd place me on their galleon, or whatever type of ship they had.

The pirates either weren't speaking, or the box was incredibly sound proof. Eventually, I was lulled into a dreamless sleep, waiting for whatever was going to happen next. It seemed like an entire lifetime passed before I was suddenly hoisted up again, my trunk swaying every which way before it finally landed on a wooden floor with a loud clunk. There were voices now. I could hear them. Why hadn't I been able to before? Someone was pushing me across the floor, which I soon realized to be the deck of a ship.

So, we had arrived. Now my only question was if I got to come out or not.

"You there!"

Randall's voice shot out in the din and I flinched, my heart starting to race again.

"Yes, Captain?"

"You were assisting the last doctor on board before he died. I'm promoting you to surgeon. Come with me."

"Yes, Captain."

Again, I was lifted up and carried somewhere else. It was like a guessing game, trying to figure out what the hell was going on.

"Set it down there," Randall ordered. "Carefully.

You've had your fun. Now get out, both of you."

Footsteps shuffled away and I held my breath, waiting for something to happen.

"I want you to take care of what's inside this chest," Randall said evenly. "If it dies, so do you. Do you understand?"

There was a brief hesitation before the man finally agreed, his voice sounding somewhat strained.

"Good," Randall said. "Get to work."

More footsteps went out of the room, leaving me in silence once more. Suddenly, the chest began to rattle, the lid creaking open.

Fearful, I tried to pull back as far as I could, blinking in the light at the shadow looming over me now. The man sucked in sharply, freezing for a second.

"Oh my god!" He removed the gag from my mouth and I coughed, eyes watering as I sucked in a good, deep breath.

"Sammy?" he asked tentatively.

It was then that I saw whom I was talking to, my eyes fully adjusting and shock almost knocking me out again.

"Mark?"

Mark Bell

This wasn't possible.

Samantha continued to stare at me from her tiny prison, her body beaten and bloodied. For an instant, I wondered if her ghost had finally found me again and was torturing me once more. Blinking hard, I waited for the vision to subside, but it never did.

A strange rush of emotions filled me, causing my eyes to prickle. She was alive! By some happenstance, fate had brought us back together. Her dress was torn in several places, gore splattered over the fabric—some of which looked like it might not be hers.

"Mark?" she questioned again, but I couldn't even answer her. My mouth refused to form words as I stared at her, trying to accept what I was seeing before me.

Anger coursed through me, seeing her in such a state, but my surprise kept me rooted to the spot, mouth hanging open like a sail without wind. Fear touched the back of my mind, for both her and me. Something told me Captain Randall wouldn't find me necessary to keep around any longer if he found out I knew his captive. What did they want with her?

Curiosity also slapped me across the face. How long had she been in this time? Had it happened in the Pit? Did she know how? What had she been doing since the slip? Were there more time travelers?

Most of all, there was a radiating sense of peace that burned me from the inside out. It touched every part of me, causing the tears that now fell freely down my face. My hands shook beneath its power, my knees giving out as I crumpled to the floor. The feeling urged me to reach out and take her in my arms, to hold her and share my relief. Not even hesitating, I followed the instinct, gasping as her hands clutched the front of my shirt, wrists still bound together.

I wasn't alone anymore.

"How are you here?" she asked, her voice muffled against my shoulder. "How?"

"I don't know." My fingers felt her hair, long and frazzled, even more wonder filling me as I held her.

Common sense raised its head and nudged me, the realization of her situation hitting me full force.

"Here, let me untie you," I spoke, releasing her quickly and setting to work on her bindings. "Then I can look at some of your injuries."

Randall had left us both in the room the ship used as a surgery. It wasn't large, or even adequate for such a task, but there was a table for patients to sit on and a desk for the few scant instruments the last doctor had left behind.

Frowning, I pushed thoughts of Abel Martinez from my mind. He'd been a good man, despite how he'd met his end.

Sam's eyes seemed to burn into me as I worked, quickly freeing her and pulling her from the trunk. It was immediately obvious that she'd either been clubbed over the head at some point, or her ride here had been a bumpy one, judging by the lump under her hair. Carefully, I led her wobbly form to the makeshift bed and sat her down, grabbing a lit candle off the supply table and holding it in front of her face.

"Open your eyes, wide," I coached her, trying to watch the dilation of her pupils and determine if she had a concussion.

"How are you here?" Her voice held an air of anger and I paused, looking at her in surprise.

"I told you; I don't know. It just happened."

"How are you here, on this ship?" she clarified. "Working for Thomas Randall? Do you have any idea who he is?"

"A bit." Feeling somewhat miffed, I went back to observing her eyes until I was satisfied her head injury would be fine. "I was pressed into service, along with the former doctor."

"Pressed?"

"This ship fought and boarded the one I was on," I explained. "After they took all of the goods, they decided they needed a few men for the crew as well. The doctor and I went, as well as another man. Everyone else was killed."

Appearing aghast, she pulled away as I tried to feel the spot as well. "You went willingly?"

"Yes. No. I did what I needed to, to survive. You of all people should understand that, I think." Staring pointedly, I waited for her to relax and let me continue my evaluation.

My emotions were still a roller coaster as I touched her, drinking in the presence of someone from my own time. It didn't seem like it would have mattered much, but it did. I couldn't explain it, but it was as if my soul had found a missing piece in the image of someone who knew completely what had happened to me. Not just that, but someone who understood the situation wholly, because it had happened to them, too. A person who knew what a cell phone was, who would understand television and movie references, or know exactly what I meant when I used slang from the twenty-first century.

Several minutes passed as I checked her, happy to find that she was mostly banged up and not mortally wounded. "I think you're going to be okay," I told her, stepping away and giving her some space. Being by her was like being drunk, not knowing what to do or say, but having so much I needed to express.

She nodded, biting her bottom lip, her hands resting against her stomach. Her eyes were troubled, something bothering her more than the abuse she'd taken from the crew. What had they done to her? Balking, I instantly worried someone had touched her in an intimate way.

Pirates were not above rape.

"Were you hit there?" I asked her, hoping she would quell my fears for her.

"Yes. Kicked," she said, her voice strained.

Sighing in relief, I felt my posture slump some as my muscles relaxed. "You'll probably have a bruise, but I don't think anything too bad happened, based off your other injuries. It'll be sore for a while, though."

She nodded again, her eyes tearing up, and then took a deep breath, seeming to calm down some. "Mark—" She hesitated, eyes glancing toward the open door.

Taking the hint, I got up and closed it, checking to see if there was anyone in the hallway. Once I was sure we wouldn't be overheard, I motioned for her to continue.

"I'm pregnant," she whispered, her eyes wide with fear.

It felt like I'd been shot in the head, the words causing me to stare blankly for a moment before I shook myself roughly.

"It's only a few weeks along," she hurried to say, seeming to tremble. "But I was kicked in the stomach. Is there any way . . ." Her words trailed off as she covered her mouth, tears starting to roll down her face.

Nodding, I shoved my startled and slightly outraged thoughts into a box and closed the lid, tight. "Lay down," I ordered, crossing to her side. "There's no way for me to know for sure, but I can feel around where you were kicked and try to see if there was internal damage."

She did as I asked, hiccupping, and stared at the ceiling.

The good news was that wombs were made to protect babies. Based on the condition she'd arrived in, the trauma had probably occurred before she was put in the box. She would have noticed bleeding if she were miscarrying.

Feeling through her dress, I tried to be gentle, watching as she flinched. Whoever had kicked her hadn't spared any force. Unfortunately, just as I'd thought, I wasn't able to tell anything.

"We'll just have to wait and see how it goes," I told her comfortingly. "That's the best we can do. How are you feeling?"

"Sick," she replied, laughing slightly. "That's a good sign, right?"

"I guess." My experience with pregnancy was limited to my time as a paramedic, before I'd decided to become a history professor. Even then, I'd rarely actually had to use any of the skills I'd been taught. Since being here, I'd picked up small things from other healers, but not so much about this.

"Sammy," I started, my frustration getting the better of me. "Whose baby is this? What on earth were you thinking, getting pregnant? We're not from this time! We have to be careful!"

"Excuse you," she said, her tone instantly dangerous as her expression morphed into a glare. "It's my *husband's*."

I didn't know how many more surprises I could take today.

"Your husband?" Stepping back, I looked at her like she was crazy. "You're married?"

"For over a year," she said briskly, frowning at me.

"How long have you been here?"

Her face softened at that. It was obvious that we had a lot of talking to do.

"Almost two years. You?"

Gulping, I turned my back to her, hands clenching into fists. "Ten," I said softly.

Hearing her small gasp, I glanced over my

shoulder, getting some satisfaction from the expression of sorrow on her face.

"How?" she asked. "How did it happen?"

Chuckling some, I shrugged, moving to face her as I leaned against the wooden wall. "It's a mystery. I was in Arizona and got caught in a dust storm. When it ended, I was in another time. Of course, it took me a little while to figure that out. It wasn't a fun period.

"I was in the desert, no city in sight. For a while, I thought I was dreaming. Then I started to wonder how I could have wandered so far away during the storm. It didn't feel like I'd gone that far—I'd been at a hotel in the middle of the city. It didn't even seem possible.

"I got sick. There was no water, no food, no anything. I remember laying in the dirt and looking up at the sky, watching vultures circle around. That was when they found me."

"They?" Her eyebrows raised in surprise.

"The Apache Indians." Smiling, I could easily recall their faces when they came across me, even though I'd been in a haze of sorts.

"I didn't understand it then, but they argued about whether or not to take me to their village. The leader, Taklishim—Grey One—thought I was too far gone to bother with. A few of the party agreed with him, but there was a young man who refused to go without me. He said I must be either an offering from the gods, or I was lost and they were being tested to see if they were kind at heart."

"What was his name?" she asked, caught up in the story.

"Runs With Wolves." The twenty-three-year-old

boy and I had become close friends in the time I spent with the Apache. I often heard his loud laugh in my sleep, the picture of his tan face and brown eyes bringing memories of campfires and ridiculous stories he told to try and impress the woman he'd loved, Singing Bird. It was obvious to everyone but him that she wanted no one else; when she sang, her voice always had a way of conveying her love for him, no matter the tune or group she was with.

Coming out of my memories, I saw Sam staring intently, waiting for me to go on.

"I stayed with them for two years," I continued. "Once I was healthy, I worked as a servant, but was well taken care of. Over time, I was treated like a member of the tribe. They called me Snake Eyes, because of the way I was squinting when they rescued me." My smile grew wider then, a laugh caught in my throat.

"The Apache were like a family to me. After two years, though, I started to feel . . . useless. It was clear to me that I'd traveled through time somehow; I had a basic idea of when I was. Runs With Wolves could tell I was unhappy. After a while, it was decided I would leave and go home. Or least, what they thought was my home."

"You never told them the truth?" She sounded more melancholy, even though there was nothing she could have done.

"Does your husband know the truth?" I asked, raising an eyebrow cockily.

"Yes, he does." Smiling ruefully, she shrugged. "It's a long story. Not ten years long, though, so you finish yours first."

Nodding, I continued the tale, relieved to finally talk about what had happened to me, all those years ago.

"Runs With Wolves traveled with me when I left the village," I began, remembering the man with fondness. His strong features were easily recalled in my mind, long black hair hanging freely past his shoulders. Sorrow had touched his features when we parted, but I knew he would be fine; he had a new wife and a child on the way. I was just another memory for him to forget.

"I don't think so," Sam disagreed when I said as much. "You lived with him for two years. He saved your life! You have to have been more than just a memory."

"We were like brothers," I confirmed. "But once I left . . . I don't know. I never really belonged there. I felt like I needed to hold on to who I really was. In the process, I kind of stopped myself from becoming part of the tribe. Runs With Wolves didn't seem to care, but others did."

"Did they ever say anything to you?" Her voice was quiet and calm, not pushing in any way as she asked her questions.

Gratefully, I smiled at her, shrugging my shoulders. "No. They didn't have to. I never participated in anything special or sacred to them, not until Runs With Wolves wedding, anyway. To everyone else, I was just a slave who had worked his way to freedom."

Thinking back for a second, I saw the flames of the powwow fire, heard the chanting and celebrating on the night of my friend's nuptials. His new wife, Singing Bird laughed delightedly as a young girl braided wild flowers into her hair. The memory easily sucked me in, bringing me to the happier moments of my life in the past. Thinking on to what had happened afterword, though, I quickly felt my stomach souring.

"Where did you go? When you left?" she asked, helping me find my place in the story again.

"We made the trip to Mexico City," I continued, blinking hard and refusing to open them until the desert celebration had faded back into the darkness where I wanted it to stay. "Once I was somewhat settled, and he'd made the trades he wanted, he went back home." Carefully, I locked the two years spent with the Indians back in their box in my mind. I'd never returned and didn't see any reason why I would in the future.

There was still nothing I could do to better myself or them.

"I can't imagine how hard that must have been." Sam stared at me with a dejected look. "To leave the only family and friends that you had in the world. It was very brave of you, albeit unneeded."

"It wasn't unneeded," I replied, more forceful than I'd intended. "There was nothing else there for me. I had to go, or I would have lost myself."

"Because they were so blood thirsty?"

Staring at her blankly, I tried to decide if she was serious. After a moment, I realized she really believed the stories that had been told about the natives.

"The Apache only fight when they need to, Sam. There was maybe one battle in the entire time I was there, and it lasted maybe a day. Just because history says something is true, doesn't mean it is. You're more likely to make a trade with an Apache than go to war with one."

Surfacing to the front of my mind, another memory surged through me.

"Fight only when there is no other choice," Grey One had said, nodding wisely. "Life is the greatest gift we have. Do not take it unnecessarily."

"I'm sorry. I didn't mean to upset you." She spoke quickly, eyes wide at my sudden fierceness.

"It's not you," I sighed, rubbing a hand over my face. "Someday the Apache will be made into sob stories and villains. Life as they know it will be destroyed, all because someone decided they needed to spread hate."

"You sound like one of them to me." Her confession caught me off guard and I stared back with a slack jaw, not knowing what to say. Her words hadn't been an insult—she hadn't meant them that way—and they touched me in a way that was surprising.

"Thank you."

"So, you spent two years with the Indians and then moved to Mexico City. What happened next?" Grinning, she encouraged me to continue, but her eyes still held the pain she felt for me.

Thinking back, I felt a pang of the loneliness and

destitution I'd suffered with while in the great city. The citadel was magnificently huge and powerful; a center for education and religion, but none of it had been for me. "It was . . . simple," I told her, shrugging. "The first year was the hardest. Most everyone knew I had come from the north, after living with the Apache. Work was scarce. I wasn't much more than a beggar, really."

Breath catching, her eyes widened, a hand going to her heart. "How? How did you survive if you had nothing? Why weren't you able to make more, or even find more?"

"I didn't try." Laughing slightly, I looked away from her confused and affronted face. "I don't want to change the future, Sam. What if I did one tiny thing and it changed the entire world as we know it? No, I kept to the shadows on purpose."

"I'm sure the people of our time will be so happy to hear that you starved yourself for them," she replied, somewhat snottily. "Sacrificing your own well-being for something that might not have made any difference."

"I didn't starve. There were enough odd jobs that I stayed fed." Feeling like I wasn't explaining well enough, I frowned, not knowing how to put into words that particular year of my life. Sometimes, I'd wished I'd stayed in Arizona, where it was less likely that I would have changed anything. At the same time, I'd really enjoyed the freedom of being on my own, as poor and lonely as I was.

"Keep going," Sam said, obviously frustrated as well. She wasn't understanding why I did what I did. Why should she? She had apparently let herself be adopted into this era without any issue at all.

"There was a woman named Angelina." Pausing, I allowed myself to picture her in my mind, closing my eyes and sighing heavily. Her laugh tinkled in my ears like bells, big brown eyes staring at me happily. Swaying her hips gently, she motioned for me to come inside, the smells of dinner wafting out of the door behind her. Hunger for more than just food washed over me, my own chuckle responding to her beautiful form. More than anything, I wanted to take her in my arms and hold her close.

But love was not something I could risk.

"Her father was a pastor at a local church. They offered me a job tending the garden and a place to sleep inside. I never did decide if it was because they really needed the help, or if they were trying to help me out. There wasn't anything else for me to do, though, so I accepted."

"And how long did you stay there?" I could see her thinking, the timeline she was forming practically written on her face.

"Another year." Smiling, I silently said goodbye to the memory of Angelina, whisking the smell of her natural perfume back into the recesses of my mind, where they had been kept for the past five years or so.

"Why did you leave? Were you not happy there?" Her mild curiosity had returned, the annoyance at how I'd allowed myself to live seeming to diminish.

"I was more than happy," I confessed. "But it was time to go. I don't know how to explain it."

But I did. The images were all there; a child wrapped in my arms, Angelina's happy face smiling at me as she cooked dinner, holidays spent with her father, a house in the hills, everything. Loving her felt so natural, but there was too much time between us. My flight from her had been in the dead of night, without any goodbyes, a pack of my few belongings flung over my shoulder. Bumping right along with the cart I'd given the last of my money to take me to the coast, I remembered the coolness of the air that night, the smell of smoke hanging in the air, mixed with the chicken stench from the cage beside me.

Slowly, the smells changed to that of the sea, the sounds those of birds who frequent the waters, and the cart dropped me off on the docks, ships stretching down the shore, resting in the bay, their anchors resting on the ocean floor.

"At that point, I decided it was time to use the knowledge that I had. Understanding ships was easy enough; I'd studied them for years. I knew where the pirates liked to frequent, or at least where the history books had said they would be. Going to sea gave me the stability I'd wanted. I had a place to live, a steady income, and I got to see the world." *And there were no women to fall in love with*, I added silently.

"So you've been a pirate for six years?" Her eyebrows rose and I knew what she was thinking. How was it possible, for her to have been a pirate herself for the last two years and never run into me at the usual ports?

"No. I've only been a pirate for the last year." Moving to her side, I sat down, clutching the edge of the table. "I joined the crew of a vessel named *Raggedy Maiden*. I liked it so much, I remained a member until she was set upon by corsairs a year ago."

"By Randall, you mean." Glowering, she shook her head, her lips taking on a hard appearance. "That must have been close after I last saw him."

"They took the ship, naturally. I was waiting below deck, with my friend Abel. He was the ship's doctor."

"Steady, Mark," Abel had whispered, watching as I fidgeted at the surgery door. He held a pistol in his hand, and his large form pressed against the back wall, sweat shining on his Spanish skin. "We don't know what they want. I'll hand over the tools if it will keep us alive."

"Damn pirates," I growled. While I'd enjoyed studying them and learning in my own time, I found them quite the nuisance in this one. "You'd think they would recognize when to let things go and when to keep going."

"We'd been trying to outrun them for three days," I said, looking over at Sam. "The Navy regularly patrolled the area we were in, but it didn't seem to matter."

Thinking back to that day, the few moments that had altered the course of my life yet again, I suddenly felt grateful that it had happened. The events had led me back to Sam, as horrible as they'd been.

"We'll be fine," Abel said reassuringly. I heard the slight tremor in his voice, though, and pulled the hammer on my gun back, just in case.

The fight above us did not last long. Silence filled the air, the absence of sound making me even more nervous than I would've been otherwise. When the door in front of me finally opened, I started pulling the trigger, only to have the gun knocked to the side by a cutlass.

Cursing, I staggered away, holding a newly acquired cut. It didn't appear too bad, but it stung some, the mark stretching from the top of my wrist to the base of my thumb.

"Gentlemen," a voice easily distinguishable as English said politely. "There is no need for violence here." The man strolled into the room, taking in its contents with a frown. His long, black hair was braided and pulled over his shoulder, a splatter of blood on his cheek that was obviously not his.

"I'm looking for crew members," he said, motioning to someone out the door who came in and started taking everything out of the area.

"No, thank you," Abel said ferociously, his gun still pointed at the man. The pirate, however, continued on as if nothing were happening.

"You'll be given a fair share of every profit. Leave when we stop at port. And, you'll have the honor of sailing under myself, Captain Thomas Randall." He smiled, a sickly, evil expression, and I felt my breath stop for a second.

It was him. This was the pirate whose ship would sink in the Gulf of Mexico within just a few years. All of the questions I'd been trying to answer in my own time sprung up instantly, despite having been forgotten about for almost a decade.

"I'll join." I heard myself speak, the words coming out before I even realized what I was saying.

Abel gasped behind me, his eyes wide, and I gave him a quick, pleading glance. Slowly, he lowered his gun and nodded. "I'll go, too," he said stiffly, glaring at me.

Glancing away, I stared at Randall, hoping I hadn't just killed us both. Abel was one of the people I trusted most since arriving here. It was both heartening and frightening to see him put that same trust in me.

I was now a pirate, on a ship that I knew would sink, with a friend who thought we'd made the switch just to survive and get home.

"What happened to Abel?' Sam's voice brought me out of my thoughts and back to her. "He's not here any more."

"He died. Nine months ago." Flinching, the sound of the pistol that shot him rang in my ears. "Randall had him burned with the rest of the ship we'd taken."

There it was. The last of the weight I'd been carrying around for ten years lifted off my shoulders. Someone knew what had happened to me. With the epistle finished, I looked over at her, relieved to have finally shared it all.

"And now you're here. I don't think Randall would be happy to find out I know his captive, too."

She frowned, taking everything in as she nodded. "You can't let him know, Mark. He knows about me, about how I'm from the future. If he discovers you are, too, he'll keep you around, but it won't be in the condition you are now."

Flinching, I got the message, loud and clear. If I was found out, I wouldn't be part of the crew anymore; I would be one of their treasures.

Silence hung between us, and I found myself thinking of the state things were in and how I'd gotten here. Suddenly, a memory from my own time surfaced and my mouth dropped open, my eyes practically bugging out of my head.

"Sammy, you've gone and married yourself to a pirate!"

"How did you know that?" Leaning back in astonishment, she regarded me with a cautious curiosity, as if she didn't quite trust me all the sudden.

"I found a record of your marriage, back in our time. That's a whole different story about how I came across it, but I know you're married to Tristan O'Rourke. Do you have any idea what kind of man he is? Stealing a ship and turning pirate! And you've trusted him with the truth!"

"You have absolutely no idea what you're talking about," she replied coldly, standing and glaring at me.

"Do you care to enlighten me?" I shot back. "I mean, you're pregnant with his child! You've changed the future, Sam. That baby could grow up and get married, have kids, start a whole different line that never existed before. What if one of those people turns out to be the next Hitler? You could have practically destroyed everything that we know!"

"Shut up!" It was the first time she'd raised her voice at me and I didn't like it. I could tell she was getting worked up quickly, though, and bit back my retort.

"First, do you know if Tristan . . . is he still

alive?" Fear flashed in her eyes, but she held her strong stance, her fingers forming tight fists at her side.

"Why wouldn't he be?" I asked, caught off guard yet again.

"Your ship just came from England, didn't it?" she asked through clenched teeth. "Tristan and a whole crew of men went to intercept it. They never returned."

"If anyone ran into them, I didn't know about it," I replied honestly. "But, if he were dead, I would have heard about it. People have made more than a few threats against him over the months."

She relaxed some at that, closing her eyes and taking a deep breath. "I hope you're right." Her voice was soft, scared even, and I suddenly realized that her marriage wasn't just some fling she'd joined to pass the time. She really loved the man, despite his character flaws.

"I broke into Oak Isle and climbed into the Treasure Pit." The change in direction of the conversation was somewhat dizzying, but I stayed with her.

"I know. They caught you on camera—even if you'd gotten out, they would have had enough proof to lock you up."

"It wasn't about getting the treasure." She sighed, sitting down again in a defeated sort of way. "I did it for Dad. He should have been the first one to see what was down there. I wanted to steal from McCreary what was taken from my father."

"You made it down there before it flooded." I'd long accepted that fact, since the vase that had surfaced in her place had basically confirmed the notion.

Nodding, she looked at me seriously. "I've been down there now, too. I helped build the Treasure Pit."

Unable to respond, I stared at her with what I was sure were eyes so wide I looked like an owl.

"The first time—our time—I found a vase at the bottom and opened it. I later learned that it was Pandora's Box. Instead of killing me, it decided I was worthy enough to know the answer to the question I had. It sent me to this time, where I would find out what was in the Pit."

"A vase?" Insides going cold, I turned away from her. "With Greek marks?"

"Yes. How did you—oh no. It's not in the Pit anymore, is it?"

"I don't know where it is." Peering over my shoulder to her, I shrugged. "Somewhere in a motel lost and found, I would imagine."

With a confused expression on her face, Sam waited for me to expound, but the realization hit her before I was able to gather the words.

"You had the vase and opened it," she breathed. "And it found you worthy enough to save, too. What question were you trying to find the answer to?"

Laughing, I ran a hand through my hair in frustration. All these years, I'd tried to think of how a dust storm could be a time portal and it had never occurred to me that the sand had nothing to do with it. "I was wondering what happened to you. They never found your body and I felt like I was seeing your ghost everywhere. It was like a nightmare. I would sleep and you would be there, saying my name. I wasn't even in Maine anymore; I was running, trying to get away from the past. Apparently, I just wasn't going far enough into it to figure anything out."

Sighing, she stood again and walked over to me, putting a hand on my shoulder. "Don't think about it too much," she said gently. "If I've learned anything while I've been here, it's that everything happens for a reason. And if I really was haunting you . . ." Her words trailed off and she squeezed me, stepping away.

"If we could find the vase again, we could go home," I mused, feeling a little of the desperation I was always pushing away bubble up. "Wait a minute, you said you helped build the Pit. If you found it in the bottom, you must know where it is now."

Her stare told me that she did, but that it wasn't going to be any help.

"The Pit is closed off. The vase is in the bottom. No one else will get to it until I climb back down in the future." She smiled, small and apologetic, wincing as a small cut on her lip tore open.

"What else was down there? Is that it?" I needed something, anything to keep the anxiety away. It wasn't possible for me to accept I was never going home, not yet.

"It's the treasure of the Knights Templar, just like Dad thought." She sounded like the old, excited Sam I'd known, the girl who helped me search the swamp and scan the beach every day for months.

"What?" All of her talk about Randall, and the fact that her husband was a pirate, had made me sure that my theory was the correct one. "It wasn't a pirate bank?"

"It was." She laughed at my confusion, holding a hand up to stop me from speaking. "Tristan is a pirate, yes. But he's also a Knight, and he was hiding their treasure on the island there. Randall was part of his team." Her face grew dark then and she looked toward the door, pausing as if she were listening for someone. After a moment, she continued, a serious tone to her quick speech. "He joined the Black Knights, Mark. They're horrible people and they want the treasure. Tristan and Thomas have a personal feud, though. We have to get off this ship as soon as possible. If Tristan is alive, I promise, he will come for me, and when he finds us, it will be a bloodbath." She shuddered, a memory that was lost to me flashing across her face. "There won't be anything I can do to stop him from killing every single member of the crew."

An icy finger of fear brushed against me. Her face held all the promise it needed to; she loved her husband, but he was a man who should be feared by his enemies. The talk I'd heard about him here had made him sound like he was someone who would easily be taken care of. Now I wondered how many of those statements had been made to try and calm those who were told they would be facing him someday.

"Sam, I—"

The door flew open, halting my questions, and we both jumped, caught off guard by the man in the doorway.

"Legion," I breathed, using the nickname the one eyed pirate had given himself. "You scared the shit out of me."

"I heard you had a woman in 'ere," the old, stick

thin man said, scratching his leathery skin. "Looks like it's true."

"Bugger off," I said sharply, stepping in front of Sam protectively. "Captain said I'm supposed to fix her up and keep her alive. I don't want your dirty hands touching her."

"I wasn't plannin' on touching 'er with me hands, savvy?" Laughing, he rubbed his glass eye, the pupil rolling around in an unpleasant manner.

"Back off," I warned again, putting a hand on the pistol in my belt.

"Lighten up, Snake Eyes."

His use of my Apache name made my skin prickle. When I'd been pressed into service, I'd refused to share my real name, just as I'd had when I joined the merchant business. As far as anyone was concerned, I was a white man who'd grown up among Indians.

Taking a step forward, he all but leered at Sam behind me, licking his lips in anticipation.

"Take one more step and you'll be missing both eyes." I'd whispered, but the fierceness in my tone made him pause, looking at me with greater caution as I pulled the gun out and pointed the barrel right at his head.

"You'd deny your mate the lovin' comfort of a woman's breast?" he asked in surprise.

"I'll deny you anything that could cost me my own life."

A stare down commenced, my finger itching to pull the trigger. There were always fights on this pirate ship, none of which were ever settled by lawful means. The crew thought they were their own masters and I'd been in more than my share of arguments, as had everyone else. It seemed that Legion was remembering this as well, a hint of anger passing through his eyes. I'd cut off the finger of his cousin not three weeks earlier, and it seemed like justice was coming to call.

I didn't know how, but I could always tell the instant a conversation became a fight. It was as if the air changed, red filling my vision, or if someone had whispered to me when something was coming. As it was, I easily dodged the knife that was pulled on me, the tip skipping over my shoulder and tearing my white shirt.

"Son of a bitch," I muttered, looking at it. I'd just spent a good portion of my money I'd saved up to buy the damn thing when we were in London.

Scurrying out of the way, Sam shoved herself into a corner as I lunged forward, clocking the man over the head with the butt of my weapon. She was unusually quiet, and I soon forgot she was there altogether, focusing on the task at hand.

Legion, stumbling under the blow I'd given him, fell to the floor, grabbing my ankles and taking me down with him. His nails dug into my legs as he struggled to climb on top of me, his fist punching me soundly in the stomach.

Grunting, I jerked my leg up, laughing in satisfaction as my knee connected with his face in a magnificent spray of blood. Screaming, he released me, his hands grasping at the broken nose in fury.

Seizing the moment, I got my feet under me again, lurching toward him and pinning him on the ground. His jaw cracked when my knuckles met it, then a barely audible grunt escaped through his thin lips as I punched him in the chest. His hands were fumbling, reaching for something, anything, and I crushed one under my knee when it came close enough.

Obscenities flew from him, murder in his good eye, and I instantly realized he'd managed to pull another knife from his boot. Grabbing him by the wrist, we wrestled over the blade for a second, life and death hanging in the balance.

Unable to get a good enough grip to make him drop the blade, I resorted to another trick—twisting his arm as hard as I could, I didn't stop until I heard another crack, his wrist shattering under my touch. The knife fell to the floor, his howls rising even more.

Blood pounded in my ears, my vision blurry with the adrenaline from fighting, every nerve calling out to finish the deed. The hunger for death overtook me, my fingers wrapping around the blade.

Legion could see it in my eyes. His face went dark, a hiss surging from him, his undamaged arm holding me back the best it could.

The knife slid across his throat easily, exactly as I remembered from the last time I'd cut a man's neck, when we'd attacked a ship a month ago. Warm blood washed my hand, his body going limp beneath me.

It was done.

Breathing heavily, I stood up, hovering over him as I watched what was left of his life flee. A puddle was forming underneath him, but I couldn't seem to care in that moment. All that mattered was that I'd won. I'd lived to fight another day, in a world where you had to kill or be killed.

"Oh, Mark," Sam's voice said from behind me, full of fear.

Turning, I saw her, staring at the body with a blank expression. When her gaze moved to me, though, it held more pity than I could handle.

"You've become just as much a pirate as the rest of them," she said, sadly.

Breathing heavily, I looked down at the body beneath me, the gory blade still clutched tightly in my fingers. Red liquid dripped from my knuckles, softly splattering on its host's unmoving form. Vaguely, I was aware of more people joining us, shouts falling on my deaf ears. All I could see or hear was the blood, the very thing that had burned so hot in myself, now shed by the man before me.

Life is the greatest gift we have. Do not take it unnecessarily.

Grey One's words echoed in my mind. Was Sam right? She hadn't sounded like she blamed me, but there was a condemnation to her words that stung. Had I taken a life just because I could, or had it been truly necessary? Would Legion have left after only being roughed up? Now I would never know.

I thought I was protecting her, but going over the fight in my mind, it was easy to see that wasn't true; I'd let the blood lust overtake me. Hadn't the same sense been in Legion's eye as well, though? If I hadn't have killed him, surely it would be me bleeding out on the floor right now.

The noises around me seemed to pop and fizzle

back into existence as I blinked, glancing up from the corpse. The brown walls faded into nothing as I stared at the group of men who had shoved their way through the door, more that I couldn't see still shouting for details from outside. Some of them wore expressions of shock and boredom, others rage. Eyes were either trained on me, or the not-so-dearly departed lying on the planks beneath me.

"What have you done?" It was the dead man's cousin, his stump of a finger still crudely bandaged up and wrapped around his drawn knife. Face contorted into a mix of anger and grief, his dirt streaked form glared up at me, inches from his relative. A pang of guilt washed over me, but I stood my ground.

This was no time for apologies.

Those who had found Legion a friend or ally were obviously readying themselves to fight for him, swords being drawn as they stepped forward, growls resonating in their throats. Defensively, I held my blade out, refusing to move even an inch and show them the terror they wanted from me.

"What's going on down here?" Captain Randall's voice boomed over the crowd, his form shoving through the throng. The men fell silent and darted to either side to make way; he was the only person we all truly feared. When he reached the front, he paused, taking in the scene. His gaze traveled over his captive once, slowly, before moving on to me. He then glared at the floor, lips pursed, before straightening to his full height and sneering at me. "You've made quite the mess here, Snake Eyes. Do you care to enlighten the crew as to why?"

I'd seen him use this type of interrogation before.

His easy manner made the victim think they were safe from harm. It was how he'd convinced Bobby Jones to confess that he'd stolen extra rations.

Bobby was gone now, beaten to death after Randall had left him to his fellow shipmates, who were extra hungry after we'd skipped a port to make it to England in the time frame Randall wanted.

"He attacked me first, Captain," I replied, trying to keep my voice steady. "I'd be dead if I hadn't defended myself."

His eyes narrowed as he studied me. Distinctly, I had the impression that wasn't what he wanted to hear. It was as if I was part of some game, only no one had told me about it.

Steeling myself, I waited for him to question me further. Instead, I watched as he turned toward Sam, his expression turning to that of mild glee.

"Missus O'Rourke," he said, his voice dripping with sticky sweetness. "Would you be a dear and tell me what happened here?"

Glancing back at her, I could see Sam glaring at him, her arms folded and stance strong. She looked like she'd been through hell and back, and yet, she still wasn't going to take any shit from him. She seemed stronger than when I'd last seen her, and I found myself wondering exactly what she'd been through in the past two years.

"They fought. He won." Well, that was gruff and to the point. She *really* didn't like him.

"Yes, but what were they fighting about?" There was an edge to his tone, an unspoken threat that we all heard. It was never a good sign when the captain used that tone. Behind him, the crew shifted uncomfortably, the sound of it enough to make them dread him more.

"Legion wanted—how did he put it—the comfort of a woman's breast." Her own voice was tight and full of hate, the answer coming from barely moving lips.

Captain Randall laughed, the sound booming in the space as he faced the men behind him. Joining in, his crew forced out a chuckle, not wanting his wrath to turn on them.

"And Snake Eyes, why was this arrangement not satisfactory to you? Did you want her for yourself?" His cold gaze of pretend merriment moved to me and I felt the hair on the back of my neck stand up.

"Snake Eyes has never touched a woman in all the time we've known him!" The shout came from the back of the group, causing real laughter to break out as Randall watched me, his mean smile still in place.

"I know." The quality to his voice now held a death threat and I felt my face whiten. He continued to grin, the situation not dire to anyone who was watching from the outside, but everyone in the room seemed to know that I was seconds away from being shot.

My initial assessment of his appearance had been wrong. This wasn't just a fight between mates to the captain—it was a fight over Samantha, and that was something I suddenly realized he would not tolerate. If I didn't have a good enough reason for killing a man in her defense, I would be dead before we even left port.

"She's pregnant," I blurted out, hearing her gasp

behind me. "You told me to keep her alive and I thought Legion might put too much stress on her. He wouldn't take no for an answer, so I did what I had to." Holding my breath, I waited to see if the partial truth would be enough.

He froze for only a second, betraying his shock, but then recovered, slipping into his friendly demeanor. "Pregnant? Why, Sam, is that true?" Striding over to her, he pinned her against the wall, standing just close enough that she couldn't move anywhere else. "Who's the baby's father?"

Sam spit in his face before I even knew what was happening. "Tristan will come for me," she hissed, shoving him away. "And when he does, you'll all be dead."

Randall wiped the spittle from his face, glowering at her. All traces of the friendly show he'd been putting on vanished. "I know he will," he whispered back. "In fact, I'm counting on it."

I saw the slap coming, turning away in pain and anger for her just before she was hit. The sound echoed through the cabin and I flinched, hearing her fall to the floor with a small yelp.

"However, I don't plan on doing any dying, and neither do my men."

Afraid that if I looked in their direction my face would betray my feelings, I stared forward, jaw clenched.

"There will be no sex with this woman," Randall said loudly, coming into view as he headed for the door, the crew parting to let him through again. "Anyone who tries will be shot, if Snake Eyes doesn't kill you first. Do you understand?"

"Aye!"

The rousing chorus of agreement followed him out onto the deck, no one wanting to question his reasoning as they slowly shuffled away, until only Legion's cousin and close friends remained. Without saying a word, they took the body, glaring at me and making intermittent hissing sounds. Finally, only Sam and I were left.

Turning around, guilt grabbed hold of me again as I watched her sit on the ground, cradling her face in her hand. Randall's slap had split her lip open even more, the tears in her eyes revealing to me just how much it had hurt.

"Are you okay?" I asked quietly, offering a hand to her.

"Fine. I've had worse than a slap." Ignoring my help, she shoved to her feet, as if she were trying to prove that she could take care of herself, no matter the circumstance. Looking at the puddle of gore on the ground she nodded toward me. "Are you going to clean that up?"

"Hmm? Oh." Staring at the spot, I suddenly realized I was still clutching the blade, clenching it so tightly in fact that my fingers ached.

Without another word, she crossed to me, laying her hand on top of mine. "Let it go," she said softly. "It will be okay."

Surprised, I nodded, struggling to relax my grip. After a few seconds, the hilt slid from my hand, clattering on the floor. A rush of air moved through me and I staggered somewhat, the adrenaline high I'd been experiencing coming to an instant stop. Guilt spread through me once more, aided by the tender way she continued to hold my hand.

"You're okay," she kept saying, coaching me.

It felt like I was coming undone. Whether she knew it or not, it wasn't just the feelings I'd suppressed during the last few minutes that were coming up. It was everything; all of the things I'd shared with her and the moments I'd kept for myself. Each pain and fear, every hatred and love I'd felt since traveling to this time gushed from me, leaving me a shaking mess.

Her arms wrapped around me, her tone that of a soothing parent as she stroked my hair, apparently knowing that I needed that right now for some reason.

"You're not alone," she said firmly, her touch strong and reassuring.

And then I understood. She may not have known everything, but she knew the feeling. It wasn't just me that was finding comfort; she was with someone from her own time as well.

We were not alone.

The ship left port that night. It was a blow to Sam's heart, which was apparent. I didn't know if she'd expected her husband to show up before we even got away, but I hated to tell her he might not even know of her disappearance yet.

As the French coast faded into the darkness behind us, I racked my brain, trying to think if I'd heard or seen anything that would suggest the Black Knights on board had met with the ship Sam claimed had been sent after them.

The crew's time in London had seemed as normal as any other. We'd taken the long boats in and went our separate ways for the few days we had to ourselves. There was no talk in the streets of any dueling or group fights and when we'd returned, everyone appeared to be in good health, hangovers aside. Frustrated, I was forced to accept that I had no idea if Tristan O'Rourke had met with anyone or not.

Through all this, my mind kept going back to the shipwreck in The Gulf of Mexico, a ship that would surely be the one I was on now. Having Sam on board and learning the few brief things I had from her, it sounded to me that someone would come for her, be it Tristan or someone else. The two ships would meet in the bay, and one would be burned and sink.

Looking over at my friend, I couldn't help feeling a little worry over her. She'd curled into a ball and gone to sleep, her arms wrapped protectively around her stomach. Whatever trouble we were in to, it wasn't a situation suitable for a baby. She must have been so scared, without Tristan and in the hands of their worst enemy.

Wrong, I corrected myself. *She's in my hands, now.*

Smiling softly, I thought of her father, Michael. I was sure, if he'd been able to say it, he would have been happy that she at least had me.

Footsteps announced someone heading our way and I turned, jumping as the door shot open.

"Bring her," the quartermaster said, his hulk like form turning to leave. "Captain wants to talk."

Captain Randall's cabin stretched across the whole backside of our ship, the cherry wood stained interior the only part of the entire vessel I ever considered fine. The large window in the rear showed the inky black sea outside, along with the stars glittering in the sky above. That was the only section of the room that conveyed openness and freedom, though.

The hammock bed, in the far left corner, gave the appearance of having never been used, the ropes hanging listlessly, as if Randall were some kind of being who could survive without sleep. A large desk was bolted to the ground in front of the window, a few other bookcases and trinkets lining the walls. The floor was bare, with scuff marks from the door passing over the entryway standing out as the only difference in pattern. Overall, it was a very bland place, but at least it had sufficient room for meetings.

Samantha stood before the group I'd often seen gathered here, her head held high, despite her obvious beaten state. Ignoring jeers and catcalls from the pirates, she had eyes only for the captain, her mouth pressed into a straight line.

Turning to leave, I planned to wait right outside the doors, in the hopes I'd be able to hear something of what they had to say to her. To my great surprise, I was stopped.

"We have a sort of club here, Snake Eyes," Randall said, a knife in one hand, the point resting against the desk he sat at. Sitting there, with his wall of muscles around him, his red coat glowing in the light of the lanterns, he looked like a devil, sent to take my soul.

For an instant, I felt the longing for Devil Dancers, the Apache who would beat drums and shout during powwows to keep evil spirits away. However, I was sure that a few Indians wouldn't be a problem for these men.

"We've been watching you," Randall continued, digging the point of his blade further into the wood. "As you've been watching us. It would seem that now is the time to rectify the situation."

Oh, damn.

"What do you mean, Captain?" I kept a straight face, trying to find my best Apache warrior impersonation to intimidate them with.

"You showed great . . . initiative today, with Legion. I had no idea that there was so much fire in you. I thought all of your promise had fizzled out when your doctor friend died. Truth be told, I expected you to be dead a long time ago. But you've surprised me in many ways now." Leaning forward, he folded his arms, the dagger forgotten.

"Thank you." Well, if this was an execution, he'd caught me off guard with his compliments.

"How would you like to join our club?" Randall

asked easily. "There are certain benefits, of course. Two extra shares of any loot, information on where we're headed, and, of course, kingdoms at your command."

"Kingdoms?" Laughing, I looked between them, waiting for the others to join in the joke, but none of them did.

"Yes, Mister Eyes, kingdoms."

Captain Randall rose then, striding around the desk and stopping in front of Sam. His expression was one of several emotions, rage and revenge among them. With one swift movement, he reached out and grabbed her around the throat, squeezing hard.

Gasping, her fingers instantly went to his wrist, scratching and clawing in an attempt to get away. Strength was on his side, though, and he lifted her in the air, holding her there for a second before dropping her to the ground.

"Where is the lost treasure?" he hissed, staring down at her. When she didn't answer, he kicked her in the side, knocking her over as she screamed; he'd hit a spot that was already tender. "Where is it?" he shouted.

"I don't know," she wheezed, looking up at him, fury rolling off her.

"Wrong answer." The growl made her blanche, and she tried to push away, crawling over the floor as his foot stepped on the back of her dress. "Take her," he told the men around the desk.

It took all of my self-control not to lash out and protect her, my hands curling into fists at my side as I watched them haul her up and drag her to the table, bending her over it, her stomach pressed painfully against the edge, and holding her head and arms against the surface.

"Now," Randall said, coming back to his seat and picking up the knife. "I will ask you again. Where is the treasure? I know you know—that senile Grand Master started something after you met with him. What did you tell him?"

"He was just showing me the Temple, you idiot!" Her reply was snarled almost, spat out as she struggled against those holding her. "If he started anything, I have no idea why."

"You're lying, Sam." He sighed as he spoke, almost as if he were bored, sitting down in his chair and looking at her. Suddenly, he lashed out with the blade, slicing across her right forearm.

Screaming, she fought harder, trying to pull away as the blood rolled over her skin.

Trying to conceal the trembling of my hands, I clenched my jaw; ignoring the red filter I was now viewing the interrogation through. My entire body was calling out for me to fight for her, to save her from her torturers, but I knew I would be dead the instant I tried. Who would protect her when I was gone? No, it was better that I did nothing. If Sam was still anything like the girl I'd known in our own time, she would understand.

"Where is it?" Randall roared, dropping the weapon and slamming his hands on the table. Grabbing her by the hair, he yanked her up, shoving aside those who had been restraining her, and slapped her hard across the face, practically plowing her into the ground with the force of it. "Tell me!"

She seemed to have barely any strength left as

she pulled herself across the floor, laughing slightly as she stared at him over her shoulder. "Did you really think I would tell you?" she asked breathlessly, her features dark. Chest heaving, she turned her whole body to look at him, scooting backward until she hit the wall. Blood smeared across her face as she reached up and pushed her hair away, trying to see him better. "There's not anything in this world that would make me do what you want, you murderous, lying bastard."

I couldn't see Randall's face, but I could tell from his posture that he was positively seething as he watched her. His hands shook; her blood soaked into the sleeve of his jacket, and his breathing was labored, as if he'd just finished running laps. "You tell me what you told those filthy beggars masquerading as knights, or I will cut that baby out of you and eat it for dinner."

Even some of the Black Knights behind him visibly recoiled, horror washing their features as they watched him. Sam's eyes had gone wide, her body freezing as she regarded him, the blood still slowly dripping from the shallow cut on her arm.

"You wouldn't." Sam hesitated. "That would kill me, too, and then you'd have nothing." She was scared though, her hands covering her stomach protectively as she pressed herself harder against the wall, as if she would fall right through it to freedom.

"Nothing but the satisfaction of knowing you were dead," he replied haughtily, motioning for one of his men to give him back his dagger. Slowly, taunting her, he came closer, the metal tip seeming to shine in the light, until he was kneeling right in front of her. "Tell me," he ordered again.

She clamped her mouth shut in reply, kicking out and catching him in the arm. However, he'd been expecting that, his free hand clamping down on her ankle and yanking her toward him. The scuffle that ensued looked more like an attempted rape than anything else, his form holding her down as she screamed and fought against him. The fabric of her dress ripped more, the bodice falling open and revealing her corset underneath. With one swift motion, Randall cut the ties down the front, rendering the device useless and shoving it aside.

My foot slid forward, my heart pounding as I watched. One man noticed, regarding me with warning, and I bit my lip, trying to keep from yelling out. It was taking every ounce of strength I had not to run to her side.

Come on, Sam! Give him something, or we'll both be dead come morning!

The blade drew across her stomach, barely even drawing blood, but she was screaming like she was dying, writhing beneath him, her hands clawing at him. "I don't know!" she screeched, tears rolling down her face. "I told him a guess, that's all!"

That was enough for him. Immediately pulling the knife away, he sat back, pinning her legs down. "Good." The tone of his voice made me picture his sick smile, his lips twisting like any villain in a super hero comic I'd ever read.

"M-Mexico C-City," she stammered, holding still under him, fear in her large, wide eyes. "In m-my time, they found evidence that Montezuma had his slaves bring the treasure back after the Spanish l-left."

Captain Randall didn't answer, instead standing and moving away from her. "Very good, Samantha. I knew your motherly instincts would work to my advantage." He turned to face me then, his expression just as wicked as I'd been imagining. "What do you say, Snake Eyes? I have an opening in my crew. Join me—join us—and you will become a Black Knight of the Order of the Templars, the one and true faction dedicated to the liberation of the treasures of this world. When the riches are in our grasp, you will have the kingdoms I promised. In fact, you can have anything you wish."

It wasn't really that much of a choice. They would kill me if I said no, especially after what I just witnessed. Sam was also lying to them, which made me think it might be better if we had an inside look into the plans of the group. A quick glance to her form on the floor behind him confirmed as much in my mind.

"When do I start?" I asked easily, forcing a smile.

The group laughed heartily and Randall gestured for me to come over to the desk. "Welcome to the brotherhood." He made a motion to someone and held the chair out for me, nodding in encouragement as I paused.

Sitting down, momentary panic grabbed hold of me as another crew member locked their fingers around my wrist, yanking my arm out. "Hey!" Surprised, I tried to pull back, but Randall put his hands on my shoulders.

"It's nothing," he spoke smoothly. "Just a mark, so others will know you're one of us."

The man he'd pointed to stepped forward, leaning over my arm to look at it. "There," he said, his voice low and quiet. "Just above the elbow."

"Good," Randall cooed.

It was then that I became aware of something resting in the lantern, a long metal rod with a design at the end of it. It must have been there before we even came in, warming up for just this occasion.

The bastards were going to brand me!

"You said everyone has this mark?" I asked uneasily, trying to think of how I would explain to any of our rescuers that I wasn't actually their enemy.

"Everyone," Randall replied, showing me his own wrist. The mark was a cross with a spot in the middle, just like the gold ring he wore.

And the one the journals at the Mission had said he'd been wearing.

"It will only burn a lot," the brander said, snorting as he pulled the rod out and advanced toward me.

"If you say so." That earned me a few laughs, and I steeled myself for what was about to come. When the hot metal touched my skin, I drew in a deep breath, suddenly feeling many hands on me, holding me steady. It must have only lasted a few seconds, but it seemed like hours, my body begging for me to make it stop and soon. When the rod was finally pulled away, it was if all my energy had been sapped and I slumped in the chair.

"Here." There was a ripping sound, followed by a curse from Sam, and another member of the group passed over the strip from her dress. I watched as they tied it around my raw flesh, feeling slightly dazed and in shock.

"Today, you became a member of the elite," Randall was saying. "You swore to support the new world order and all her riches. Your life is now devoted to the gods and the power that man has stolen from them."

"Aye!"

"Amen!"

"Praise be to the gods!"

Every single member of the group congratulated me then, one by one, helping me to my feet and moving me toward the door. They pushed Sam along behind me, until Randall finally called for quiet again.

"Get some rest," he told me, as if I were his best friend. "Your orders are still the same. You know how important she is—do not let her die, or your life will be forfeit."

Feeling thoroughly dismissed, I nodded, grabbing her by the arm and yanking her out the door with me.

I'd never felt so afraid of a cult before, and now I was a willing member.

My brand was a third degree burn with flair, the edges of the mark burning horribly for days to come. All I had to doctor it with where herbs, which weren't as good as modern day antiseptic and soothing lotion might have been, but they helped some. The little bit of lavender I'd picked up in London had to stretch a long way, which meant I would have to use less than I wanted. Had I chosen to receive such a mark in my own time, I probably would have thought it looked awesome, displayed proudly on the same arm as my skull and crossbones tattoo. However, the sight now gave me an uncomfortable feeling, as if I'd somehow mistakenly sold my soul.

Sam, on the other hand was both unlucky and fortunate in her healing. It was like every place someone had touched her left a bruise, her skin turning a dark purple and yellow that made her look like a zombie when I saw her in the dim light. However, there was plenty of tobacco to chew and place on the worst of the marks, which seemed to be helping to ease some of the pain, if nothing else. Her dress had been too destroyed to try and piece back together, so I'd rounded up some clothes for her, bullying the smaller members of the crew into handing some of their things over. As I watched her now, standing on the deck, the wind blowing the hair away from her multicolored face, I frowned at her state. Brown pants bunched around her waist, tied clumsily with an extra rigging rope, her white shirt looking more like a nightgown as it puffed out around her. She appeared to be drowning in the fabric, her feet bare and dirty on the planks beneath her.

A few of the crew heckled her from all sides as they went about their duties, the quartermaster doing nothing to stop them. I hadn't expected him to, but it would have been nice if someone showed her a little compassion. Every time a Black Knight crossed her path, she covered her stomach protectively, dropping her head so she wouldn't have to make eye contact. Preferably, I would have kept her inside at all times, but Randall insisted she come out and get some sun. In my mind, it was partially because he wanted to torment her, and also because he really did want to keep her alive and healthy for his purposes.

Watching her closely, I felt she had already lost some of the strength she'd arrived with. The defiance she'd shown her captors was astounding, but the longer she remained with them the more it dwindled. It was as if she had forgotten the fire inside herself, the flames dimming to those of barely warm coals.

Three days had passed since we left France. I knew she only agreed to come out because she wanted to stand and watch for her husband's ship. Her belief that he would come strengthened me some, and so, with her in mind, I went into the captain's cabin for a meeting I'd been called to.

"She'll be fine, aye?" one of the other men said, watching as I glanced over at her hesitantly. "No one will bother her while the captain wants her."

Nodding, I shut the door, trying to steel myself for whatever it was we were going to talk about.

The man, Flanagan was his name, smiled a gap-filled grin at me, leaning up against the wall by the entrance. He'd either lost his shirt somewhere, or had abandoned it willingly, his bare chest streaked with sweat and grime from climbing the rigging to the crow's nest several times a day. Spots of curly, red hair brushed across his pecs, matching the short crop on top of his head. His striped pants would have made him appear somewhat comical, if it weren't for the sword at his waist and the pistol belt slung over his shoulder.

Turning my attention away from the Irishman, I peered around the space at the rest of the room's inhabitants, feeling intimidated by them. Sam hadn't said much to me in the way of what they all wanted out of this treasure they were going after, but I knew it couldn't be anything good.

"I say we ask 'im, that's all," one of the other pirates, a man called Greybeard, was saying. "Captain's done nothing but support us. What difference does it make if we don't know the whole plan?"

"And I say it's not right to follow a man in the dark," the man across from him spat. He was a newer member, someone we'd picked up in London and I didn't know his name yet. He looked much cleaner and wise than the others around him, though, which immediately made me think he might be the right one

254

in this argument.

"What do ye mean, Black?" I knew who was speaking now. It was the quartermaster, Gordon White, who always made me think of a certain other large, green man who was hulking over everyone else, and was really not a nice person when he was angry.

"What do you think I mean?" Black shot back, huffing indignantly as he pushed his short, blonde hair out of his face. "We followed orders blindly under the Dogs, didn't we? And look where it got us! We didn't know anything and the treasure was right there the whole time! Captain Randall ought to tell us the truth. We're all part of the brotherhood; why is he the only one who gets to decide anything? We should have a say!"

"He has a point," Flanagan said, speaking up from his self-assumed post by the door.

"See!" Black pointed at him, a smile on his face. He'd found an ally and wasn't about to let him go. "Tell me, Flanagan, how did the captain's last attempt at getting the treasure go?"

"Not so good," he responded easily, acting as if he were simply indulging the conversation for the sake of passing the time.

"Not so good." Black turned to each person in the room, looking them in the eye before he kept going. "Not so good! He had the head of Medusa in his hands and let it go! You all saw him! You were on that island for weeks, digging that stupid pit to the treasure, only to watch your friends and family slaughtered by the Dogs! And what did Randall do? He dropped the one weapon he'd managed to grab down there and ran. We could have used that shield in countless ways to gather the rest of the treasure. Did he care? No! He goes on and on about how he got the ichor, but to what end? Now he wants to go after another treasure and we don't even know where it is—he doesn't know."

An uncomfortable murmur spread through the group. It was clear that many of them agreed with what Black was saying. Somewhere along the way, Randall had goofed up, and his crew wasn't happy about it.

"Who are the Dogs?" I asked Flanagan, not quite following the conversation.

"Templars," he whispered back, raising a finger to silence me as he watched the conversation continue.

"The shield won't matter once we have this treasure," Greybeard argued back. "And Captain knows that. That's why he left the other things instead of grabbing as much as he could. What do you expect 'im to do? Them Dogs were down there fighting 'im. He's lucky he got what he did."

Randall's supporters voiced their approval to that statement, White included.

"How do you even know if you're telling the right story?" he demanded of Black. "You weren't even there!" Stepping out of the mass to join his opponent in the middle of the room, he gestured to all of us. "I was there—one of the first to join Randall's cause when he plucked me out of that Hell in Africa! You may not agree with how Captain Randall does things, but you can't deny that he gets the job done! If those Dogs hadn't shown up, we would be richer than any king on Earth, right now! It's not his fault that we met opposition. We knew we would; it was a dream to think we would make it off before anyone else arrived." He thumped his chest as he continued, his beefy hand clutched into a large fist over his white shirt.

"You didn't hear the things that Dog we had with us said. I did! I was with the Captain the whole time, right up until he climbed down into that pit. If you knew what I did, you would know he did all he could for us, for the treasure. You wouldn't be standing around, arguing because you don't know what port we're going to stop at next. This is bigger than stopping at damn port—bigger than you and bigger than me. Captain is the only one who knows the plan because he's the only one he can trust to keep it safe."

"A captain who can't trust his crew can't be trusted by anyone else," Black retorted loudly, speaking over the impassioned man. "Secrets should not be kept from your brothers!"

The argument was coming to a head, heated discussions breaking out among other members present as Black and White continued to go at it in the middle.

"Just wait," Flanagan said, nodding for me to join him at the wall. "It's going to get real good here in a second." He tilted his head toward the door, a smile on his face, and reached into his pants pocket, pulling out a grimy cigarette and twirling it between his fingers.

Frowning, I watched, as he seemed to stare into nothing, his ear pointed toward the door. Finally, it dawned on me what he was doing.

"How long has the captain been outside?" I asked softly, leaning against the wall as well and trying to look unconcerned with the fighting going on in front of me. It was possible to do, as long as no one pulled a knife or gun.

"A good while," he said back, laughing under his breath. "Methinks Black won't be with us much longer."

When I didn't reply, he nudged me with his elbow, winking in a knowing manner. It didn't matter; I knew what he'd meant.

It wasn't likely that a man who was openly talking about defying the captain and committing mutiny would live through the night.

"Why doesn't he just come in?" I finally inquired, impatient for the yelling around me to stop.

"He's listening," Flanagan replied simply, shrugging. "Who knows why he does anything? No one here, that's for sure."

"Do you think he can even hear anything through all this?"

"He can hear," he said, nodding. "That he can."

Curious, I leaned a little closer to him, keeping my voice as soft as possible for him to hear over the racket. "Which side are you on?"

He looked at me in surprise, putting the cigarette back in his pocket as he stood up straight. "Why, the captain's o' course. Who else?"

Grinning, I bobbed my head, wanting to seem like I was a friend to him as I stepped out in front of the entrance His loyalties were still in question in my mind, but there was no time to press him more under the cover of the shouting.

"Gentlemen." Randall's voice drew our attention as the door opened, his presence causing an instant silence in all those present. Black pants stretched into matching, calf high boots, a red, billowing shirt draped from his torso, the sleeves gathered at the wrist. Around his waist, a dark, leather belt housed his gun and cutlass. His black hair was pulled into a thick tie, hanging over his shoulder like a horsetail. He held himself like he was a great ruler, here to speak with his people, the sun illuminating him like a god from behind.

Suddenly, I wondered if that was more or less how he saw himself.

"Mister Eyes." He waited for me to step out of his path before coming further into the room, the door falling shut behind him. It was as if he hadn't heard a thing anyone had been saying, his air easy and carefree as he walked up to White, nodding for him and Black to leave the center of the room. He paused then, seeming to think for a moment, and took a deep breath.

"As many of you know, when the Black Knights were so unjustly destroyed in the thirteen hundreds, those mutinous Dogs who dared to call themselves Knights stole our treasure out from underneath us. They tortured our brothers! Roasted them over open flames! Locked them in their own Temple to rot! They thought they had won. But they had not!"

This was met by a few grunts and murmurs of agreement, the men too involved to really celebrate anything he was saying. I had the small impression that he started every speech somewhat like this, and I listened on, curious as to what he wanted to share.

"God called his men back to the good fight, and the Black Knights rose again. And again, and again! Here, today, we stand, those who are willing to do whatever it takes to share the truth of God and his powers with the world."

His voice was impassioned as he spoke, his hands moving with the words as he rotated to look at each of us, speaking to the group as a whole.

"We infiltrated the Dogs' camps, became part of their crews, earned their trust. And we have now in our possession, ichor—the blood of the gods—and none will take it from us!"

Actual shouts rang out, the men who had supported him in the argument staring at him like the god he was acting the part of. Watching them all, the dynamics of the group became clear to me; this ichor was the only thing keeping Randall in the leadership position. Those who reinforced him did so because he'd managed to bring back a piece of the treasure. Everyone who didn't want him at the head of their organization didn't care one bit about some tiny thing he'd taken.

"We found part of the treasure," he continued, staring at each man in turn. "It was within our grasp! When the Dogs came, it was only us that survived the massacre. They tried to end us again, to take what is rightfully ours, to stop the progression of man. And still, we prevailed.

"Brothers, I come to you at this moment, to finally share the plan you have been longing to hear since I first told you we would be kidnapping O'Rourke's wife."

Turning to face me, he smiled triumphantly,

holding his hand out toward me as he went on. "Snake Eyes. You have joined our brotherhood. Our ways are a mystery to you. Allow me to explain just what it is we are doing here."

Surprised, I nodded, wanting to hear what his goal was just as much as everyone else. His strategy was sound, too. He'd heard the crew arguing, even if they didn't realize it, and decided to give them what they desired before a mutiny ensued.

"Samantha Green O'Rourke." He was back to moving about the room, addressing his crew, his brothers-in-arms. "Mister White, just what is this woman? What did we learn from the Dog we captured and extracted information from on our way to Oak Isle?"

"She's from the future," White answered promptly.

"Why would that help us now, as we are no longer in search of the riches in Oak Isle? Mister Black?"

Black seemed to shrink back, his earlier bravado fading away under Randall's gaze. "Captain?"

"Why would a woman from the future be an aid to us now?" Randall repeated patiently, only a hint of venom to his tone.

Black peered around the room, as if he expected someone to help him, and then swallowed hard, staring back at his captain. "Because she knows things we don't?"

Randall glared at him hard for a moment before slowly nodding, moving away. "She knows things we do not. But, everyone here except Snake Eyes knew this already."

Thankfully, I'd maintained enough sense to act adequately surprised as they revealed who Sam was to me, my eyes wide as I looked between all of them, as if searching for confirmation.

"You see," Randall continued, addressing me. "That's why we needed her to tell us where the treasure was last night. That's how she knew its location."

Pressing my lips into a thin line, I stared at him, hoping he would take my silence as agreement to his actions.

"Unfortunately," he sighed, turning around. "Dear Samantha lied to us." His attention snapped back to me, fire in his eyes. "Isn't that right, Snake Eyes?"

"What?" I asked blankly, trying to hide the instant panic his question brought.

The entire group shifted, staring at me, mirroring the surprise I felt as they waited for me to explain my traitorous deeds. Except, I didn't have any idea what Randall was talking about. Samantha had lied, that was true, but how did he know I knew?

"You knew she was lying and didn't say anything," he said again, his voice more forceful and accusatory.

Had he heard us talking about how I was from the future, too? Did he just bide his time, waiting for the right moment to bring it up? Swallowing hard, I shook my head, denying his statement.

"I didn't know."

"Yes, you did!" The shout caught me even more off guard and I fought my instinct to step back and let him cool down.

"How could I have known something like that? Do you think she told me? I'm one of her kidnappers!" How did you defend yourself against the unknown? It seemed like I was reaching for straws, trying to grab onto anything that made sense.

"Weeks ago, the Dogs Grand Master started looking for information on a place further north than the city—a place where you spent a lot of time with the Natives. According to our man inside, they are protecting the treasure." He snarled his explanation out, the crew gasping in all the appropriate places as his eyes burned into me.

Thankfully, he couldn't have said anything else to make me feel calmer.

"Oh." I almost laughed, stopping at his look and clearing my throat instead. "I was only with the Indians a few years, as a slave."

This gave him pause. I'd never really shared much about my life prior to joining the shipping business and there was no way for any of them to dispute what I was saying.

"Why would they let their slave go?" he finally asked, eyes gleaming with triumph as he found what he thought was a hole in my story.

Shrugging, I smiled, knowing it would infuriate him more, but not caring. "I worked myself to freedom. They may be fierce, but they aren't savages. A job finished is a job paid. In this case, payment was my permission to leave."

Some of the men quietly conferred behind him, mostly in gestures. They'd heard stories of the same nature and believed me. Randall, on the other hand, was becoming more irate with each passing second.

"If they ever spoke of a treasure, it wasn't around me. I'd swear so on a Bible, right now," I added, trying to placate them all.

The captain glared at me darkly before turning, obviously upset that he hadn't been able to out

264

someone and show how much power he had to his faltering men.

"I always thought ye were some Indian heathen, Snake Eyes," Greybeard said, sympathy present in his speech. "Er—do ye have a Christian name? Or do ye prefer the Indian one?"

The grin I gave him was tight at best, but I nodded all the same. I'd shared part of my past and now it was time to keep the story going. "Mark," I told him. "I used to be called Mark. Snake Eyes is fine, too, though."

"Mark." The man smiled at me, almost in confusion.

With a sigh of frustration, Captain Randall pulled the pistol from his belt and shot Black straight through the forehead.

Shouting in surprise, the men scrambled away as the body toppled over onto the floor, a thin line of blood dripping down the face that was now pressed against the ground.

"If I ever hear mutinous talk from any of you again, you'll be joining Mister Black in a sail, shark bait flung off this ship. Now get out, all of you." The phrase sounded more like a declaration to have a tea party in the garden, his voice smooth and almost song-like as he dismissed us.

The Knights scurried toward the door, eyes wide, some angry, but none of them argued. I didn't blame them; I wanted out of here as fast as possible, too.

"Not you, Snake Eyes," he called, stopping me as I was inches from freedom. "You stay."

Freezing, I kept my back to him, watching as the rest of the men filtered out, dispersing across the deck in a hurry. Sam was still where I'd left her, watching the group with interest.

"Close the door," Randall ordered.

Stepping forward, I did as he asked, ignoring her darkening features as she watched me stay behind. There would be time to explain later.

Hopefully.

Having barricaded myself inside with the monster and Black's body, I turned, trying to remain nonchalant and look straight ahead at the only other living man in the room. Randall sat down behind his desk, his still slightly smoking gun resting on the wood surface. It wasn't lost on me that it could have been me he'd shot, if I'd giving any inclination I wasn't telling the truth.

"Do you know why I let you join this crew, Snake Eyes?" He was studying his fingernails, as if I wasn't even good enough for him to look at.

"Because you needed me?" I asked, hesitantly.

"Because you lived with the Indians. You speak their language and know their ways. I let your doctor friend join because we needed someone who knew medicines. And I let the other mate from your ship join because he killed one of my best fighters.

"I've been planning this trip into the desert for a year now. Everything I've done, everyone I've taken under my wing, each little instance and event has been thought out months in advance. It was clear that I would need some kind of guide to get me to the treasure. When I found you, I thought it was another sign from God, blessing my path."

He did stare at me then, his expression cold, eyes dead. "Now, based off your testimony before the men, you don't possess the things I need from you. If I'd known you were a slave, I would have killed you on that ship and kept searching for someone to lead me."

My mouth stayed firmly shut. He was trying to get a rise out of me, I knew it, but I wouldn't give it to him. If he'd wanted me dead, I would be. That much had been made clear with Black.

Unable to help myself, I glanced down at the body, eyes still open in what looked like shock. Randall caught the action and laughed, leaning back in his chair like some giant corporation head in a mafia movie.

"I'm not going to kill you, if that's what you're thinking," he said helpfully. "While you don't have what I initially needed from you, there is something else you can do that I can't."

"Sir?" I didn't like where this conversation was going, or the way his tone seemed sugarcoated all the sudden.

"Our captive has a fighting spirit, as I'm sure you've noticed by now. For us, that means we will have a hell of a time getting her to tell us exactly where the treasure is. That's where you come into play."

"I don't understand." Shifting from one foot to the other, I watched him curiously, returning the gaze he had locked on me. "You want me to beat her?"

"No." Standing, he took the blunderbuss off the table and put it in his belt, turning to look out the window. "She's too valuable. As much as I believe she could do with several more good beatings to put her in her place, I think we need to use a different tactic."

He paused, glancing over his shoulder at me, smiling. "I want you to woo her."

Blinking, I reached up and jammed a finger in my ear, wiggling it vigorously to loosen any earwax that was impeding my hearing. "I'm sorry, did you say *woo* her?"

"I did." Turning back to the window, he missed my incredulous stare and gaping mouth. "I want you to court her. Make her love you. She will tell you anything you want to know."

"She's married!" I blurted out, wondering why he couldn't hear how crazy his plan sounded.

"To a man who held her captive on a pirate ship, yes, I know."

Soundless words flew from my mouth, eyes bugging out of my head. I didn't know what to say. What could I say? I knew there was no way she would ever fall for anyone besides her Tristan, not with the way she spoke of him.

"Do you understand your orders, Mark?" The use of my real name snapped some sense into me and I shook myself, trying to think of how to answer.

"I . . . I will do my best, Captain."

He moved, facing me again and smiled his friendly-but-very-dangerous smile. "I believe you will. I don't have room for useless things on this ship."

With a flick of the wrist he dismissed me, sitting at his desk. "Send White in to take care of this disappointment," he said, gesturing to the man he'd killed without a second thought.

"Yes, Captain."

Practically fleeing from his room, I hurried out the door, closing it tightly behind me and turned, jumping slightly at the crowd gathered around.

"Ye're alive," one of the crewmembers said in surprise. "I thought ye were the one he shot."

"Where's White?" I asked, ignoring the looks.

"Here." He appeared, a bucket and sponge in one hand, a grim look on his face. "The lot of you, get back to work. You can't expect to catch a ship with ours in such bad shape, now can you?"

Slowly, they peeled off in their own directions, casting mutterings and backward glances my way. Sam stood where I'd left her, facing away from me as she stared out over the water. Sighing, I went to her, touching her on the shoulder and motioning for her to follow me.

"Time to go under," I said gruffly. "There's going to be a funeral and I don't want you up here for it."

She nodded, apparently having already heard someone was shot, and went without another word. As soon as we were in the surgery, the door shut and locked for privacy, I told her everything that had happened, including the fact that I was now supposed to be getting her to tell me things through affection.

"That dirty rat thinks he has everything figured out," she spat, sitting on the table and checking the cut on her arm. It had healed nicely, but the scab had been itching, judging from the scratch marks around it. "But, he did know a lot more than I thought he did."

"What are we going to do, Sam?" I asked, feeling slightly desperate. "He wants information, and if he doesn't get it, I'll be the one who pays."

She paused, looking at me seriously. "We'll give him what he wants," she said calmly. "You can make it look like you're hitting on me when we're not alone. I'll understand. In the meantime, we need to come up with something that sounds enough like the guesses I gave the Grand Master for him to be satisfied."

Falling silent, she seemed far away for a moment, her eyes almost glazing over.

"What are you thinking?"

Coming out of it, she focused on me again, frowning. "There were only four people in the room when I told them what I knew from the future—myself, Tristan, the Grand Master, and the man in charge of trying to find the treasure, Captain Lomas. I know that neither Tristan nor I are a spy, so it must be one of the others. Captain Lomas, most likely. It makes me angry, to think that I gave Randall exactly what he wanted without meaning to."

"It's not your fault," I offered. "You didn't know."

"No, but I should have been more careful. I said too much. Tristan tried to warn me, but I ended up sharing everything I knew, or thought I knew, about it." She smiled a sad sort of look at me, her arms wrapping around her knees and hugging them to her chest. "I just hope the Knights make it in time to stop Randall and his men."

"This is ridiculous," I muttered, feeling like the palm of my hand was burning as it rested against the small of Sam's back.

She shifted, obviously uncomfortable as well, but someone was watching just then. The man grinned as he chewed on a sliver of wood he'd peeled off the mop he was using to swab the deck.

"Warm waters, eh, Snake Eyes?" he called, breaking out into cackled laughter, turning and going back to his chore.

Fighting the urge to roll my eyes, I shifted away from her, leaning over the railing instead as we both studied the horizon. Our act made me feel a sort of dizziness, like I was sick. There was always someone around when we would touch or talk to each other, as we'd planned, but it felt like everyone was easily spotting our lies.

But that wasn't all.

Swallowing hard, I glanced at her, checking to make sure no one was coming to bother us, and turned to sit against the rail instead, folding my arms and locking my gaze on the far side of the ship.

My feelings weren't fake—at least, that's what I

was starting to think. There was no way there would ever really be anything between us. I knew that very well. Yet, when I took her hand in mine, or heard her slight laugh as we spoke of whatever we wished, it was more than easy to imagine she actually was falling for me. Even now, standing beside her as she watched for any sign of a ship around us, it felt like I was full of hot electricity, the feel of her skin on mine making me fizz with energy.

Stop, I ordered myself, shaking my head slightly and moving to gaze over the water again. *You're being stupid. Not only is she married, but she's almost young enough to be your daughter. You're letting your excitement at having found someone from your own time get to you. That's all.*

Breathing in deeply through my nose, I looked down at my brown boots, sliding the toe of one over the deck with ease. It wouldn't have been so bad if I'd had other duties to tend to, but Captain Randall had given me none. Samantha was all he wanted me focusing on, as he'd said to me when I asked if there were other things I could do to clear my head. Every now and then, someone would need help in the surgery, but that was it. Each second I had was spent with her.

Shaking my head, I tried again to shove the thoughts from my mind, glancing up at the exact moment I heard her take in a sharp breath.

"What?" I asked, searching for the culprit of her shock, my hand going to the dagger in my belt. "What is it?"

"Look," she breathed, nodding toward the watery expanse in front of us.

Confused, I searched in that direction, almost missing what it was she'd seen. "Well, I'll be damned," I muttered. "Do you think it's—"

"Sails!" The watchman in the crow's nest waved frantically, pointing to the ship Sam had spotted seconds before him. "Sails off the starboard side!"

It was like dropping a piece of cheese into a group of hungry mice. Men started climbing out of every opening, running up stairs and scaling the rigging to get a better view. Others crowded us at the railing, shouting excitedly as they strained to see the tiny speck in the distance.

"Make way, you scallywags!" Randall, having emerged from his cabin, stationed himself just a few feet from us, a telescope in hand. Raising it to one eye, he paused, seeming to examine the vessel for longer than normal. "How far out are we, Mister MacTavish?"

The navigator, who was peering through his own scope, turned to the captain, exhilaration in his eyes. "It can't be more than a league or two, sir."

Turning to the crew around him, Randall grinned, snapping his looking glass shut. "To the oars, men! We've got a ship to catch!"

A sound not unlike that of a crowd cheering at a sporting event erupted, feet slapping over the ground as we hurried to our spots. For an instant, I was lost in the enthusiasm of impending battle, but then Sam's face filled my mind.

Feeling somewhat faint, I turned to her, trying to spot her among the mass of bodies pressing down to the lower decks. Thankfully, she'd stayed put, frowning as she watched the wave of people move ahead of her. Struggling through the press, I made my way back to her, taking her hand firmly in mine.

"Come on. It won't be safe up here for much longer."

"I've taken a ship before, Mark," she said sharply, ripping her fingers away.

"What are you doing then?" I asked, exasperatedly. "You know what's going to happen!"

"That ship could be Tristan," she hissed, staring off at the vessel we were about to chase down.

"I don't think Randall is so crazy as to attack his pursuers head on." Even I heard the hesitance in my voice. Everything I'd learned over the past few weeks had led me to believe we were trying to outrun the Knights Randall knew were coming after us. However, deciding in an instant to turn and fight back instead seemed like something he would do as well.

The brute would do anything if he thought he had a chance at winning.

"Snake Eyes, get Missus O'Rourke below deck and find your oar!" Turning, I saw Randall taking the wheel of the ship, his expression elated as he started the advance toward our target.

Nodding quickly, I took her by the hand and towed her after me, thankful that she only put up minor resistance.

"He has dark hair," she was saying quickly, with a desperation about her that made my heart hurt. "And he won't be looking for people to fight—"

"He'll be looking for his pregnant wife." Cutting her off, I motioned for her to go down the steps onto the gun deck, and then to the galley and crew quarters, before instructing her past the oar deck and into the hold. "Stay here," I ordered her sternly. "I'll come back when it's over."

If I'm not dead, I added silently to myself.

She smiled, a sad sort of look and then hugged me, squeezing tightly. "Tristan said the same thing to me the first time I was on board when they took another ship. Be safe, Mark." She hesitated, whatever she was about to say fading from her lips.

Pulling away, I smiled tightly. "If it's the Templars, I'll bring him," I promised. "Here." Pulling the dagger out of my belt, I handed it to her, wrapping her fingers around it with care. "Just in case."

Heart pounding, I hurried up to the oar deck, slipping into my place between the men already hard at work. It was backbreaking labor, rowing a huge boat like this while the wind pulled us along, but it was part of what made this boat so good for pirating. We were a lot faster than our prey, easily catching them when a normal ship might have taken hours or days to come alongside their bounty.

"Put yer back into it, ye rats!" One of the men roared, spurring us forward.

Thoughts of Sam, hidden beneath me, slid from my mind as I threw myself into the chore of rowing, sweat soaking my clothes within just a few moments. We were yelling together as a group, the sound keeping time so we would move at the same pace.

"We'll have her in half a league!" MacTavish shouted down to us, his cry echoed by several of the men. As one, we seemed to speed our movements, if that were at all possible, heading forward with only one goal in mind—the fight that awaited us.

"Keep speed!" The call came from above again,

echoed by those closest to the stairs. "They're trying to run!"

A breathy laugh shook from my chest and I tightened my grip on the section of oar in front of me. The men around me were buzzing with the same heat I felt, aching to run up top and see what was going on. We would be part of the action soon enough, as long as we kept moving forward.

After what felt like a lifetime, sweat running into my eyes and plastering my hair to my head, the next orders came. "To the guns! Put the fear o'God in them, men!"

The group worked together with efficiency and ease as we flooded up the stairs to the gun deck, each man quiet as we took up our spots. The ship we'd run down was noisy in comparison, the shouts of her men reaching my ears as I crouched next to a cannon, ready to load it at an instant's notice.

The man next to me nodded and I grabbed the ball, thrusting it down the front of the weapon. Another man used a long pole to shove it in further, while someone poured gunpowder and another readied the wick.

"Open the hatches!"

Jumping up, I undid the latch that kept the tiny window closed before helping to slide the massive cannon forward, its end sticking out of the ship now.

A breath passed, the craft across from us still trying to flee as we came up on her port side, gunshots firing over the railing toward us. A groan to my left suggested that someone had been hit, but I didn't have time to check; the entire ship was in our view.

"Fire!"

I didn't even know if the command had been repeated, or if it was Randall himself ordering us around. With a roar, our cannon shot forward, the ball flying toward the other ship and smashing into her side with a satisfying crack. Other shots landed easily as well, my crew not stopping to watch as we loaded and fired again.

The next ball took out their main mast, the wood cracking apart and falling over like a twig, sails billowing through the air before they landed in the water. The beam had fallen on the opposite side of their ship, but there was a cracked railing I could see. Judging from the shouts of the men, it had also broken through two decks. The waves from the sea would soon be flooding in and their boat would be at the bottom of the ocean come nightfall.

The havoc with the mast had allowed us to steer closer. Nets were being thrown, ropes tying the two ships together in haste—we couldn't let them sink before we got what they were carrying.

Climbing out of the window, I jumped across onto one of the nets, loaded gun in hand, and clambered up the side of the boat.

"Get back, ya filthy pirate!" Someone yelled above me, slashing down with their sword. Narrowly avoiding being hit, I ducked and moved to the side, pointing my pistol at my attacker and shooting before he could even blink. His body slumped forward, the shot having caught him in the chest, and he slowly slid over the rail into the water below.

There was no time to think about what I was doing, or the life I'd just taken. My brain and body were in the place I'd been surviving from for the past ten years—kill or be killed.

Climbing on deck, I found myself to be one of the first of our crew on board, a slew of angry Englishmen brandishing swords and guns of their own as I advanced toward them. The mast had already made messy work of a few of them and there were almost seventy-five men coming behind me. It didn't even seem to make sense to me to hesitate in anything.

A man with light hair and blood on his forehead ran at me with his sword out, words streaming from his lips that I didn't bother understanding. Drawing my own blade, I parried his first attack, sidestepping and slicing across his back with ease. The red that appeared on my blade made me feel a kind of elation, my senses urging me forward, my arm swinging back and forth, cutting down anyone who got in my way.

Without hardly any effort, the fighting was suddenly done. It had passed in a blur, the end finding me on the gun deck, a stranger's blood dripping down the front of my head. No one had surrendered. It had been a fight to the death and every last man on board had been slaughtered. It was like I couldn't even remember what I'd just done, the red fading away from my vision as I beheld the carnage left behind.

"Well done, Snake Eyes," Randall said behind me. Turning, I stared at his own battle torn form, his jacket cut on one shoulder and a flash of gunpowder on his cheek. He nodded in approval to me, standing over the man I'd just finished.

Suddenly, I remembered Sam, her words coming back to me full force.

"Are they Dogs, Captain?" I asked him huskily, looking at the dark haired man whose blood I now wore.

"Unfortunately, no. Hopefully next time." He laughed, gazing toward the gash in the side of the ship. His eyes narrowed some as he studied it, and then he turned, calling up to those above. "Get the cargo! Bring it all aboard and then burn what's left of this mess."

"Burn?" I said in surprise. "Why? She's going down on her own."

"It'll leave a message for the Dogs following us," he stated easily, leaning over and going through the pockets of the man he'd killed. "A calling card, of sorts."

"I thought we were trying to get away from them." I spoke carefully, not knowing exactly what was safe to say to him about this.

"Only for a time." He straightened, studying me with a kind of cold self-absorption.

"Don't you think they'll kill us all if they catch us? I mean, that is what they do, isn't it?" I felt somewhat like a schoolboy, waiting to be scolded by his teacher for asking so many questions, but I couldn't help it. There was something about this moment that was telling me to ask him the things I wanted to know. Maybe it was the camaraderie of having just fought together, or maybe it was even because he seemed to be in a good mood. Either way, he motioned me forward, a grin covering his face.

"You've never seen it, so you wouldn't know. The Knights Templar have a treasure so massive that it took an entire fleet of ships to move it. They've been hiding it from the world, from me, and I'm finally finding out their secrets. We are, together. I promise, more answers wait on the ship that's coming for us."

"More answers to where the treasure is, so we can steal it," I said slowly, not quite understanding his excitement.

"Not steal," he corrected me. "We're going to liberate it. These things were meant to be used, to be seen! When that ship finally catches up with us, I'll have all I need to know in order to get what I want."

"You want the information the men have," I said, finally catching on. "Not just for the treasure you're after now, but for the other ones, too. You mean to take the information from them, but only when they least expect it."

"You're a smart man, Snake Eyes. Yes, I intend to attack when they think they have the upper hand. Right now, we have it. Samantha O'Rourke is our biggest bargaining piece. When the time comes, we'll use her."

Numbly, I followed the stairs down into the hold, finding Samantha just where I'd left her, watching as other members of the crew stacked our stolen loot into place, securing it with ropes and nets. The knife I'd given her was tucked into her makeshift belt, her arms folded across her chest as she leaned against the wall, watching them.

Clearing my throat, I continued to stare at her, feeling a sense of calm and regret settling around me. It was like she was my anchor, the one person who had managed to make me feel like my old self, the man who had been buried beneath all of the mulch and false identities, sacrificed in order to remain alive. As she turned to look at me, her eyes slowly widening, the pain in my heart grew.

The faces of the men I'd just killed seemed to reflect in her gaze.

Pushing away from her spot, she came to me and touched my forehead. "Are you okay?" Her voice was full of worry and shock, her fingers covered in blood as she pulled them away.

"Yeah." I sounded hoarse, like I hadn't said anything in years. It felt like I'd been locked away for just as long. Maybe I had been, never fully realizing it until right then.

Now, she was here, her face sympathetic as she took my hand and squeezed it gently. Her hair spread across her shoulders, long and wild, not like I'd ever seen before in our time. Skin, tanned from being at sea, brushed against mine—skin that had felt things from my century.

Here was a person who had been flung into the past, but somehow managed to keep herself, when I'd so desperately lost myself. Samantha was the only thing that could bring me back. Standing here with her, watching, as she looked me over, her bottom lip caught between her teeth in worry, I knew she was the savior I needed.

Blossoming inside me, the realization grabbed hold in the pit of my stomach, flooding me with warmth. Breath caught in my chest, and I allowed myself to look at her the way I'd been longing to. I devoured her image hungrily, memorizing every detail, giving into the hope and relief that she supplied me with.

"Come on. Let's get you to the surgery." Her voice barely permeated the haze that was surrounding me, the sound of my heart beating filling my ears. I didn't even realize I was following her, clutching her hand tightly as she led me away from all that I'd become lost in. Each step seemed to peel off another protective layer I'd swaddled around my consciousness. Faces flashed before my eyes, battles, lonely nights, Devil Dancers, each a memory that had added to the shell I carried. By the time we reached our destination, everything was gone. I was the man dying in the desert, vultures circling overhead, expecting to eat my corpse.

Patiently, I waited for the face of Runs With Wolves to flood my vision, to remember what had happened to me, to know why I had done all of the horrible things I'd carried away and locked out of my awareness. When the face finally came, though, it wasn't my Apache friend I saw.

It was Sammy.

"You're hurt," she was saying, the front of her shirt covered in blood from my clothes. Slowly, my environment seeped back in. She'd sat me on the table, her hands exploring, touching every part of me, the gory signs of my battle washing her in red. "Your forehead," she said again, speaking a little slower. "What happened?"

Blinking, I stared at her, not knowing what to say. For a moment, I couldn't remember anything but her, standing in front of me, hands outstretched to help.

Saving me.

"Shot," I finally managed to spit out, the image of a sailor pointing a gun at me and firing flitting through my mind. The shot barely grazed me as I rushed forward and cut him down. Now that I thought about it, the spot was burning fiercely.

She nodded, moving away to the other table, pulling things out and looking at them. A ripping sound reached my ears and I watched as she soaked a strip from her shirt in a bucket of water, picking the barrel up and hauling it over to me. Without saying a word, she began to wipe away the mess, softly, the liquid turning darker each time she put the rag back in to wet it again.

Love burned in me and I closed my eyes at her touch, reveling in the feel of it. It didn't matter what our ages were, or that she was married, or that I would never have her in this time or any other. I loved her, even though I desperately wanted not to, revulsion at my own feelings trying to stab at me through the cloud of emotions crowding her. But, how could I not love the woman who had saved me? She brought me back to myself—she understood exactly what it was to be a person lost in time. There had never been another so like myself in my whole life. In the same instance, there had never been anyone so different, so perfectly fitted into the parts of me that were jagged and rough. For as long as I lived, she would be the one who filled those holes, the one whose face I would see when I needed rescuing from the darkness.

"Mark?"

Opening my eyes, I let myself fall into her gaze again, drinking up anything she would give me.

"Are you okay?" she asked urgently, grabbing my face and leaning in close. Staring into my eyes, she turned my head to each side, frowning, before releasing me and stepping back. "What can I put on your cut to stop it from hurting?"

"It doesn't hurt," I replied thickly, suddenly wondering if maybe I had lost a lot of blood and that was why I felt so strange, on top of all of my personal feelings coming to the surface.

"You're crying," she pointed out, looking like she didn't exactly believe me.

Surprised, I reached up and touched my face. The

moisture that I'd thought was blood was in fact tears. When had I started that?

Looking back up at her, I opened my mouth to reply and found myself at a loss for words. The faces of the men I'd killed came to mind again and my newly revealed self felt the full brunt of what I'd done, no layer of protection in place to convince myself I'd acted as needed.

"Sam," I started shakily, feeling the tears as they gathered in my eyes.

"It's okay," she said quickly, leaning forward and wrapping her arms around me firmly. "I think you're in shock. Everything is fine."

"Those men." Holding her tightly to me, the wall of emotions finally burst, and I sobbed against her shoulder. I cried for the lives I'd taken, the life I'd forced myself to live, and the life that had been lost in the desert, all those years ago.

Mark Bell had died that day and the man who'd replaced him was not someone I wanted to be.

Now, with Sam's help, I was crawling to the surface, fighting through the demons that tried to hold me back, breathing life into Mark Bell when it should have been impossible to do so.

But nothing was impossible with Samantha at my side. It was her strength that brought me back, my love for her that made it possible to dig my way out of the pile of hate and fear I was buried under.

I didn't know how long I sobbed, or why I was having such a powerful reaction, but she never let me go. Her arms stayed around me, comforting phrases whispered in my ear, her hand brushing through my hair. There was no judgment from her, no condemnation for behaving in such a manner, which made me love her even more.

As I finally started to calm down, new resolutions formed like concrete inside me. Randall meant her harm on some level and it wasn't going to happen as long as I was around. No one would lay a finger on her again, even if it meant that I fought every single Black Knight on this ship in her place. Her husband would see her returned in good health and happiness if it killed me. Samantha would be reunited with her Tristan if it were the last thing I did, because it would be the one thing that would make her happiest. She would be safe with him, safer among the Templar Knights, and that was enough to calm my aching heart as I thought of losing her completely.

Truth be told, she was already lost to me, and I knew that, but it didn't hurt my resolve at all. Everything I did from this point would be for her and in her best interests.

"Sorry," I mumbled, regretfully leaning away from her and wiping my face with the sleeve of my shirt. The action only made me dirtier and I laughed, sniffing as I tried to compose myself.

"Don't be sorry." She smiled, a gesture that seemed more understanding than anything else, and continued her work, wiping my face off again. "You did what you had to do. We've both done it. Sometimes it just catches up with you, that's all." Her tone was so dismissive and final that I believed she truly didn't hold anything against me.

"You were all right in the hold?" I asked, anxious to know how the battle had been for her and to make sure I wasn't accidentally missing her own wounds in my overly emotional state.

"I was fine," she replied, nodding. "No one even came in until it was all over. I was worried when you didn't come right away."

"Sorry," I mumbled, instantly chastising myself for not being the first one to return. Of course she would have worried. Why had I let myself get caught up in the fight? Why hadn't I stopped and thought about what I was doing?

"You're here now. That's all that's important."

Her words made me feel light and a bit dizzy. Actually, maybe that was my gunshot wound.

"Am I still bleeding?" I asked quickly, grabbing onto the table as the room started spinning around me.

"A little," she answered in a matter of fact tone. "But not bad. I don't think you'll even have a scar."

A knock at the door interrupted my reply and we both turned to see who it was, the action making me feel like I needed to vomit.

"What's this?" Captain Randall stood in the doorway, looking just as he had on the ship when he'd told me part of his plans. "Are you injured, Snake Eyes? I thought you were fine just a while ago."

"He was shot in the head," Sam replied, folding her arms as she glared at him. "Didn't you notice the blood all over his face?"

He seemed somewhat put off, but the excitement from the catch had put him in a good mood. He came closer, glancing me over with interest. "I don't think I realized it was yours, Snake Eyes. I'll send White in to tend you. He was our unofficial doctor before you showed up."

"I can handle his injuries just fine," Sam said through clenched teeth.

"What's the matter?" Randall sneered at her, having finally decided to acknowledge her presence. "Have you fallen for your captor yet again? Poor Tristan will be devastated to hear that you've forgotten him so soon."

Her hand snaked out so fast that I didn't even have time to blink before she'd struck him across the face, a red mark instantly blossoming across his cheek.

"We both know who wins in a fight between the two of us," she hissed back, daring to enter his personal space and speak right in his face. "Or don't you remember? I've beaten you once. I could do it again."

This Sam was somewhat frightening. There was a flash of what I'd just gotten rid of in myself, the darkness that we had to use to survive at times. It was news to me that the two of them had dueled before and I watched the exchange with mild alarm and interest.

Randall smiled, a laugh shaking him as he straightened, looking down at her. "You only won that fight because you had men to back you up," he said coldly. "Do you really think you won because you were better than me?" His voice sank dangerously low and he stepped forward, making her move against the table, her hip brushing my knee. "It didn't make sense to kill you then, so I didn't. It was luck that you managed to land a blow on me at all."

He moved even closer, causing her to back up

out of what seemed to be instinct, wedging herself between my legs, almost entirely blocking my view of him.

"Victory or death, Missus O'Rourke," he breathed, taking a piece of her hair in his hand. He rubbed it between his fingers, eyeing it as if he were truly interested in its qualities and the woman it was attached to. "As of yet, you have not experienced either."

"I hope you burn in Hell." Her voice held only the tiniest bit of fear, but he heard it, just as I did, and laughed gleefully.

"Haven't you noticed?" He motioned all around us. "We're already there! Look outside—the fires of the Devil burn across the water."

"You would compare yourself to Satan?" She seemed appalled, pressing against me like she wanted to be as far away from him as possible.

At the moment, I rather thought he was embodying the father of all evil, the expression on his face one that could turn people to stone. His entire body was tense, angling all of the hatred that was rolling off him toward us.

"Even Lucifer was an angel, thrown from Heaven for believing in a cause unworthy to God. Tell me, what does that sound like to you?" His eyes searched hers eagerly, his tongue darting out and licking his lips as he waited for her to reply.

"You're no angel, Randall," she whispered bitterly. "And the things you did were not a worthy cause."

"Who are you to play God to my plans?" he snapped, raising a hand to strike her.

"Stop!" Surprised by the sound of my own voice, I was shocked to see I'd grabbed his wrist before he could hit her, my free arm snaking around her and holding her protectively. Trying to think of a good reason for why I would have stopped him, I let go of them both, nodding at him. "She'll be fine enough as a nurse. If you rough her up now, I'll have to put up with White's prodding. My head hurts bad enough as it is."

He glared at me, clearly not happy to have been interrupted, but backed away all the same. "Very well." Then, peering back at Sam, he gave her a look of condescension, laughing lightly as he took his leave. "This devil has things to do elsewhere."

"We can't sell the goods in Veracruz," White announced, a good majority of the crew agreeing with him. "They'll spot us as pirates right from the start. Captain's ordered a pit stop on the way, to empty the hold and recharge before heading on."

A buzz of excitement washed over the group again, the men grinning like fools.

"Is it Nassau?" Flanagan asked, showing a rare amount of enthusiasm. "Tell me it's Nassau!"

"Boys." White beamed at all of them, just as thrilled as the crew anxiously awaiting his reply. "We're headed for Nassau's white, sandy shores!"

Cheering, the men clapped each other on the back, chattering excitedly, their duties forgotten for the time being.

"Three days of leave, for the whole crew!" White yelled over the din, creating even more uproariously loud celebration.

Chuckling, I watched the masses below, scratching around the edges of the scab that was forming at my hairline. Sam had been right; the bullet graze wasn't too bad, but had bled a lot because it was a head wound.

Glancing behind me, I caught sight of her, standing at the very rear of the deck, looking out over the water as usual. I'd given her one of my own shirts, a black fabric that fit her better than what she'd been wearing previously. While her bruises had faded, she still had the look of a ragged prisoner, her glowing happiness that I so longed to see sinking further and further away each day.

Aside from waiting for Tristan to come for her, I knew she was worried about the baby. When the morning sickness started to go away, she'd confided in me that she felt her sudden lack of symptoms had meant something was wrong. That had been a few days ago, with no throwing up or nausea to speak of. I'd done my best to reassure her it was normal—she was nearing the end of her first trimester, from what we could tell—and she should have been starting to feel better. However, I couldn't shake my own worries that something was wrong.

Rolling waves and calm seas brought us to Nassau in another week, the island's pale beaches and blue waters overloaded me with a sense of excitement I hadn't dared feel since Sam came aboard. I considered trying to sneak her away while we were anchored, but in the end decided it would be too much of a risk. The place was always overrun with pirates, who wouldn't think twice about raping her, even if I was there to defend her. Randall would probably hunt us both down and kill me. Tristan might never find her if he was chasing after the ship, as well.

So, we found ourselves in a long boat, being rowed toward land with Randall at the helm, three more vessels full of cargo behind us. The harbor was a flurry of activity, as was the beach, pirates littering almost every space the eye could see. Shacks rested against the tree line, old sails strung over the tops of the huts like a giant canopy. Beyond the shoreline was the town, bustling with activity and sound. It appeared just as it had the last time I'd been here, except for the large, imposing, castle-like structure resting on the small hill beside the port.

"The fort is new," Randall called, pointing to the building. "Is it the Navy's? They're doing a rather poor job if it is."

"Private investors," White answered calmly, rowing as if it cost him no effort at all. "Ones willing to turn a blind eye in trade for good profits."

"Do you know them?" Randall asked, curious.

The two fell into a conversation about the powers that controlled this place, palm trees swaying on the sand in front of them, seeming to welcome us to the den of thievery.

"Are you okay?" I asked Sam quietly, worried by the pained look on her face.

"Fine," she breathed. "Just a backache. I'm excited to sleep in a real bed tonight."

Frowning, I thought of the room we would be renting in the brothel. Randall, apparently, had also thought Sam might try running away while on land. The whore house was the best place to lock her up, seeing as how any man who went in there was immediately occupied by some woman who wanted his money. The Templars wouldn't hardly be able to move one inch without being detained long enough for us to make our escape. However, even if Sam did somehow manage to get away, anyone here would turn her in; Randall would pay to have her back.

Making landfall, the crew split up easily, used to completing their individual jobs when they were on shore. The cargo would be sold to the harbormaster and then we would all be free for the next three days. It was likely the majority of men would spend their share of the loot in the brothel, having sex and getting wasted drunk, which meant I'd be spending my time off with the lot of them anyway.

Helping Sam out of the boat, I held her hand firmly in mine, keeping her close as we followed Randall to our destination. She didn't seem to mind, her eyes wide as she took in everything around her.

"Never been to Nassau?" I guessed, smiling at the glimpse of the old Sam I saw in her. The expression of wonder she wore now was one I'd seen in our own time, whenever we worked together in the Pit. She still looked so beautiful now, even in dirty, men's clothes that didn't fit her.

"No," she confirmed. "It feels a lot like Tortuga, though. And the village on Madagascar."

"I imagine the people here are doing the same things they were there." I chuckled, secretly adoring the way her fingers felt in mine, wishing there were some way we could stay together. As always, my self-loathing over loving her reminded me that she was married and in love with another man. Shoving reality from my mind, I resolved to simply enjoy the moment while it happened, future problems be damned.

Stepping through the doors of our latest prison, my eyebrows rose at the flurry of activity before us.

The building, a stone structure two stories high, was by far one of the busiest establishments I'd seen as we passed through town, with the bar coming in at a close second. Topless women paraded their breasts in front of a slew of patrons, the men reaching out and touching the waitresses and even pulling them onto their laps for a kiss. At the bar, drunkards laughed over some card game that was taking place, betting on who would win. The stairs to the rooms were in constant use, either by women leading men up, or patrons leaving after their lusty meetings.

"How can I help you?" An older woman, wearing entirely too much makeup appeared magically at our side, eyes swiping over the group. Her perfume was so strong that it caused me to forcibly fight the urge to gag,

"Your best room," Randall told her coolly, reaching into his coat and procuring a bag full of coins. Shaking it gently, the sounds of the money clinking together inside made her eyes widen with hunger and happiness.

"Will you be wanting a girl to go with it?" Her tone was casual, but I didn't miss how her gaze seemed to pause on Sam for a second, a frown pulling at her lips.

"No. It's not for me." Looking over his shoulder, Randall nodded for me to step forward. "It's for my friends. They'll be staying a few nights and I want them well taken care of." He jiggled the purse again, as if reminding her about the money involved. "You'll be paid handsomely for watching after them for me. Especially the girl."

The woman's eyes narrowed and she turned her

attention to him, seeming to be assessing his character. Finally, after what felt like an hour of holding my breath, she nodded, reaching out and snatching the bag away from him. "She'll not take one step without me knowing. Follow me."

Pushing through the crowd, she yelled at a few people to behave themselves, laughing loudly as she went up the stairs. It wasn't hard for us to follow, the crowd staying parted to allow Randall and his sinister air to pass through.

Finally, we reached our room, located at the end of the hall. It was a rather large space, with sparse furnishings, but it held the comfort that a hammock on a ship lacked.

"Your meals are paid for and the privy is out back," Captain Randall said as he watched Sam sit down on the edge of the mattress. "If I hear one word of either of you leaving before it's time to set sail, I promise Nassau will be the last place you ever set eyes on."

"Yes, Captain," I replied, leaning one shoulder against the bedpost. "I'll make sure she doesn't try to leave."

He regarded me with a cool and calm interest, his eyes flicking between the two of us for a moment. Ever since I'd stopped him from slapping her, he had seemed to hold less trust in me. Perhaps he'd realized I had real feelings for her. Or maybe he thought I was trying to take some of his power from him. Either way, I'd been given much less information than normal, and he'd stopped pressing me for details on what Sam knew about the treasure.

Without another word, Randall left the room,

shutting the door firmly behind him and plunging Sam and I into our three-day "vacation."

Sighing, she fell back onto the bed, staring at the ceiling with a blank expression. Following suit, I moved to the other side, lying so our heads were together, and remained silent.

"I don't suppose you brought any books or cards," she finally said, moving onto her side to look at me.

"As a matter of fact, I did." Getting up, I went to the small bag I'd brought with me. It had some clean clothes in it, as well as an extra knife and gun. Before we'd sailed in to port, I'd gone to a couple members of the crew and paid them off with my share of the loot for their cards and dice, knowing there wouldn't be much to do during a three-day confinement indoors.

Shuffling the cards, I motioned for her to join me at the small table, dealing out a hand for each of us. After a few hours, I was surprised to find that Sam was quite good at gambling.

"Where did you learn to play so well?" I asked after a particularly nasty loss on my end.

"Tristan," she answered, laughing. "He plays with his grandmother every time they get together. She's the master, but he's beaten her once or twice. He taught me how to do it, for practice. I'm afraid I'm not that much of a challenge for him, though." She grinned, mixing the deck again and dealing out the cards.

Our dinner arrived after dark, a delicious pile of roasted pig, bread, and tropical fruits. Wine had also been delivered as our drink, but the waitress was nice enough to bring some water up when I asked her.

"She likes you," Sam said after she left. "She kept tossing her hair for you."

"She likes every man here." Chuckling, I sat back down, pouring her a glass of water. "She works in a whore house. It's her job to like every man she meets."

"I don't think that's true." Tearing off the crust of her bread, she chewed on it thoughtfully. "It's her job to sexually arouse and please every man she meets. She doesn't have to like it."

"You really want to be technical about prostitutes right now?" Grinning, I passed the cup over to her, enjoying the banter.

"Actually, no." Standing, she brushed off her pants and nodded toward the exit. "I have to go to the bathroom."

"Oh." Gulping down the bite I'd just shoveled into my mouth, I pushed to my feet, hurrying to open the door for her.

As I'd suspected, the ground floor was even more packed than when we'd arrived, our crew making the most of their leave. Slipping out the rear entrance, we found the privy with ease—it looked like an old outhouse and stank like one too—and I waited outside while Sam did her business.

After an unusually long time seemed to have passed, I cleared my throat, embarrassed. "Is everything okay in there?" I asked with as much discretion as I could.

"Yeah." Her voice was strangely high and strained, with a quiver I hadn't heard earlier. Before I could ask again, though, the door opened and she came out, her features a mask.

Not saying a word, she led the way inside, hurrying up to our room. When the door was closed, the mask broke and she looked at me, tears in her eyes.

"I'm bleeding, Mark." Her voice caught and the tears started rolling down her face. "The baby—it's d-dead."

"What?" Going to her side, I took her in my arms, holding her as she shook. "Are you sure?"

"There's b-blood." She was struggling to speak, a panic so strong shaking her that even I felt it.

"How much?" When she didn't answer, I pulled away some, staring at her sternly. "Sam, some bleeding during pregnancy is normal. It could be nothing. I won't know how to help you if you don't tell me."

She nodded, hiccupping as she tried to stop crying, a shaky hand brushing across her face.

"It wasn't a lot, just a little spotting, like I'd started my period."

"What color was it, bright or dark red?"

"Bright r-red."

Bringing her to me again, I held her tight. Bright red was fresh blood. If there wasn't a lot, she could just be experiencing some break through bleeding. There was no reason to think she'd lost the baby—yet.

"Okay, here's what we're going to do," I told her firmly. "You are going to stay on bed rest the entire time we're here, do you understand?"

Nodding, she seemed to calm a little.

"Everything is fine. This could be normal. I want

you to remember that, alright?"

Slowly, I coached her down from the panic attack and sorrow she'd been feeling, getting her tucked into the bed. I knew my words and actions would only have a small effect on what she was feeling, but it was all I could do.

"If you start having cramps or bleeding worse, we'll figure out what to do next then," I told her reassuringly. "Right now, you need to rest. Let your body figure out what it's doing and how to take care of you."

"Thank you, Mark." Her voice was quiet and I could see the fear in her eyes. I hated not knowing how to help her find out what she wanted to know, how to tell her if her child was going to live or die.

But, most of all, I hated that I wasn't who she needed to be with right then. All I could do was pray that Tristan would find us soon.

As we sailed away from Nassau, headed for the coast of what would one day be the independent country of Mexico, I felt like crying again. Not for myself, but for Sam, who was currently in the surgery, probably lying just as still as she had the entire time we were on land. We were both too afraid to say what we thought was happening—that the bed rest hadn't made any difference.

Her bleeding hadn't increased, just the occasional spotting continually showing up to worry us. Cramping had joined in the mix as well, but the pains were few and far between. Symptoms like morning sickness and fatigue had remained in the past, too. There was nothing we could do to physically check the baby; it was still too young for her to be able to feel its movements and the heartbeat wouldn't be strong enough to try and listen to with a makeshift stethoscope.

All we could do was wait and see what would happen. Maybe the bleeding would stop, or she would deliver the baby, small as it was, and we would move on from there. It was my sincere hope that everything would be fine. She may have only been a few weeks along, but Sam was obviously attached to the kid already. I'd seen the way she touched her stomach and heard her whispering softly to the child when she thought I was sleeping. It was the only thing keeping her from trying to escape, the only thing making her go on as she waited for her husband, not knowing when or if he would come. If she lost it, I didn't know what would occur.

"You seem reserved, Mark." Captain Randall joined me at the bow of the ship, an orange in his hand. He rarely used my real name, which made me think I was about to be scolded for something. "Where is our lady friend today?"

"She's not feeling well." It was a short answer, but one I hoped he would leave alone for now. However, Thomas Randall wasn't one to let his questions go completely unanswered.

"What happened while we were on land?" he asked tersely, throwing his peelings over into the water. "Something is different. I want to know what it is. I'm your captain—your brother—so tell me."

Sighing, I peered around to see if anyone was nearby. Up ahead, a man sat in the rigging, seeming to rest in the light of the sun after climbing up and releasing the sails when we set out. Behind us, a few people stood around a barrel of rum, laughing as they drank freely from the newly acquired luxury. In our immediate area, there was only the two of us, and I looked him in the eye frowning.

"She's losing the baby," I told him softly. "Or she might be. I don't know. She needs a midwife, someone who can better tell her what's going on."

I didn't know why I always told him the truth.

Maybe it was because I thought he would uncover any lie I uttered, or because I thought it was best to just have things the way they were, rather than try to remember some elaborate story I'd concocted. Either way, I knew this was important. He would have to listen to me, to get Sam the help she needed, if he wanted her to stay alive long enough for whatever plans he had.

Of course, there were no midwives at sea, which meant I was about to find out what he thought of the whole thing.

"Is she sick?" He didn't ask out of care and his tone made it apparent. She was spoken of as if she were goods for trade.

"Not yet, but she will be if it continues on. If she really is losing it, the baby needs to come out soon. If it doesn't, she could get an infection. That would make her sick enough to kill her if it's not taken care of."

He stared blankly at my answer and I belatedly remembered that he wouldn't have any idea what the word infection meant. It didn't matter, though; he had gotten the message well enough.

"How long before you know if she's lost the child?" he asked abruptly.

"If she keeps bleeding like she is, I can't say for sure. It could still go either way."

Without even stopping to think about it, he shared his plan with me. "We will sail on to Veracruz. If she hasn't gone either way by then, we will find a midwife for her."

"That's almost two weeks!" I argued. "She needs someone who knows how to take care of her now, to

303

help calm her down before she loses it."

"Then I suggest you make sure she doesn't get to that point," he shot back coldly. "Brotherhood or not, I gave you a task to do—keep her alive and find out what she knows. I don't think I have to tell you what happens when you fail at both."

Snapping my mouth shut, I leaned away from him, trying to keep my eyes from narrowing. There was nothing more I would have liked to do besides punch him in the nose. Samantha was possibly entering into a life or death situation and all he cared about was if I'd managed to find out where the treasure really was.

Taking a slice from his treat, he placed it in his mouth, the juice rolling down his chin as he bit into it.

"I haven't asked her where it is yet," I said through gritted teeth. "She isn't to the point where she would tell me anything."

"I didn't think she ever would be." Swiping his arm across his face, he caught the extra liquid on his sleeve. "It's obvious to any idiot with eyes that she's in love with that idiot Dog, O'Rourke. She's taken to you for some reason, though. She trusts you. And you love her." Raising an eyebrow, he waited for me to deny it.

I didn't give him the satisfaction.

"She has a pretty face." Continuing in an offhand manner, he slowly ate his fruit, looking over the water. "A woman unlike any other I've come across. Of course, she would be, since she's from another time. But she's still the beguiling sex that has done nothing but underhand progress from the start of all time, exotic or not. You would do well to remember that, Snake Eyes. She will turn on you the second she doesn't need you anymore."

Shaking with fury, I bit my tongue, facing away from him instead of replying.

"Don't believe me? I've seen her do it. If you think she's an innocent, maybe you should ask her about when we left her in La Coruna, what she did to her own husband." He laughed, a low, throaty sound, and stepped in front of me again. "She slept with the captain, right under O'Rourke's nose, and then left without saying a word. In all my life, I've never figured out why he forgave her for it."

"Perhaps your information is wrong," I replied, as coolly as possible.

"Perhaps. You should also ask her about James Abby, the man she left for dead in the pit on Oak Isle. If you wanted, I could tell you about the men I watched her kill personally, cutting them down without a second thought."

His words were sinking in and he knew it. A strange sort of triumph gleamed in his eyes as he continued to drag her through the mud, making outrageous claims against her character.

At the same time, I felt my own heart hurt at his words, my brain unwilling to believe what he was saying. Sam would never hurt anyone! But, a small voice in the back of my mind reminded me of what I had done to survive here. It was more than likely that she'd done her fair share of regretful things in order to make it by.

"Men are waiting for us in Mexico City," Randall said, returning my attention to him. "Once we arrive there, we'll have all we need to continue north. You and I will follow the path of the last, great Black Knight—and we will find the treasure. The world will be at our fingertips. Would you let a woman keep you from that?"

His words brought a realization to me and I shook my head, wanting him to leave. "No, Captain. I wouldn't."

"Good." Even if only mildly convinced, he nodded, looking past me to something up by the helm of the ship. "Make sure she doesn't die." Without another word, he pushed past me, heading toward whatever had caught his attention.

Hurrying below deck, I slipped into the surgery, closing the door behind me and held a finger up to my mouth. Sam, from her spot on the table, stared at me questioningly, arranging the blanket so she could sit up.

Stepping closer, I whispered quickly, not wanting to risk any chance of a long, drawn out conversation that someone would overhear.

"Randall already knows where the treasure is," I said quietly, right in her ear. "He has men waiting to join us in Mexico City. He said they'd be following the path of the last, great, Black Knight. He's not waiting on any information from you."

"Cortés," she breathed. "But if he already knew, then why has he been insisting that I'm the only one who knows?"

"I don't know. But, if he's not keeping you around for information, there has to be another reason." A conversation from earlier flashed through my memory and I tried to make more sense of it.

Samantha is our biggest bargaining chip, he had

said. Bargaining with whom? Tristan and the Templar Knights? If what Sam had told me about them was true, they wouldn't be doing any kind of trade. They would simply wipe out the Black Knights before they could advance any further. Randall didn't seem the type to just let her go, either. No, he hadn't been talking about a trade with Tristan when he'd said that.

Unfortunately, I had no idea who he *had* been talking about. I had the distinct feeling that whatever it was would end up with Sam dead.

That was not something I planned on letting happen.

Almost two weeks later, the shores of New Spain sat before us, bustling with activity and excitement. Veracruz was one of the biggest ports the area had, boasting even more riches than Mexico City at times. Ships from all over the world were docked here and sitting in the harbor. We'd chosen to drop anchor, owing to the fact that we were trying to avoid being labeled pirates and our ship had no name, and row in to shore.

With our feet firmly on the ground, I gently guided Sam, my arm around her shoulders, her form wrapped in a long cloak to disguise the fact that she was a pale mess and a prisoner. The baby was definitely lost in my eyes; her bleeding having never stopped. She hadn't passed anything other than blood yet, though, and I was worried that an infection would soon set in. As we'd sailed into the harbor that morning, she'd started cramping badly and the amount of blood she was losing increased. The baby could possibly be delivered before the end of the day if she kept going like she was. Hopeful, I'd shared the information with Randall, explaining that we needed to camp for the night before setting out, to give her time. Surprisingly, he'd agreed very easily.

"I know a place," I told Randall firmly when he opened his mouth to speak. "An old church, on the outskirts of town. There's enough space for the whole crew. Send some men for food and water. Someone needs to find a midwife, as well."

He frowned, not liking that I'd so openly ordered him around, but listened all the same. "You lot!" He yelled at a group to his right, pointing. "Get some food! Bring it to the old church outside town."

"I know of a midwife here, Captain," MacTavish said sheepishly. "I can ask for her if ye'd like."

"Go." Looking at me, Randall smirked, as if waiting for me to give him something else to do.

"Do you feel well enough to walk, Sammy?" I asked quietly, finding one of her hands with my free one and squeezing slightly.

"I think so." She was flushed, her cramps having increased some as she moved about and came ashore.

"It will all be over soon," I assured her, glancing out over the city in front of us. "I promise."

The walking was slow, which seemed to annoy Randall to no end, and he eventually disappeared, slipping off into the crowd with the rest of the crew without a word. Assuming that they knew the place I had told them about, I kept right with Sam, stopping whenever her fatigue dictated she needed to. Buying a few items from sellers along the way, I tried to ready myself for anything she would need help with. By the time we arrived at our destination, the sun was setting.

The church had been abandoned for longer than anyone could remember, an old building that was forgotten as the city developed. A bell tower, missing its namesake, glowed in the evening sun, the sky orange around it like a halo. The front doors looked rotted and beaten, but held shut as if only the will of God kept them going. Weeds had overgrown the paths and steps, giving the entire brick façade the appearance of a crumbling ghost house.

Laughter and singing floated out of the windows, the smells of cooking meat making my mouth water. Happy that the crew had already arrived and settled for the night, I sighed, ready to deal with whatever the evening would bring us.

Relief washed over me as I led Sam inside, thankful to know that her physical suffering was only hours away from being finished—hopefully. She hadn't indicated that anything was better or worse, but my gut told me that this was the night she would lose the child.

"Snake Eyes!" Flanagan called from beside a fire, over which a pig was roasting. Next to him, a woman sat, running her fingers through his hair. "It took you long enough!"

A few of the other men greeted me as well, the company and respite having put them in as good a mood as Nassau had.

"Captain had a room in the back saved for the

309

lass," Greybeard said as I passed him.

"Thank you," I told him honestly, wondering if he could see how tired I was. It would have been nice to have nothing more to do than sit on the wooden benches around the fires in this old chapel, but Sam needed me, and I wasn't going to let her down.

"Where's MacTavish?" I called over everyone, searching for him. Spotting him in the far corner, we made our way to him. The expression on his face didn't make me excited to hear what he had to say.

"Where's the midwife?" I asked him, desperately noticing his lack of womanly companionship.

"She wouldn't come." He shrugged, taking a swig from the glass bottle in his hand. "Said she can't risk working for pirates. Bad for business, or something."

"What?" Panicked, I looked at Sam, who seemed like she was ready to sit down and cry.

"She did send these herbs, though," he said, digging through his pocket and pulling out a crumpled sack. "Said they would help her with the pain. Sorry, Snake Eyes."

"She doesn't need medicine, she needs someone who can check her and tell her what's going on," I replied, frustrated.

Glancing around the room, it became obviously clear to me that no one was going to help us. Randall was nowhere to be seen. No woman in her right mind would risk coming here if she didn't want to be grabbed upon by one of the crew.

Taking a deep, steadying breath, I took Sam's hand and pulled her along to the back of the space, to the room I'd been told was waiting for us.

Please, God, I prayed as we passed an old crucifix on the wall. *Help me know what to do. Help her through this.*

"How are you feeling?" Putting my own desperate worries and anxieties aside, I gently guided her into the room that had been reserved for us.

"Crampy." Frowning, she placed a hand over her stomach. "Like I'm having a bad period."

Pursing my lips, I kept my thoughts to myself, yet again. She knew what was happening—the expression on her face said as much—but I didn't want to blurt it out for some reason. It was as if saying it out loud made it more real than it already was.

"Do you need anything?" I pressed, looking her over.

"I don't think so." She appeared somewhat pale and exhausted, but other than that, it was as if nothing were occurring. I never would have known what she was going through if she hadn't told me.

Glancing around the room, I frowned, feeling half thankful for the privacy and half annoyed she was still being treated as a prisoner, even if she was a very well taken care of captive. A fire burned in the hearth, sweltering hot, but a welcome comfort. There was only the table and a few chairs, an old picture frame broken and sitting in one corner. Everything else had been cleared out by some mystery person, either tonight or sometime in the past when the place was abandoned. It made everything feel cold, impersonal, and old.

Suddenly, I wondered if Sam felt deserted now.

"Hey," I spoke up, smiling. "Do you need more clean rags? I can go wash some for you in the well, if you'd like. Or do you not want to be alone?"

"Actually, I'd like a few minutes, if you don't mind." Grimacing, her lower lip trembled some and there was a flash of moisture in her eyes. "To get ready, I mean."

Feeling my own emotions catch, I nodded, hesitating to leave. "It's going to be okay, Sammy. I know it's hard, but it'll be okay someday. It will always be your baby."

"I know." Sniffing, she grinned at me, eyes shining brightly. "It's just hard to think about the future now. Everything I'd been planning for isn't going to happen. Tristan—all I can think about is Tristan. He was supposed to be coming home to his pregnant wife. Instead, he returned to no wife and now he has no baby."

She didn't have to say what else she'd been thinking and feeling. The words were practically hanging over her head like a neon sign. She had no Tristan, no baby, and it was obvious her heart was in shambles.

Stomach twisting, I stepped forward, taking her into my arms as a tear rolled down her cheek. "I'm here, Sam. I'm not going anywhere. I promise."

"I know." Voice trembling, she retreated,

straightening the back of her shirt and staring at the floor. "Thank you for that."

"Do you still want me to go out for a while?"

"Yes, please."

I studied her once more, trying to decide if she would truly be okay, and then left the room as she'd asked, grabbing a handful of rags out of my bag by the door.

Shutting her into solitary confinement behind me, I sighed deeply, my shoulders slumping a bit. It was as if the crew didn't even notice me, going on with their loudness and partying in the chapel. Their actions were probably highly offensive to those who were religious, but they didn't care, like always. I found the atmosphere to be too much for my taste, though, and went outside, searching for fresh air and some semblance of quiet.

The well wasn't far from the church, tucked into a tiny grove of trees that hid it from the main road. This, too, had crumbled over time, the bricks broken around the top, some of the stones having fallen to the ground. The plants felt more overgrown here, like the jungle was trying to consume anyone or anything that entered. Allowing myself to be enveloped by the greenery, the sounds from inside the chapel fading into the background, I set to work, finding the old bucket and tossing it inside the hole.

Thankfully, the container didn't have any holes. As soon as I'd brought the liquid up and had a drink, I began washing the rags, silently thinking over everything I'd learned and been through in the last while. It seemed so much like a blur and yet in the same instant as if it had all happened in only one day.

Where would we go from here?

Would Tristan and the Templars ever catch up with us?

"You look like a man plagued by demons, Snake Eyes."

Startled, I peered up, staring into Randall's face on the other side of the grove. "Captain. I didn't hear you come."

"No worries." Striding over to me, he sat on the edge of the well, staring down into the depths. "How does your fair lady go?"

Frowning, I glared at him for a second before grabbing another rag and scrubbing it together forcefully. I'd never enjoyed being teased, let alone by a brute like him. "She's fine. Resting."

"Good. We'll stay through tomorrow night, as well. Beyond that, I can't give her any more time to sit around."

Curious, I glanced back over to him, laying the cloth I'd just finished across a fallen branch to dry. "Why are you being so generous?" Waiting for the answer, I regarded him with a cool and calculated stare. He'd proven many times that he didn't ever do anything unless it benefited him personally.

"I want her to live." Sounding genuinely surprised, his eyes widened and he stood, returning my gaze. "I told you, we need her."

"For what?" I pressed. "You already have a direction you want to go. Are you really waiting for her to tell you where the treasure is?"

"Watch yourself, Snake Eyes." His tone was still friendly, but it held an edge to it, a resonance that warned me I was getting into dangerous territory.

"I'm sorry," I replied automatically, stepping back a pace. "I only meant . . . I don't understand why we keep her. She's slowing us down. If there weren't company and food for the men, they'd be in a rage over having to delay for her. Do they know something I don't?"

Laughing, he shook his head, motioning to the church. "That lot? No. You're better informed than any of them. They do what I say, or die. You are my brother-in-arms, Mark. Out of the entire crew, I have confided in you the most. Do you know why that is?"

"I have no idea," I confessed. Something about the way he was speaking made me uncomfortable, like I was slowly being led into a trap.

"I like you," he said simply. "You aren't afraid to do what you need to. It's a good pirate, the man who will put aside everything to obey his captain. I need men like you behind me."

The near mutiny I'd witnessed came to mind at that, the crew fighting over whether or not they could trust Randall to do as he said. It occurred to me that I'd never done that; I'd always believed he would do what he said he would. If the Templars arrived to thwart him, that was another thing. However, if he had no outside force to stop him, I truly believed that Thomas Randall could accomplish whatever he set his mind to. It was what made me wary to go against him.

I may have been the one they called Snake, but Randall was a true predator, hiding in the grass.

"You have me, Captain." Swallowing hard, I nodded at him, trying to think if there'd been any further signs of an uprising. Anxiety over being away from Sam so long was starting to eat at me as well and I fidgeted, ready to go back.

How much longer would he want to stay and talk?

"You're a good man, Snake Eyes." Grinning, he sat down once more, apparently appeased with my promise. "I've a mind to promote you, when this whole mess is over with. Granted, no one will have a need to be a pirate once we've finished what I have planned. We'll be living like kings—gods."

"Thank you, Captain." Silently, I wondered exactly what that plan was. He wouldn't tell me all of it now, though, that much was clear.

Standing abruptly, he made to leave, pausing at the tree line of the grove. "You know," he said in an odd tone. "You remind me of her sometimes."

"I'm sorry?" Bewildered, I stared blankly at him.

"Sam. There's something about the two of you that feels the same, but I haven't quite put my finger on it yet."

Heart suddenly racing, I swallowed, continuing to stare. "I don't know what you mean."

"I'll figure it out eventually." Smiling, he left, his footsteps fading into the darkness.

Gathering the wet rags, I followed after him, trying to calm the panic that had taken over at his words.

What if he did find out how we were similar? Would he kill me for lying, or would I become a prisoner like Sam?

Sammy.

Speeding up, I practically raced through the doors of the church to her room, looking around wildly to make sure no one had bothered her while I was away. Talking with Randall had left me on edge, the discussion making it easy to imagine her being attacked while I'd given her the time she asked for.

"Everything okay in here?" I asked, coming in and returning to the solemn environment.

However, it immediately became clear everything was not okay. Her shoulders were shaking, her body collapsed on the table. That wasn't the most alarming part, however. It was the sight of Sam's hands covering her face, blood smeared across them as they stifled her wailing.

"What is it? What happened?" Rushing to her side, I glanced her over, trying to assess what had happened in my absence. Had someone come in here? Was she hemorrhaging? Going over every inch of her, I desperately searched for what was wrong, before I finally saw it.

The baby was tiny, so tiny that it could have fit in the palm of my hand, the head not even reaching my fingers. Resting on the table, between her legs, it was smeared with blood as well. Carefully, I picked the small child up, marveling at it, my eyes drifting from the small figure to Sam.

"I f-felt something c-come out," she said, sobbing even harder, her face still hidden. "And when I l-looked, it was the b-baby."

Shifting my gaze to the child again, tears pricking me. It was a girl, her pale skin somehow so perfect while still underdeveloped, the veins of her body showing through the somewhat see-through flesh. Her eyes, still fused shut, looked peaceful somehow.

The chord protruding from where her belly button would have been was dark, leading up into Sam's pants and the placenta I assumed she still needed to deliver. It seemed like something had happened with the baby's nutrition source, but I didn't know if it had been a natural occurrence, or something brought on by the beating Sam had received when she was kidnapped. I did know for certain that the child had passed away within the last week, judging from its size.

"It's a girl," I said quietly, brushing my finger across the tiny forehead.

"Oh." The announcement seemed to have shocked Sam some and she uncovered her face, staring at the two of us.

Turning to let her see, I showed her the child, smiling sadly. "Here." I told her, giving her my free hand to help her sit up. Once she was somewhat comfortable, I passed the baby to her, laying it against her chest.

The sound she made could have destroyed even the coldest of beings. I watched as she cradled her child beside her heart, weeping for her and the life she would never have. Shedding a few tears myself, I rose and gathered the string and scissors I'd bought earlier in the day, cutting the chord for her and tying it off.

"I'm going to go outside, to the chapel," I whispered, knowing that she wouldn't be paying much attention to me. There would be time to take care of her soon enough, a space where I could make sure that she was going to be okay. Right now, she had to be alone with her daughter, to say goodbye and to tell her whatever it was she wanted her to know. "You still need to deliver the placenta. It should come on its own in few minutes. I'm going to give you a few moments with your daughter. Just call if you need me. I'll be right outside." She briefly acknowledged my words with only a nod. "I'm so sorry, Samantha."

Tears washing her face, she stared down at the baby, caressing the fingers of one hand.

Slowly, I got up and headed for the door, wishing I could block out the sounds of sadness behind me. It wasn't just the baby Sam had lost; her fighting spirit had also faded from her gaze

I didn't know if it would ever be back.

The coffin wasn't much more than a small box I'd managed to craft out of a few pieces of wood, the lining a shirt I'd scrubbed with well water until it looked clean enough. It wasn't even the size of a shoebox, and I hated that it wasn't an actual, professionally made resting place for the baby.

Sam, taking the care only a mother could, washed the little girl and wrapped her in a soft handkerchief from one of the shops in the city. As we stood together, beside the large tree she'd picked to lay her child to rest under, I could see her knuckles turning white, the grasp she had on the box so strong it almost kept her hands from shaking.

Using a knife and a flat rock, I dug the deep grave, wanting her to have the comfort of knowing the tiny bundle wouldn't be pulled up and destroyed by animals. It wasn't hard, nor did it take very long, but it seemed like time was moving slower these days. The sun had risen high in the sky by the time we were ready to say goodbye.

"Does she have a name?" I asked softly, staring down at the hole with her.

"Rachel Dawn." Fresh tears fell as she closed her

eyes, hugging the makeshift box to her chest.

Sensing she wasn't ready to let go yet, I picked up the stone I'd been using and set to work carving her name into its surface. By the time I had it deeply etched, I could hear the crew gathering their things inside. Randall had given us most of yesterday and today to take care of this, which was a surprising show of compassion from him. We'd been joined by more men while we were here, which made me think it was probably more for his recruiting benefits that we'd stayed so long.

Finally, hesitantly, Sam knelt on the ground, kissing the top of her daughter's coffin, and bending over, she set it in the bottom of the hole. Shoulders shaking, she stayed there for a second, arm stretched out fully, her fingers still touching the box. It was hard not to kneel next to her and hold her, but I knew she needed to do this alone.

Her strength was fading in the fight against her demons—battles I couldn't finish for her, even if I wanted to. If she ever wanted to come out of this stronger than before—the kidnapping, beatings, losing her child—she had to pick herself up and find the power she'd let go along the way.

"Rachel Dawn," she said again, clearer, as she straightened. "Rachel Dawn O'Rourke. I'll make sure your father gets to come here and meet you." Grabbing a handful of dirt from the pile I'd made, she sprinkled it over the grave, grabbing another one as soon as she was finished. Eventually, she was sliding whole armfuls of the earth into the pit, burying her baby while she silently cried.

Toward the end, I helped her, packing the soil as

she moved it. A small mound appeared in its place, and I set the carved headstone at the head, shoving it into the ground deep enough to keep it from falling.

We sat there for a long time, observing at our handiwork, and a silent heat in the air made it feel as though I were suddenly suffocating. The need to get away from all this sorrow was overwhelming, but I wouldn't leave without her. When the sounds of the crew preparing for departure could no longer be ignored, Sam stood, turning her back on the gravesite, and headed toward the commotion.

The crew, which had started with around thirty men, had doubled in size once we hit land. It was unclear how many of the newcomers were Black Knights before joining, but every new face I saw had a brand somewhere on his person. A few of the familiar faces, which had not been members of the society previously, now sported the marks as well. Of the original party from our ship, it seemed that only three or four did not know they were the minority in a band of brothers.

Uncomfortably, I watched as they loaded our supplies and belongings into carts, ready to walk the rest of the way to Mexico City. They laughed and joked together, and there was an excitement floating around that I hadn't noticed before. At sea, the men were worried the Templars would catch us. Now, it appeared they all felt relaxed and ready for anything.

How many more recruits waited for us in the city? Judging from their carefree attitudes, it was obviously enough that the crew believed they could win the fight if the Templars arrived.

Glancing over at Sam, I saw her climbing onto

the front of one cart, sitting down carefully. She hadn't delivered a fully-grown child, but was still sore, understandably. The bleeding had slowed considerably, as well, allowing me to breathe a little easier on her behalf. It seemed that she would survive—just as she always had.

I couldn't help grimacing when an image of her husband, or how I pictured Sam's Tristan, flitted through my mind. As I made my way to her, set on driving the cart she'd picked, it reminded me that she had gotten along with his help.

"Snake Eyes!"

Turning, I frowned at Flanagan and his dark green shirt, his arm waving me over energetically. The woman I'd seen him with our first night here was hovering in the background, seeming unsure of what to do. Her demure, almost virginal looking, white dress was somewhat misleading, based on the thoroughly sexed appearance of the rest of her.

Grumbling under my breath, I changed course, making a beeline for him. They were standing under an archway, hidden halfway in shadows, giggling and whispering together as I came upon them.

"What?" I asked, trying to ignore the strong stench of alcohol wafting off the pair.

"This is Francesca," he told me, hiccupping slightly and laughing as he threw an arm around her shoulder.

"Pleasure," I responded dryly.

"She's comin' with us. Joining up! What say you to that?" His eyes narrowed and he stilled for a moment, like my answer was truly important for some reason.

"Uh . . ." Glancing between them, I caught a slight expression of determination I'd missed before, something that told me it was probably a very bad idea for her to come with us. "What does Captain Randall say about her coming?"

"He doesn't care." Flourishing his hand, Flanagan bent and picked up a bottle on the ground near his feet, draining what was left of it in two seconds flat. "Women always join the caravan to the city."

"Well, then I guess it's fine." Giving him a look of disgusted confusion, I moved to leave, surprised when he put a hand on my shoulder and yanked me back.

"Good. Great man." The words were slurred. "I need a man on my side in case old Capítan decides to come after her."

"Capítan?" Further lost on his meaning, I peered between them, trying to figure out just what it was he was asking I volunteer for.

Just then, a breeze ruffled through the area, and the sun shone down on us for a brief moment. A dazzling light emanated from Francesca's side, instantly drawing my attention to the gaudy ring on her finger. Putting the pieces together, I felt my stomach turn with anger and worry.

"You didn't!" I hissed, backing them further into the corner, making sure no one else was paying too much attention. "The captain of the guard's *wife*? Are you trying to get us all hung?"

"Relax, Snakey. I ain't done nothing. She's here of her own free will."

"It's true," she said with almost too much

sincerity, speaking to me for the first time. "I 'ate my husband! 'e beats me sometimes." She presented her cheek, showing me something non-existent, and then turned her big doe eyes on me, pleading silently.

"No offense, Madam," I replied coolly. "But if your husband catches you with us, he'll do more than deliver a beating to every single person here." Glancing over my shoulder, I felt a chill go through me at the sight of Sam. She was already in so much danger; being caught by law enforcement with pirates would brand her as one of us, and she could be hanged as well.

"How about a trade, then?" Flanagan asked, his own eyes on Sam when I glanced back at him. "You help me keep the men off my woman and I'll make sure they don't bother yours."

"Captain Randall has already told them to leave her alone," I answered, practically snarling.

"She was pregnant then," he pointed out. "She's not now. Half the men here weren't around when he said to leave her be, either."

His words seemed to zap right into me and I visibly recoiled, staring at him in horror. "She's just delivered a baby!" I said, aghast. "They're more civil than that."

But they weren't. Even as I said the words, I knew it was a lie—one I had to tell myself to keep me from turning around and gunning them all down, one by one. I would do it, too, if it would keep her safe. One against sixty didn't sound like great odds, though.

Glaring back, I saw the pirate's grin curling over his face, his arm around his prize once more. In the shadows, he seemed like some kind of devil, here to make a deal with me that would never work out in my favor.

"Deal," I told him roughly, moving away. I couldn't leave her alone for more than a few seconds, now that I'd realized what kinds of thoughts were being spread around.

"That's my man!" he laughed, the sound echoing off the stones behind me, replaying in my ears as I climbed onto the seat next to Sam and took the reins in my hands, slapping them across the backs of the horses tethered to our cart.

Calls of protest broke out as we began to move, both from men still trying to load the wagon and from those in front of us, scurrying to get out of the way. Further up, I met Randall's eyes as he watched, astride on his own steed, his gaze pointed and a frown on his lips. It took me a second to realize his scrutiny wasn't for me, but for those trying to catch up behind.

"Get on the road, you sea rats!" he roared, drawing a pistol and waving it over his head. "We have a treasure to find!"

The men cheered, along with the few women who were riding along, and everyone surged forward, suddenly ready to be gone.

"Are you okay?" I asked Sam, falling in line behind the captain as we rode out into the jungle-like terrain in front of us, the well-worn road wide and ready for our travels.

She didn't answer. Peering over, I felt a stab at my heart again, watching as she turned and stared in the direction of her daughter's grave until the church was long gone from view.

I should have been used to the heat, especially
after living in the desert for so long, but it felt like I
was drowning in my own sweat. Bugs buzzed in my
ears and around my face, causing me to swipe at the
little monsters every half-second as I pushed through
the foliage. The mountains we were currently camped
in lay just outside Mexico City, which meant our
week-long trip would soon be over, and I would be
able to go to the bathroom without worrying about
leaving Sam out in the open.

At the moment, Sam was with Flanagan and his
runaway, though, allowing me a moment to slip
away, further than I normally would have gone,
seeking silence from the never-ending party that had
been carrying on every night. Flanagan had kept his
promise, making sure both women were left alone,
except for those whom they wanted to see.

Having finished what I set out to do, I turned and
started back toward the loud, boisterous camp, when I
heard the voices.

"Did you think you would get away with it?"
Randall's voice was low and clear, the malice present
in it so strong that I froze, thinking for a moment that

he was talking to me.

"I knew there was a chance I wouldn't." The strange voice with a South African accent I hadn't really heard before, replied with ease, despite the hate in it that matched Randall's own.

There was another noise, one I'd come to recognize as a pistol whip, and a groan from the unknown man.

Carefully, I inched toward the sounds, eyes straining in the darkness, until I saw the group. They were in a clearing, the moonlight shining down on them just enough for me to make out features. Randall stood with a gun in his hand, flanked by two men—White and one of our newest to join the crew. In front of the captain, a man knelt with his hands tied behind his back. He was someone we had just picked up, his face not one I was familiar with.

"Who did you tell?" Randall asked calmly. "When did you send word that you'd joined us?"

The African man didn't respond, hanging his head in response, as if he were waiting to be shot.

"Tell me!" The shout rang out and I flinched, unprepared for the murderous tone he spat out.

Still, their captive did not respond, this time looking Randall in the eye and smiling. With a flash, Randall pointed the gun and shot him in the thigh, breathing heavily in anger as the man cried out and fell over, squirming in agony.

"Tell me, or so help me God, I will hang you from this tree and leave you here for the birds to peck at. No one will ever find you—any family you have will forever be tormented, wondering what became of you. Who knows how long it would take you to die?

You could starve for weeks, begging death to come for you."

"Or I could talk and you'd give me the mercy of a quick death now, is that it?" The man's chest was heaving, his eyes full of pain, but he'd managed to stop writhing. Taking a slow and steady breath, he rolled back onto his stomach, struggling to his knees. As he rose, he spat on the ground in front of Randall, laughing a crazy, half maniacal cry of pain. "You might as well shoot me. You're not getting anything from me."

Randall paused, his eyes narrowing as he studied the man, and then he turned to his companions. "Get them," he said simply, putting his gun in his belt.

The henchmen ran off, thankfully neither in my direction, and returned moments later, carrying some rope and a few other unidentified things. Randall stared around the clearing, seeming to pause slightly as he glanced over to where I was.

Breath catching, I froze, not knowing if he'd seen me lurking or not, and waited for him to move on.

"There." Pointing at the tree a few feet in front of the one I'd chosen to hide behind, he nodded to his men, going to untie the hands of their prisoner.

Moving slightly to get a better view of what was going on, I tried to think if there was anything I could do to help the man. I didn't know what he'd done, but it was clear Randall hadn't been very pleased about it. Showing myself would risk meeting the same fate. I wasn't ready to die, as horrible as that made me feel for not intervening.

"You're going to tie me to a tree and leave me?" The man scoffed, rubbing his wrists as Randall guided him along with the barrel of his gun.

"Does that seem like a fitting death for a Dog, White?" Randall asked.

I strained to hear exactly what they were saying. If the man was a Templar, did that mean others were close by? If they were, why weren't they coming to save him?

"No, it doesn't," White answered happily. "Too easy."

"I agree." Randall thought for a moment, staring at the Knight as he leaned against the tree. "I do believe he should have the holiest of executions."

Laughing, his men began stringing their ropes around the Templar's arms, tossing the ends over the branches above and hoisting him into the air. The African screamed as he was stretched, his back scraping up the trunk of the tree, his shirt ripping on the rough bark. It was a miracle that his arms didn't simply tear off, the strain he was bearing visible even in the dark. As soon as Randall motioned that the man had been raised high enough, the extra rope was tied securely around his ankles, pinning him to the tree in true crucifix fashion.

Horrified, I watched on, frozen to the spot in fear. They were leaving him here to either starve or suffocate to death, the position he was in making it difficult for him to get a full breath.

"The Order will come for me," he rasped out, staring down at the three men like some avenging angel who had been thwarted.

"Let them. You'll be dead before they ever find you." Randall pointed the gun up one more time, firing a single shot into the man's chest. From his gasping, it sounded like one of his lungs had been punctured, blood soaking the front of his shirt. The captain had aimed well, though; he wouldn't bleed out too quickly, allowing for the torturous death Randall had wanted him to suffer through.

Heart pounding, I turned from the scene, hurrying back toward the camp as fast as I could. They would be returning soon, and I didn't want to be discovered missing. The man was as good as dead anyway.

"Best to not end up the same," I muttered to myself. As the light from campfires appeared through the trees, I breathed easier, knowing that I would be safe from Randall's fury.

For a time, at least.

Coming into camp, I did my best to not look like I'd just seen a secret execution of a Templar Knight, arranging my features into a passive expression. Anyone who did notice my return quickly ignored me, their present company and conversations much more exciting than that of a man who had just returned from taking care of his needs.

"Is everything alright?" Sam asked as I sat by her. "You were gone a long time."

"Got the shits, Snake Eyes?" Flanagan asked, much less delicately.

However, the comment made Sam laugh and I stared at her in surprise. She hadn't truly made a sound like that in several weeks, and her eyes were shining with mirth. The sensation faded quickly, but it lightened my heart to see it.

"I'm fine," I told her, smiling. "I was looking at the stars, that's all."

I couldn't tell her about what I'd seen, and as I caught sight of the captain and his team returning to camp, I decided not to tell her at all. The knowledge would only trouble her, as it troubled me. The man hadn't said anything that really told me what I didn't already know, except for the fact that the Templars had managed to get a spy in our midst.

No, if I was going to tell her, I needed more information. It was obvious what I needed to do if I was going to get it, too.

Slowly, the camp died down around us, Sam and I curled up in the back of the unloaded wagon. Her breathing was even and deep when I slid from the makeshift bed, making sure she was covered well before I disappeared into the woods again.

Moving as quickly and quietly as possible, I checked my knife as I made the short hike to the clearing. As it began to show through the trees, I slowed, looking for any signs of movement, heart thundering in my chest.

It was almost a certainty that if I was caught, I would be strung up beside the mysterious man.

Breaking into the space, I gathered all of the courage and determination I had and walked up to the crucified stranger, clearing my throat to announce my presence.

He lifted his head a tiny bit, looking at me from under hooded eyelids, his breath rasping through his mouth like he was having an asthma attack.

"I know you don't have any reason to trust me," I whispered. "But I need to know if the other Templars are close. It's important—I've been waiting for over a month."

"I see your mark, Black Knight," he growled, his voice shallow and wet sounding. "And I'll not fall for any of your tricks."

"I'm not a Black Knight, I mean, I am, but—" Frustrated, I shook my head. Unable to help myself, I glanced around, checking to see if anyone had come back to make sure he was still alone. "I'm a spy. I didn't even know about all of this until a little over a month ago."

He regarded me coldly, disbelief in his eyes. "Go away," he finally said, dropping his chin to his chest again.

"Are the Templars coming for Samantha O'Rourke?" I was hissing now, agitated and fearful about being discovered.

"Of course they are." He laughed, sending himself into a coughing fit that sprayed tiny flecks of blood from his mouth. "Any man who doesn't think so is a fool. I'd run now if I were you—her husband isn't likely to take to the man who's been hovering around his wife with puppy dog eyes."

"What?" Damn it, was it that easy for *everyone* to see how I felt about her?

"Get out now," he said again. "Before it's too late."

"I can't." Stepping closer, I craned my neck to stare up at him. "I'm *like* her. From the same . . . time." I'd never told anyone else the truth before. It was as if the statement hung in the air, waiting to be challenged. Surprisingly, I found myself waiting for him to laugh again, to treat me as if I were crazy.

Instead, his eyes widened, studying me over with renewed interest. "Prove it," he gasped.

334

"And just how am I supposed to do that?" I asked crossly. Impatiently, I held the knife out, showing it to him. "Look, I saw what they did to you earlier. You're dying and there's nothing I can do to stop that, not without medicine and instruments from my own time, anyway." Hesitating, I found myself not wanting to say the next part.

"But you can stop my suffering now," he breathed, finishing the statement for me.

Seeming to consider for a moment, he closed his eyes, struggling to breathe, his body twitching in its held up state. Holding my own air, I waited for him to decide what to do.

"I'll tell you." Choking, he coughed again, his body trembling from fatigue and abuse. "I've nothing to lose either way. Black Knight or not, this is the truth—I never sent word that I'd joined up."

Not expecting that answer, I froze, staring at him with what must have been a dumb expression.

"There was no time," he explained. "I'd planned on sending word from the city, but was caught before I had a chance. I'm sorry; the Templars aren't anywhere nearby."

It became clear to me then just how much I'd been relying on the wonderful force of good Sam had been telling me about to burst in and save us. Every morning, I'd committed to protecting her for one more day, to loving her silently until her husband came to take her away from me. Now, to hear that they weren't going to be arriving any time soon, it was like being punched in the gut. How could I protect Sam from whatever Randall had planned for her? How could she continue to survive through her

335

losses if she didn't have the man she loved to help put her back together?

"Thank you," I told the man numbly, staring out over the grass of the clearing.

"Someone will send for them," he said in what I thought was his attempt at a comforting tone. "They will come."

Looking back at him, I inhaled deeply. "What's your name?"

"Ayo." He smiled grimly, nodding at me and the knife I held. "Make it quick, yes? I would like to leave this place sooner rather than later."

Silently agreeing, I stepped forward, reaching up toward his neck "Thank you, Ayo. May God be with you."

It was over quickly.

The warehouse in Mexico City wasn't far from the church I'd lived in and fled from. The thought made me anxious, like I owed it to Angelina and her father to go and apologize to them for leaving. Maybe I would have, if Sam hadn't been with me.

Since learning the help I'd thought was coming actually wasn't going to be here any time soon, I'd found I wanted to keep her with me even more. Flanagan wasn't cutting it in my mind, our deal be damned, and she wasn't safe with the group she'd been saddled with when Randall took her almost two months earlier. Every time someone looked at her, I had to fight the urge to reach for a weapon, reminding myself that we'd made it this far without her getting hurt even more. There was a definite difference in the sexual attention she received since she'd lost the baby, as disgusting as that was to the both of us, but the men kept their distance, thankfully.

"Do you think we could get any food in here?" she asked me, glancing around at the tiny room we'd claimed when we arrived. It had a few chairs and what appeared to be an old, ratty bed in one corner, but that was it. The wooden door faced the hallway, the large open space that most everyone else occupied located just beyond that.

"If we're lucky. I don't know if the new people brought anything with them." By my count, there had been another ten men waiting for us when we arrived, playing cards on a barrel with a slab of wood placed over the top of it, an oil lamp illuminating the proceedings.

Randall hadn't cared to share with us how long we would be staying. Most of everyone had set up around the new crewmembers for the night—with only a few of the other couples searching out tiny spaces and rooms for privacy. I knew what it must look like, me taking Sam in here alone, but it was the only way I felt I could really protect her.

"Are you okay, Mark?"

Her soft voice brought me out of my thoughts and I glanced over at her, sitting in one of the chairs by the back wall, the bed to her right side. Worry creased her brow as she watched me.

"Something has been bothering you. What is it?"

"Nothing." How could I tell her that rescue wasn't imminent? That we were stuck with pirates and murderers for the foreseeable future?

Balking, I thought of the man I'd killed, the first one since I'd cried over my past in her arms. Should I tell her that I was still the same, no-good-murderer as before? I'd only committed the crime at Ayo's agreement, but it still felt like a dark deed.

What if I'd been able to save him? A punctured lung and a few gunshots didn't have to be fatal. If Randall had found out I'd cut him down and doctored him, though . . .

338

"I'm fine, really." Forcing a smile, I leaned against the wall, listening to the racket of games and gambling in the main room.

She didn't believe me, but dropped the subject, staring at her hands in her lap.

"Hey." Softening some, guilt coursed through me for shutting her out again. "How are you? You're the one going through everything."

"I'm okay, I think." There was a note of the despair I'd seen in her as she held Rachel to her chest and she sniffed, rubbing her nose with the side of her hand. "I'm not really bleeding anymore. I thought I would for a few weeks."

"You probably lost a lot of the lining while you were spotting and then miscarrying. If you count that, it's been three weeks total. That's not a bad time. You'll probably lose a little here and there for a few more."

"Did they teach you that at paramedic school?" Laughing, she gazed up at me and sighed.

"Actually, yes, they did," I replied in mock defensiveness.

"Thank you, Mark." The sincerity in her voice caught me off guard and I gaped, surprised that she would say it with so much feeling.

"Of course. You know I wouldn't let anything happen to you." Pushing away from the wall, I walked over to the bed and flopped down on it, immediately regretting my decision as dust clouded the air.

Chuckling, she waved her hand in front of her face, smiling at me in a way that made my heart stop. "Really, though. You've saved my life more than once, and even in our own time when you kept me from going into the Pit when it collapsed. I don't know how I'll ever repay you."

"Don't," I said immediately, sitting and staring at her. "Don't act like you owe me anything. You *lived*—that's all I wanted. I don't need anything more than to know you're in the world and okay."

If there had been no Tristan, no pirate hostage situation, no anything but us, it would've been easy to kiss her then. Her face was so sweet and soft, her eyes wide as she watched me, only a few inches away. My hands ached to hold her, to cuddle her against my chest and run my fingers through her hair. Drying quickly at the thought, like I was a man dying of thirst, my lips tingled with the image of her mouth on mine. Heart racing, I felt myself leaning in, slowly, as if every millimeter was killing me.

Jerking back into the present, I blinked, and then looking away, I stood so quickly she jumped.

"What is it?" she asked in alarm.

Glancing at her, I tried to focus on the things that would help me remember what our situation was. Her black shirt was dirty and torn on one shoulder from getting caught on a branch as we rode out of the mountains. The pants she was wearing belonged to Flanagan, who had been more than happy to tell everyone I'd let her get in his breeches. The shoes I'd bought for her in Veracruz were muddied from our trek as well, tied to her feet with little care for whether or not they stayed on.

She was a prisoner, a captive among this crew.
Married.
Not mine.

"I thought I heard something outside," I lied, moving toward the door. "I'm going to go check it out. Will you be okay?"

"I'll stay right here," she said by way of reply, eyes still wide as she stared at me.

All but fleeing the room, I practically threw myself out into the hall, gulping down the smoke heavy air as I pressed myself against the wall. I'd come so close to doing it, to touching her in a way she wouldn't want, and it scared me. Where was my self-control? What the hell had I been thinking?

The way she had looked at me—had she felt it, too? The draw, the need to be touched and loved by someone? It was as if her gaze had burned into me, uncovering all of my secrets and declaring they didn't matter to her.

Swallowing hard, I knocked my head against the wall once, frustrated. I needed real fresh air, not the smoky crap everyone was inhaling here.

Moving down the hall, I ignored everything I passed, pushing through the doors and into the night.

"You all right?"

Whipping around, I stopped short in front of Flanagan, the way he was tying his pants suggesting he'd come out to use the bathroom.

"Yeah. Could you keep an eye on Samantha for a while? I need a break."

Something in my face must have convinced him it was dire, because he nodded without saying anything, staring at me quizzically. "She in the room?"

"Yes." Turning away, I started walking down the street, needing to go somewhere that she wasn't,

341

fleeing the woman who made my life worth living so she could live her own in peace.

"Where are you going?" Flanagan called after me.

"Church," I yelled over my shoulder, saying the first thing that came to mind.

Striding down the roads I'd once known so well, I made my way to the chapel, wondering if Angelica and her father still lived and worked there. What would I say to them if we ran into each other? In that second, it didn't matter, so long as I could get my head on straight again before I returned to the warehouse. Randall would probably be pissed when he found out I was gone, but that wasn't important.

A few moments later, I found myself outside the stone and stained glass building, staring up at the bell I'd helped ring so many times. The garden was still growing on one side; I could smell the flowers Angelica had loved so much through the wall that protected the space from the street. Despite it being after dark, the doors were open, as they had so often been, the place of worship beckoning for me to come in and sit a while.

Jogging up the steps, I ran a hand through my hair and straightened my shirt, suddenly wanting to appear somewhat presentable. As I came through the door, I noticed I was the only one here, a few candles lit by the entrance as prayers from those who came before me. The benches at the back were empty and waiting, so I sat down, breathing heavily as I folded my hands and did what I always did at church—I thanked any god or gods who might be listening and asked for help with my current situation.

After a while, I became content to just sit and stare at my old home, smiling as I relived the good memories I had of the place. This had been my most peaceful time in the past, besides when I lived with the Apache.

Shouting outside drew my attention a while later and I frowning as I tried to hear what was being hollered.

"Capítan! Capítan!"

Flanagan's voice reached my ears and I shot to my feet, turning to the doors in horror. He was outside, running like his life depended on it, smoke billowing into the air behind him as an unknown building burned.

"Sam!"

I was sprinting before my mind could even comprehend what was happening, racing toward her, praying I would make it in time. If the Captain of the Guard found her there with all of those pirates, she would be thrown into prison, hanged as a thief even. She'd said she worked as a buccaneer before; did she have a warrant out for her arrest? Cursing myself, I sped up, feet slapping against the pavement.

The warehouse came into view, shining like a beacon. The roof was on fire and mass panic had ensued on the ground. Men darted every direction, some openly fighting in the streets. Apparently, the Capítan had brought his entire guard with him.

Shoving past one pair of fighters, I made a beeline for the door, punching someone in the nose as they tried to grab me. There was a satisfying crunch and blood ran under my knuckles, but I didn't have time to stop and admire my handiwork.

Inside was even more chaotic than what I'd just witness in the streets. It was a full on war, swords clanging as blood flew in every direction. Screams of dying men met my ears, part of the ceiling suddenly collapsing in and smothering three or four people underneath.

Panicked, I dove into the hall, rushing toward Sam's and my room. Someone shouted behind me, the sounds of pursuit reaching my ears, and I threw myself into the bedchamber, slamming the door shut.

"Mark!"

She was standing against the back wall, a pointed chair leg in her hands. Apparently, she'd bashed her seat to pieces so she could defend herself.

"We have to get out of here, now," I told her urgently. "It's the Captain of the Guard, if he finds you here, you'll be tried as a pirate."

Glancing around, I cursed myself. I'd picked this room because there was only one way in. Any second now, whoever had followed me down here would burst through and take us.

"What do we do?" she asked, seeming to come to the same conclusion.

Filled with the fear of having to watch her die, I grabbed her hand. This was the only moment we were going to have before it was all over.

"I love you, Sammy."

Bending down, I kissed her full on the mouth, feeling her freeze under me, but not even caring. Kissing her was like drinking sunlight and whiskey. I felt I was falling through time all over again, melting against her. She was everything I needed and wanted, and I had to let her know before we were torn apart.

Her hands fisted against me, pushing me away, and I felt my heart break. It was like an explosion in my chest, an ending to everything I'd ever wanted. The moment was over; she wouldn't allow any more.

The world around me popped back into focus, the sounds of battle and screaming filling my ears again.

Wait, that was *Sam* screaming.

Bewildered, I looked down at her hands, still grabbing my chest, pulling on my shirt, her words incoherent. Blood washed her skin and there was fear in her eyes as she looked at me.

Confused, I fell to my knees, not understanding why she was trying to hold me up. Words wouldn't form in my mouth and I felt my consciousness sliding away into the darkness, the phrase at the tip of my tongue.

I've been shot.

My chest felt like it had been blown to bits. I guess that was partially true.

Groaning, I rolled my head back, grimacing at the pain I felt in my ribs. Someone had tied me to a chair, my ankles secured to the front legs and my hands bound behind me. The position made me feel like I was being cut in half from the pressure on my lungs.

There was also a bag over my head.

Apparently, Capítan planned on getting some revenge before sending us to trial.

"What is your name?" The man's voice had a Spanish accent and was full of cold business.

"Snake Eyes," I rasped, finding that my voice sounded like a dying dog by comparison. "Could you at least take the bag off my head? I'm not going anywhere."

A pause followed, then footsteps, my eyes greeting the blinding light of the early morning sun shining through the window as the cover was torn off. Blinking rapidly, I squinted, trying to make out my companions. In the end, I settled on one calculation.

One me.

Five them.

The room was small and brown, with only the one opening. I assumed there was a door somewhere, but couldn't see it. The figures crowded the room, standing almost shoulder-to-shoulder. It felt a little like an alien abduction scene from a movie, to be honest.

Wincing from the brightness, I nodded, touching my chin to my chest. "Thank you."

"Snake Eyes. Is that your given name?" the Spanish man asked again.

"No. It's . . . uh . . ." Scrambling for a fake identity, I kicked myself for getting caught. Of course, if some record book somewhere showed that a man named Snake Eyes had been hanged for piracy, it probably wouldn't make anyone familiar with Mark Bell pause. "Ben," I finally answered. "Ben Lowe."

"Well, Señor Lowe. You stand to be convicted of piracy. How do you plead?"

Another thought grabbed hold of me and I straightened, wincing as my chest stretched with me. "Where's Sammy? Is she okay?"

A hiss from one of the men in the rear of the room answered and I glared at him, trying to see his face but he was hidden behind the light.

"How do you plead?" Spanish Man's tone demanded I answer him, but right then I was feeling rebellious. What did I have to lose, anyway?

"Where is Samantha?" I asked, louder.

"Shut up!" It was the same man who replied earlier. This time he moved closer as he spoke, someone putting out a hand to restrain him.

"Sam?" I yelled. "Sam!"

347

Angry Man moved forward and punched me in the jaw, making me see stars and yelp at the contact. He stepped away quickly, as if he knew he'd crossed some line, and I opened and closed my mouth, trying to make sure my jaw wasn't broken.

"Order!" Spanish Man yelled, slamming his fist against the wall. "There will be order in this court!"

"Court?" Confused, I tried to glance between the five of them, my head still spinning. "This doesn't look like any court to me." Where was the crowd? Pirates were always tried and executed publicly, to discourage others from taking up the profession.

"Señor Lowe," Spanish Man said, growing more impatient by the second. "Do you plead guilty to piracy?"

"Yes." I ground the answer out, knowing I would be convicted either way. "Under the flag of Captain Thomas Randall. You didn't happen to catch him, did you?"

All of the men in the room seemed to growl at that, their forms shifting dangerously in the light. I took that to mean no and laughed slightly, closing my eyes against the headache that was forming.

"Do you know where Thomas Randall is?" Spanish Man asked tightly.

"You didn't get him? That sucks." My body was threatening to pass out again and I let my head fall back, ignoring the outcry of fresh pain from my gunshot wound. They obviously didn't want to listen to anything I had to say that wasn't what they wanted to hear. Unfortunately, I had no idea where Thomas Randall was now.

The men conferred quietly with each other and I

suddenly hoped that maybe I would just be shot and have it over with. That sounded better than torture, which I was beginning to think was a viable option for these guys. Remembering Sam, though, I sat up, trying to lean forward and look at them.

"Is Samantha okay? I don't mind answering your questions, but I'm not saying anything else until I know where she is."

"Ye'll not be seeing her any more," Angry Man spat. "Why would she want to, after what ye tried to do?"

"Huh?"

"You also stand accused of rape, Señor Lowe," Spanish Man added, sounding particularly happy about it.

"What?" Outraged, I tried to shove my chair across the floor, wanting to stand up. "I would never!"

"One of our men walked in on you trying to force yourself on the lady," Spanish Man informed me smoothly. "It was clear that she was a prisoner of the crew. You would argue with an eye witness?"

Aghast, I stared at them with an open mouth, trying to make out the faces that would accuse me of such a horrible thing.

"I wasn't forcing myself on her! I love her!"

Angry Man jumped forward at that, grabbing me by the collar of my shirt and yanking me off the floor, chair and all. For the first time, I saw his face; complete with the green eyes and hair that Sam had told me about so many times.

"That's *my wife* ye're talking about," Tristan O'Rourke growled at me. "And if I were ye, I'd watch what ye say about her. Samantha is *mine*, no matter what ye claim."

He was truly terrifying, suddenly making me see how he could have done all the things she swore he had. If I were Thomas Randall, I would have stayed as far away from him as possible—which was probably why my captain was nowhere to be found at the moment.

Tristan had a fierceness about him that practically shouted how he could kill anyone he wanted, and right now, that was me.

His face was covered with a short beard, eyes burning with rage, and I knew it was only his self-control that kept me alive at this moment.

"You're him," I said in awe, feeling both affronted and relieved at the same time. "Tristan."

"Put him down, O'Rourke," Spanish Man said, sighing unhappily.

Glowering, Tristan did as he was asked, stepping away from me.

"Señor Lowe—"

"My name is Mark," I said, interrupting him. "And there's been a misunderstanding."

"A misunderstanding?" Tristan scoffed, folding his arms as he looked down at me.

"Yes. I'm not who you think I am." Licking my lips, I tried to gather my thoughts coherently enough to explain before I passed out again.

"And who would that be?" His tone was belittling and infuriating, causing me to take a deep breath before I continued.

"A Black Knight," I responded, knowing they would have already seen the brand on my arm. "But I promise, that's not what I am. I'm like you—just not a Templar."

"Like us?" Tristan leaned forward, smiling evilly. "Ye're no better than the hair on a dog's ass."

Biting my tongue, I glared at him. Had he not talked to Sam? Hadn't she told him who I was? "I was protecting Sam until you came," I started, only to be interrupted by his laughter.

"I'm the one who saw ye kissin' her, man. That's not what I would call protection."

The other men in the room just let him goad me. It was like they weren't even there, his words biting and harsh as he spoke to me. As insulted as I felt and so incredibly angry, I pressed on, my voice only shaking slightly.

"I knew her from before she was taken," I forced out. "We were friends."

"Ye're a liar!" Tristan yelled, getting in my face again. His patience for me was not very large, it would seem. "There's hardly been a day that she hasn't been with me since ye took her and carried her here! Who knows what ye did to her, aye? Tell me, so I can make sure the same happens to ye." His eyes were burning dangerously, his hands clenching and releasing over and over, chest heaving as he stared at me, hate and disgust written across every feature. "Ye say ye know her, huh? How many times did ye beat her and rape her before ye felt comfortable saying that? Did ye pass her around like some toy, doing whatever ye wished? Ye love her? Ye don't even know her, ye no good, pig shit, son of a bitch!"

I was done with this crap. Sam may have loved the jerk, but I sure didn't.

"I've known her longer than you've even known she existed," I spat out, leaning forward the best I could. "Before she drowned herself in the Treasure Pit and ended up stuck with you as her dirty, pirate, bastard of a husband!"

A shockwave coursed through the room and he visibly drew away, eyes wide and stunned. Smiling in satisfaction, I huffed a breath out of my nose and frowned.

Don't do it, I told myself, fighting down the urge to poke the bear one more time. *Don't do it!*

"And you know what?" I heard myself saying, my lips curling into a grin, as I looked him in the eye. "I quite liked kissing her. She's got very soft lips."

His forehead met with mine in a sharp crack and I crumpled, watching the sun quickly fade away as the darkness took me into its cold embrace.

Samantha O'Rourke

The bed beneath me was soft and warm, calling for me to sink further into the dreamless sleep I'd been experiencing. Sighing, I rolled over, relishing in the feel of the silky shift I wore, the fabric brushing my skin like angel fingers.

Shift?

Freezing, I tried to think of what was going on. Where was I? What had happened last night? Then, like floodgates bursting open, the memories of the raid on the warehouse rushed through my mind, the image of Mark shot and bleeding under my hands standing out the strongest. He'd pulled me over with him when he fell, and I'd knocked my head on the ground, which was the last thing I remembered.

Opening my eyes hesitantly, I looked around the space, surprised to find the room nicely decorated and homey. Four posters and a canopy sat around me, a soft breeze blowing in from the open widow, the wooden shutters cracked a tiny bit to let the light in. Flowing curtains swayed gently, cocooning all around me. There was indeed a shift on my person, causing me some alarm as I thought of who might've changed my clothes.

Searching my memory, I saw his face, the smoking pistol still clutched in his hand. There was dismay in his features, his form rushing toward me in that tiny room.

"Tristan," I uttered breathlessly sitting up and placing my feet on the cool, wooden floor. Suddenly, this place and my appearance made sense. He was here—he had finally come! Somewhere in this building, my husband was taking care of things, waiting for me to wake up and find him.

Standing, I swayed slightly, putting a hand to my sore head. Nothing was going to stop me from marching out and locating the man I'd been yearning for, though.

A sound at the entrance made me pause. The handle turned, the door sliding quietly across the floor, and he materialized in front of me, as if simply thinking of him had summoned him to my presence.

He was wearing black boots and pants, along with a white shirt, the neck untied and hanging open. Blood was stained across his chest, dry and dull in the morning light. A gun belt was still draped across one shoulder, his sword in the sheath at his waist. His hair, which had always seemed so nice and smooth to me, look frazzled, like he'd run his hands through it so many times that it now stood on end no matter what. His beard was short, but full; he hadn't shaved in a while, it would seem.

All of this was secondary to his eyes, the green color shining with unshed tears as he looked at me, full of pain and anguish. Relief rolled off him as well, hitting me like a wall, and I could just see the past terror he'd been living in while we were apart.

"Samantha." His voice cracked, lips trembling, and he shut the door, locking it behind himself.

Bursting into tears, I threw myself into his arms, holding him so tightly I worried I might've been suffocating him. Huge, gasping sobs overtook me, his hands pressed into my back, holding me off the ground as his face buried into the crook of my neck. His own cries were muted, soaking my slip, muffled against me.

"I was so worried ye were dead," he said, fingers digging into me, refusing to let me move even an inch from him.

It didn't matter; I never wanted to be anywhere else ever again.

"When I came back and ye were gone—" He broke off, a strangled sort of cry coming from his throat before he fell silent, simply holding me.

"I thought you might be dead," I whispered. "You didn't come back and no one would tell me what had happened. The day I decided to try and find out was the day they took me."

"I walked into the house two days later." Gently, he set me down, brushing his fingers over my cheek as he looked at me. "Ye can't imagine what it was like, coming back to that. No one knew what had happened. I wanted to run them all through myself. How could something of that magnitude have occurred and no one realized?" A few tears still ran down his face, wetting his beard.

"I came as fast as I could, Sam, I swear. I'm so sorry I wasn't there to protect ye. Can ye ever forgive me?"

This brought fresh tears to my eyes and I buried my face in his chest, not even caring about the gore he still wore.

Instantly, the image of Mark, covered in blood, popped into my mind and I gasped, pulling away. "Where's Mark? Is he okay?"

Unexpectedly, Tristan's face grew dark, his expression turning dangerous as he stiffened. "He's alive, if that's what ye mean. Lomas is still holding him for questioning. There were . . . complications during his first interrogation."

"Interrogation? Complications?" Confused, I stared into his eyes, not understanding the emotions I was seeing there.

"I knocked him out," he said crisply, but his shoulders hunched slightly, like a child who knew they were about to be scolded. "The man provoked me," he added quickly, a flicker of annoyance passing over his features. "But . . . I did the same to him first. I'm sorry, Sam. I don't trust the bastard one bit."

"Whoa." Staring at him seriously, I took his hands in mine. "Bastard?"

"What else am I supposed to call a man who claims to love my wife, who I saw kissing ye? He's lucky I didn't shoot him again on the spot. If we hadn't needed information, I would have happily taken care of him." Tristan growled slightly, the fire returning to his eyes, and then he sighed, looking up at the ceiling.

"I wasn't kissing him," I replied, minimally irritated. "He caught me off guard. I had no idea he felt . . ." Letting my words trail off, I moved closer and wrapped my arms around his waist. "It didn't mean anything, not to me. I'm sure he knows that, too."

"As soon as he identified himself as another time traveler, Lomas ordered him into a safe room. Ye can see him later, even if I might not like it." It wasn't much of an acknowledgment of the situation, but it was something.

Exhaling, I took a moment to bask in his embrace once more, feeling like I was in a dream. We were finally together again! I'd always known he would come, but the waiting had nearly killed me.

"What happened in London, Tristan?" Curious, I stared at him, smiling in encouragement.

"There was a coup," he replied, letting a long breath pass between his lips slowly. "One of the crew had been working for the Black Knights the entire time; he was an assistant to the Grand Master and knew everything. Some of the other men on board had joined the ranks with him and they all attacked before we even made landfall. By the time we got to London, we had men who desperately needed a doctor and Randall wasn't where our information said he'd be."

"Was one of the scouts secretly a Black Knight?" My stomach turned at the thought. How could there be so many of them among us and we not know? How were they communicating without getting caught?

"No. The rat had left before we could get there. It took two weeks just for us to recover enough to sail home, once we'd searched everywhere possible for the scoundrels."

"And the traitors you caught?"

"They won't be a problem any longer."

Frowning, I knew what that meant. They were all dead, either killed during the coup or executed afterward. The Templars were insistent that the entire dark faction be destroyed.

"How are ye feeling?" he asked me, pulling me close once more and resting his chin on the top of my head as he changed the subject. "Sick? Is the baby doing well?"

Stilling, I felt my insides go cold with horror and dread. Of course he wouldn't know—I'd been too early for a real baby bump to show. Mark would have been too busy defending himself to tell anyone that he'd helped me through a miscarriage. Tristan stood before me now, a man happy to have his wife and child safe in his arms, and I was going to have to tell him that his daughter hadn't made it.

"Can we sit?" My voice sounded high and trembling.

"Of course!" Quickly, he led me to the bed, smiling as he joined me, grasping my fingers in his own.

How did I even start? What words could I use to explain how everything had happened? I wasn't even ready to revisit the moment myself. What if I broke down and couldn't do it? Gulping, I cleared my throat and looked at him, frowning.

"Tristan, I—" Tears welled in my eyes and I closed them, shaking my head, trying to shut out the anguish that fought to overtake me again. "Sorry," I gasped, sniffling through the whole mess crashing around inside me.

"Oh, no." The phrase was almost whispered, his

hand tightening around mine. "Please, lass, tell me the babe is okay?"

"I lost it," I said, opening my eyes and staring at him. "I don't know if it was something I did, or Randall and his men. I'm so sorry, Tristan. Truly. I wish—I don't know—I can't . . ."

Crying, I let him pull me into his embrace, his hand smoothing my hair as I wept against him once more. Not a word came from him, but I could feel the slight tremor to his touch, murmuring to me of the pain he felt.

"And ye're okay?" he finally asked, his voice husky. "Ye've recovered, I mean? There's nothing to worry about with ye?"

"I'm doing alright," I confirmed. "Or at least as well as I can, given the circumstances."

He sighed, relaxing some, and I took a deep breath, trying to steady myself.

"She was beautiful. I named her Rachel Dawn."

"After my mother?" He sounded surprised, the grief in his voice doubling. I knew it wasn't because he was upset over the name—he was touched.

"And mine."

We fell silent, simply content with holding each other for a time, allowing our combined presence to strengthen and uplift us. When my tears finally stopped falling, he laid us back across the mattress, his arm around my shoulders, holding me close to his heart.

"What did she look like?" he asked quietly, turning to watch me. "A normal child, but smaller?"

"Kind of."

We talked about her for hours, how she had

looked, what it felt like to hold her in my hand and cradle her. I described everything with the greatest detail I could muster, from the events leading up to the delivery to her tiny grave under the trees by the church. He traced the skin of my hands, outlining her shape as I explained it, exclaiming at how tiny she had been.

"And Mark helped you with all of it?" He sounded suspicious, making me wonder just what had been said between them during their earlier meeting.

"Every single thing." Smiling, I pressed against him, wishing there was a way to be even closer than we already were. I'd missed him so much, had been so scared I wouldn't see him. To have him with me now was everything I could have wanted, even if I'd had to tell him about Rachel.

My stomach growled unexpectedly and he chuckled, kissing my forehead. "Are ye hungry?"

"A little. I can wait, though. I want to spend more time with just you." In response, my stomach growled once more, louder this time, as if in protest.

"Hang on," he ordered, sliding away and standing up. "I'll have someone bring something in."

Going to the door, he cracked it open, muttering softly to someone on the other side. I hadn't realized we were being guarded, feeling completely at home with him.

"They'll have something here soon."

"We have a guard?" I asked, not able to help my curiosity.

"Yes, but let's not talk about that right now. I have a surprise for ye. It's coming up with the food."

"A surprise?" Smiling lightly, I fought the urge

to laugh. What could he have thought to bring me when he left to chase down my kidnappers? I didn't need gifts or surprises. Being done with Randall was good enough for me.

There was a knock at the door and he opened it wide. The tray of food appeared first, followed by . . .

"Abella!" Jumping to my feet, I ran to her, hugging her tightly just as Tristan took the meal from her. "You're alive!"

"*Oui*," she responded, laughing. Her arms encircled me as well, warm and welcoming. "Monsieur O'Rourke found me."

"She'd pulled the dresses out of the wardrobe and bandaged herself up," he said, staring at her with respect.

"I would have died if he'd come any later. Samantha, I'm so glad that we finally found you. I've been so worried."

"How are you even here?" I asked, stepping back and staring at her in awe. "You would have had to leave with almost no medical care."

"I wouldn't let them go without me," she said truthfully. "Not after the way you sacrificed yourself to try and help me. That reminds me, Monsieur O'Rourke?"

He smiled at her, raising an eyebrow at her formalness. "Yes?"

"Mark Bell is awake. Captain Lomas had me examine his wounds. He's going to be all right, but they want you to come to talk with him. Samantha, too, if you feel up to it."

As enticing as visiting Mark sounded, I frowned at Tristan. It didn't feel like we'd had enough time

361

together. I wasn't ready to leave this room and go back to the work we needed to finish. If I'd had my way, we would have stayed here forever, just holding each other.

"I think we'll stay here a while longer," Tristan answered, seeming to catch on to my feelings. The expression in his eyes said he felt much of the same. "I'll send word when we're on our way."

"Then I will leave you alone to enjoy your meal." Curtsying, Abella grinned happily and quickly left, closing us into solitude once more.

"Come, sit down. Ye look like ye're starving." Holding the tray and taking my hand with the other, he led me to the bed, sitting me down with the order not to move.

"I love you." Gazing up at him, it felt as though my heart might burst from happiness. Everything was broken and wrong, except for him. As long as Tristan was at my side, I could do anything.

His features softened and he rejoined me, taking my face in his hands. "And I love ye." Brushing his lips against mine softly, he seemed to put all the tenderness he possessed into the touch, holding me as if I were china that might break.

Finally, I felt the cracks that had been forming in my heart start to heal.

Mark grimaced as I hugged him, emitting a breathy laugh over my worry. "I'm fine. A bit roughed up, but it'll be good."

"You've been shot," I argued. "In the chest! It's a miracle that you're even alive."

"The bullet was stopped by one of his ribs," Abella said behind me. "They had a doctor look at it when they first brought him over. It really is a miracle."

"See!" Smiling at him, relief coursed through me. A broken rib was easily survived and much preferable to a punctured lung or gouged heart. He would be sore and need time to heal completely, but the only real risk he faced was infection, which was something he knew how to avoid.

"You had a doctor look at me?" he asked Tristan, glancing past me to my husband for the first time. Surprise tinged his features, along with disbelief.

"I couldn't have ye dyin' before ye told us what ye knew." Tristan's voice was somewhat strained and I was astonished at his distrustful expression.

"Thank you." Mark sounded equally hesitant. "I don't think I'm ready to die, just yet."

Turning to watch Mark, I frowned at the marks on his face. His jaw was bruised, as well as his forehead. Tristan admitted he'd knocked him out again, but it looked like more than just that. What passed between these two while I wasn't there?

"Captain Lomas asked that we let him know as soon as you were awake," Abella piped up again. "Shall I go get him now?"

"Uh . . ." Mark trailed off, meeting my stare. "Is there any way Sam and I could talk alone for a moment, first?"

"Sure," I replied easily, smiling gently at him.

"No," Tristan said at the same time. Stepping to my side, he folded his arms, his jaw set in a way that made me think he wasn't going to change his mind.

"Why not?"

He examined me, gaze softening some at the genuine curiosity in my voice. Pausing, his eyes darted toward Mark, but then he sighed, releasing his stance. "I just got ye back, lass. It was awful enough, leaving ye alone while I helped take care of the hostages. Now that I have ye again, I don't want to be without ye if I don't have to."

"It probably doesn't help that I told him I love you, either." There was some distant laughter in Mark's eyes. "I wouldn't want to have my wife alone with anyone who had done that. That's what I wanted to speak to you about—apologize about, anyway."

"Apologize?" These two were full of curve balls today.

"I'm sorry for the way that I told you, for how it happened." He flinched in pain, moving away to sit down, leaving me beside my husband.

Truth be told, he had caught me so off guard with his declaration, I hadn't even known what to do or say. Preferably, I would have liked to never mention that moment again. Such a conversation was sure to hurt his feelings and, even though I knew he would want the truth to be out for everyone to see, I didn't want to have to tell him there was no chance of us ever being together.

"I've always known what my place in this was," he said, smiling as if he could read my mind. "You love your husband. Anyone with eyes can see the two of you want and need nothing but each other. Telling you how I felt and acting on it was never part of the plan. Every day, I woke up resolved to keep you safe and alive for him." He nodded at Tristan then, who was watching him with a narrow stare and hard-set lips.

"But ye did tell her," Tristan replied, a dangerous air about him. "And acted on it."

"In my defense, I thought we were both about to be tried and hanged as pirates." Mark glanced pleadingly at me then, his eyes begging me to listen to what he had to say. "I have been running since the day they told me you drowned on Oak Isle, to Florida, Texas, and even back in time. The Apache let me go, Mexico City allowed me to flee, and when Thomas Randall took my ship, he let me run right into his crew and his plans. I got tired of slipping away. When I thought of you, convicted and dead, I didn't want to hide my feelings any more. Your husband wasn't coming. All I wanted was for someone to know how I really felt before I disappeared completely."

He shrugged, resting against the back of his

chair, hands folded in his lap. "I shouldn't have said anything. I'm sorry for the position I put you in and the hardship I caused for your family."

I wanted to say there had been no hardship, but looking over at Tristan, I could see there was. Mark's apology seemed to have gotten to him the most, his brows furrowed as he stared at my friend. I couldn't read what emotions he felt, or guess at his thoughts, but it was clear that he hadn't liked what he heard.

"You don't need to run anymore," Abella offered kindly in the absence of my reply. "You are with people who will take care of you and treat you as one of their own. I know Samantha—I know Tristan, too—and they would not want you to flee now. Stay. Let us help you."

She had picked up on another meaning I'd missed in Mark's words; he was offering to leave. Staying with us was either too painful for him, or destructive to my marriage.

"Don't go," I said suddenly. "Please."

"Why? I can't do anything to help. I shouldn't even be in this time to begin with. Who knows what I've changed over the past ten years?" He laughed, humorlessly, and shook his head. "I'm better off on my own, where I can make sure I don't screw up anything important."

Still not knowing what to say to him, feeling awkward over the whole affair, I huffed, trying to think of a way to convince him not to go off on his own. It was true that there would never be anything romantic between us, but he was still my friend. I wanted him to be kept safe.

"Mark is a historian," I told Tristan, who was

opening his mouth in confusion. "A pirate historian, to be specific. He knows more about what's going to happen on the oceans over the next one hundred years than anyone else I've ever met."

"Which is exactly why I should stay away from you and your pirate husband," Mark argued. "I'd already found a record of you when I was researching Randall's shipwreck. The future is changing because we're here and I'm not okay with that!"

"What did ye say?" Tristan butted in, stepping forward in an excited way.

Mark, startled, stared at him like a deer in headlights. "We're changing the future," he started.

"Not that." Cutting him off, Tristan waved to Abella, who promptly left the room without another word. "Randall's shipwreck?"

Eyes widening, the man from the future gazed at the man from the past, and he nodded. "Of course. The ship that sent her down was a Templar vessel."

Quickly, Mark relayed his expedition in the Gulf of Mexico to Tristan, detailing the boat and Mission, as well as the records he'd discovered at the site and in other parts of the world. "I know where he is," Mark spoke, astounded. "I know where Randall is going."

"That's good to hear." Captain Lomas stepped through the door, Abella behind him, and entwined his fingers behind his back. "All traces of the Black Knights have vanished from the city and there is no trail to follow. We estimate that around fifty men managed to flee the coup at the warehouse. I've been readying the men to follow them to the north on foot. We can catch them within a few days, I'm sure of it."

"They aren't going north on land," Mark explained, shaking his head as he stood up. "They're on their way to Veracruz and their ship."

"We have to leave now," Tristan continued for him, turning to the captain and putting up a united front with Mark. "It's already been almost two days. If they're smart, they've been running through the night and taking limited breaks. They'll reach their ship in another day, at least."

Lomas looked between all of us, thinking hard. "*Sí*," he said finally. "We'll leave within the hour."

The Order was amazing when it was on a mission. Each member of the party had a job, and they did it with ease and finesse that Randall's crew lacked. Where the Black Knights made up for their shortcomings with violence, it was like the Templars had none, merely achieving anything they set out to do.

The pace of our trip back to Veracruz was fast. Everyone was always on the lookout for Randall and his men, but what Tristan had said appeared to be true; they had already reached their ship and sailed away. So it was, after three and a half days of practically non-stop trekking across the lower end of North America, we reached the Templar ship and set sail toward the tiny Mission Mark assured everyone was waiting for our arrival.

Unlike the warship I'd last traveled on with the

Order, this boat was medium sized and fast, the bow breaking through the water with hardly any effort. I watched the skies with a hopeful heart and pleading prayer whenever I was on deck. It was now hurricane season and we couldn't afford for a storm to blow in and slow us down. If the worst were to happen, though, and we were caught in the gale, I felt fairly confident we would hold together enough to make it through.

Hopefully.

"We're only two days behind them, with any luck." Tristan wrapped his arms around me from behind as we stood at the bow of the boat. "The wind is good. We'll catch them."

"What happens when we do?"

Mark had said there would be a fight. Randall's vessel would be burned to the decks and sink, leaving almost no trace of anything for more than three hundred years. However, fire was the Black Knight's calling card. Who was to say that it wouldn't be our craft Mark would work on, confusing his data and naming the wrong crew as the losers in this battle?

Unfortunately, Mark and I seemed to be the only people who thought that might be a possibility. Everyone else took what he shared as pure truth, especially after everything I'd said about the Treasure Pit had turned out to be right.

"What if I'm wrong?" he'd said to me, his face hidden in the darkness of the crew quarters where we were all camped out. "What if I'm leading these men to their deaths?"

"We won't know until we get there," I replied, unhelpfully. "Try not to think about it."

369

"Samantha?" Tristan's voice brought me back to the present, worry in his tone. "Are ye okay?"

"Yeah, I'm fine. Just thinking about where we're going and what Mark said." Sighing, I reclined my head against his shoulder, staring out over the water. Blue reflected down from above, not a cloud in sight.

"Mark."

Tristan hadn't exactly been mean to him, but he wasn't really welcoming Mark into the ranks. Sometimes they would share a glance and I knew there was a struggle in my husband to accept that he wasn't a danger or threat to us. Sometimes, I wondered how it must appear to him, the two of us, time travelers, sitting and talking together. Was I still the same Sam he'd left in Paris? Did I look different to him?

He had no comparison for Mark, though. He hadn't seen him when he was ten years younger, laughing and carefree as he tried to solve a mystery that had intrigued him for most of his life. All he saw now was an aging man, with crow's feet that appeared whenever he smiled and some flecks of gray in his beard.

It was still strange, to see my friend aged so much in the short time since I'd been away. It wasn't short for him, though. Ten whole years had passed in his life, completely changing him from the man I'd known into the fierce presence he was now. There was a reason no one had bothered me on Randall's ship—Mark didn't seem like someone you would want to mess with.

"Do you hate him?" I asked Tristan softly, curious.

"Hate him? No." He sighed, putting his chin on my head, like he so often did. "I think I perhaps envy him some, or even feel jealous, but I don't hate the man."

"Jealous? Why?"

"He gives ye something that I can't—a companion from yer own time. No matter how much ye tell me and explain it, I'll never know what it's really like there. He does. He's also held my only child."

"And you'll never get to," I finished for him, sadly.

There hadn't been time to stop and show him Rachel's grave. In all honesty, I hadn't wanted to when we were close by. I wanted him to meet her without the burden of his duties to the Order hanging over his head, or thoughts of having to catch Randall. We both needed the time to sit beside her and mourn, and our current situation didn't allow for that.

"I'll hold her in my heart, always."

His words brought tears to my eyes and I spun in his arms, resting my forehead on his chest. The wound was so achingly fresh for the both of us, but we had each other to heal with.

That was when the cry came from up above, the sound that would draw every man onto the deck, anxious to see what would happen next. It was a vibration that seemed to echo around us, filling me with anticipation and fear.

"Sails!"

Mark held the spyglass up to his eye, studying the ship in front of us carefully. It seemed as if everyone was waiting with bated breath for him to say whether or not it was the vessel we wanted. Tristan stood beside him, observing the small spec in the distance with his naked eye.

"Is it his?" he asked Mark, leaning toward him in an attempt to keep their conversation more private.

Captain Lomas, who hovered on the other side of the group in his Blue uniform, tilted his head as well, listening for the answer.

The men conferred for a moment, whispering among themselves. Anxiously, I anticipated the verdict, pondering why Mark didn't just tell everyone the Black Knights were only a couple miles from us. I recognized the flag they flew on the back of the ship—the laughing skull with blank, white eyes. Even from this distance, I could just barely see it, my memory helping me fill in the gaps the space between us created.

"Is it them?" Abella asked next to me, whispering as well.

Checking to make sure everyone standing right

next to us was occupied, I looked across the deck. "Yes," I uttered back, barely moving my lips.

Nodding, she fell silent, biting her bottom lip on the inside of her mouth. Her hands betrayed her nerves, though, twisting in the front of her brown dress as she stared out with the rest of the crew, waiting. It was no wonder she would be worried; the last time she'd had an encounter with Thomas Randall, she'd been shot.

How much did she know about the Order, I deliberated? She'd never really acted like she knew everything, but she didn't seem to be in the dark, either. I assumed that Tristan had taken her to the Temple with him for help, and she was here on this ship. We made no effort to hide what it was we were going after, or what was at stake should we lose. No, she had to be aware of who she was with. By now, I was sure she knew I was from the future, if she hadn't already figured that out on her own somehow.

"It's them," Mark finally said, loud enough for everyone to hear.

The crew bristled with excitement and agitation, some moving to grab their weapons and ready for battle.

"We won't be pursuing them just yet," Captain Lomas yelled over them.

"What? Why?" The shout came from one of the men who had gone to arms, his pistol already half loaded in his hands.

"The time isn't right," Lomas explained. "The wind is good for us, which means it's good for them. Señor Bell has told us they have oars to help their cause, as well. If we give chase now, they could easily lose us."

"We want to maintain the element of surprise," Tristan added, continuing on at the Captain's approval. "Right now, they think we've gone after them on land. The few men we caught and questioned told us that Randall ordered all those who survived to head north, out of the city."

"But they changed direction and headed back to sea after re-grouping." Mark stepped forward, the glass still in his hands as he looked down at it. After a moment, he raised his head, appearing to stare at each person in turn as he began again. "I worked for Thomas Randall for over a year. His specialty is in deceit, not weapons or running. He will do whatever it takes to get what he wants, even if it means losing time or men.

"I have seen what remains of a ship at the bottom of the ocean. One of us will be taken under in battle. I know that thinking I have knowledge like that is hard for some of you to believe."

It wasn't. The Templars understood there was truth in all things. Even as he said the words, I watched the men wave him off. They would trust whatever he told them about the future, especially after I vouched for him.

"We're not to the place where the fight is going to happen." Mark visibly swallowed, pulling back for a moment and then went on. "It's important that we don't change the future. If I don't come study the wreck, I won't make it to this point in time. There will have been no reason for me to learn the things that helped me decide what to do here. Everything will change, maybe even the world as I know it. We have to wait until we're in the bay."

Captain Lomas nodded in agreement, pursing his lips, and then looked out over deck, eyeing the sails overhead. "Tie them down," he ordered, motioning up with his hands. "We can't keep the element of surprise if they see us coming. We need to back away."

There was only a second of hesitation, the crew appearing to think over everything they'd just been told, before they burst into a flurry of action. Riggers scaled the ropes like rats, speeding up the masts and tying the sails down. Almost instantaneously, I felt our progress in the water halt, our speed dropping to practically nothing. In the distance, the pirate ship sailed on, seemingly unaware of us hunting right behind it.

Leaving Abella on the top deck, I moved to follow Tristan, who was going below for some reason. I'd lost Mark in the movements of the crew, thinking he must have gone into the Captain's Cabin with Lomas to discuss how things should happen further. As I came down the stairs, though, I heard him calling to Tristan. Apparently, he was already down there as well.

Curious, I paused on the steps, wondering if I should go back up and leave them be, or if it was okay to let myself in on the conversation. It soon became clear that this wasn't something I needed to be a part of, but my feelings got the better of me. Sitting on the step, I listened intently, not wanting to miss a thing.

"Thank you for backing me up," Mark was saying. "I didn't think Captain Lomas was going to listen to me."

"Lomas likes to think he's the only one who knows what's going on," Tristan responded, laughing. "Sometimes, he needs the extra push."

"Really, though." It sounded like someone had stepped forward, or away, but the movement stopped at Mark's words. "Thank you. I know you've had a hard time with me being here. I don't blame you, at all. It means a lot to me that you would help me even with everything going on."

"I appreciate that ye can see why I wouldn't want ye around," Tristan returned amicably. "But I don't blame ye for loving Samantha. Just like ye understand where I am on the matter, I understand where ye are."

"You do?" He sounded cautious and wary, the words more doubtful than believing.

In response, Tristan chuckled again, sighing. "I love her, too, aye? I know what it is to look at her and want her more than anything in the world. Ye can't help it, even if ye have to fight it. Loving her is like breathing; it's easy to do without even thinking, but if ye ever try to stop, ye've started down a path that will quickly kill ye."

"You've never watched her love another man in your place."

Mark talked so quietly I almost didn't even hear him. The sadness of his voice spoke to me in a way the words hadn't, though. He was hurting, hurting because of me, and I would never be able to do anything to fix it for him. Perhaps that was why it pained him so much, because he knew there would never be anyone but Tristan for me.

"No, I haven't." The compassion in Tristan's

voice surprised me, but it made my heart overflow with love for him. He could have shut Mark out entirely, but here he was, not only talking about it, but being kind to him as well. "And for that, I do not envy ye."

The two of them paused in their conversation, making me wish I'd also sat somewhere that I could have seen what was going on.

"I guess I'll get going," Mark finally said, his tone somewhat strained.

"Wait." Tristan sounded hesitant now, but there was a desire to his speech that I recognized immediately. He had something he wanted to say, but didn't know how to put it into words. When that happened between us, we always managed to figure out what it was together. Now, I wondered if Mark would understand whatever it was that was so important.

"Thank you," Tristan started quietly, his tone gaining some strength. "For taking care of her. She told me everything you did. I—" Faltering, he let silence stretch between them again. After a long moment, he cleared his throat. "Thank you for loving her and taking care of her how I would have. I couldn't be there for her. I'm glad that you were the one to do it."

I could hear it all in his voice, the fear and anger he'd shared with me, the mourning over his daughter, the hate towards Randall and what he'd done, and his uncertainty toward Mark. He wasn't usually pressed to find words to express himself, but I felt he'd managed it this time.

"You're welcome. Thank you for coming when

you did." Mark sounded somewhat emotional as well, and I smiled, happy that they were working everything out.

"I'm not sorry I shot ye, though," Tristan added gruffly.

"I would expect nothing less than for you to shoot anyone you saw kissing your wife," Mark replied seriously.

And, just like that, the spell was broken. The men laughed, a relief that even I could feel. They headed in the same direction, talking about plans for when we arrived in the bay, and the conversation drifted away from me.

Standing, I went back up to the top deck, looking for the ship on the horizon. It had already disappeared and I wondered exactly how long it would be before we were back together, reprising our battle on Oak Isle more than a year earlier.

"Do you need anything, Samantha?"

Turning, I smiled at Abella, nodding for her to join me. "I think it's safe to say you're not my maid anymore," I told her, laughing. "You don't need to wait on me."

"Truthfully? I don't know what else to do." She giggled, tucking a strand of her long hair behind an ear. "You don't need my assistance getting dressed anymore, since you insist on wearing pants while on board. The cook doesn't need help. The crew does all the cleaning as it's assigned to them. I don't know anything about how to sail. Even as we get ready to track down this ship and fight, all I can think about is how I don't know anything to defend myself. Captain Lomas says we should be at battle in two days' time and I feel like a sitting duck, just waiting for someone to pick me off and be done with it."

"You've been helping Mark," I offered, trying to make her feel better. "Making sure his wound is okay and all that. I'm sure he appreciates it."

"The only reason I know anything about taking care of gunshot wounds is because I had one myself." Grinning, she blushed slightly, shaking her head. "Mine wasn't anywhere near as bad as his, either. The shot grazed me along one side. It bled badly, but nothing else. Most of all, I was just weak from shock and blood loss."

Those sounded like Tristan's words coming out of her mouth, more of an explanation to herself as to how she had survived the ordeal.

"I just want to be useful," she continued, staring at the water as it lapped softly against the hull of the ship. "What am I if I can't be worth something to someone?"

"You're worth a lot to me," I told her seriously. "Maid or not. You're my friend. You matter."

"Friend to a time traveler." She smiled crookedly, looking back at me. There was a light in her eyes and a determination that flared up in that second, making my own eyes widen. "Will you teach me how to fight, Sam? All this time, I kept thinking that I lived for some reason. I lived through my father, through your abduction. God must be saving me for something and I want to be ready for whatever it is. I want—" She blushed even harder, clearing her throat, her form straightening. "I want to be like you."

Her words made me feel unworthy of her praise, but I was honored at the same time. No one had ever

told me they wanted to be like me before. It was . . .
surreal.

"I have to be honest, Abella. A lot of what I've
been through—and the resulting outcomes—have
been luck. I don't feel like I'm the great person some
have made me out to be. But, I can help you learn
how to fight, if you really want to. It's a good idea,
especially when you think about where we're
headed."

She made her agreement clear, biting the inside
of her lip again. "When can we start?"

"I'll ask Tristan when he thinks he can help. His
input will be nice to have." *Especially since I'm rusty
when it comes to sword fighting*, I added silently. The
last time I'd really handled a blade was on Oak Isle,
fighting Randall in the Pit.

Practically beaming, she curtseyed, turning to go.
"I'd better change," she explained. "I don't think a
dress is proper attire for a combat lesson. Thank you,
Sam. From the bottom of my heart."

Watching as she left, I smiled, seeing Tristan
approaching out of the corner of my eye. "Abella
wants us to teach her how to fight," I told him,
leaning back against his chest. "For some reason, she
wants to be more like me."

"She already is like you," he stated, not surprised
by the request in the slightest.

"And how do you know that?"

"When she found out I was leaving with Lomas
and his crew to come after you, she insisted she go
along. It was such a persuasive argument that even
Lomas fought for her to travel. I had never seen
anything like it, except from you."

"So you agreed to let her join because you saw me in her?" Chuckling, I turned around to look at him, taking his hand in mine.

"I never would have let her come if I hadn't."

Impatiently, I waited for the long boat that had been sent out an hour before to return. Our destination was just ahead, hidden behind a rocky shoreline that kept us out of view of our enemies. Right now, somewhere in a small rowboat, Mark and Tristan were with three other men, surveying the bay for the ship we hoped was there. Every now and then, an irrational thought would pop into my mind—what if they were caught? What if the Black Knights weren't here?

The presence of Abella helped to steady me more than ever as she stood beside me, watching the waters. Her two days of training wouldn't have prepared her in any way for what was about to happen, but she carried a small sword all the same, a pistol on her other hip. After a few minutes, she would shift, as if she were uncomfortable in the brown pants I'd given her, but other than that, she showed no sign of worry.

"They'll be back soon," she assured me, smiling tightly. "And then this whole nightmare will be over."

Biting back a contrary response, I nodded, thinking it best to not speak of Randall and his ability to escape when it should have been impossible. This was either a single battle in a long war, or the end of an epidemic. Only time would tell.

A few moments later, I saw the small craft, rowing steadily toward us from around the rocks. A breath I didn't know I'd been holding let loose and my shoulders relaxed, my hand leaving the hilt of my sword.

As the men climbed aboard, I found myself eagerly waiting with the rest of the crew to find out what they'd learned.

"The ship is there," Mark announced at last, grinning. "And she's empty, save around five men."

There was no cheer, everyone wanting to stay quiet while in hiding, but a shot of energy coursed over everyone, bringing smiles to their faces.

"Are you sure?" Captain Lomas looked at the group with a hard expression, clearly wanting detailed statistics on what was going on.

"I climbed the side of the ship and looked myself," Tristan replied easily. "There's hardly anyone there, and only missionaries on shore."

"The rest must have moved on to the mountains," Lomas said, taking in the information. "Those left behind will be guards until they return. The fight should be easy enough. Once the vessel is taken care of, we can unload our provisions and follow after the rest."

"It won't be easy," I piped up. "Especially now that it's monsoon season."

"There will be a lot of rain, dust storms, and other weather anomalies to be wary of," Mark agreed. "The Superstitions are at least a month away on foot.

If we want to catch up before they reach the treasure, we're going to have to be smart. It's very easy to lose men in the desert."

"Then we'll count ourselves lucky that we have two people who have lived there to get us through." Tristan smiled as he spoke, obviously feeling confident about the endeavor. It was no wonder; when we'd had our fight on Oak Isle, there was no time window to stop Randall from getting in. He'd been there for weeks already, digging down to the treasure. Now, there was a chance we would stop them before they even got to their destination. With the Black Knights out of the way, the Order could safely reclaim the treasure they had lost, maybe even leaving it where it was, if it was guarded enough.

"O'Rourke," Lomas spoke, turning to him. "What do you say? Shall we sail in now and get this taken care of?"

"I think so," he agreed. "Surprise is still ours. There's no need to wait for nightfall to attack five men."

Lomas smirked, drawing his sword and moving to everyone else. "Man your stations!" he yelled, heading toward the helm.

Men darted every which way, the sails billowing out above us, catching the air and pulling us forward with a sudden tug. Grabbing onto the side railing, Abella and I watched, the wind blowing our hair back from our faces as we came around the rocks.

And that was when all hell promptly broke loose.

It was an ambush; the Black Knights were already aware we had arrived. Cannons fired from the enemy ship, barely missing us. On shore, more guns suddenly appeared, shooting as we made what had now become a suicide run down the shore. One blast hit our center mast, cracking the top off, the highest of our sails swinging down and hanging precariously over our heads.

"Get away from the edge!" Tristan screamed, ducking as another shot flew over our heads and landed in the water on the other side of us.

Throwing myself on top of Abella, we hit the deck as another cannon took out the banister, inches from where we'd just been standing.

"Fire!" Lomas shrieked the order, desperately trying to turn the ship around, but the loss of our topsail had slowed us down by so much that we were hardly even moving. As he shouted out orders to fight back, another cannon blasted from the pirate ship, which was now headed toward us, and it hit true; the helm burst into pieces, flying into Lomas's face and knocking him back.

The world seemed to slow down around me as I watched, bits of wood and rope flying in every direction as we were hit, over and over again. Lomas lay unconscious or dead, blood dripping from his left ear. Tristan was stumbling down the stairs, narrowly avoiding being hit. Abella was screeching underneath me, terror in her eyes as I tried to shield her with my body. Mark was nowhere to be seen, but I could hear him shouting among the other men below deck.

Finally, I saw someone raise a gun, aim, and fire at the shore, smiling in anxious panic as the shot apparently hit whomever he'd been targeting. Another rifle fired behind me, answered by cannon blast from below.

Grabbing Abella, I hauled her to her feet, pulling her along beside me. "Load the firearms for them!" I yelled at her over the din, pointing to the men who were trying to get shots off on the men on shore.

Not needing any prodding, she picked up the nearest rifle and set to work, flinching as a small round returned from the nearby shore.

Glancing over the edge, I tried to count how many cannons were lined up on the beach. There weren't many, thankfully. Beside me, one of our snipers fired, missing his target by a long shot. Swearing, he reached back for another weapon, grabbing it from Abella and aiming again. Even though his shot should have hit where it was supposed to, he still missed; the guns weren't accurate like they would be in the future. Short of standing right in front of your target, there was no way you could guarantee what you were aiming at would be hit.

"We need people on the beach," I said suddenly, drawing the shooters and Abella's attention. "We need people on the beach!" I repeated, motioning to the eight cannons spaced across the sand.

Another mortar fired from below us, hitting the side of the enemy ship with a resounding crack. The hole it left behind was enough to give hope to anyone—we hadn't lost this battle yet.

Tristan ran up the stairs then, seeming to have noticed the same thing I had. Without a second thought, he flung himself into the water, swimming hard.

"Cover him!" I ordered the man next to me. "There!"

One of the pirates on the beach had pulled out his pistol and was pointing it right at Tristan. There was probably a good thirty feet between them, but I wasn't willing to take that risk.

Neither was the sniper. Pointing and firing, he shot the ground in front of Tristan's would-be attacker, causing him to jump back in alarm. Our other shooter shot at him as well, missing terribly, but stopping the man who had been coming to help the Black Knight.

Watching the men on the beach draw their guns, it occurred to me that Tristan wouldn't be able to fight off all of them by himself. Just as I vaulted myself over the edge of the ship, I heard Mark's cry of alarm and dismay. Now wasn't the time to play it safe, though, and I'd fought pirates before.

Swimming steadily, I trusted that the men on the ship would watch my back for me, trying to ignore the cannon that fired from the Black Knight's ship and landed in the water ten feet away. Heading in a different direction than my husband, I made landfall within minutes, gasping for air and drawing my sword out. The powder in my gun was useless now, but I grabbed it by the butt as well, thoroughly intending to club someone over the head with it.

The first man I reached had come to the waterline to meet me, a knife in his hand and three teeth missing from the front of his smile. Dodging his first thrust, I swiped my sword across his abdomen, not stopping for even a second as he fell to his knees behind me. A gunshot whizzed past my head, striking the next man in the neck and I silently thanked whoever it was that had shot him for me.

387

The Mission was a hundred yards away down the shoreline, free of cannons and full of missionaries. They would have supplies and weapons to defend themselves with and I intended to claim the building as a strong point for the match. Finishing off the last man who had been working the cannon in front of me, I made a dash for the cover of the building, bursting through the doors and sliding to an instant halt.

Carnage covered every inch inside the building, blood splattered over the walls. The missionaries were all dead, the gruesome sight of their bodies piled in the courtyard. It was unclear how long they'd been deceased, but I was sure it was recent. Tristan had said they were alive when he scouted—

"Hello, Samantha."

Skin prickling, I turned, my gaze falling on Thomas Randall who was clothed in the robes of a priest, his hair combed back and tied smoothly. A smile that made my blood run cold covered his face. It was impossible to ignore the touch of blood on his fingers as he held a hand out to me.

"So nice of you to join me. I was worried I would have to go out and get you myself."

"Stay away from me," I warned, brandishing my sword.

"How sweet," he replied, laughing. "You still think you can beat me."

Icy disdain filled my voice. "I can damn well try." Glaring, I hoped the frantic pounding of my heart wouldn't give away how scared I was.

"If you insist." Shrugging, he threw open the robe around his shoulders, revealing his normal clothes underneath, splattered and stained with gore. The material flew out behind him like a cape as he drew his sword, sidestepping and beginning to circle me.

Gulping, I watched him, waiting for any signs of him lunging, palms sweating as he continued to sneer at me, his eyes carrying a darkness that made me want to vomit.

Shooting forward, he brought up his sword, swiping it past my face as I leaned away, barely missing my cheek. Tristan had done something similar in our lesson the day before, though, and I easily shifted my weight, ducking under his arm and stabbing up toward his stomach.

Parrying my blow, Randall shoved me in return, spinning around, his blade flashing in the light as he yanked it down, barely missing my back. The sword cut into the dirt, kicking up dust as I tried to return the attack.

Easily deflecting me again, he laughed, striding forward and shoving me down to the ground with his free hand. "You're a little slow, Sam," he noted. "Been a while since you were in a fight?"

Growling, I scrambled to my feet, thrusting my blade toward him. Every time I thought I had the advantage, he somehow came out on top, shoving me to the ground again. After my face met dirt for the fifth time, I suddenly realized what he was doing.

"You're playing with me!" Huffing, I stepped away, trying to catch my breath as I looked at him. He didn't even seem bothered, let alone gasping for air like I was. Our fight was costing him no effort whatsoever.

"I thought you might enjoy a chance at believing you could win." His voice was smooth and full of humor, eyes shining with mirth as he spoke. "It's so much more fun when your prey doesn't give up immediately."

Infuriated, I charged him, screaming, the end of my cutlass pointed right at his heart. Anger flashed across his face and he slammed his sword up, deflecting me. This time, however, he turned the blade sharply, pulling my only weapon from my hand and throwing it across the room like it was nothing. Grabbing the front of my shirt, he threw me into the brick wall, smashing my head against it and holding me there.

"Don't move," he ordered, the sound of a gun cocking ringing in my ears. "It would be a shame to kill you, but I will do it."

"Listen very carefully," Randall said quietly, his breath hot on my neck and the barrel of the gun pressed against the side of my head. "I'm going to let you go now. If you fight, I will shoot you. If you scream or try to run, I will shoot you. If you do anything other than what I say, I will shoot you. Understand?"

"I'm not stupid," I growled, resisting the urge to struggle.

"That's a good girl." Slowly, he released my head, stepping away far enough for me to turn around, but still holding the gun to my temple. "Now, I want you to look out that window there." Motioning to the opening on the other side of the courtyard, he smiled, waiting for me to comply.

Nose twitching in anger, I slowly made my way to where he'd indicated, imagining all the while how I could get the gun away from him as he followed me with it. As soon as the bay came into view, though, I became preoccupied with what was going on outside.

"What do you see?" he prompted, sounding lazy and bored.

"The two ships are still fighting," I told him,

trying to see if either had gained any headway over the other. "It looks like yours might be falling behind."

That was somewhat of an overstatement. The two parties were still firing on each other, the blue sky awash with flying cannon balls and smoke from the weapons. The water in the bay was sloshing between the two, rocking back and forth as if it were trying to choose which one to take under. The Templar ship was firing everything she had, breaking apart the other ship slowly, but surely. However, the Black Knights were still fighting hard, dealing just as much damage, though they had fewer cannons.

"What about the beach?"

Searching across the sand, I felt my stomach tighten at the sight of Tristan, bleeding and still fighting his way through the men around the last cannon. It looked like he and a few other allies had managed to gain control of the land, stopping the firing on the Templar ship from there and giving them the edge they needed to fight back fully. Gratitude for the men who had come to his aid filled me.

"You're out of cannons," I announced triumphantly. "Tristan's stopped your men there, too."

"Wonderful." He sounded like he meant it, the word rolling off his tongue with ease and clarity.

Confused, I turned my head slightly, my gaze meeting that of the end of the gun.

"Look at the ships again," he ordered, jerking the barrel toward the window. "Use the spyglass on the sill."

Glancing down, I frowned at the object. Had he

been here watching before? Either way, I grabbed the metallic tube and stretched it open, peering through to the bay again.

There was some kind of commotion on the Black Knight's ship. There were people fighting on board there; someone had swum over and attacked them on their own ship. Gasping, I yanked the glass away from my face, only to lift it again, feeling sick.

Abella, sopping wet and bleeding from a cut on her face, brandished her sword, a cry I couldn't hear leaving her lips as she brought the sword down on the man in front of her. By her side, Mark fought another, ruthless disgust written on his face. His blade ran through his victim, sliding in and out with ease. Turning, he charged a man who had been running for Abella, tackling him.

Faltering, Abella stumbled over something, falling out of sight. The man she attacked raised his blade high, slamming it down with an impressive amount of force.

Frozen, I stared with wide eyes, not believing what I was seeing. Mark resurfaced, fighting the same man, who he had in a headlock, but he hadn't noticed Abella yet. Heartbroken, I waited for him to see that she had been killed, to do something to avenge her.

Suddenly, she popped into my view, her shirt torn and bloody, but she was alive. Exclaiming in surprise, I watched as she faced her attacker, holding her sword at the ready.

"What do you see?" Randall asked, some agitation in his voice. He poked the gun at my head and I flinched.

"The men on your ship are dying. In just a

moment, the ones firing the cannons will have to stop to fight. Your ship is going to sink." Relief coursed through me. Mark had been right—it was the Black Knight ship that went down, not ours. Everyone was still alive, too, thankfully.

"Good." Sounding very pleased, Randall grabbed my shirt, yanking me away from the window. "Come on."

The look on his face said it all. Shocked, I stumbled, yelping as he whacked me in the of the head with the pistol.

"You want them to sink your ship and kill everyone," I gasped through the pain. "You planned this entire thing!"

He didn't answer, merely smiling at me and shoving me through a door, into the hallway behind it.

"Why? Why would you sacrifice men you need to get out of this mess? You can't honestly think you can win all on your own!"

Stopping, he pressed the gun against my head again. "Be a dear and shut up," he said coldly. "Outside, now."

Doing as he asked, I clutched the spyglass to my chest, wondering if I could use it to hit him or something. There would be more space to maneuver once we were outside and away from the building. Quickly, I put together a plan, praying I would have luck on my side.

Hurrying out, I glanced at the bay, trying to hide the fact that I was looking for some place open enough to try and wrestle him. He was heading for a break in the trees, ignoring everything around him.

Sensing that it was now or never, I tensed, ready to jump into action.

A loud explosion in the bay caught me off guard and I spun around, gulping at the fiery cloud reaching high into the sky. Randall's ship was on fire, sails and masts crumbling under the heat, the entire thing engulfed in flames. Raising the looking-glass, I felt my knees giving out as I watched Abella stumble across the deck, screaming, and jump into the water. Desperately, I searched for Mark, not seeing him anywhere. Finally, I found him, floundering in the water, Abella coming over to help keep him afloat. His face was red and burned, but other than that, he seemed okay.

"That was unexpected," Randall mused, watching the spectacle as well. "But, if anything, fire is a good way for the ship to go out. Come on." Grabbing the only weapon I had, he snapped it closed and put it in his pocket. "Into the trees, now."

"Where are you taking me?" I asked evenly, obeying as the gun came in view of my face once more.

"Right now? Nowhere."

We disappeared into the cover of the foliage on the shore, slipping into the forest that stretched out in front of us. After walking a short distance, Randall finally stopped. "Look up," he ordered.

There was a black bag suspended from the tree, tied to a high branch. Staring at it, I felt my fear increase a hundred-fold. He had definitely planned everything that had happened today.

And we had followed right into it.

"Climb up and get it," he told me, shoving me

into the trunk. "If you so much as think of falling on me while you're up there, I'll shoot you."

"What if I already thought about it?" I grumbled, grabbing onto a low branch and hoisting myself up. My hands stung from one of the falls I'd had during our sword fight, but the climbing was otherwise easy. Glancing to the ground, I saw he had moved out of the way. I wouldn't be able to do anything short of throw something at him. How would I escape if I fell out of a tree after being shot?

Retrieving the bag, I scurried down the tree and tossed it at his feet, frowning at the barrel still pointed in my direction.

"Open it." He kicked it toward me, smiling in what I normally would have considered a pleasant manner.

Picking the satchel up, I looked inside, almost surprised to see the cloth and ropes it held. Of course, he had made me hike out here and get my own bindings.

"Turn around and put your hands behind your back." Stepping forward, he waited for me to do as he said, quickly pulling out a length of rope and tying my hands painfully together once I had. "Now, open your mouth." He didn't really pause for me to listen on that one, shoving a wad of cloth in my face, choking me with it as he pushed it past my teeth. Another strip was tied around my head, covering the entire lower half of my face. Finally, he pulled the last piece of binding out, knotting it around my waist before he wrapped it around his arm.

If I'd been able to talk, I would have said something scathing about being led around on a leash.

"I can't have you running off, now can I?" Grinning, he picked up the now un-cocked gun and put it in his belt, tugging me sharply toward him. "Be very quiet. We have listening to do."

Slowly, we moved through the trees, stopping just out of sight of the beach.

"Sam!" Tristan was yelling my name, panicked and fierce. "Samantha!"

"She's not in the Mission." Mark's voice reached me. "Something is wrong. All of the missionaries are dead. This is not what was supposed to happen here!"

"I don't care about your damn future," Tristan spat. "Sam is gone! Randall's taken her—again." There was a hint of defeat in his tone and I felt my heart drop.

Unconsciously, I pulled on the rope that held me, causing Randall to hiss under his breath. Pulling the gun out, he pointed it at me, sending the clear message he was in control.

Falling still, I listened hard to the faraway conversation.

"You don't understand," Mark was saying. "The journal I read was written by a missionary. Now he'll never share that you were here. I'll never read it and . . . all of this will have never happened." He sounded puzzled, and I could easily see his face of concentration in my mind.

"We can fix the future later,' Tristan argued. "Right now we need to get Sam. Have the crew search one more time."

"We've searched the entire area," Mark replied. "There's no use in looking again, not when we know where he's headed."

So that was why we'd taken our walk out into the woods. We were staying away from parties that would be scanning the beach. We'd also gone in a direction they hadn't anticipated. Unless they widened their perimeter, they'd never see our tracks.

"What are ye doing?" Tristan finally asked, frustrated.

"The journal," Mark spoke, rubbing his head in frustration. "I think . . . I think maybe I wrote it. It had so much information and descriptions we normally wouldn't have found. I think maybe this all did happen and I covered it up. I changed the future on purpose, so that I would find out all of the things I needed to know."

Wishing Randall hadn't heard so much, I glanced over at my captor, grimacing.

"Snake Eyes is from the future." He breathed the phrase out slowly, quietly, and his eyes narrowed. "Of course. And you've known him in both times, haven't you? That's why he was so protective."

It was a tiny bit satisfying, knowing that we'd managed to fool him over at least one thing. However, now that he knew, I was pretty sure he planned on making us pay dearly for lying to him.

"That can wait," Tristan growled. "We have to leave now if we want to catch them. Ye said yerself, this trip could be more than a month long. I don't know about ye, but I'm not waiting another month to make sure my wife is alive."

"I agree," Mark said instantly. "We should leave now. Abella is tending to Lomas; she can tell him where we've gone when he wakes up."

"Then grab yer things," Tristan ordered. "I'll not

wait another second to find them."

Breathing heavily, I tried to listen for any other sounds from them, but they were gone. Tristan and Mark were heading off to save me.

But they were going the wrong way.

We followed them. After the first couple days, I began to see Randall's wisdom in doing so. He was still getting where he wanted to go, but without being chased from behind. Tristan and Mark were so concerned with rescuing me they wouldn't be backtracking. He was free to go along without always looking over his shoulder.

Every night, he would ungag me and feed me a little food, always leaving my hands bound and the rope around my waist. After two weeks, I was beginning to feel like I had no skin left in either place.

"Why are you doing this?" I asked, watching as he mixed together a stew that he'd made from a rabbit he caught earlier in the day.

"Are you ever going to ask me for specifics, or will you remain vague and without answers for the entire trip?" Smiling slyly at me, he turned his attention to his small fire and pot, our tiny bag of essentials on the ground beside him. It had been tied on another tree along the way, which he had retrieved himself.

Surprised, I thought over what he'd said. I hadn't expected him to reply at all, especially since he'd ignored the question every night up to now.

"Why do you want the treasure that's hidden here?" I asked, wondering if I'd phrased it the way he wanted.

"Closer," he muttered, shaking a finger. "You can do better than that."

Frowning, I stared, not sure what I was supposed to say. "Um . . ."

Thinking, I remembered him in the bottom of the Treasure Pit, furious because something was missing. The memory brought everything together for me and I sighed, knowing what to say. "What do you want that's in the cache?"

"That's a good question." Chuckling, he leaned onto his elbows, staring at me like a wolf—a predator. "The answer is good, too. Do you really want to know?"

"Why would I ask otherwise?"

He smiled, obviously pleased that I was playing his game of reasoning with him. "Very good. I want the same thing I took from Oak Isle."

"Ichor? But you already have it." Confused, I watched as he paused to dish out some of the stew, sniffing it delicately. My stomach growled in response and he laughed, staring at me pointedly.

"Am I not feeding you enough?" He was putting on a friendly act for some reason, teasing me. "And yes, I already have the ichor. That's not exactly what I'm after this time." Slurping the hot food out of his bowl, he finished it quickly, getting himself another helping.

Puzzled, I watched him, waiting for him to explain it to me.

"Do you know what the Black Knights stand for?" he asked me, in an unexpected turn in the conversation.

"Murder?" I offered, rolling my eyes.

"Yes. Naturally." He sipped his soup slower this time, savoring it for a few seconds after each taste. "Power, and greed—the ultimate control over the lives of those around them. What greater control is there than the ability to take someone's life? To decide who will continue on and who will fall by the wayside? I'll tell you—none."

Appalled, I stared at him with my mouth open. "That's absurd! Killing someone isn't a show of strength, it's a spectacle of weakness and contempt. To murder another human being is the worst thing you could do. You've ended a life, a person's ability to choose what their existence will be. Only a coward would think murder was an acceptable path to dominance. There's no one to stand against him, to prove whether or not he's worthy of such titles and recognition. Would you want someone who tricked their way into position to be your ruler?"

"That is precisely my point. I would indeed want that person to be my ruler, because they have proven they are the smartest and most valuable through their plotting. This is how the gods became rulers; they took what they wanted and killed anyone who got in their way. You met Zeus—tell me, do you think his special jar was a just and kind present for a regular man who did nothing but better his own life by stealing fire? Was it appropriate that every evil thing be released on the world because of that?"

"Zeus is a god, though," I argued. "There's not

anything you can do about gods. They do whatever they want."

"Isn't there?" He grinned, his expression practically begging me to figure it out.

"You want to drink the ichor out of the Holy Grail, so you'll become immortal. That's how you plan on fighting against the power of the gods?" As of yet, he'd never actually confirmed that was his plan. Holding my breath, I waited for him to answer, feeling my anger spike as he took another sip.

"God holds the supreme power—the decision of who lives and dies. In fact, every god does. The capability resides in their very blood. That is what I want; the power of all the gods. And I intend to take it by whatever means necessary."

Staring at me pointedly, he fell silent, waiting.

Thinking, my mind a-jumble after everything he'd just said, I tried to put the pieces together. If he wanted the power of all the gods, he needed their blood, which was where the strength resided. Ichor was the blood of the gods, which he already had.

Wait, no. Ichor was the blood of the *Greek* gods. Which meant there was more blood he needed to gather.

"You want to replace all of them," I breathed. "Absorb the abilities of each of them, until you become so strong that you're the greatest being that exists. That's why you need the Holy Grail to drink it from. That cup held the blood of Christ, the Christian God and Savior."

The treasure we were going after wasn't gold or weapons. Somewhere in the Superstitions, the blood of the Norse and Ancient American gods were waiting for him, locked away in a vault that he desperately wanted to get into. He'd planned everything from the destruction of his own ship and crew to my kidnapping in order to get there. If I could just figure out my part in it, I might be able to stop him before he got it.

"Very good, Samantha." Filling the bowl again, he came over to me, holding it up for me to drink from. "I knew you would get it, given enough time."

"What's my part in it?" I asked as soon as I'd finished up my share, happy to not feel hungry.

He clicked his tongue, shaking his head. "Don't ruin all the fun of the mystery," he said lightly. "You'll find out soon enough."

Two weeks later, I recognized the peaks of the Superstition Mountains ahead of us, their familiar shape both relaxing me and filling me with fear. Rain clouds stacked above it, the same storm that had nearly drowned us two days before having apparently decided to hover over our final destination. The brown and green of my desert home was beautiful and bleak—a reminder of days gone by.

The air was heavy and wet, filled with mosquitoes that landed on me every time I blinked. I was being eaten alive and had no way to soothe the horrible scratching their bites induced. The rope burns around my wrists had turned into raw, bleeding wounds, making me want to weep whenever I moved them even a millimeter.

Randall, on the other hand, seemed as happy as could be, whistling as he dragged me along behind, never slowing down or stopping to rest. "Today is the day," he said to me cheerily, over his shoulder.

Inwardly gagging, I didn't bother making any kind of sound in reply. My face was sore from the wrap being around it, and I preferred being quiet to listening to his crazy plans for world domination and godlike power.

"Now, Samantha. I know you're excited to see your husband and friend again. You don't need to act like you don't care around me. I'm ready to see them, too. In fact, I'm pretty sure they're right over that ridge up there. Mark was kind enough to stop by our camp last night while you were asleep. He didn't want to wake us, though, so he left without saying anything. I imagine he's planned a very exciting reunion for all of us with Tristan."

His words made me stumble, causing me to fall to the ground and cut my knee on a jagged rock. Panicked, I struggled to my feet, staring at him with wide eyes as he watched me, amused by my clumsiness.

"Here, let me help you," he said, grabbing my arm and yanking me upward. In a flash, his gun was pressed to my temple, his arm tight around my waist. "You're not going to move, are you?"

It sounded more like a threat than a question and I shook my head, too tired to fight back. His beard tickled my face, his breath warm on my skin as his eyes glanced around, a calculating look to them.

"Show yourself or she's dead!" he yelled,

standing his ground. After a few seconds, he smiled and I assumed that the men had appeared on the ridge, just as he'd suspected. "Wonderful. Come down, with your hands in the air."

Their footsteps soon reached my ears and I almost cried from relief, I was so happy to know they were near, despite the circumstances.

"Let her go," Tristan called, apparently still keeping his distance as much as he could. "Ye're already here. What else could she tell ye?"

"You don't know what you're dealing with, Randall," Mark added. "Let her go and maybe we can work something out."

"You mean with the Indians you've got hidden up there, waiting for us?"

The stillness weighed heavily on me after he spoke, and a sort of despair settled over my heart. How were we ever going to get the upper hand on him if he somehow figured everything out before we did it?

"Don't look so surprised," he continued, grinning. "You lived with the Apache for two years, Snake Eyes. I haven't seen a single one since I set foot on their land. Of course, you would ask them for help. It's only natural. However, now I'm going to need you to ask them where the treasure is. I'd be quick about it, too, if I were you."

I was a bargaining chip, I realized. The only thing that kept anyone from killing him was the fact that I was tied to him with my life hanging in the balance.

"They don't know," Mark replied quickly. "But they've agreed to let you search for it if you hand her over to us."

"Do you think I'm stupid?" Randall snarled.

Suddenly, an arrow shot through the air, landing in the ground at our feet, my cry of shock muted by the gag in my mouth. Faster than I could blink, the gun against my head cocked, pressing harder against me.

"Don't think I won't do it." As if to emphasize how serious the situation was, lightning flashed in the sky above, the thunder clapping so loud it made my eardrums feel like they were bursting.

Instantly, a voice I didn't recognize called out in a different language.

"He says wait," Mark called. "Will you meet for negotiations?"

Randall eyed whomever it was behind me, his heart beating a little faster as he held me close. The feeling gave me hope; maybe he was nervous and would slip up somewhere along the way. Giving a curt nod, he stepped forward, making sure I was still securely in his grasp. We walked a few feet and stopped, waiting for something.

The strange man spoke once more, spouting off a rapid string of strange words, which Mark quickly translated.

"I am Runs With Wolves. Our people and the gods forbid what you ask. It would be better for you if you left now and did not anger them further. Already, the mountain tells you to leave, spitting lightning out from inside."

"I'm not leaving until I get what I came for. Show me where the treasure is and I'll personally make sure you and your family are never bothered by the gods again." It seemed like Randall was slipping, his voice jagged and rushed instead of the cool, manipulative style I'd become accustomed to. This was the Randall I'd seen in the bottom of the Treasure Pit, angry because the things he sought weren't all there.

Mark relayed the message and waited for his friend to answer, the emotion between all of us heavy.

"You can not direct the gods," Mark translated. "No man can. If you insist on knowing where the treasures lie, you must journey into the mountain, to the heart, where the lightning lives."

Randall was shouting now. "Tell me where the entrance is!" Yanking me around, he faced the group, shoving the end of the gun under my chin, but not before I caught the murderous gleam in his eyes.

Mark acted like he was ready to reach out and grab me, his eyes angry and hands clenched into a fist. Beside him, an Apache man with half his face painted red stared at me blankly. There were feathers in his hair and a leather jacket hanging open on his bare chest. Tristan stood further away his body in a battle stance, teeth bared as he watched the conversation.

Mark said something in Apache to his friend, pleading. The two seemed to argue for a moment before Runs With Wolves threw his hands up in the air and turned. Raising one arm, he pointed at the mountain.

"The rock that looks like a man," he spoke clearly, shaking his head.

"Thank you, my friend," Mark replied sincerely, placing a hand on his shoulder.

Runs With Wolves added something in his native tongue once more and began walking away, motioning to the area around him. Slowly, other men slid out from behind rocks, following him as he departed.

"The rock that looks like a man?" Randall asked, still bristling.

"He pointed right at it," Mark explained, gesturing to the mountain. I've been there before. He says the entrance is supposed to be in the canyon behind it."

"Take me," Randall ordered, pulling my head back slightly and snarling at him. "Now."

Hiking up the mountain was brutal. Randall refused to let me go, which was smart on his behalf, but incredibly painful on mine. We couldn't go more than three steps without Tristan threatening to rip his bowels out because of the whimpers I made. I'd never felt so helpless in all my life.

"This is it," Mark said, yelling over the wind that was picking up. "The rock that looks like a man!"

Glancing up, I could see that the storm was really getting started, lightning flashing overhead as rain began to sprinkle down on us. The stone we'd stopped at didn't really look like anything to me, but I supposed the image was in the eye of the beholder. As far as I was concerned, it was a big brown blob of nothing.

The canyon just beyond it was small, more of a crevice in the rocks than an actual canyon. Palo Verde trees covered it, as well as prickly pear cactus, both of which were the beautiful green the desert acquired when it received rain. If I'd come at any other time, I would have thought it was a nice place to stop and take a break or have a picnic.

However, we weren't exactly having a pleasant

day trip.

"Now let her go!" Tristan yelled, stepping close to us and grabbing one of my shoulders.

"Back off," Randall snarled, jerking me away. "I'm not done with her yet."

Moving the gun to my temple, he glanced between the two of them. "Snake Eyes, you did what you had to do," Randall said, somewhat calm. "I can respect that. If you'll join me now, I'll forget all about your mutiny. We can split the treasure down the middle and make a run for it."

"Why?" Mark asked, completely thrown off by the offer. "There's not even anything here! Look around you, Randall; this is a dead end."

"I like you, Snake Eyes," Randall said, backing up slightly as Tristan loomed over him. "I think you should get what you want. Of course, what you really want is Samantha, isn't it—all for yourself, to love and cherish for the rest of your life? All it takes is a small fee to me and she can be yours."

Mark stared at him like he was crazy, flinching as another round of thunder clapped overhead, the rain gaining strength.

"Kill Tristan!" Randall screamed, all his patience suddenly gone. "The vault needs a blood sacrifice to be entered and it's either her or him, your choice!"

Bucking wildly, I tried to get away, suddenly terrified that he might actually shoot me after threatening however many times over the course of this trek. As I scrambled, I could see the revelation hit the two men in front of me like a ton of bricks.

Someone here was going to die, and at this point, it was very likely me.

The two civilizations that had hidden this treasure believed in sacrifice. No one would be able to enter until there was blood on the ground—Randall would end me without a second's hesitation.

Tristan was already lunging for me, terror in his eyes, the image of me seeming to reflect in his gaze, small and vulnerable. However, Mark was a fraction faster than him. Jumping forward, he grabbed Tristan by the hair and yanked him back, pulling a dagger out of his belt.

The knife flashed in his hands, drawing across Tristan's throat from behind, blood smearing across his neck as he fell to his knees, eyes bulging.

Mark had just killed my husband without a second thought.

Shoving him over the rest of the way, Mark glared at his victim, face down in the dirt. Chest heaving and eyes wide, the revelation of what he'd done seemed to slap him across the face and he staggered back as the storm broke overhead, dropping all the moisture it had in a ferocious torrent.

Screaming, my legs crumpled beneath me, the cut in my knee stinging as I hit the ground, not able to believe what had just happened. The gag in my mouth choked me, muffling the almost inhumane sounds I was making, looking at the body of my husband in front of me. Tears fell from my eyes faster than the sheets of rain, soaking us all clean through in seconds.

"I'm sorry, Sammy," Mark was saying, his words coming to me like they were being beamed from a different planet. "I'm so, so sorry."

Trembling, I looked up at him again, wishing I

could strangle him with my glare. The sentiment appeared to share well enough and he took a step back, his own hands shaking.

"Come on," Randall ordered, grabbing my arm and getting me on my feet. "There." He nodded to the tiny canyon ahead of him. A small opening had appeared on the other end, a cave that disappeared into darkness. Shoving me forward, he marched me across the space and into the hole, Mark following close behind.

My heart felt like it was shattering.

I couldn't breathe, not with the way I was crying. Each movement I took made me want to fall and perish right there, to stop the pain I was feeling. Every day, I'd lived with the fear that Tristan would die and I would have to go on without him. Nothing could have prepared me for it to happen like this, though. Not at the hand of Mark, my most trusted friend.

"Cut it out!" Randall hit me in the back of the head with his gun, pushing me even faster, my feet tangling beneath me. Stumbling to the ground, I made no move to get up. There was a light ahead, but I didn't care. Everything I wanted was bleeding out on the ground outside.

Disgusted, Randall turned to Mark. "Take her," he said simply, handing the rope he'd used to tie me to him. "She's served her purpose. O'Rourke was the one I wanted dead. I knew if I had her, he'd follow me anywhere." Stepping over me, he continued on without another backward glance, disappearing into the light.

"Sammy," Mark whispered urgently.

A fire lit within me as he bent over and pulled on binding around my wrists, cutting it with his knife. Sore as I was, as soon as he'd freed me, I rolled over, kicking him in the groin and knocking him to the earth. Not even bothering to remove my gag, I climbed on top of him, wrapping my fingers around his throat, squeezing as hard as I could.

"Sam," he gasped, fingers digging at mine. "Sammy!" His voice was fading, his skin turning red in the dim light and I growled, leaning forward so I could exert more pressure. He was struggling for air, squirming to get away, but couldn't.

"My . . . blood . . . Sammy!" He was slapping my arms now, holding his hand in front of my face. All I could see was red, though, a call for revenge burning so hot within me that I suddenly felt like I was at sea again, waiting to take a ship we'd cornered.

Those were the only times I killed, the only times I'd had to, and the bloodlust I felt in those moments was speaking to me now, urging me on as he struggled to get free from beneath me.

"Sammy! Sam!" He started to pass out and I snarled angrily, tears falling. He wasn't even fighting back, the coward. He was going to let me kill him, rather than deal with what he'd done.

"Samantha!"

Tristan's voice hissed my name and I jerked in surprise, instantly letting go at the sight of him. He was standing in the tunnel, staring at me with wide eyes, the blood on his neck barely even there. Soaked to the skin, he looked like a wet dog waiting to come inside from the weather.

Beneath me, Mark coughed life back into his

lungs, rubbing his throat. The action smeared blood all over him and I finally saw what he'd been trying to show me. There was a cut on his hand, the one he'd used to slice Tristan.

He'd cut himself and spread his own blood as the sacrifice in order to save us both.

He hadn't murdered the love of my life.

Sobbing, I tore the gag off my face and out of my mouth, hurling myself into Tristan's arms.

"It's okay," he said soothingly. "I'm okay."

"I'm fine, too," Mark rasped.

For some reason, that made me cry harder. Staring toward him, I opened my mouth and closed it over and over again, unable to find adequate enough words to express the horror I felt at for having nearly killed him.

"Ye almost strangled a man to death over me," Tristan uttered in amazement, laughing out of what sounded to be disbelief and respect. "That's the most pirate like thing I've seen ye do in a while."

"Sorry," I mumbled into his shirt.

"It's not me you should apologize to." There wasn't any chastisement in his voice, only awe. He studied me like he hadn't in a long time, like he knew I could take care of myself, no matter what happened.

The thought was a revelation to me as well. I'd felt like I'd lost myself, my ability to protect what was mine, ever since Randall had taken me from my home in Paris. I'd let Mark shelter me, and then Tristan when we were back together. When Randall had taken me again, I hadn't even fought back to the best of my abilities. At the moment, I hadn't realized it was because I thought I couldn't.

Now I felt the power I'd always had returning to me, reminding me of what I was capable of. With it came a touch of fear—I had almost strangled Mark to death.

Bloodlust had burned within me and I had listened.

"Mark, I—"

"There will be time for apologies later," Mark said, interrupting me. "We have to go, right now, before Randall gets whatever it is he's looking for."

"It's a vial," I told them, pausing to swallow and wet my lips. "Two of them, like the ichor. I'll explain later. We can't let him get away with them, though."

Nodding, the two of them drew their swords, heading down the hall with me between them. I had no weapon to speak of, my fingers curled into fists should the need to fight arise. As we came around the bend and into the light, I sucked in a breath, not ready for what I saw.

It looked like the catacombs, with skulls lining the entire path, stretching down further than I could see. The bones seemed to stare at us with their empty eyes, as if waiting to jump out and grab whoever was closest. Every couple of steps, arm bones reached out, the attached hands holding the flaming torches that lit the way.

"They said the treasure was buried with two thousand Aztec soldiers, sworn to protect it for all time," I whispered, walking slowly through the spectacle.

"I'd say there's enough here to be at least two thousand," Mark agreed. "Do you think . . . will they come to life and defend it?"

"I believe in the power of magic," Tristan answered, glancing uneasily to each side. "But Randall's already been through and they haven't moved. That says to me they aren't likely to wake up but . . . the sooner we get past them, the better."

His discomfort spurred Mark and me on and we half jogged through the line of remains, slowing as the walls returned to stone. The sounds of someone riffling through things reached our ears and Tristan held out a hand, moving to the front of the group.

Motioning for silence, he snuck forward, disappearing around the bend. Following suit, Mark and I dashed after him, abruptly stopping dead in our tracks, narrowly avoiding Tristan, who was also staring at the sight before us.

The cave was one of the biggest I'd ever seen, including the ones they talked about on the television science channels. The ceiling was so high up I couldn't even see it, long stalactites hanging over the space like booby traps waiting to be sprung. Gold laced through the walls, shining brightly in the firelight that burned from torches anchored in the stones.

As if the cavern itself weren't magnificent enough, there was the treasure.

Mounds of gold sat heaped together, ancient jewelry and art pieces simply lying in the pile, as if carelessly forgotten. Gems twinkled like stars, randomly dropped across the ground. They lined the floors, draped across stone tables, and shone in the waters of a small spring that bubbled in the corner. It looked like there were bounties from every ancient American civilization here, stored away where their

417

people thought they would be safe.

The Norse items were easily spotted as well, weapons and armor set out like prized possessions, bone horns, and beautiful furs that I'd never seen before tacked onto the wall.

The tabard of a Crusader, bearing the mark of the Order of the Knights Templar, rested among the trove as well, held up on a stand in honor.

Randall stood not far from us, a shiny, golden belt around his waist, cradling what appeared to be a small figurine in his hand. Carefully, he slid it into his pocket, reaching out for the pair of gloves that matched his belt.

"Stop right there, Randall," Tristan said loudly, stepping forward.

Stiffening, the villain turned, eyes narrowing at the sight of his foe. For an instant, his gaze flickered over to Mark as anger rolled off him in waves.

I knew with a certainty Randall would never offer to let him come back to the Black Knights again.

"You should have left when you had the chance." Pulling a long sword out of the mass of weapons in front of him, Randall held out the blade, murder in his eyes.

With a shout, Randall lurched forward, swinging his sword quickly down.

Jumping up to meet him, Tristan lifted his own blade to parry, growling. As the two blades met, there was a magnificent crash, the air suddenly crackling and shining with the pieces of Tristan's weapon.

Randall had shattered it into what looked like a million tiny pieces with one brutal stroke.

Yelping in surprise, Tristan backed away, tossing his useless pommel to the side. Wide eyed, he held his arms out protectively, blocking Mark and me.

"What's the matter?" Randall smiled wickedly as he advanced. "Don't you have anything else to fight me with?"

Stunned, we all watched him, not sure what to do. There never would have been any possibility for Randall to do such a thing before. He wasn't strong enough, let alone skilled enough to explode metal with one blow.

Firelight glinted in the belt around his waist and I frowned, zeroing in on it. "It's the belt," I said to the other two. "It's enchanted to make him stronger, or something."

"Remove it from him!" Mark stepped around Tristan with his own blade, revealing some hesitation.

"I think I'll kill you first, Snake Eyes," Randall said, stopping as Mark moved up to meet him. "No one double crosses me and lives to tell about it." Spitting on the ground, he settled into a battle stance, sneering as he prepared for the attack. It was like he was playing a game with us.

"There's a first time for everything," Mark muttered in reply, his response bringing a grin to my face.

Frowning, Randall lunged, apparently deciding to make the opening move after all. Mark danced out of the way, sidestepping and almost slipping on the coins all over the floor.

"Sloppy," Randall breathed. "You can do better than that, can't you?" Circling around, he watched Mark like a hawk, eyes shining with glee.

As the enemy's back faced us, Tristan leapt toward him, darting for the table of weapons. Moving quickly, he almost made it past Randall, who noticed the attempt seconds too early.

Catching Tristan around the waist, he threw him back toward me and into a rack of artifacts. The objects crashed to the ground around him, rolling over the floor and out into the hallway. Dazed, Tristan shook his head, struggling to his feet in the mess.

Suddenly, the floor beneath us rumbled, shaking slightly, and a terrifying noise barreled down the corridor at us. In my mind, the only thing I could liken it to was the sound of an army heading into battle.

"What is that?" I yelled, covering my ears.

Face going white, Tristan grabbed me by the arm. "The warriors," he said weakly. "They're supposed to guard the treasure and keep it from leaving." Motioning to the objects that had rolled out of the room, he looked around frantically. "We can't let anything else leave this room!"

"Shit," I muttered, knowing he was right. "Get those things back in here, quick!"

Turning from the entryway and the sound racing toward us, I surveyed the room. Mark was still doing a good job at distracting Randall, despite the ear-splitting shouts echoing off the stones. The display closest to me was full of coins, but the table behind Mark had swords.

Staring at the weapons, one of them seemed to glint in the light, like a sign from the gods, and I jumped into action, feeling as if Fate were trying to tell me now was the time to get moving.

Running full force towards the fight, I dropped to my knees and slid under Randall's arm through the dirt, rolling once to reach the table. As my hand wrapped around the handle of the sword, I turned to face my kidnapper and abuser, ready to seek the revenge I deserved.

Mark stumbled backward as I advanced, kicked by the magically strengthened pirate, and fell against a stand of golden statues, tumbling them out of their case and all over the floor. Blood dripped from his lip as he stilled, staring up at the ceiling like he had no idea what was happening for a moment.

"Hey!" I screamed at Randall, bringing his attention to me. "Suck on this!"

Using both hands, I swung my sword at him, surprised when our two blades met and mine held together. He was definitely tougher than me, knocking me aside with ease, but my sword stayed in one piece. Apparently, it was made of the same stuff his was, or enchanted in some way.

Stabbing toward me, Randall yelled, gnashing his teeth together when he missed me by inches.

"Too bad stronger doesn't mean faster, huh?" Goading him, I moved in a circle, breathing quickly as I tried to think of how to get the belt off his waist.

Growling, Randall lunged at me again, cursing as I slipped out of the way.

"Sam!"

Glancing to the entrance, I saw Tristan and Mark, both holding objects that had rolled out of the room, standing at the entrance to the cavern. On the other side of them, a skeleton stood, staring down at them.

Blinking, I froze, everything forgotten for a second. My brain wasn't exactly sure that I was seeing what my eyes said was there. The bones were a dark gray and smooth, the figure simply standing at the mouth of the cavern, watching the two men. Behind it, another impossible body appeared, and another, and another.

The warriors had come to protect their treasure.

"Drop the artifacts!" I screamed, watching as the magical beings raised the swords in their hands.

Tristan and Mark didn't need telling twice, practically throwing the things on the ground and running further into the space, grabbing the first weapons they came across.

The undead army charged into the room, swords

flying, their roared battle cry turning into the sounds of combat. They were like a never-ending wave, more bodies flooding into the room. Soon, I couldn't even see the two men in the middle, their shouting the only sign they were still alive amongst the chaos.

Empty eyes circled to me then as one of the warriors stepped out and charged at me. Panicked, I jumped out of the way, slashing the figure across the spine as it passed. To my surprise, the steel passed through the spine without hardly any effort, the skeleton tumbling to the floor in two pieces. Surprisingly, it didn't move afterward, the curse that had reanimated it apparently broken.

"Break them apart!" I called, trying to see what was happening in the mass of bones surrounding the men. "It kills them!"

Bringing my attention back to Randall, I stared, the spot where he'd been standing now empty. Glancing through the room, I saw him, rifling through more cabinets, dumping things out onto the ground, searching for the vials he'd come to claim. Everything he touched didn't seem to have any value to him as he threw it aside, moving quickly. His eyes darted toward the army every now and then, as if agitated or afraid, his speed increasing as he returned to his task.

Charging him, I shouted, swinging my sword down and catching him in the belt. The metal didn't even dent, though, and he spun around, punching me in the face. It felt like being hit by a bus, plowing me into the ground as I saw stars.

Struggling up, I shook my head and lifted the heavy sword, feeling dizzy on my feet. My nose was throbbing, maybe even broken, blood trickling into my mouth, but I didn't care. Lunging forward, I tried to hit him yet again, only to be easily blocked; my motions becoming more and more lethargic. The blow to my face had doubled the weariness fighting the skeleton had given me, while the belt seemed to supply him with endless stamina.

"Give it up," Randall scoffed, shoving me down to the ground as he leaned over me. "You couldn't stop me when I had human strength. Do you even know what this is?" Pointing to his waist, he laughed, shaking his head. "This is the belt of Thor, you idiot girl. It gives the wearer his strength. As long as it's on me, you won't stand a chance."

"Then I guess I'll just have to try harder to get it off," I growled, shoving to my feet and leaping forward again.

We did our best to hit one another, but somehow never landed a blow. The frustration was building between us, and I dropped to the floor, narrowly avoiding having my head taken off.

One of the skeleton beings vaulted over me, screeching like something from the worst of my nightmares, and began dueling Randall, driving him back against the wall. Seizing the moment, I looked around for anything that would help me get the belt off his body and away from his clutches.

Instead, my eyes landed on Mark, trapped in a corner by three of the warriors. Struggling to keep a hold on his sword, he was basically just trying to block anything that came his way. A cut ran down one side of his face and his knuckles were bloody, but it was his eyes that told me he really needed help.

There was a fear and desperation to them that I'd never seen before, a call for assistance I couldn't ignore.

Searching the table of weapons again, I saw the gloves that matched Thor's belt and the hammer that sat above them. Hoping I could pick it up, I made a run for them, slipping one glove on and grabbing the short handle of the legendary artifact.

"Mark!" I screamed, throwing the other glove in his direction.

He'd just managed to worm his way out of the corner, slashing at the bones in front of him, when he heard my cry. Turning, he saw the glove flying through the air and reached up, catching what was probably the best throw of my life. Hoping I could do it again, I hefted the hammer off its head and threw it as hard as I could.

It was like magic.

He slid the glove I'd given him on, raising his hand, and the hammer literally curved to go to him. As soon as the handle was in his grip, Mark swung it around, knocking the heads off of the three enchanted guards. Lightning burned around the metal, zapping to pieces the one guard that had been trying to sneak up behind him.

Wide eyed, Mark gave me a thumb up before returning to his task.

Examining the other side of the room I watched as Tristan dropkicked an arm, apparently having resorted to dismembering anything he could grab to stay alive.

A crumbling sound drew my attention back to Randall, the dust of the skull he'd just crushed drifting down from his fingers. "Give me that glove," he growled, heading for me with a bloodthirsty gleam in his eyes.

In that instant, I realized he did want some of the other treasures that were here. Mark had told me the crew wasn't happy he'd lost the shield with Medusa's head on it before. Now he had a whole room of things to pick from, items that would secure his leadership position among the Black Knights, despite the fact that most everyone who followed him ended up dead.

Holding my sword up, I glared. "No. You can't have it."

Roaring, he charged me, swinging his blade like a madman at anything that got in his way. Nimbly jumping around, I did my best to stay away from him, not even bothering to retaliate.

Suddenly, a bullet shot past me, striking him in the shoulder and I glanced back, surprised that either of my companions had managed to load a gun and fire it under their current circumstances.

Captain Lomas stood at the entrance of the room, covered in bruises and bleeding from his hairline, the liquid running down his scarred face. His pistol was aimed right at Randall, a grim look of satisfaction on his face. He was soon blocked by a skeleton figure, which he immediately began dueling with. Another Templar slid into the space behind him, pulling one of the guards away from the group Tristan was grappling with.

That's when the realization hit me.

The Order had arrived and was fighting their way in from the outside.

With a thud, an arrow soared streaked across the

space, stabbing into another skull, the Apache man who'd fired it appearing among the Knights. He let out his own battle cry, yanking a small axe out of his belt as he charged the nearest warrior. Mark, shouting something in their language, moved through the mess to meet him, the two of them dueling the macabre creations together.

Turning back to Randall, I smiled triumphantly, holding my sword up. "Too bad you let them kill all your men," I said, goading him. "You probably could have used some help becoming king of the world."

Shot, bleeding, and raging mad with his chest heaving, Thomas Randall glared at me. "I could still kill you, you know," he puffed, stepping closer. "There would be others."

"Others?" I asked, faltering for a second.

"Others proven worthy by the gods," he explained, grinning in a sickly kind of way. "Those worthy of my presence. Zeus already marked you, when he let you come back in time instead of destroying you. Of course, if I kill you now, I'd never get the satisfaction of knowing I took something that belonged to O'Rourke and broke it so completely."

His words didn't make sense for a second and then I almost threw up, looking at him in disgust. "I'm not yours to play with," I told him fiercely. "And I never will be."

"We'll see." Laughing breathlessly, he shrugged his shoulders, as if throwing off the pain from being shot. "Snake Eyes was proven worthy, but he won't do for what I need. He'd only get in the way of me taking you."

"You'll never take me anywhere again." The

cold defiance in my tone made his nostrils flare in anger and I knew our talking had ended.

Charging once more, our blades clashed, clanging against each other and joining the din of the battle going on all around us. There was no opportunity to look at the others, or to see if we were about to be attacked by the skeleton guards. All that mattered was to me was stopping Randall, right now.

Pushing him into a corner, I layered all the pressure I could on him, hacking away, punching, kicking, and doing whatever I could to keep him occupied. The golden belt still glittered around his waist, just out of reach. As I tried to sidestep him and grab it, he turned, catching me under the chin with the pommel of his sword.

Stunned, I arched through the air as I fell, twisting around. The water of the spring was waiting to break my fall—the gem-lined basin, sharp and unforgiving. Dropping my sword, I flung my hands out to catch myself, cutting them on the rocks as my face dunked into the liquid.

Fingers pressed against the back of my head, Randall held me under the surface, and I screamed in frustration, the sound escaping as giant air bubbles from my mouth. Struggling against him, I opened my eyes, struggling to find something, anything I could grab and hit him with.

Two tiny vials shone from the bottom of the pool, their dark red contents sending a thrill through me. They almost blended in with all of the jewels around them, sparkling just as brightly. For half a second, I reached for them, finding them just out of the grasp of my fingers, and then I was yanked out of the water, coughing and sputtering as I tried to see straight again.

Randall dropped me on the floor, kicking me in the ribs as he growled, but then he stopped, his eyes trained on the pool. Slowly, he knelt down and dipped his hand in the water, reaching until his entire shoulder had been submerged.

Drawing the two bottles out, he stared in wonder at the diamond cases, the lights still shining off them as he examined the small items. It was as if he'd forgotten everything going on around him, the danger he was in.

He was completely devoted to the blood, curling his fingers around it protectively.

I, however, had not forgotten what was going on.

Gripping my sword, I raised it high over my head, standing as I did so, and brought it down as hard as I could, pressing harder as the blade met his skin. It crushed through bone, severed veins, and came out the other side, Randall's hand falling to the floor, the vials still in it.

Screaming, he grabbed at the bloody stump, stumbling away from the edge of the pool he was now coloring red with his own gore. His cries echoed off the walls, overpowering those of the other fighters, practically paralyzing me as I stared at the now useless appendage that lay in front of me.

"My hand!" he cried in anguish. "My hand!" Shaking, he gaped up at me, the color fading from his face as blood pumped from him, the artery in his left arm now disconnected.

"I'm sorry," I said, surprised to find that I meant it. Slowly, the realization of what had just happened seemed to wash over me and I jolted myself, knowing I needed to get the vials to safety.

Reaching down, I pulled the bottles from the detached hand, turning to find Tristan and Mark. The room was still a mess of fighting, and I worried that most of the objects kept here were being destroyed in the process.

Suddenly, someone grabbed me from behind, yanking me by the hair and I cried out, dropping the vials. Randall was right there to catch them, scrambling across the ground. Shoving the first one he grabbed in his pocket, he grasped the second in his hand, gasping for air as he stood. He looked ready to topple over, blood still slowly spurting from his wound, his skin so pale he looked like a ghost.

Panic seized me and I slapped at him, knocking the vial from him, the glass stopper in the top shattering as the contents splattered against the wall.

"No!" Randall screamed, running over. Even with the belt, his energy was spent, his body collapsing along the stones, tears seeping from his eyes.

"The world could have been great under me," he said hoarsely. "I had so many . . . plans." Reaching up, he touched the blood on the wall with his stump, his breathing slowing as he died right in front of me.

My breath caught, everything seeming to freeze in that moment, our eyes meeting as the life slipped from him. A film covered his, the lights in them growing darker, fading into almost nonexistence.

And then, just as slowly, the glow started returning, his skin turning pink, and then the tan I knew him to regularly have. Air filled his lungs as he gasped, his back arching as his body twitched, his remaining hand grasping at nothing. Before my eyes, the stump I'd given him started to heal, the bleeding stopped, skin growing over the clean cut.

"What?" Stumbling away, I tried to understand how he was still alive, how he was coming back from the dead. My gaze raked over him, searching for any explanation.

And then I saw it.

The blood on the wall had disappeared.

As I'd been watching him die, breathing in the peace his death offered, the liquid had absorbed into him, healing him from the inside out.

Standing, he stared at his wrist in wonder, the amputation site perfectly rounded and without scars. It was as if he'd never had a hand in the first place, the skin flowed so smoothly together. Glancing up at me, he smiled, the wicked grin that made my stomach twist in horror.

"The blood of the gods runs in my veins." It wasn't a question or a statement—he said it like a power phrase, a declaration meant to strike fear into people's hearts.

It worked.

Backing up, I felt my body hit the wall. There was nowhere left to run and no telling what he might be able to do with the essence of a god running in his veins now. If he could heal himself, the odds were no longer in my favor.

Stepping closer, he reached for me, wonder on his face, and I slammed my eyes shut, not wanting to see whatever it was he planned to do with me.

Heart pounding, I held my breath, steeling myself

for the touch of his fingers, for the sound of his voice in my ear, for him to force me to go with him again. He thought I was his chosen one, picked by the gods, worthy enough to be in his presence. What would I have to do to get away this time?

But there was nothing. No touch, no words, not even a movement of air. Slowly, I opened my eyes and peered around the room.

Thomas Randall was gone, and he'd taken the blood of the gods with him.

The skeletons seemed to fade and fall apart, the brightness of the room dimming some. It appeared that, without the essence of those who had enchanted them, the warriors became simply bones, breaking into pieces and laying still at last. All around me, Templars stood dazed, beaten and tired, appearing confused as to what was happening.

"Tristan!" I yelled, pushing through the crowd in his direction. "He's getting away!"

My husband turned to look at me, just as shocked as everyone else. His face was covered by the blood trickling out of his hairline, his shirt missing a sleeve. Despite his haggard facade, he glanced to the entrance of the cave as soon as he understood what I was saying, his hands tightening around his blade. By the time I reached him, he was already running down the long tunnel, hurdling fallen Aztec warriors, shoving stunned Templars and Apache out of the way.

Feeling like my lungs might burst from over-exertion, I followed him, the light from outside a pinprick in the distance. Sounds of rain still cascaded softly down on the mountain, the rumble of thunder rolling through the sky. Randall's form was barely visible, a shadow racing toward freedom ahead of us.

Reaching the mouth of the cave, Tristan skidded to a halt, throwing his arm out and catching me before I went any further.

Gasping, I looked out into the storm, marveling at the sight in front of me.

Randall stood in a Viking style boat, the golden belt still around his waist. Lightning flashed as he took the helm, waving at us with his stump, and the entire vessel rose into the sky, disappearing into clouds above without a sound.

"What the hell?" I muttered, watching the clouds with fascination and dread.

"I think that covers my own feelings," Tristan agreed, peering at me with identical confusion.

"Where is he?" Captain Lomas burst past us and into the rain, turning around wildly, his sword raised. He looked a little like a zombie himself, he was so beat up, a crazed glimmer in his eyes.

"Did you catch him?" Mark stopped on the other side of us, breathless, the hammer still clenched tightly in his gloved hand.

Tristan stared at me, his mouth opening and closing in bewilderment, and then stared up at the sky.

"He's gone," I said, to Lomas.

"What?"

"He . . . flew away." Tristan sounded like he didn't believe it, even though he'd just seen it. "In a ship."

"I'm sorry?" Mark stepped forward, eyeing the cut on Tristan's head like he thought it might have impacted his vision.

"It's true. There was a Viking ship and it just flew into the sky." Swallowing, I glanced at Lomas.

Sighing, he nodded, sheathing his sword. "*Skíðblaðnir*."

"Bless you?" I said, confused.

"No. *Skíðblaðnir* is the name of the ship. He must have taken it from the vault." Running his hands through his wet hair, Lomas shoved back past us, seeking refuge from the weather.

"How could we have missed him taking an entire ship?" Mark sounded just as baffled as I was. Tristan, meanwhile, continued to stare at us all blankly.

"It's a magical ship," Lomas explained. "Besides being able to fly, it can be folded up to fit inside your pocket when you aren't using it. The Norse considered it their finest vessel, able to travel over water, land, or air, and hold whatever you needed, no matter the size or weight."

"Are you sure that's what we just saw?" I pressed.

"I've spent my lifetime as a Templar searching for this treasure and studying the contents of it," he snapped, glaring at me. "If you saw a ship fly away, trust me, it was that one."

"He was still wearing the belt," Tristan finally said, seeming to come to his senses.

"Thor's belt," I added, grimacing as Lomas's face turned a deeper shade of red.

"What about the vials?" Mark asked, closing his eyes tightly and rubbing the bridge of his nose.

Biting my lip, I stared at the three of them, not replying.

"*Dios nos ayude*," Lomas muttered, crossing himself.

"I had them," I said, stumbling over my memories of the fight. "I cut off his hand to stop him from taking them, but—"

"You cut off his hand?" Tristan stared at me with wide eyes.

"Yes! He was dead; I watched him bleed out from it. But one of the vials had spilled and . . ." Frowning, I took a deep breath. "He absorbed it."

Lomas grabbed me by the front of the shirt, yanking me to him as he stared in my eyes. "He did what?" His voice was dangerous and low, gaze burning furiously into my own.

"Get yer hands off her," Tristan growled, pulling me back. "It's not her fault that things didn't go as planned."

"It is," I replied, miserably. "The wound I gave him is where it absorbed into. He was completely healed, except for his hand returning." Shrugging helplessly, I let my sword fall from my hands, clattering to the ground.

Distracted, Lomas looked down at it, a suspicious expression crossing his face. "This is the blade you cut him with?"

"Yeah. Why?"

Bending down, he picked the weapon up, examining it with careful eyes. "This is *Dáinsleif.* I'm sure of it."

The name tugged at something from my memory and I frowned, thinking back to my many literature classes. "The sword that can't be sheathed until it's killed someone?"

"Or given them a wound that will kill them, *sí*." Pausing for a moment, he seemed to think it over to himself, nodding. "Of course. That's why his hand didn't grow back—you hurt him enough to kill him. The blood he absorbed couldn't override the magic of the sword. The power of the gods was already at work there."

"What will happen now that he has the blood inside him, though?" Mark questioned, bringing up the question I hadn't wanted to ask.

"I've no idea," Lomas replied. "But it can't be good."

Falling silent, the four of us continued to watch the storm, the sting of our defeat hanging over our heads.

And it was my fault.

"You need to see a doctor, lass," Tristan finally murmured, taking my hand in his and examining my wrist.

"I'm not the only one." Smiling softly, I looked over his bloodied face, feeling my heart lighten some despite the position we were now in. We were together and that was all that mattered.

"There are men inside who need assistance as well," Lomas spoke up. "We'll have to make camp in the valley and assess our damages. There are the Apache to deal with, too."

"They don't need dealing with," Mark spoke up roughly.

"On the contrary. They are now part of this entire ordeal; their secrecy must be obtained, or they will face the consequences."

"Funny, I bet they're thinking the same thing

about you." Glaring at the captain, Mark folded his arms. "This is the riches of their people. It belongs here, where they can take care of it."

"What?" Lomas exclaimed. "Where it's not protected? That would be disastrous to the artifacts that remain!"

"It's not unprotected," he replied evenly, not seeming to care that his suggestion had angered the captain. "The Apache know what this place is. They've been the first line of defense for hundreds of years, even when they didn't know if it existed or not. They'll keep guarding it now. If you try and move these things, you'll not only be disturbing a cursed treasure, but the final resting place of all the Aztec warriors we just fought with. Let the tribes take care of their own."

"It's not a bad idea," Tristan agreed.

"I promised Runs With Wolves I wouldn't let anything happen, if I could help it," Mark added. "It needs to stay here."

"Snake Eyes speaks words of wisdom." The entire group turned back, watching the Indian man make his way to us. His eyes smiled, his strong form reaching out for Mark. Pulling his brother into a hug, the two men remained silent, breathing together after their battle.

"Who would have thought you'd be calling me wise someday," Mark finally said, breaking away.

"Not I." Runs With Wolves laughed, looking out to the storm. "But, I never thought this place was real, either. It seems I was mistaken about many things."

"I don't feel comfortable leaving the treasure here." Lomas asserted himself to the man. "It's my job to make sure it is taken care of, not left in the desert to rot."

"It stays here," Mark answered, his voice unwavering.

"No, it doesn't!"

"It does," I offered. "It will be safe here. All the stories in my time say it's just a gold mine; no one will ever find it. The Apache will keep it hidden and secret."

"The future can be changed. Our fight at the Mission proved that well enough." Lomas's voice was haughty and condescending, his expression one of triumph.

"Actually, I don't think it does." Mark sighed, rubbing his face, and then stared at his brother. Speaking quietly in Apache, he told Runs With Wolves something that made his eyes widen, his mouth pressing into a thin line.

"It is the truth?" the Indian asked, glancing between Mark and me.

"Yes," I replied, knowing then he'd been told we were from another time.

"I wrote the journal at the Mission," Mark started again. "The missionaries were always dead and Randall never paid them to let him leave his ship. I made up the story, so I would search out the right information. I'm the reason I went back in time. Without that book, there would have been nothing to find."

Frowning, he looked down at the ground. "I've wanted to go home for the longest time, up until Sam showed up in my life again. I don't think I can now, though." Glancing at the rest of us, he smiled tightly.

"There's something more important here, in this time. Randall needs to be stopped, and I think I can help. I know a lot about ships, about pirates. I need to stay here."

"Are you sure?" I asked quietly. "This is your one chance, Mark. If you write that journal, there's no going back. You'll have set your life on the course that brought you to this point."

"I'm sure." Decided, he grinned for real. "However, I'm going to spend the night with my Apache family, if you don't mind. It will take a few days to settle things here, and I've missed Singing Bird's cooking."

Runs With Wolves chuckled at that. "My wife," he explained to the rest of us. "She will be happy to have you, Snake Eyes. We all will. Our children have longed to meet you." The two men fell into an easy pattern of conversation, talking about the life Mark had abandoned here as they made their way back to the treasure vault.

"I'll organize the men," Lomas stated, moving to follow them. "We need a thorough list of everything here." Eyeing the sword he still held, he frowned. Then, suddenly, he held it out to me. "Take this. If you were worthy enough to do battle with it, you should keep it. At least we'll have one thing from this god forsaken mountain to prove we actually found what we were searching for." Still muttering to himself, he put it in my hands and left, shaking his head.

Holding it gently, I gazed back out the tunnel entrance, the rain slowly stopping.

"Are ye okay, Samantha?" Taking the weapon,

Tristan leaned it against the wall and squeezed my hand.

"Yeah." Sighing, I shook my head. "It's my fault that Randall got away. I should have kept fighting, but I froze instead."

"Thomas Randall with the blood of a god flowing through him." He pursed his lips, brow furrowed. "Methinks the next time we meet we'll discover what he can do."

"Do you think we'll see him again?" I asked, surprised. "He has a means of getting around that we can't double now. If I were him, I'd stay out of sight."

"He'll be back," Tristan said positively. "We'll be ready for him. I'll not underestimate what he's willing to do for power any longer."

Pulling me into his embrace, he kissed my forehead. The action made my nerves calm and I leaned against him, overflowing with relief.

We'd done it; we'd made it back to each other, despite being torn apart for so long. Tristan was still mine and I would always be his.

"Ye better enjoy the next two months while we head back to France," he suddenly said, tilting my face towards his and kissing me softly. "We have a lot of work to do once we get back to Paris."

"Work?"

"Aye. There are six more treasures out there, which means six more vials Randall wants to steal. I intend to stop him from getting any of them." He grinned, some excitement returning to his face.

"Six more treasures?" Just the thought made me sleepy. But, as always, the curiosity started burning within me. "Where are they?"

"I don't know exactly," he stated. "But I have a few ideas."

"Pandora's Box isn't hidden away any more, either." Frustrated, I tried to think of how we were going to solve all the problems that were rising around us.

"That's something the future will have to deal with, I'm afraid." Moving to head inside, he towed me along beside him.

"Tristan?" I suddenly asked, laughing slightly. "Does the Order keep records of everything?"

"Of course," he responded, slightly stunned. "Why?"

"I need to get a message to the future," I said slowly. "And I know just who to send it to."

Acknowledgments

As usual, I have no idea who to thank, because so many people were involved in making this book, haha!

Thank you to those readers who messaged me so excitedly after Swept Away released. I loved talking with you about the alternate history theories and research I'd done. Those conversations are part of what made me so excited to get to work on Carried Away.

Thank you to my family, for forgiving me after I completely disappeared into the writing cave for weeks on end. Thank you to Jake—I quite literally feel that I couldn't do hardly anything without you.

Thank you to my wonderful beta readers and editors! Raquel Auriemma, Kayla Hyden, Vonnie Hudson, Julie Engle, Heather Garrison, Annie Angelich, Tyanne Romney, Kysee Weatherford, Kassidy Carter, Lacey Weatherford, and Belinda Boring. I love you all so much! Thank you for listening to my crazy ideas and putting up with all of the drafts of this story I asked you to read, haha!

~Kamery

About The Author

Kamery is not the person who grew up dreaming of the day that she would clutch her very own novel to her chest, tears brimming over the rims of her eyes as she thought about how she'd written it herself, finally! In fact, anything remotely like that didn't even happen until she was actually holding her first book in her hand, amazed that she'd written it and wondering how on Earth she'd managed to do it when it hadn't ever occurred to her to write one until months before. Surprisingly, though, it was just what she never realized she loved doing.

When starting out in life, Kamery had (and still has) big dreams to perform on Broadway. She loves music and acting very much, while she and dance have a love/hate relationship; she would love to do it and every form of dance decides it hates that about her, haha! The one constant she always had between the performing world and the book world were the stories, tales that transported her to other worlds and made her feel like she really could do anything. Finally, she decided she wanted to do that for someone else and sat down to write.

It's been a few years since she held that first book, realizing that she really liked writing and wanted to do more, but the love that blossomed in that moment has only grown. Currently, Kamery works from home in the White Mountains of Arizona, while taking care of her two adorable kids, a girl and a boy, and talking her sweet husband Jake's ear off about the insane amount of characters in her head who are ready to fight to the death for a chance at their own novels. She also gets together with other authors in the family and they all gab together, making up The Royal Court of the Queens of Romance. It truly is a wonderful life!

Visit www.kamerysolomonbooks.com for more information!

12070650R00248

Made in the USA
San Bernardino, CA
08 December 2018